P9-CFY-452

And They Lived...

Also by Steven Salvatore

Can't Take That Away

And They Lived...

STEVEN SALVATORE

BLOOMSBURY

NEW YORK LONDON OXFORD NEW DELHI SYDNEY

BLOOMSBURY YA
Bloomsbury Publishing Inc., part of Bloomsbury Publishing Plc
1385 Broadway, New York, NY 10018

BLOOMSBURY and the Diana logo are trademarks of Bloomsbury Publishing Plc

First published in the United States of America in March 2022 by Bloomsbury YA

Bloomsbury books may be purchased for business or promotional use.
For information on bulk purchases please contact Macmillan Corporate and
Premium Sales Department at specialmarkets@macmillan.com

Library of Congress Cataloging-in-Publication Data
Names: Salvatore, Steven, author.
Title: And they lived . . . / by Steven Salvatore.
Description: New York : Bloomsbury, 2022.
Summary: Chase Arthur is a hopeless romantic, but he's also struggling to figure out his gender
identity and recover from an eating disorder. When Chase starts his freshman year of college,
he has to navigate being away from home, missing his sister, and finding his squad,
and will have to learn to love—and be enough for—himself,
while discovering what it means to truly live.
Identifiers: LCCN 2021032180 (print) | LCCN 2021032181 (e-book)
ISBN 978-1-5476-0819-5 (hardcover) • ISBN 978-1-5476-0820-1 (e-book)
Subjects: CYAC: Universities and colleges—Fiction. | Gays—Fiction. |
Gender identity—Fiction. | LCGFT: Novels.
Classification: LCC PZ7.1.S2543 An 2022 (print) | LCC PZ7.1.S2543 (e-book) |
DDC [Fic]—dc23
LC record available at https://lccn.loc.gov/2021032180

Book design by Jeanette Levy
Typeset by Westchester Publishing Services
Printed and bound in the U.S.A.
2 4 6 8 10 9 7 5 3 1

To find out more about our authors and books
visit www.bloomsbury.com and sign up for our newsletters.

To every queer person who grew up
never seeing themselves in fairy tales but still dreamed of
being swept off their feet in a Technicolor love story:
this is for you, go find your adventure

To Steve, who swept me off my feet and made me
believe I was worthy of being loved:
together *we* lived

And They Lived...

1

✶ ONCE UPON A TIME ✶

My mother is trying to get me killed.

"So, what do you think?" Mom asks, bouncing on the balls of her feet. I've just gotten back to my new dorm room suite with my twelve-year-old sister, Taylor. She couldn't sit still for the short amount of time it took to unpack my entire life, so I'd taken her on a walking tour of the campus. We were gone for *twenty minutes*, which apparently was long enough for Mom to put a scrolly decal on the wall just above the head of my extra-long twin bed that says Once Upon a Time. She might as well have gotten one that says Live, Laugh, Love.

"I think I'm going to get the shit kicked out of me before classes start," I say.

"Chase Arthur, watch your language." Mom nods toward Taylor, who rolls her eyes.

Taylor looks awkward and innocent—still incubating in the stage between ugly duckling and beautiful swan—but I know better.

"Sorry. But . . ." I stick out my tongue and gesticulate wildly toward the wall. "Seriously, Mom. *Why*? You *know* the rules."

I swipe my phone from the desk and pull up the email about move-in day. "Only adhere things to the walls with tacky stuff." My fingers pinch the air.

Mom waves her hand dismissively and glances toward the corkboard above my desk at my high school Drama King picture. "Oh, relax, you're such a drama queen."

I was not in the drama club or anything like that. I was crowned Most Dramatic, aka Drama King, aka the person most likely to cause a *whole scene* and then gossip about it later. Which, fair.

The picture is ripped down the middle. Missing in action: Leila Casablanca, my former best friend, voted Drama Queen. We haven't spoken in months, and I seethe when I think about how I'll probably run into her because she just had to come to *my* college. But I love this picture of me, so I keep it. Seriously, I fucking sparkle in a tiara.

"The sign peels right off," Mom continues, ripping the *e* at the end of *Time*, so now it reads Once Upon a Tim.

"You're gonna get me written up by RA *Tim*," I say. RA Tim is so cute I could cry, so, okay, that wouldn't be the worst thing.

"It's a sign," Taylor chimes in, reading my mind, her legs dangling off the edge of my perfectly made bed. "You should make a move."

My face heats. "Taylor!"

Mom goes silent. Then, "You know to use protection, right?"

My eyes widen. "*Ahhhh, whenareyouleaving?*"

Taylor erupts in a witchy cackle.

This is why we requested an early move-in. It's better that we get all this embarrassing crap out of the way now before other people have to witness it. My three other suitemates arrive tomorrow with the rest of the freshman class, but Mom, in her infinite wisdom, knew I'd be an anxious mess and would need to carve out my space first.

"You'll miss me when I'm gone," Mom says.

"When ya going?" I won't admit this out loud, but I *will* miss her.

Taylor goes quiet. Her face scrunches up the way it does when she's about to cry. It amazes me how, no matter how old she gets, she never loses the ability to cry on a dime. What sucks is that I'm the reason for her tears now.

"Hey, stop." I hop onto the bed. Mom sidles up on her other side. "I'm not going to be gone forever. I'll be back for your birthday and maybe Thanksgiving and definitely Christmas and probably a bunch of weekends in between because, seriously, this place is a hole."

Which obviously isn't true because this campus is *everything*.

But it elicits a mucusy giggle from Tay. I'll take what I can get.

Mom sucks a long breath through her nose and glances out the window. The sky is streaked with a late-summer hot orange. "We really should get on the road, Taylor-bean."

With that, all the frustration and exhaustion from packing up my entire existence back home, driving four hours upstate, and unpacking said existence into this tiny room is replaced by an overwhelming sadness that sucks all the air out of the room.

I don't want them to go.

I'm not ready for this.

The finality of it. That once they walk out of this suite and out of this dorm and get into their car, they're gone, leaving me behind.

"You could stay. My suitemates won't be here until the morning. There's—"

Mom grabs my hand and squeezes. "As much as I want to move in here for the rest of the school year—" She pauses, clearly contemplating it. "I think we should get on the road."

"What're you gonna do, alone?" Taylor asks.

I know it's not meant to be a serious gut punch, but . . . I stammer, "Chill. Me time. Maybe I'll do some sketching. Get a jump on some animation projects I wanna start this semester." Be a strong, independent person and all that.

What'll probably happen is I'll end up watching a marathon of Disney movies on my laptop and falling asleep in a puddle of tears because there's nothing to do when the campus is practically empty. The sportsball people have been moved in for a few weeks already, but I can't honestly imagine me, uncoordinated queer AF Disnerd Chase Arthur, just, like, wandering up to the athletes' dorm being all, "Hey, wanna party? I got the *Moana* sing-along on iTunes." The thought alone makes me break out in a cold sweat.

"Sounds like a *great* time," Taylor deadpans. She mashes her glasses up the bridge of her nose.

"He'll call Rae," Mom says. "Won't you, sweetheart? She moved into her dorm last weekend, right?"

"I told you this already," I begin. "Rae and I made a pact that we would not call or see each other until at least the first full week of school is done. You know, so that we give each other time to find ourselves or whatever."

"In one week, you're going to find yourselves?" Taylor's glasses fall to the tip of her nose again. She purses her lips as she turns toward Mom. "He'll call her the second we leave."

Rae Ackerman is my actual best friend. She goes to the pristine "little" Ivy League school Laurene University, which is, no joke, two miles away from me at CIA, Cayuga Institute of the Arts. We didn't design it that way. She didn't tell anyone, not even me, that she even applied to Laurene, let alone that it was her first choice, because she was so superstitious. She told me it killed her to keep it from me, especially when I told the entire senior class, the janitorial staff, teachers, school board, and the flock of pigeons that posted up outside our high school that CIA was my number one and that if I didn't get in, my future career as Walt Disney Animation Studios' head animator was DOA. Rae is my more practical other half. My very tall, very extra other half.

"You don't know me," I say with a smirk.

"I packed a surprise for you," Taylor whispers. "Top drawer, next to your socks."

My eyes narrow at her. "The fuck?"

Mom slaps me playfully upside my head. She snaps her fingers, a cue for Taylor to get off my bed, get her shoes on, and ready herself for a car ride home filled with tears and an inevitable playlist of Disney musical numbers to remember me by.

As if it's my funeral.

But they do a great job holding themselves together. At least until our slow march out of the suite. And into the hallway. And down the stairs (because Mom is way too antsy for the elevator). And out the main entrance of the dorm. And into the empty parking lot to her car, where, upon arrival, she looks at me and bursts into tears.

I'm talking Niagara Falls–style bawling.

Her face, hot from the setting sun, is so red I'm worried she'll pass out, and it's not like Taylor can take the wheel while they're driving home.

"I'll be fine, Mom. I'm good." I puff out my chest. "Totally. Great, even."

I learned a long time ago, right around the time Dad dropped off divorce papers to Mom's job and moved a few towns away and started dating a woman whose government name is Krissy(!), that sometimes it's best to pretend to be okay around Mom. It makes it easier on her.

"I'm sorry your father flaked." Mom sounds more upset than I am. "I was sure he'd be here to help and see you off."

"You're surprised? Par for the course. Which is probably where he is today: golfing."

She shakes her head, avoiding Taylor's disenchanted gaze. "Call me every day?"

"Mom!" Taylor snaps. "That's ridiculous."

"Okay, every other day!" Mom cries. "I just want to make sure my firstborn baby is alive." She grabs my chin. "Every other day?" But it's not a question.

"Every other day," I repeat.

"And please eat, b-but . . ." Her words teeter on the edge of her tongue. She struggles to hold it back, her eyelids twitching. We're so close I can practically hear her thoughts: "But please don't overeat, and if you feel the urge to, don't. Call me. Or seek out a therapist on campus. You're gonna do that, right?" Last week, I overheard her talking to Taylor, saying, "Chase needs to make sure to watch for the freshman fifteen. It's real. It was on *20/20*. I saw what it did to Marcy's son Jamie, and let's just say I think she's mispronouncing *fifty*." As great as Mom is, she's often the proverbial verbal bull in a china shop when it comes to saying the absolute worst things without realizing they can cause me utter devastation. She means well, and I always forgive her because she knows not what she does. Thankfully, she's exercising *some* restraint today.

Mom shakes it off, then leans in close so Taylor can't hear. "Please make sure you wear protection when you have sex. I left a box of condoms under your pillow—I didn't know your size, so I guessed a sensible average—and I also got you some lubricant because they told me at Planned Parenthood that for, you know, it's not naturally . . ." She motions with her hands and finally says, "Wet."

Ohmygod, how do I make it stop?

My shoulders tense, my mouth slacks, my entire body goes into multisystem organ failure. Within seconds, I am deceased—new record for Mom.

She plants a big kiss on my cheek that smacks. "I love you. Be safe. Call your sister."

"She's right there." I point to Taylor, who doesn't hesitate to run back over and fling her arms around me.

"I'll miss you," she says. "But only because you're the only person who still plays Barbies with me."

Right. All her friends are way too cool for that "baby shit." But honestly, there's nothing more therapeutic than a good old-fashioned hair-styling sesh followed by a fashion show set to a super gay mashup of Dua Lipa's "New Rules" and "Prince Ali" from *Aladdin* that I made on GarageBand.

I've done a few stop-motion films with our combined dolls. My favorite is the one where my Prince Naveen doll from *The Princess and the Frog* and Kristoff from *Frozen* get glammed in subtle frosty make-up and play husbands whose lives come apart when they both fall for the same gender-ambiguous Ken doll. Until they become a throuple. It was avant-garde. High fashion. Art. And very, *very* gay. It was kind of major when it went viral. I included it in my portfolio alongside another viral short, and I think it elevated my college application. Who said you can't make your obsessions work for you?

I wonder if Taylor will still put on Barbie fashion shows without me.

"You'll come home for my birthday, right?" she asks.

"Wouldn't miss it." I have no idea if Mom will be able to afford a bus ticket home in October, so close to Thanksgiving break, but I'll walk if I have to. I'll just have to convince Rae, who has her car at Laurene, to come with me. Taylor is obsessed with her, and Rae has always thought of Taylor as a little sister, so it should be an easy ask. I kiss the top of her forehead. "Love you, sis."

Taylor whispers, "Go find your adventure."

Adventure is our code name for *love*. Because I'm *that* desperate that we had to find a way to talk about my love life all the time without me seeming like an obsessive mess. It might be super weak and cliché and cheesy, but all I want is to fall in love. Have an adventure. But I'm me, which means I'll probably graduate a loveless virgin.

Taylor knows I daydream about falling in love, and she's never judged me for it. Probably because she witnessed the dissolution of our parents' marriage, too, so to us, nothing is more far-fetched and magical than finding actual love, the kind that doesn't up and leave at the first sign of trouble, but instead holds your hand on the battlefield. It's an adventure we know nothing about.

"Don't become an asshole," she says, peeling herself off me and slumping to the car.

"Don't become a mean girl," I say back.

"*Boo, you whore,*" she says in her best Regina George.

Mom clenches her jaw. "Language! My god, you kids!"

"What?" I say, "*You* showed us that movie."

Mom opens the car door and leans on top of it, clearly not wanting to get in. Then she looks at Taylor and says, "*Get in, loser, we're going home.*"

"Oh, *burn,*" I say. Mom always did love a good movie reference.

This is a good moment to walk away. End it on a funny, happy *Mean Girls* line. I blow an air kiss, suck in a breath, and make my way back toward the dorm.

I don't turn back, nor do I stop walking, until I'm barreling down the hallway toward my suite. I can't. If I stop, I'll go back, and they'll be gone.

They're already gone.

And I'm alone.

Now, this is the point where most people might blast some music, strip down to their boxer briefs, and eat Flamin' Hot Cheetos and ice cream simply because they can. But all I feel is the resounding silence of Mom and Taylor's departure.

Once the metal door to the suite clicks behind me, I take a look around. The suite smells faintly like lemony bleach, thanks to Mom obsessively cleaning both bathrooms, and a little bit like fresh wood chips and dirty socks. The common room is stark, save for one uncomfortable couch and two equally uncomfortable chairs, all with low-to-the-ground wooden frames that look like slightly elevated Tinkertoys—but far less colorful—with rough, grayish-blue cushions. There's a TV stand on the opposite wall. At either end of the common room is a doorway to a two-person room. Right now, it feels empty. Un-lived-in. Save for the micro-fridge, a microwave-refrigerator hybrid, and the latest PlayStation console that my suitemates decided I would bring.

Heading back into my room is like stepping into *Walt Disney's Wonderful World of Color*. Half the room is covered in posters of my favorite animated films, from *Sleeping Beauty* to *Beauty and the Beast* to *Moana* and *The Nightmare Before Christmas* on the Disney spectrum, to *Spider-Man: Into the Spider-Verse*, *Spirited Away*, *Paranorman*, and *Coraline* from the more experimental indie studios. I guarantee a lot of my classmates in the animation program are going to give me flack for being a corporate hack with dreams of working for Disney one day, but I don't care.

The other half of the room is bare—for now. I wonder what my roommate, Benigno, will bring with him. He's mentioned on the CIAChat that he loves football, and the way he texts is super masc, but he's also a major Ariana Grande stan, so who knows. When I casually brought up the fact that I'm gay in the suite group chat, all three of my future roommates—Aaron, Xavier, and Benigno—were super cool about it, though Benigno was fairly quiet, which makes me glad I didn't bring up that I also think I might be nonbinary. Or genderqueer; I'm not sure. I haven't figured it out, untangled all the ways I feel slightly different than every other guy I know, and I definitely haven't figured out the whole pronoun question, which, why can't I just be he and him *and* nonbinary? Either way, it'd be my luck that Benigno ends up being a super straight-cis-dude-bro who is queerphobic and has a chiseled body.

Stopping in front of the mirror built into the sliding closet door, I try not to hate every square inch of what I see. From this angle, I look like unbaked bread dough, and—

No. This is what my old therapist told me to avoid. *Don't compare your body to food. Instead, focus on what you like.* Okay. I like my hair. It's got this wavy, swoopy thing going. But, uh. That's all I got. Then the other thoughts wander in: *You're too masculine and lumpy, but not masculine enough to be a real man.* I shudder at the term *man* and all the expectations that come along with it that I'll never meet.

You're broken, the voices say, *fat, ugly, not nonbinary enough, and*—

Nope. I can't fuel this thinking.

I wish I could just call my old therapist and unpack all these fears, but we had our last session a few weeks ago, and she told me it would be best if I found someone new here. She even looked into the free therapy CIA offers as part of tuition costs. But the thought of diving into the crap relationship I have with my dad, body image issues, eating-disordered past, and the question mark that is my gender identity feels too overwhelming. I'll do it. Just not today.

This is supposed to be a new start, a place where I don't have to be anyone but the person I want to be. But that feels daunting, and I need a reprieve from all the voices in my head.

My fingers twitch as I paw at my phone. Instinctively, I pull up the only person I know will be a comfort and a distraction. Though I hesitate about FaceTiming her due to our pact, I can't stop myself.

Rae's face pops on my screen, her eyes wide, her tongue wagging. She looks exactly like middle child Alex Dunphy from

Modern Family, thick-framed nerd glasses and all. "What the hell do you want, slore?!" It's good to know a week apart hasn't changed her.

She seductively tussles her wavy brown hair, which gets caught in the silver Star of David necklace around her neck. She yanks on it and yelps, "*Ouch! Fucking shit bitch!*" and all the sexy just goes right out.

"I am neither a slut, nor a whore," I say. "Yet. Unlike you."

"I beg to differ, you sexy beast." Rae winks as she settles post–hair struggle.

Rae and I have what Mom affectionately labels a "very inappropriate relationship." When we're together, we act like a married couple deep in the honeymoon period. There's lots of handsy behavior on both of our parts, and we talk to each other like we're in some low-budget BDSM porn about to get it on. But she's very much a girl, and I'm very much into guys. It's our friend fetish. Nobody gets it, and I love that.

"No, *you're* sexy!" I say. Then I go silent, my cue that I need to talk.

"All right, what's wrong?"

"Sorry, I know I'm breaking our pact—"

She cuts me off. "Excuse me, slore, but that pact was one-sided. I never agreed to such a thing, and this past week without seeing your face has left me feeling a ferocious void the likes of which not even my boyfriend's ginormous cock can fill."

My eyes widen. "Rae! Did Bubbeh Harold make a move?"

Rae met her boyfriend, Harry, at a freshman orientation mixer at Laurene just after high school graduation, and they've been together ever since. Granted, he lived in California, so their relationship has existed purely over the phone for the past two months, but apparently, they're making up for it now.

"No, I'm still a big ole V," Rae says.

I hear a muffled voice shout, "Tell Chase I'm working on it!"

"Harry says hi." Rae flips the camera so I can see him, dressed in a dadesque polo shirt and ill-fitting jeans, sitting at Rae's dorm room desk, glasses at the tip of his nose. I'd say he's a total zayde, but his prudishness reminds me of Rae's bubbeh.

"Wait a second, why the hell is *Once Upon a Tim* stenciled on your wall?" She closes her eyes and sighs. "Mama Arthur did that, didn't she?"

I burst out laughing. "How'd you know?"

"Is that like, some sort of gay mating call to all the Tims out there?" Rae asks.

"Wait. *Tims* is a great code word for hot guys."

"Yes, yes, it is," she says. "Enough stalling. What's up? What's wrong? Talk to me."

"I'm bored!"

"Do you need me to come over there?" she asks. "I can be on the bus in ten minutes and at your dorm within a half hour. And yes, I did already map out bus routes and schedules because one of us had to."

Not going to lie—I did the same thing already. "Or you could take your car?"

"My mom doesn't want me to use the car too much. According to her, it's 'Emergency Use Only.'" Rae lives and dies by her parents' strict rules, even if they don't make much sense. I mean, I'm so close by, her mom would never know. Except Rae would tell her because she tells her mom everything, and then she'd have to endure a lecture about car safety and mileage and spending too much time seeing me instead of studying, and I'm exhausted already on her behalf. "You know Mama Ackerman, she'll know if I so much as turn the ignition." She pauses. "Is this an emergency?"

"Nah, I'll be okay. One night alone won't kill me."

"You sure?"

"Yeah. I just wanted to see you."

"Awwwww, you *do* love me!" She brings her lips to the camera and smooches the air. It sounds wet and gross, and I love it.

"Shut up. Do not."

"Deny me, and I won't give you that sweet, sweet lovin' next time I see you."

"Yes, you will."

"You're right, I will." She starts to laugh again. "Harry is giving me the most fakakta look right now."

"Harry, get used to this!" I shout.

She flips the camera again so I see him. He says, "You two are wild!"

"We're a package deal," Rae says. "You want me, you get Chase."

He buries his face in his hands.

Between gulps of laughter, she says, "Listen, sweetie, I should go." She flips the camera back to her, and her face is changed. She's wearing her stoic, serious, "I'm done joking" mask. "Harry and I have to study for an exam on Monday, and yes, before you say *anything*, I do actually mean study."

"Don't classes *start* on Monday? And you have a test already?"

"Welcome to Laurene!" Harry shouts.

I want to thank her for offering to ditch Harry—and studying, which is a Big Deal for Rae—to be with me. That's Rae, though.

She'll drop everything for me, even if it's not in her best interest, which is why I won't press her to come.

"Welcome to the hardest environmental science program in the country," she adds. "Love you, boo. And just try to, like, relax. Why don't you sketch your feelings? You know I love a good angsty Chase original." Silence zips between us for a beat. "What're you feeling?"

"Very *Alice in Wonderland*. Like, I've fallen down the rabbit hole, and I'm stuck in this room, alone, with no way out."

"Who *are* you?" she says, mimicking the Caterpillar.

"*I hardly know, just at present—at least I knew who I was when I got up this morning, but I think I must have been changed several times since then,*" I recite by heart. Dad used to read that book to me every night when I was a kid. Back when he was, well, a *dad*.

"I already know who you are. You just have to be brave enough to show the rest of the world." Her face scrunches in a way that tells me she's about to read me like my favorite book. "And when you're ready, the boys will flock."

"Ha," I snort. "I wish. I'm not even thinking about *that*."

Which is a lie, of course, and she gives me The Look. Arched eyebrows, pursed lips. Rae and I used to stay up all night talking about how, once we got out of our small town and into the larger world, we'd find men who'd sweep us off our feet. She found hers. I'm still waiting. I don't even know what my dream man looks like, but that doesn't matter. What matters is that the experience is grand and sweeping, epic and life-altering, a montage of us set to an Alan Menken/Howard Ashman musical number with dancing cutlery and singing woodland critters.

"It's harder than you make it look."

15

"Oh, shut up," she says. "Let me come there and sweep you off your feet."

"I said no!" I protest. "Go study!"

"Fine, but I love you dearly."

"Parting is such sweet sorrow," I say. "Love you, too."

When the call ends, the silence in the suite reverberates in surround sound. Who *do* I want to be here? The Chase of yesteryear was out and seemed loud and proud, but inside my broken, misshapen body was a fragile mess of a person just trying to keep himself together. I love Rae, but I was always slightly out of place amongst a group of cishet girls. I felt small, unworthy of being noticed as anything other than Rae and Leila's fat friend who loved to gossip and draw. None of the cute, out gays even glanced my way because, for most of high school, I hid what I thought was an ugly, fat body under baggy clothes and suffocated my loneliness in food. I never gave myself a fair shot. This is my chance to shift *my* perceptions of myself. Start fresh. Be the fully realized, cartoon, Technicolor version of Chase Arthur I see when I close my eyes or open up a sketchbook or Autodesk Maya, my animation software.

It's time to find my adventure.

Then I remember Taylor said she put something in my sock drawer. I shuffle to the dresser. When I yank it open, I see them: the Prince Naveen and Kristoff dolls, still glammed up, still half-naked and abtacular, looking like queer gods in their own fairy world. Taylor has a knack for knowing what I need before I do.

After propping up the two prince dolls (hand in hand, of course, because they're boyfriends), I grab the nearest sketchbook and the plastic carrying case where I keep all my pencils, charcoal, chamois cloths, stumps, and tortillons. There's nothing like the crisp scent of fresh paper and a new pencil; it's woody and earthy and clean. Sparks fly as my fingertips glide across the page.

The tip whisks fluid and free, brave and bold; the only thing in the world that matters right now is my art, and through it, I can be whoever I want, do whatever I want, live authentically on and through the page.

Stroke after stroke, swipe after swipe, I breathe life into the emerging figure. The muscles in my arm strain. I lean back, tilt my head, and close my eyes as images project on the backs of my eyelids. It looks like me, but it's still far away. I have much more work to do to fully realize who this character is and what their story will be, but it's a start.

I glance up at the shirtless Disney dolls holding hands, and there's a pang in my chest. I want that. Maybe not the brazen shirtlessness—because the thought of a guy seeing my bare body is triggering AF—but the prince. To be the star of my own fairy tale. To not just see myself in the animation I love but to see a love story for the ages unfold, musical numbers and grand marriage proposals, knights in shining armor and all. This, being at CIA, is my chance to create it for myself.

Loose, relaxed, I push down on my fingers, listening to them crack one by one. The air is ripe with fresh graphite dust; I breathe it in and let it invigorate me as I get back to work, the first steps in creating a world, an adventure that belongs entirely to me.

For me.

I don't know what it looks like yet or if it involves a Prince Charming, but it's a start.

2

Freshman move-in day on campus looks a lot like the opening sequence of *Beauty and the Beast*. In this scenario, I'm Belle, wandering around her little town (the dorm suite), trying to mind her own business (nosily snooping at everything my new roommates and their families are bringing in) while the chaotic townspeople (hysterical parents) are so worried about their daily routines (literally running to claim free space like animals) that any disturbance sends them into a tizzy. I may not be a smart girl who reads (gasp!) in an ass-backward patriarchal town, but I am a queer person in a hot-pink T-shirt with an image of a shirtless Prince Adam (the human version of Beast) on a Grindr dating profile with the screen name B_My_Guest alongside the caption *Prince in the Streets, Beast in the Sheets*. My presence and the extremely colorful half of my room are enough to distract them from their missions.

Honestly, it's overwhelming. Parents and siblings and grandparents of virtual strangers buzz around me, and I can't remember any of their names. But I do learn a good deal about my suitemates in a short amount of time.

Aaron is the first to arrive, and he basically looks like a young

Instagram version of Gaston, all burly and muscly, parading around in one of those tank tops that's cut so far down the side, he might as well be wearing nothing at all. Which wouldn't be the worst thing. Half of his stuff is "packed" in garbage bags instead of suitcases. He wastes no time unloading a small set of free weights in the common room and telling me I can "use them whenever, fam."

"Nice. Thanks." Because I totally work out.

His two older brothers are busy carting in cases of beer disguised in empty Capri Sun boxes. Their parents both make a few judgy under-the-breath comments about our small "elite" arts college, and I catch the mom looking at vaguely racist Facebook memes as I come out of my room. That's my cue to stay far, far away. I doubt Aaron mentioned to his family that one of his suitemates is very, *very* gay.

Xavier arrives next with an older sister, his grandma, and an aunt, and immediately he's quite possibly the coolest person I've ever met. He's quiet at first, dancing around Aaron and his family, who don't say much to him. But he's quick to decorate half of his dorm room with the most stunning portraits of Black women I've ever seen. The lighting is electric and layered and exquisite. Then I see his cameras and photography equipment and the signatures—a sweeping *X* with a cool squiggle—on the bottom of the portraits, confirming they're his work. Xavier looks like Michael B. Jordan in his tight white tee, black joggers, and Ray-Bans—indoors!— through which he stealthily checks out Aaron. Don't think I didn't notice *that*.

Once they're unpacked, they each go out for lunch and shopping sprees at the nearest Target with their respective families, leaving me alone yet again. Both Aaron and Xavier asked me to tag along, but that would have been super awkward, so I stayed behind.

The only person who hasn't shown up yet is my actual roommate.

"Where the hell do you think he is?" Rae asks over FaceTime. "Do you think he saw just how gay you are and ran screaming? Or maybe he saw how hot all your suitemates are, including you, and simply couldn't measure up."

"Yes, that's exactly it." My voice falters as I walk around the quiet suite, now filled with boxes and suitcases and knickknacky crap that wasn't here last night.

"Relax. I'm sure this Benigno character is cool," she says. "And if he isn't, I'll come over there and kick his ass. I do have a—"

"A black belt in karate, yes, I know," I finish for her.

She's silent for a few minutes. "Guess who I heard from today?"

There's a thrum in my chest that unsettles me. Rae only talks like that, all cryptic, when Leila reenters our peripheries.

"What'd she say?"

"Just that she misses me and hopes we can hang soon." Rae's eyeballs nearly roll out of her head.

"Cool, cool. What'd you say?" I ask.

"I told her that I hated her face," Rae deadpans.

"Shut up. You did not."

"What do you *think* I said?"

"Knowing you, you told her you can't wait to chill. Right?" I say. "Which is totally fine. Just because she was a shitty friend to me doesn't mean *you* have to stop being her friend."

Rae and I were a package deal before Leila entered the picture, but once she wormed her way into our tight twosome, we became an inseparable throuple. I mean, our ship name was *Raeilachase* for crying out loud. Rae is allowed to be friends with Leila without me. I don't think Rae has figured out how, especially when she's so fiercely protective over me.

"Whatever," Rae says. "Time will tell."

That's Rae's answer for literally everything.

There's a click at the front door of the suite.

"Someone's here," I whisper.

"Oh, leave me on and prop me up so I can see," Rae says.

"Okay, creeper. Get me thrown in campus jail," I retort.

"Sounds hot."

"You really need to stop watching bondage porn," I whisper as the doorknob twists. I peep my head out of my room. "Okayloveyoubye!"

Just as the call ends, the door propels open with such force that it bounces into the rubber stopper against the wall and rebounds directly into the person who flung it. I hear a muffled "fungool!" followed by a throat clearing and a more controlled motion that allows the door to slowly open, revealing a tall, lanky, scruffy-looking Italian guy.

"'Sup, bros?" His voice is way lower than I expected, and it's got this inauthenticity to it, the way a girl might imitate her meat-head boyfriend. He walks with a kind of stiff swagger, chest puffed out like he watched some old John Wayne movies, but he's way more Woody from *Toy Story* than the Duke.

He sees me and looks like a deer in headlights. His back straightens and shoulders pull back. The duffel bag hanging off him falls to the floor.

"Nobody's here," I say. "Just me."

His gaze dips to my shirt, and a smile cracks his face wide open, the tension melting away. "Ohmygod, you must be Chase! That shirt is everything."

Gone is the deep voice, replaced by a natural, higher pitch. He skips over his bag and flings his arms around me. He's so much taller that the hug is a tad awkward, but it's not entirely unwelcome. When he pulls back, he lets out a long breath and sticks his tongue out. "And your hair! It's giving McDreamy vibes. Sorry, I obsessively rewatch old episodes of *Grey's Anatomy* at night and cry. Fair warning."

"Benigno!" I say as if he's an old friend.

"Please don't call me that. Benny. *Please*."

"Benny. Cute."

"Benny Gorga, at your service." He bows.

"Gorga? As in Melissa Gorga, sister-in-law to Teresa Giudice from *Real Housewives of New Jersey*?"

"Ohmygod, they are true queens" Benny says. "No relation, but could you even imagine? Also, can I just say, I was like, ugh, I have to be all masc-for-masc, but you are just a queer lil delight? Ohmygod, I'm making a horrible first impression." He shakes out his arms, and he looks a lot like those inflatable tube men at car washes flailing in the wind. Then he closes his eyes and whispers to himself, "I am centered. I am blessed. I am the master of my own fate. I am thankful for all of life's bounty."

Wide-eyed, I stare, not really sure what to do.

This is the person I'm going to be sharing a room with.

At least he's gay.

Taking in one last breath, his eyes open. "Is this our room?" He points to the space behind me, and I nod. He pushes past me.

"It's like Disney threw up in here. This is truly the gayest thing I've seen in a really long time. And I looked in the mirror this morning. Who is Tim?" He points to Mom's decal job. "Ohmygod, is that for the hot RA because, let me tell you something . . ." A moan escapes his lips as he turns back to me. "Have the other guys seen this?"

"Yep."

"And they're cool?" he asks.

"Yeah, and I get vibes from Xavier. Not Aaron, though. At. All."

He lets out a sigh of relief, and I realize the whole sports-loving, masc-texting Benigno was just an act of self-preservation. I feel that in my bones.

"Ohmygod, really? Is Xavier hot?" Benny crosses his arms and leans in like I'm about to spill the hottest tea ever brewed.

"Beyond."

"And all the parentals? They're not mildly homophobic?"

"I didn't clock anything. But it could go either way with Aaron's parents."

Benny nods. "Well, this suite is certainly the Gay Agenda we all want. Here I was psyching myself up for a straight frat house." He links his arm with mine and pulls me toward the door. "Can you help me with my bags?"

"Yeah. No parents?"

He groans. "Single-parent mom couldn't get off work, so I had to bus it across state lines from Massachusetts with *all* my bags. It was *beyond* tragic."

It takes us an hour to lug all his shit upstairs from the dorm lobby into our room and tuck it away. He has a few posters that

I help him hang—one of Ariana Grande that he had planned to say he jerked off to if any of the guys questioned him (then do the sign of the cross so she'd forgive him for such blasphemy), and two of his favorite movies, *Clueless* and *The Godfather*. He's a music theory major who plays the saxophone and wants to "make albums of smooth instrumental music that straight couples have vanilla sex to." The more he talks, the more I get him. He's pure gay chaos. I love it.

When we're finished, he spots my half-naked prince dolls.

"Ohmygod, this is so kinky," he says, grabbing Naveen and running his fingers over the abs and getting lost in the doll's eyes. "This reminds me, should we, like, develop a system for when we're hooking up?"

"Hooking up? Us?" My mouth goes dry.

"Oh, sweetie, no. Not you-and-I us." He giggles. "Like, me with a guy, you with a guy. Like a sock on the knob or something."

I nod to the door. "I got a whiteboard?"

"Perf." He carries Naveen back to his bed and falls back against the mattress. It creaks so loudly, he screams in concert with it. "I feel *so* bad for whoever shares this wall."

"Are you, like, planning an orgy?"

The Grindr sound buzzes on his phone. "No. I'm looking for my husband, Chase."

"Right." Something tells me Benny's version of love and mine are wildly different.

"Ohmygod, are you a *virg*?"

My cheeks get hot.

"You are!" He jumps up. "That's adorable! Okay, I'll be your wingman. I love this journey for us!" His phone buzzes again, but it's a regular text ping. "Come on, we're going out to meet the masses."

"What?"

He doesn't respond, instead beelining right out of the suite.

I think about what Taylor whispered to me before she left with Mom. Maybe this isn't some grand adventure, but everyone has to start somewhere, and I don't feel like being left behind on the first day. "Wait up!"

3

"Where are we going?" I follow Benny out of the dorm room and into the blistering August sun. The campus is buzzing as thousands of students—new and returning—settle in. Some parents still dot the hordes of young bodies, but for the most part, it feels like a wholly encapsulated world, one defined by prestige and competition, populated by The Chosen—those who worked their asses off to get here, those whose parents paid their way here, and everyone in between. We exist outside larger society, and together, we're taking part in the construction of an ecosystem that's entirely ours. It's weird, and my chest flutters as I think about how this ecosystem doesn't consist of anything I once knew: Mom, Taylor, Rae, even Leila. The Leila I *thought* was my friend, anyway. My high school self is gone, and I feel like I have to come up with an entirely new persona.

Benny's neck nearly snaps as we pass by a group of shirtless guys playing Frisbee, sweat glistening off their bodies. "What'd you say?"

"Where. Are. We. Going?"

"We're meeting a few friends."

"How do you have friends already?" I ask incredulously. "You just got here."

"Ugh, it's such a complicated thing." Benny gestures wildly with his hands and continues, "This guy I used to hook up with also goes here, but we're not hooking up anymore because he's 'straight' now or whatever. But we're friends." He stops cold. "Actually, that wasn't so complicated. He texted me and asked if I wanted to hang out because a bunch of people in his dorm are going to this river thing in the woods. That sounds vaguely *American Horror Story*, but I guess there are cliffs you can jump off."

"I'm not wearing a bathing suit," I say immediately, my mind reeling.

I'm in full freak-out mode. When things like this are sprung on me, I tend to turn around mid-journey because the discomfort of being out of control is not a feeling I enjoy. I like to have all the facts. I like to plan, mentally and physically. My brain needs the opportunity to map out all the potential scenarios before I dive right in.

"Sweetie, underwear is a whole thing," Benny says. "I mean, our capitalist culture tells us we have to buy bathing suits just to go swimming when underwear, which is like, a fifth of the price of a cute Andrew Christian bikini, exists."

He waits for me to respond, but in my head, visions of random strangers laughing at me in my boxer briefs dance on repeat.

"Or you could go au naturel."

Benny must register the absolute fear smacked across my face because he instantly softens and pulls me to the side of a dorm building, out of view of prying eyes. "All right, calm down. I was joking.

Babe, you're hot. Who cares what people think? You don't have to swim. Just be all . . ."

He wiggles his body in a way that I think is supposed to imply sexiness, but all I see is a creepy old man doing a "come hither" thing.

"I don't . . . what is that? What are you doing?"

"Be cool!" he says. "Like all nonchalant. Honey badger don't give a shit."

"First, *that* was nonchalant?" I ask, and Benny shrugs. "Second, 'honey badger don't give a shit' is literally the best video on the interwebs."

He smiles. "Ugh, I'm so glad you know that. My mom was obsessed with that video when it came out during the Stone Age. You feel better?"

Nope. "Yeah, but if people make fun of my underwear, I know where you sleep." I wish I could tell him that it's really my soft upper body that paralyzes me.

"Oh, come on, it can't be *that* bad. Let me see 'em," he demands.

"Benny!"

"Relax, we live together." Something about his tone and the soft, reassuring way he looks at me tells me I can trust him.

"I already hate you." I unzip my super-short jean shorts and shimmy just enough so he can see the fire-engine-red boxer briefs with the tiny cardinals that Mom got me.

"They're super cute! Who doesn't love birds, and honestly, you're probably gonna find a cute guy to comment on them, and I'll be a jealous wreck who will plot to destroy your wedding." He says it without a hint of irony. "Now zip your pants before someone thinks we're hooking up. I'm not about to get cited for indecent exposure on our first day."

"Exposure?!" My hands involuntarily cover my belly.

He sighs. "You're so cute. *Like a Martian.*" Hot honey drips from Benny's lips as he does his best Regina George. Then he leans in, "You have nothing to worry about. Breathe." His encouragement does make me feel a touch better, despite the anxiety bubbling inside me, knowing I may soon be half-naked in front of strangers who could judge me.

Since CIA is situated in picturesque central New York, tucked into the Finger Lakes Region, it's ripe with great expanses of untouched woods, rivers, and lakes and an incredible number of pristine gorges with impressive waterfalls that carve into mountains. I love fresh mountain air—the distinct sharpness of the pine, the way it feels so much lighter and crisper than it does where I grew up, in a small town outside New York City. It does something to my lungs.

It doesn't take us too long to find the trail and stumble upon a group of CIA students hanging at the edge of a cliff, sprawled among boulders and in patches of dried pine needles. One in particular stands and pulls Benny into the broiest bro-hug I've ever seen, and my entire body shudders with secondhand embarrassment as Benny tenses.

Benny yanks on my arm. "Chase, this is my friend from back home, Rhett. Rhett, Chase is like, my new best friend. And also my very cute roommate."

Rhett is all tight mousy curls and brown puppy-dog eyes and a serious stank face that I hope is not for me.

"Nice," Rhett says in a vaguely Southern accent that's not at all Massachusetts like I expected. I can tell by the way he sizes me up and then avoids looking at Benny that he's still struggling. With what exactly, I don't know. But it wasn't long ago that I *was* Rhett, trying to figure myself out, crushing on boys, and not quite fitting into the role everybody shoved me into. He'll get there, too. Or he won't. But it's impossible not to notice how Benny stares at him like a lost puppy just wanting to be pet by his person. Suddenly, I feel super protective over Benny, and I'm not even sure why because we've only known each other for a few hours.

"Not sure where my roommate Jack, is, but uh . . ." Rhett scratches his head. He looks like one of the nondescript boys in those Instagram ads for basic polo shirts. Very much the boy next door who doesn't care about his appearance. And Benny eats. It. Up.

Rhett, who I quickly find out was born and raised in Alabama and then moved to Massachusetts in middle school, motions toward the others and introduces us to his dorm mates, and my heart literally stops beating when I see *her*.

Leila Casablanca.

My former best friend.

She lies lazily atop a rock, cooling herself with an ornate paper fan with gold detailing. She pulls a cigarette out of her bag and lights it. One of her new "friends" lectures her about how bad cigarettes are for the environment, and for a second, she listens. But, in true Leila fashion, she bursts out into an "I'm officially quitting smoking . . . *eventually*" soliloquy, one I've heard a million times before.

"This is my last puff. I need to make it count," Leila declares, rising to her feet. "For the *planet*." She steadies herself on the dirt, holding the cigarette as a beacon of power, the source of her strength. "Never again shall I suckle at your delicious, delectable teat."

Leila has been smoking for two years, and she only tried it

because she was auditioning for the fall play at our high school, a postmodern— whatever the hell that means—interpretation of Tennessee William's *A Streetcar Named Desire*, when we were juniors. She wanted Blanche DuBois so much that she spent weeks watching the Marlon Brando film over and over, reciting her monologue, and smoking. It started with one and became a sort of ritual: capture the moment of a scene, take a drag.

With one last, great puff, her head dips, and she smushes the butt into the face of the rock. The smell—and the fake theatricality— turns my stomach.

She flips her hair as she snaps back to attention. Legend has it that's how Leila Casablanca was born: flipping her hair and shaming the nurses for not having better-quality blankets in the delivery room. Leila's curvy hips and buxom chest accentuate her petite frame, and her long, wavy black hair bounces weightlessly like an animated princess's against her olive skin.

As she revels in the imagined praise, she turns and meets my gaze. Clearly unsure what to do, she stiffens.

"Mother Monster Haus of Gucci, who is that?" Benny whispers. "Because she is fabulous!"

"Ex-BFF," I whisper back harshly.

"Oh, we hate her! Hussy!" Benny hisses.

I want to laugh, but there's nothing funny about this. Seeing her was inevitable. After all, she confirmed her intention to come *here*, to *my* college, *my* animation program, without telling me she even applied. Because to do that, she would have had to admit everything else she did to hurt me. Which would never happen. It's not her style to admit faults. She's too self-absorbed to be fallible.

I just didn't think I'd run into her *this* soon.

She picks up her sunglasses, primps her hair in the reflection, and plasters the fakest smile on her face as she bounds toward us.

"Chase, how *are* you?" Her voice drips fugazi diamonds as she offers an air kiss, one for each cheek, and a rigid hug that I have to reciprocate, or I'll look like a complete ass. She turns toward her audience, who waits for her to speak before they know how to react.

This is what Leila does to people. She hooks them in, makes them feel like they're the center of her universe, and she can do so within a few minutes of them knowing her. It used to impress me until it started to unnerve me.

"Everyone, this is Chase Arthur. We went to the same high school together. He's in the animation program, too. Or is it *they*? I never can remember pronouns. No time like college for a reinvention, amiright?"

I stare at her, wide-eyed. I don't even know what pronouns I feel comfortable using. Maybe *he*. Maybe *they*. Maybe something else entirely. Right now, I'm comfortable with *he*. I tried to explain this to her last year, but she just scoffed.

Benny leans in. "Did she really just—"

"I'm gonna go for a walk."

"I'll come with," Benny says.

"No," I say quickly. "Hang with Rhett. I wanna explore a bit. I'm good."

He nods. "Okay. If you need me . . ." He waves his cell phone.

I make it a point to smile like I'm having The Best Time Ever as I walk past Leila, even giving her a curt nod. I will not give her the satisfaction of knowing she got to me. Not again. Not here.

I walk from the edge of the cliff down to the base of the river, replaying scenes from Disney's *Hercules* in my head. It's a trick my therapist taught me for when I become too overwhelmed: choose a scene from an animated film and revisit it, pausing it to dissect and examine it and analyze all the moving parts until my heart rate steadies.

When I'm out of visual range, I slip my phone out of my pocket and dial Rae, the one person who knows my thorny past with Leila. Of course, she doesn't pick up!

Resisting the urge to toss my phone into the water, I instead bend down to grab a large stick. I fling it into the fast-moving current and watch it bob and travel farther and farther away from me, blending in with the ripples. My eyes strain to follow it, but it moves too quickly. Once it's gone, it's gone forever.

I sit at the base of the river, kick off my sneakers, yank off my socks, and dip my toes into the cool water, letting the waves wash over me as they travel downstream. I focus on how the sun reflects off the ripples, and it appears as if millions of tiny gold specks dance upon the surface.

Someone behind me coughs. "Beautiful right now, isn't it?"

I turn around and am face-to-face with a pair of hairy blond legs. My eyes travel upward past his sculpted calves and navy-blue basketball shorts to a lean, muscled torso, definitely a swimmer's build, according to my periodic Google image searches of semi-naked Olympic swimmers. He has strawberry-blond stubble and messy, golden-blond hair that falls in front of his eyes. He uses his sweat to push his hair back and roughly tamps it down with a Red Sox baseball cap.

His cheeks are red from the heat. "Hey, I'm Jack . . . uh, Reid." His voice is hearty and deep but jovial.

I try to stand to greet him properly.

He cuts me off. "Stay there," he says, sitting down next to me. He takes off his running sneakers and tube socks and sticks his feet in the water. "I, uh, caught wind of your introduction." He nods toward the general area where the rest of the group probably still lounges. "That friend of yours, she's a trip."

"Not friends, but yeah. She is." I try not to sound too blunt, but I can't help it.

His leg brushes against mine. "I prefer people who don't beg for the spotlight or misgender folks." He extends his hand. "Chase, right?"

I smile when he says my name, taking his hand and nodding. Then I catch him staring at the top of my head.

He must realize it because he snaps at attention. "Sorry for staring. Did you know you have gray hair?"

"Wait, I do!?" I say in jest, and his cheeks get rosy. "I'm actually surprised you're the first to comment. I usually get the jokes right away."

Jack's cheekbones become more pronounced as he smirks. "Never met anyone not in a nursing home with a full head of salt-and-pepper hair." He winks. "Like that?"

I snort-laugh. "Nice. Never heard that one before. I was born blond, like you. But it started to change around, you know—" *Puberty*, I think, but how awkward is that to say to a cute boy? Instead, I say, "My mom says I'm an old soul."

"I like it," Jack says. "It's distinguished." He leans back, and his stomach glistens in the sunlight. He squints, and his smile ties me up in knots. "Where you from?"

"Downstate New York," I answer. "You?"

"Vermont."

"I love it there," I say. "My dad used to take me skiing there when I was a kid."

"You ski?" he asks.

"I dabble. Mom made me pack my ski clothes, just in case. But I doubt I'll use them here."

Jack laughs, and it sounds like a symphony. The sunlight hits his blond stubble, and he shines like a beautiful golden statue. I notice just one dimple on the left cheek, and when I say I'm weak, my legs are suddenly boneless. "Same. We should ski this winter. I hear there's a mountain nearby. CIA has a bus that goes there, I think."

"I hate busses." I immediately regret saying that. Out of every-thing, every sentence in the English language I could have said, I told this beautiful boy that I hate busses. Like, what? If Rae were here, she'd slap me.

He grins. "They're terrible. I'm going to have to beg randos for rides back to Vermont during breaks. It's like an eight-hour drive, and my family can't do it."

"That's rough."

That's rough? Who am I right now, a straight bro?

Jack nods toward the river. "You wanna?"

Yes. Yes, I do.

He gets to his feet and pulls me to mine. His hands are rough and large, and when he touches me, my entire body is on fire. We walk, a few feet between us, to a raised mini-cliff where, he says, the water is deep. He cannonballs in, Red Sox cap and all, and the cool water splashes on my skin and sizzles. Wading close to shore, he waves me in.

I hesitate. I'm not one for jumping into large bodies of water without thoroughly vetting the surrounding areas. Especially when I can't see the bottom and the river has an elusive brownish color to it that doesn't exactly inspire confidence in what lies beneath the surface. When I was younger, Taylor and I used to make Dad dive in and swim around for a while, assuring us that nothing murky or goopy or spiky or fishy lurked nearby.

"I'll protect you," he says, like he's reading my mind, which is a bit embarrassing. "Promise."

My mouth goes dry, and I have trouble focusing on Jack as fire blazes across my cheeks. I definitely wouldn't mind him protecting me.

Should I go in with my shirt on? Shirt *and* shorts *and* I wish I had a floor-length jacket, too. I try to steady my shaking hand, but then I remember Benny's calming presence and how he seems not to give a shit about anything, and maybe I can embody that, too?

What do I have to lose?

I tentatively pull off and fold my Prince-Adam-on-Grindr shirt like I work at a department store, trying not to overanalyze how much of a beacon of queerness I am and wondering if that's what drew Jack to me at all. I place it next to my sneakers, and suddenly I'm very aware of my bear cub body, slightly chubby but solid and hairy, not at all cut and smooth like Jack's. My breathing gets shallow, and I try to cover my belly with my arms.

"Come on!" Jack shouts, looking impossibly sexy as water droplets slide down the smooth skin of his shoulders, which of course triggers my body dysmorphia, and I'm certain I must look like an absolute ogre-troll compared to him.

Leila used to poke my stomach and make the Pillsbury Doughboy sound. For Christmas two years ago, Dad bought me a membership to the janky ten-dollar-a-month gym in the neighboring town and said we could work out together if I wanted to.

I spent years obsessing over my weight, and the gossipy digs and snide remarks in gym class and well-meaning "we should diet together" bullshit from friends made me binge and then work out obsessively or eat nothing but celery sticks or grapefruits for weeks. Up until I got hooked on laxatives.

I try to breathe and sing "Zero to Hero" from *Hercules* in my head, imagining my own transformation. Self-actualization or some shit, right?

I tremble still, but it's leveling out. I have to get out of my head.

Here goes nothing.

I want to ask Jack not to laugh at my red bird underwear as I slip my shorts off. I cover my crotch with one hand, half out of fear that I'll pop a boner and half because I'm worried that he'll judge the size of my bulge. I try to hide my belly with the other.

Oh dear god, I can't believe I'm doing this . . .

I hold my breath.

Close my eyes.

Brace for his inevitable disgust.

"Hey," he says, and my body tenses. "We match!" When I open my eyes, I see him pointing to his Red Sox hat then to my underwear, and just knowing where his line of sight is heats my cheeks, and I sigh in relief that he hasn't swum away from me yet.

Without thinking, I take a running leap and cannonball into the river, plummeting to its murky depths. My feet immediately touch something slimy and grimy, and my entire body convulses. I suck in a mouthful of water. I flap my arms like wings, but I only succeed at expediting my own drowning. Great. This is how I die, spiraling out of control in front of the hottest guy in the world. My tombstone etched in shame, with quotes from the Book of Facepalms.

"Hey, hey, Chase . . . relax," I hear Jack say. His arms wrap around me, and his legs kick to keep us both afloat.

I cough every ounce of water out of my lungs. My tense body relaxes into him.

"Can I let you go? Or will you drown on me?"

Part of me wants to tell him I'll sink without him to hold me up. Then I realize his body is pressed up against mine, and I immediately slip out from under his grip to prevent him from noticing how hard I am. Shrinkage in cold water is no match against Jack's appeal.

"I swear I can swim!" I say. "I just touched . . . something."

Jack arches his eyebrow then laughs as I dog-paddle away. With a sick backstroke, he propels himself backward and away from me.

His laugh is hearty, and I have to go underwater and swim away a bit to prevent him from seeing the goofy-ass smile plastered across my face. But of course, I'm thinking too hard, because I slip back under and inhale another mouthful.

I try to stifle my sputtering, but, yeah, I'm a failure.

"Not much of a swimmer?"

"I love swimming," I say. "Though I can see how this might look like my first time ever experiencing the majesty of water."

"*Majesty.* I like that word." He dips beneath the water and thrusts like a rocket toward me, emerging just short of my flailing arms. "You ever hear a word, and then it lodges in your brain, so you're mulling it over and over again until it either sounds like a completely made-up word or takes on a new meaning entirely? *Majesty* feels like one of those words," he says.

I love that. Too bad the moment only lasts a second.

"Chase!" Benny shouts. "Helloooooooo, where are you?! Are you dead? Is this going to turn into an episode of *Unsolved Mysteries*?"

"Who is that?" Jack asks.

"Roommate, Benny," I say. "I guess they're looking for us."

"Speak for yourself." Jack smirks this sort of half grin, and his blueish-gray eyes look sinister, but the kind of sinister that could convert the purest of boys to the dark side.

"I just want to do this for the rest of the day," I confess.

He swims by me, cutting through the water with ease. "I know what you mean." His stroke is so wide that his fingertips graze my chest. "But we should probably get out." He points up, and the sun is no longer visible, the sky turning that late-afternoon hazy gold.

Back to reality, where people other than the two of us exist.

"You first," Jack commands. "Y'know, in case you fall, and I have to save you again."

"Good call." I laugh awkwardly like old-school Goofy. I want to die. In Jack's arms, preferably. As I grab hold of a tree root that juts out of the earth, he places his hand on my back, and I instinctively lean into him for just a second, which is long enough for me to imagine our engagement—an elaborate proposal wherein he organizes a flash mob—followed by our lavish wedding at Walt Disney World's Animal Kingdom (because he seems like the outdoorsy type, from Vermont and whatnot), and then our 2.5 children, whom we will adopt domestically.

"*There* you *are!*" Benny says as I hoist myself out of the river. "I literally thought you died, and there was one brief second where I was all, 'Maybe they'll give me straight As if my roommate's body washes ashore' before I snapped out of it, and ohmygod who is that snack?" His voice dips into something sultry.

Jack jumps out of the water and shakes like a dog. He's standing next to me, and I quietly compare our bodies. His muscular, athletic, hairless. Mine hearty, thick, hairy. I quickly squeeze my wet hog-bod into a dry T-shirt, trying desperately to hide my lumpy form.

"Jack," he says. "Jack the Snack. Nice to meet you. Benny, right?"

Benny's mouth goes slack. "I am Benny. Gorga. Behneeeeeen-yo. Eggs Benny."

Jack leans in. "Is he okay?"

I shrug. "Fuck if I know."

Benny's eyes snap back. "We're all going to the dining hall if you wanna. Um, Rhett, who you know, Jack, because he's your roommate—" Beads of sweat dot his brow. "He's going, too. He was actually looking for you."

"Which dining hall?" Jack asks.

"Campus Center," Benny answers, relieved to get an easy question.

"Is Leila going?" I ask hesitantly.

Benny nods, a little deer-in-the-headlights.

"I think I'd actually like to check out the Garden Dining Hall," Jack says, reading the look on my face. "You down, Chase?" When I nod, Jack says, "Tell them to go on without us. Unless you wanna join, Eggs Benny?"

I snicker.

Benny's gaze darts between Jack and me, then he grabs me and pulls me aside. "You want me to leave you alone with this slender slice of Gus Kenworthy, right? I just wanna make sure I'm not abandoning you in a time of need or something. Or like, forcing you to dine with the enemy."

"It's cool," I say, wanting to be alone with Jack. To keep him to myself. Away from Leila. "Go with Rhett. Just be careful not to let Leila lure you in. She's known to attract all types to her woods, and they never come out alive."

"Brutal. Text me after, and we'll meet up," Benny says. "'Bye, Jack the Snack!'"

Once Benny's out of earshot, Jack says, "Hope that wasn't presumptuous."

"*Presumptuous*," I repeat. "Another one of those words."

His eyes *actually* sparkle. I cannot even make this up.

"And no, not *presumptuous*." I take my time with the word. "At all. I needed an out."

"From that not-friend, right?" he asks intuitively, drying himself off with his shirt. He flings it over his shoulder and slips his feet sockless into his shoes. "When Rhett introduced me to her earlier, I felt this . . . air of pretension. You deserve better than that."

How does Jack know what I deserve? He doesn't even know me, yet he sounds sincere. Maybe it's a line. If it is, it's working. I am so hashtag-basic right now, but *swoon*.

"Big mood. Thanks. I appreciate it."

"No worries," he says so casually and so straight-boy-esque that all my engagement-wedding-2.5-children visions vanish and are replaced by a vision of me forced to stand next to him as he marries a nondescript girl.

I really need to have a talk with myself about expectations.

Then he adds, "I'd rather hang one-on-one," and I'm right back to daydreaming.

On the walk back to Jack's dorm before grabbing food, we joke about my lack of swimming skills, which is wild because I'm actually pretty decent, but I can't exactly tell him why I was so flustered. As we're walking, a Frisbee whizzes toward me, and Jack dips quickly in front of me to catch it. With a smooth flick of his wrist, he sends it sailing back toward the girl who threw it.

I stare in awe.

"What?" he asks.

"That was quick."

"I love Frisbee. You ever play?"

"My people don't friz."

He laughs as he waves his key card and unlocks the front door of his dorm building. "I can teach you."

"Yeah, sure, that'd be cool."

"I'm gonna use the bathroom real quick and then change, and we'll go." He lets me into his dorm, which is your standard-issue two-person, one-room dorm, like the room Benny and I share in our suite, just without the common room and semiprivate suite bathroom.

One side of the room is immaculate, and the other is a damn war zone. There's a very visible invisible line drawn down the center. And it's only the first day.

Pointing to the pristine side, he says, "That's Rhett's side. He's pretty particular. Don't sit on his bed. Or his desk chair. Or touch his stuff. He'll know."

"He runs a tight ship."

"We've been here for a week already," Jack says. "Summer upstart program for extra credits."

That explains a lot.

Jack tosses me a pair of mesh shorts. "If you wanna be dry, have at 'em. You're a bit thicker—" He involuntarily bites his bottom lip. "I mean, you'll fill them out more than I do."

Something about the way he says *thicker* makes my dick chub up a bit, which is weird because, usually, that'd be enough to send me over the edge and back to therapy. But with Jack, something's different.

The thought of wearing Jack's shorts without underwear makes me all sorts of flushed. But my wet boxer briefs rubbing against my jean shorts, now with very obvious dark-blue spots like I wet myself, are obscenely uncomfortable.

Once he slips out to the hall, I strip down my lower half and hop into his shorts, which feel so warm and loose against my skin.

In his absence, I snoop. His room smells like Febreze. Dirty jeans and boxers are strewn on his side of the floor. Nike and Under Armour workout shirts poke out from underneath his unmade bed, which is decked out in Red Sox logos: his fitted sheet is blood-red, and a solid navy-blue comforter with the team's symbol stitched in the center is crumpled in a ball. He has one pillow. One! He's definitely straight. Next to his bed is a bottle of lotion and an opened box of tissues and a bar of artisanal dark chocolate, which, *okay*. Now I'm picturing him jerking off, and dear god, I have to stop because I'm getting a boner in Jack's shorts. *Must. Distract. Myself.*

There's a tall, skinny bookcase he obviously brought from home. The shelves are packed beyond capacity with books, most of which look like they're about to explode onto the floor.

I riffle through a few printout photos of his sitcom-ready, picture-perfect nuclear family, including who I'm assuming are his older brother and younger sister, and a few of him with another guy who looks our age. I can tell this other dude is very, very straight, but the way Jack stares at his friend is piercing. I know that look. On the backs of each, *Jack and Callum 2021* is scribbled in pen. Looks like fancy script, too, the way my grandma used to write. So clearly his family is from the 1950s.

Tacked to the cinder block walls, there are three crooked posters: one of Years & Years, a queer pop band I'm vaguely familiar with, one of Taylor Swift's *folklore* album, and one of Ernest Hemingway's *Winner Take Nothing*.

There's a knock on the door.

"Decent?" Jack asks before pushing open the door. He notices me staring at the Hemingway poster, and I feel him come up behind me. "Have you ever read 'A Clean, Well-Lighted Place'?" he asks.

When I tell him I haven't, he says, "It's life-changing. Hemingway is my favorite."

"Really?"

"As far as classic writers go, anyway. Huge fan of *The Great Gatsby, Catcher in the Rye, One Flew Over the Cuckoo's Nest, To Kill a Mockingbird*. And *Huck Finn*. I love *Huck Finn*," Jack explains. "There is nothing more beautiful than words."

He catches me staring, but it's not in awe. I'm pretty sure I have a very confused, fuck-you sort of look plastered across my face.

"What?"

"Don't take this the wrong way, but you just said a whole lot of stuff by dead, straight, white people, mostly men. Ever thought of diversifying?"

His cheeks turn a shade of crimson that makes him look sunburnt. "I, uh, yeah. Absolutely. Recommendations?"

I sit down on the chair at his desk; it's the only thing not draped in dirty clothes. "James Baldwin, bell hooks, Janet Mock, Ta-Nehisi Coates, Elizabeth Acevedo, Roxane Gay, Toni Morrison, Angie Thomas, Tomi Adeyemi, N. K. Jemisin. Off the top of my head."

"Noted, thanks." Jack perks up. "You're a reader? Writing major like me?"

Makes sense that he's studying writing after witnessing his revelry over words.

"No, I mean, yeah, I love to read, but I'm not a writing major. Animation—I'm in the art and design school. I just love learning. Especially about stuff I don't know personally. I have some books I can lend you. Real visual stuff that helps me with my art."

"You're a bit of a surprise, huh?" He tears his damp shirt off and shucks his shorts to the ground until he's in nothing but his briefs.

My heart jumps all the way into my throat.

After digging through his dresser drawer, he pulls out a maroon-and-white striped Rugby shirt with a yellow collar and tosses it onto his bed. He leans against the wall and waits for my response. I'm trying not to look at his lean, toned chest, but it's hard.

"I've never been a surprise to anyone. I'm just me."

"Something tells me that's not true."

That smile! Seriously, I'm weak.

"So animation? You gotta tell me more about that," he says.

I hate talking about my art. It's like whenever somebody asks me what my vision is, or what my story is about, or my style, I freeze up. I know *how* to describe it, and I know what I like. I'm a purist, an advocate of 2D hand-drawn animation where you can see the artist, the stroke of their pencil, the imperfect perfection of the brushstrokes, the way the scenery is painted like a Rembrandt. It's my dream to be the gay twenty-first-century Mary Blair, whose psychedelic pop-arty drawings still inspire Disney animation. I also love when computer technology can be seamlessly integrated into hand-drawn work, like in *Paperman*. It's not that I don't love CGI. I do—or, rather, I can appreciate the artistry—but I love pulling from different styles and periods to come up with something that fits my vision.

"I don't know," I say. "Not much to say."

"Come on." He's squinting at me like my lie is drawn all over my face. "Yes, you do."

Damn. He's not shy. *Clock a bitch, why don't ya?*

"I guess the best way to describe it is *love*, you know. Every story is a love story of some kind. And that's what I try to convey with my art. My love for the medium. My love for the characters I've created. I want to make what I never had." My face heats up, and I stop myself because, fuck, it makes me so uncomfortable to talk about myself like this. I don't want to seem conceited because, believe me, I'm far from the most talented person in the room—I'm just happy to be here. "What about you? Tell me about your writing."

Jack takes that exact moment to turn away, take his briefs off, and slip into a fresh pair of shorts. I avert my eyes. As much as I can, anyway.

"Now *that* is personal," he says, coming up to me and knocking his shoulder into mine. "Maybe once you show me your art, I'll show you some of my words."

It's a big fucking deal to share your work with other people. If I've learned anything from workshopping my own art, it's that it's a sacred act, one that requires humility and bravery. It's a lot like being exposed, and even though I've already seen a lot more of Jack than I ever thought possible after only a few hours of knowing him, something tells me seeing his naked flesh is nothing compared to reading his heart on the page. And that feels like something I'm not yet ready for. Even though I want to be.

I'm a bit breathless at the thought of this strange, beautiful man even wanting to be so open with me eventually, and it electrifies my body. I wonder if this is what all princesses feel at the start of their fairy tales when they stumble upon their princes. Or if this is just some sort of temporary spell that only fools are susceptible to.

"Ready for food?" he asks.

"I'm starving."

We settle at a corner table at the far end of the dining hall, in a spot by the large glass picture window overlooking CIA's vast sustainable food garden, something Jack says is what drew him to the school in the first place. Beyond the creative writing program, of course. He tells such rich, detailed stories about his family and their "modern cabin in the woods"-style farmhouse with a roadside stand where they sell fruits during the months when it's not bitterly cold and snowy. The way he talks about his family makes me jealous, like they're the best people on the planet. And like something out of the fabled American Dream aesthetic.

"My dad and mom are my best friends," he says. "I also have an older brother."

"Callum?" I say and then wince because how in the hell should I know who *Callum* is? Oh, that's right. Because I'm a creeper who rifles through cute boy's rooms. "I saw a picture with his name."

He laughs. "Nah, Callum is my best friend. I have a little sister who is fourteen, too. I'd do anything for her."

Okay, swoon, because same.

"Taylor, my sister, is twelve, and I'd die for her."

There's a glint in his eye as he nods like I passed some test.

"That's cool that you're that close to your parents," I say.

"Yeah, some people think it's weird, but that's how I was raised. My dad is pretty awesome. He owns a whiskey distillery, and I've pretty much been drinking the stuff since I was my sister's age. My mom hates it, but she goes along with it because, if you know my dad, you can't really say no to him."

Jack must catch the fearful look in my eyes because he quickly follows it up with, "Not like that. He's not abusive or a bad guy, but he's like the town mayor. Not actually, but I'm telling you, every-body falls in love with him because he's just like, Superman, you know?"

No, I don't. But it's nice to imagine a father can be a superhero.

"What about you?" he asks.

"I'm really close to my mom. She's the quintessential single mom, does it all. Sometimes I think she does too much. I worry about her because she puts everything into Taylor and me, and now that I'm gone, Taylor is on the cusp of being all, 'fuck you, mom, I hate you.'"

From the look on Jack's face, his sister would never say that to their mother.

"I wish I could be there for both of them to sort of, I don't know, guide them forward. That's kinda my deal in the family. And I want my mom to have a life beyond us."

"I get that," Jack says. "What about your dad?"

"Nothing really to say. We see him every other weekend." I shrug and push food around my plate with my fork. "We've always had a hard time clicking. I think he wanted a kid who played sports, and that's very clearly not me. I guess the best way to put it is, I get the sense that if we weren't related, we wouldn't choose to be friends. But he was cool when I came out, so that counts for something. A lot, actually."

That's all I'm comfortable saying because there's a lot I still haven't processed with my dad. Mostly the idea that one day, someone could just decide they're no longer in love with the person they married. Mom was devastated when he packed a bag and left. And Taylor and I got the whole "it's not you, it's me," but clearly, neither of us was enough to make him stay. He didn't even leave for another woman, which I might have understood in some weird way. He left to be alone. He *just so happened* to meet Krissy once he was alone.

Jack gets this faraway look in his eyes. Sure, we just met, and no, I don't know him, but he does seem a bit . . . lost. I can't put my finger on it, but I want to make him feel better.

"You okay?"

"Is it weird to be a bit homesick already?" he admits, and I shake my head. He looks away before returning to meet my gaze. "And that I feel a bit *less* homesick talking to you?"

"I was thinking the same thing."

I try not to overanalyze the crinkle of his smile, but I can't help that I'm already kind of maybe completely totally lost in it.

4

Benny is gone when I leave for my first class on Monday. He's an early riser, up at 5:00 a.m. for a run before heading to the music school to practice. Apparently, all the "HiNotes"—the ridiculous moniker given to all students of CIA's Highland School of Music, named after some famous composer I've never heard of—are required to log ten hours of weekly practice time outside class, and the clock starts ticking move-in weekend. Yesterday I made a joke about how he was probably meeting up with Rhett in a practice room, and he blushed and turned the tables on me and Jack.

But that's the thing. There is no "me and Jack."

I haven't seen him since we ate at the dining hall. We didn't exchange numbers, so I can't text him. He's not on social media. Fact, because I spent part of the day yesterday scouring Twitter, Instagram, Snapchat, and TikTok—so I can't even cyberstalk him. I even tried Grindr, but no such luck. None of the headless torsos matched the one now forever burned in my mind. That little freckle under his right nipple kept me up last night.

Jack's probably not even gay or bi or pan. I'm probably misreading all the signs, and he's just super friendly. Vermonters do have a reputation for being free-spirited hippies, so maybe he's one of those sensitive New Age dudes, the kind who aren't afraid of feelings but are still very much straight. Plus, I've never had a boyfriend, never even been kissed, so my baseline knowledge of Interested Men stems purely from studying straight male characters played by Chris Evans in romantic comedies.

Wow, I'm a lost cause.

The next morning, I take the long way to the visual arts building. This particular path *may* involve a detour past Jack's dorm. Because casual, not-at-all-planned run-ins happen, right? It's merely a coincidence that the other night at dinner, Jack mentioned that he, too, had an 8:00 a.m. class, so the chances that we could be walking toward the academic quad at the same time would be fairly high.

Coincidences are great ways of masking thirst.

I feel a lot like Aurora from *Sleeping Beauty*, who had a clandestine encounter with handsome Prince Philip in the woods. Then, he was just gone. The chances of Jack being a hallucination are quite strong, especially given my extreme thirst levels for a man.

Jack's room is on the first floor, nearest to the main entrance, so his window overlooks the exact concrete path I'm on right now.

Don't stop. Don't look in. Don't be a creeper.

Slow down. Casually glance. Can't see inside, crap!

Be cool. Be breezy. Keep it moving.

My heart races, a million different scenarios flashing through my mind: *What if he notices me? What if he sees me but didn't recognize me because I'm unmemorable? What if—*

"Chase!" Jack's voice booms from behind me as I round the corner to the side of his dorm. Footsteps slap against the pavement as he runs toward me.

Okay, play this cool.

I make it a point to overexaggerate my head movements in an "Oh my word! Who is calling my name?" kind of way.

His hand grabs onto my shoulder, and he squeezes.

Squeezes!

"Hey, uh, *Jack*, right?"

His face falls. Shoot. I might've been *too* breezy.

"JK, wanted to see how you'd react." I'm thinking so quickly I impress myself. "It's John, right?" Cue coy smirk.

Which he returns! Score!

"What're you doing 'round these parts?" he asks, hoisting his backpack up.

"Got turned around. It's such a beautiful morning, I wasn't paying attention." Sweat trickles down my back. I'm such a horrible liar that the words lodge themselves in my throat and sound like I'm forcing them out too quickly. So much for being smooth.

"Took me a few days to orient myself when I moved in," he says. "You'll find your way, as we all must."

"Okay, Deepak Oprah."

Jack smiles again, but it seems a bit different today, like he's struggling to contain or suppress it.

I have to actively stop myself from saying, "I missed you yesterday," because that's weird, so instead, I go for the standard, "What class you got?"

"Introduction to the Essay, followed by Introduction to Creative Writing. You?"

There's a level of excitement to his voice that I know well, because I share it.

"Intro to Digital Animation Production, then Life Drawing, but what I'm really looking forward to is this advanced seminar course where we pair up with more experienced upperclassmen to produce a full short. It's with *the* Linda McPherson."

"That sounds awesome. Wait, Life Drawing. As in naked people?" he asks.

I nod. "It's tasteful. The models make a ton of money. I could never, though."

Not that I can't use the money, of course. It's bad enough that Mom had to take out massive loans in her name to pay for my tuition not covered by the scholarship. But being naked in front of a room full of strangers, even if they are learning and not treating you like a Pornhub clip, is horrifying.

Jack is silent.

"What? You would?" I ask, knowing I'm pushing boundaries for 8:00 a.m.

He shrugs. "I got nothing to hide."

My mouth goes dry. I'm weak. I stare straight ahead, afraid that if I turn to look at him, the entire campus will explode.

"So tell me more about this Linda McPherson person," he adds.

"Oh!" Relief washes over me. "She's only the baddest of badasses in animation. She directed the film *Crumbs*, which came out last December."

He nods slowly. "Cool?"

"Yes, very cool," I continue. "We have to watch it. It's *so* good."

"Not a big movie guy," he says.

Well, I guess not even Jack can be perfect.

"I can't believe you missed it. It was the first fully hand-drawn animated feature film from a major animation studio since, like, 2011."

As we walk, I give him the rundown. "*Crumbs* is a retelling of 'Hansel and Gretel' from the point of view of the witch. My favorite part is the 'I Want' song, where the witch sings about wanting a family and to be accepted as an eccentric candy maker. I can relate to that. McPherson is a CIA alumna, too. She's like, a visionary. And she's here as a guest lecturer for the year. That's like if Hemingway popped out of his grave and taught your creative writing class."

"Damn." He sighs. "That's awesome. I like the way your eyes go bonkers when you talk about this stuff. I'm the same way."

The way he says that makes me feel like he understands me in a way not many others do. Even Rae looks at me like I've lost every single one of my marbles when I vomit about animated films.

We reach a fork in the path.

"I'm this way," I say, nodding toward the art building on the left.

"Yeah, I'm that way," Jack gestures to the lit building on the right. "Dinner tonight?"

"Sounds good!" I say, practically skipping away.

I get all the way to the main entrance when I realize we didn't solidify a time. Or a meeting place. And I still don't have his number. I glance back, but he's gone.

Syllabus day is, well, syllabus day.

We don't do much but go over course expectations in all my classes, which is not entirely different from the first day of high school, with two exceptions: (1) every professor assigns more home-work than high school teachers, and (2) every single student in my program has the same hunger to be the best artist ever. Which, great. Who doesn't love some healthy competition? But also, (3) Leila is in every single one of my classes, including the advanced animation seminar. So, like, there's competition, but then there's Leila, a whole additional layer of bullshit I do not pay tuition to endure.

Leila and I met in high school art classes, and our bond over different mediums grew. But even back then, she knew she wanted to be "a high-powered executive at a film studio who will make enough money to one day quit and open up her own studio and art gallery." She wanted to make art but was unwilling to sacrifice her bank account.

She used to focus on sculpture. Animation, she once claimed, was "never" a consideration, but when my first short got a lot of buzzy attention online, something shifted in her behavior toward me. She began sketching and painting more furiously, dabbling in software she once said was "destroying real art." She started cri-tiquing my work more harshly, hanging out with me less, and in our classes, I saw her portfolio expanding, showcasing more than just her sculpting; whenever I would ask why she was deviating from her medium, she would make a comment like "I'm broadening my horizons," and it always sounded passive-aggressive. Then she went behind my back and applied for *my* scholarship at *my* CIA program. She knew it was selective and that I needed the money; her doctor parents could afford to send her to any college in the world. Yet she got *my* spot, which forced Mom to take out exorbitant loans for me, loans she couldn't afford, so that I could be here at my dream college.

Maybe it would have been fine if Leila had just been honest with me. Told me how she was feeling. Gave me some sort of closure, because sometimes friendships end. But can't they just end peacefully, without drama and hate? She iced me out. Stopped texting, calling, being my friend. Kept her CIA application from me. Made me feel like my dreams were silly in comparison to her more "socially acceptable career path" as a "future executive." And she didn't even tell me she got in. I found out from Rae, who heard from someone outside our supposedly tight threesome. And when I discovered Leila had been saying hurtful things about me and my art behind my back, how I supposedly never supported her, and how I was playing up the "trendy nonbinary angle"—during a time I was struggling to define my identity—I knew we were over. I needed my best friends, and she acted like I didn't even exist. Rae thinks her jealousy over my online popularity made her competitive nature kick into high gear. I got the notoriety she wanted, so she had something to prove. But her going after *my* dream and *my* success meant more to her than being happy for me and standing by me as I figure out who I am, inside and out. That's what hurts the most.

And now, here we are, competing against each other. Again.

At least this time, I know it.

I catch Leila stealing glances at me from the back of the room, but I don't give her the satisfaction of returning them. By the time the seminar starts, she's practically seething, especially because she's late and has to sit in the only open seat in the room—next to me. As if being around her weren't enough, I have to suffer with her literally on top of my space. And the way she positions herself, honestly, I *can't*! She pivots her body so her back faces me, and her

56

hair, which is tied up in a messy ponytail, actually spills onto my desk. It's a small classroom, which doesn't feel right for an animation class, and I worry for a second that I'm in the wrong place. I'm about to ask someone, but then Linda McPherson breezes into the room, and everyone suddenly goes quiet.

"I'm late, I know, but I just spent an hour fighting with the ice cream vending machine." She holds up a half-eaten Chipwich. "Before you ask, yes, it *is* worth all two of my dollars."

She's wearing tight, high-waisted jeans and an oversize highlighter-yellow blazer with '80s shoulder pads and a graphic tee of Ariel from *The Little Mermaid* covered in face tattoos. Ariel's iconic red hair—which reminds me of Rachel Maddow's but edgier, with soft-pink highlights at the tips—is buzzed short, and there are gauges in her ears.

"Before we get started, no, this will obviously not be our classroom. There was a scheduling mix-up; when we meet on Wednesday, we'll be in a room with drafting desks and the proper tech so you can hit the ground running. I'll email alert you all."

I breathe a sigh of relief. Leila shifts her weight and tosses her hair so that it swishes against my desk, obviously to rile me up.

"Someone tell me," Professor McPherson asks between bites of the melty ice cream sandwich, "What's a trope? And please introduce yourselves so I know who you are. Name and pronouns."

I go to raise my hand, but Leila's hand pops up quicker, and before Professor McPherson can call on anyone, Leila just goes right ahead and speaks.

"Leila Casablanca. She and her and hers." She pauses like she's waiting for applause or something, a by-product of always being under the spotlight when we were in high school. When it doesn't come, she clears her throat. "A trope is like a common or easily recognizable element of plot, or character, or event-slash-situation in a story." Her voice is rigid and robotic, like Siri reciting a definition she found online. This is her "I'm superior" inflection.

Professor McPherson doesn't look impressed. "What's an example of one?"

"Love at first sight," Leila answers.

"Why do they work? In other words, why is something like 'love at first sight' used over and over again?" Professor McPherson asks. "And how might something like that be turned on its head?" She scans the room then points at me. "You with the gray hair."

"Chase Arthur. He/him, maybe they/them? I, um . . ." I start a little breathlessly, but she nods in affirmation. "Tropes work because our brains don't really have to do much work. We see them so often, from the time we're babies, that we automatically register their meaning, allowing us to almost predict what's going to happen in the story. Lonely princess meets a charming prince. We know they're going to end up together. The fun is how they get there. What do they survive to make their triumphant love worth it?"

"How would you turn that on its head?" she asks.

"You could use another trope," I answer. "Enemies to lovers. Hotheaded princess who wants to be a knight meets lazy prince from enemy kingdom who has something to prove to his warmonger father, so he goes after the princess, not really wanting her for anything but to spite the king, but through a series of events, they fall in love. Or maybe the princess realizes she's queer and kills the prince, commanding both kingdoms. Actually, that's way better. Dibs on that."

Everyone around chuckles, except Leila, who huffs under her breath.

Professor McPherson smirks. "That last part is something I'd love to see. As visual storytellers, our greatest strengths *and* weaknesses are the reliance on tropes. Lean too heavily on a cliché, and the audience will predict everything."

Leila's hand shoots up. "I just have to say that your film, *Crumbs*, was so inspiring. It took the evil witch trope and completely turned it on its head in a way I've never seen done before."

Professor McPherson offers a tight smile and leans back on the teacher's desk at the front of the room.

"Like, the way the witch is an allegory for how society treats LGBTQ-plus people," Leila continues. "You're an inspiration."

My jaw tightens as my teeth grind. Leila stole that line from me.

When the film came out last year, before our friendship soured, I asked her to see it with me, but she wouldn't, saying animated films were for little kids and that her sculpture was more elevated than the art I wanted to pursue. I had even tried to share *The Art of Crumbs* book with her to get her to appreciate the art, if not the film.

"You can do better than *this*," Leila had said, flipping through the original storyboards and artwork by Professor McPherson. She pointed to a particular painting in which one half of the witch was sinister and dark and dripping with erratic paint strokes, while the second half was vibrant with free and clean brush strokes.

"Seriously? This is brilliant. The duality and uncertainty in the witch's character? I wish I could do that."

Leila had scoffed, but I pushed on, telling her that the story was really about the witch creating her own found family when heteronormative society kicked her out. Leila had smiled and nodded and said, "If you say so. At least S'Morez is cute." She had pointed to the personified snack treat sidekick and giggled in a way that made me feel small for loving every single aspect of animation.

So to hear her now use my own interpretation in a class she was never supposed to attend in the first place feels like a betrayal. Again.

Professor McPherson looks downright bored as Leila finishes her monologue.

"All right, well, I appreciate that," the professor comments. "But I have to say, sucking up won't get you far in this world. You know what gets you far? Talent. You know what'll get you further? Humility. And busting your ass, taking critical feedback, failing, and then growing from that. That's what I'm looking for."

Leila sits back, deflated, but I can tell by the way she nods that she's doing her best to appear to listen.

"This seminar is a long-standing tradition for CIA's animation program, a way for the freshmen with the greatest potential to shine. This year is no different. You have been chosen through rigorous study of your portfolios by the department chair, and this year, yours truly." She moseys around the front of the room, making eye contact with all ten of us. "As you know, this course pairs with a third-year seminar. Junior animation students will be partnered with you to help create an animated short for the December showcase. This semester, I've arranged a little competition." She rubs her hands together like a dumpster-diving raccoon. "The student with the most compelling short, which will be voted on by attendees, will be awarded the standard arts endowment, and this year, the chosen favorite will also get the opportunity to participate in an all-expenses paid mentorship with me in Los Angeles either during the summer months or during a study abroad in LA at any point in your academic career, which I'm sure you know is highly popular among CIA's students."

There's a collective gasp, and hands go up almost instantly.

This would be more than a dream come true. Which, obviously, scares me. As much as I buy into "happily ever after" as a fantastical concept, something to admire and aspire to as a Disnerd, in practicality, I've learned not to get my hopes up.

People like me rarely get the storybook ending.

Professor McPherson motions for everyone to relax and continues, "Your goal this semester is to take a well-known trope and turn it upside down. No subject matter is off-limits. Your animation does not have to be family-friendly. Lucifer knows *Crumbs* wasn't. Disney turned it down because the—*cough*—queer—*cough*—excuse me—*thematic* elements weren't family-friendly." She rolls her eyes. "Fuck that. Your short just has to have heart.

"For next Monday, I want you to create a quick hand-drawn flip animation that you will present to the class. These flip-books will serve as a teaser to your story. They must be sketched and then filmed. You can use the cameras on your phones, as long as we can project your film to the class. You should also have a workable story. The ending doesn't have to be set in stone, as endings never are at the beginning," she riddles. "The junior animation majors will choose who they want to work with based on your teasers. So, whatever you do"—she looks directly at me—"make sure to wow us."

No presh.

Leila turns to the girl next to her and says, "That mentorship is mine." Then the volume ratchets up to make sure I can hear her. "I got this in the bag."

Cue internal screaming.

5

"Chase," Professor McPherson calls out to me after class.

I stop and pivot on my heels.

Leila's eyes narrow at me, curiosity piquing her interest. Her smugness is so big, it might as well be an entirely separate person she tows behind her, the way she used to lead groupies of under-classmen around in high school like ducklings.

"Ms. Casablanca, can you close the door on your way out? Thanks, dear," Professor McPherson says.

"Abso*lute*ly," Leila says with a flourish to mask her annoyance at not being asked to stay.

When the door clicks shut, Professor McPherson motions for me to take a seat. "I spent the weekend reviewing the portfolios of all the students in this seminar."

My heart drops.

I hold my breath.

This was all a mistake, wasn't it? I'm not supposed to be here, and she's about to tell me that I have to drop the class, or maybe she already removed me from the roster, and this is just her way of breaking it to me gently. If Leila were still here, she'd be smizing all the way to that mentorship.

The professor pulls up a chair and sits back, her arms on each of the rests like she's some cool jock in a '90s teen movie. "There's so much promise in your art. It moved me in a way I haven't been moved before. Sure, it's rough, and it needs refinement of skill, but that comes with experience and dedication. It's so rare that I see myself in someone else's work. Maybe that's because there are so few nonbinary animators out there. Or, rather, so few who are out and make art that reflects that." She clears her throat and fills the blanks when she says, "I watched the interview you did with *The BuzzWord*."

I let go of a breath that locked my entire body in place. "I—" I begin, but I don't know what I say to that. I didn't know Professor McPherson is nonbinary. Fuck, I've been referring to them as *she* in my head. My cheeks heat when I realize I'm now assuming that the professor uses they/them. This is some *Inception*-level thought betrayal.

"I just wanted to let you know that I'm here as a resource, something I wish I had when I was just starting out in this business."

There's an ease with Professor McPherson that I haven't ever had with another adult, which of course makes me drop my guard, something I hardly ever do when it comes to discussing my gender identity.

"Can I ask you something kind of personal?"

Though Professor McPherson's face softens, I notice a full-body tension. "Within reason."

"Right," I say. "How'd you know you were nonbinary? And do you use they/them?"

A smile stretches across Professor McPherson's face. "I sometimes use they/them, but I actually like she/her."

"It's okay to do that?" I ask. "Use she/her, even though you don't identify solely within that binary?"

She emits a nervous laugh I recognize because I do the same thing. "The one thing that I've learned is that there are no rules, only the ones you impose upon yourself. If you feel comfortable, that's all that matters."

I gnaw on the inside of my cheek for a bit and stare past her, afraid to look her in the eyes. A memory of my secret sketchbook flashes. It was filled with self-portraits of me as both prince and princess, knight and witch, male and female, and sometimes a magical combination of both and neither all at once. I used to think I was a shape-shifter because some days I would feel more masculine, others more feminine, and sometimes in-between or something else entirely. One drawing I did over and over again was a gender-ambiguous angel with dragon-like wings. They had my body but with flowing garments that hugged their curves. I wrote little stories in the margins about them, and some days, I felt like that angel: ethereal, something beyond this binary world.

But one day, when I came home from school, I found Dad in my room with the book in his hands. His eyes were red, and he started shouting at me. That I was a boy! A man! That if I needed to be reminded about that, he would knock some sense into me! He never did hit me, but it made me hate my body even more, to think that I might be like him. And if I wasn't, would he ever love me?

"You asked me how I knew I was nonbinary," she says. "How did you?"

I think about the angel in my sketchbook, the way Taylor and I would play dress up and how I'd relish the moments when I'd let her sloppily apply makeup to my chubby face, all the millions of ways I never felt like the rest of the boys but always felt out of place with the girls, too, even if I was more comfortable around them.

"I guess I just always knew, even though I didn't have a word for it until I was older."

"Same here," Professor McPherson says. "It felt like all the tension I carried in my shoulders melted when I knew how I fit with all the ways I *saw* myself but couldn't *be* myself."

"Do you ever feel like you still don't know?" I ask.

"Sometimes, but I think that's normal."

"I don't know what normal is. I don't know what pronouns I want to use. Right now, I feel most comfortable with he/him, but maybe that's just a comfort thing. I don't even know if I like the term *nonbinary*, because it's like, I do sometimes feel like I exist within the binary, but it's not stagnant, you know? More fluid, like genderqueer, which is a term I think I like. But . . . I don't know."

"You don't have to have anything figured out right now. Or ever."

"That sounds . . . horrifying," I say.

"That's *life*, Gray," she says. "Mind if I call you *Gray*?"

I shrug. "Seems fitting."

"I have to run to a meeting, but I just wanted to tell you that I'm here to help with your art or anything else." She stands up and moves to gather her belongings. "For now, if you want me to use he/him, I will. If that changes, tell me."

"Thank you, Professor." I suck in a breath. "Can I be nonbinary and use he/him?"

She smiles. "There are no rules, Gray. And there's no pressure to be anything other than exactly who you are at any given moment."

That *sounds* nice.

But the thing is . . .

I wish I knew who I was and how to be comfortable with every part of myself in every given moment. The only thing I know for sure, even more so now, is that I have to get this mentorship with her, because opportunities like this, for nonbinary creatives, don't come along every day.

And I have to fight for them when they come.

6

"You've wasted like thirty zillion trees since you started this assignment," Benny says from his bed, hanging over the edge upside down like a tree sloth. "I'm really not judging you at all, I swear!"

"I know. I just can't figure out what to do for this flip-book."

I contemplate snapping my pencil in half, but the thought of it gives me anxiety. Every time I try to draw something, Leila's face pops into my head, telling me that I'm not good enough. That she's more talented, more deserving, and then my hand freezes on the page or draws something dark and shaky, uncertain garbage.

"You need to get out of this room!" Benny says. "You've been holed up for the past three days. When was the last time you showered?"

"An hour ago," I say.

"Oh. Point still stands. Why don't you call Jack? I can tag along on whatever adventure you two have, like the desperate third wheel. Wait." He pauses, as if what he just said about himself sank in. Then just breezes past it. "I really wouldn't mind seeing that snack."

I look up from my blank sketch pad. "You just want to run into Rhett. How is he, by the way?" I haven't been able to run into Jack casually in a way that doesn't make me look like a complete stalker, so between that and the stakes of this assignment, there hasn't been any movement on that front.

Not that there is any movement to be had, anyway. We're just friends.

I think.

"Ohmygod, you savage binch. I see what you did there, and while I don't like it, I respect it." Benny rolls onto his stomach, buries his face into the comforter, and expels a muffled scream. "Rhett's in the middle of another 'I'm straight, we can't hook up' phase."

"Tragic."

"Right?" Benny wriggles his body until he manages to sit upright. "We have to go out tonight, or I'll actually die. It's Friday! There are probably a million parties we can go to where I can drink until I puke. Preferably a rosé spritzer of some kind."

"I'm thinking it might be hard to find a party that serves a rosé spritzer."

"You honestly never know." Benny clasps his hands together. "Please, I need action of some kind. Don't you have a friend who goes to Laurene?"

I nod. "I wouldn't mind a night out." I stick a finger in the air. "Hold, please." After grabbing my phone, I dial Rae, and her face bursts onto my screen.

"Yes, binch!" Benny shouts. "That's what I'm talking about! Dick and rosé!"

"Dick and rosé?" Rae asks. "Sounds like a party!"

"Harlot!" I shout.

"Says the person who made me listen to Cardi B's 'WAP' on repeat the summer before junior year," she retorts.

"You both are fabulous!" Benny hops off his bed and moves to hover behind me. "Hi, I'm Benny, Chase's new best friend!"

"Excuse you?" Rae says, aghast. "I never received your application. This simply will not stand."

"Ohmygod, it must have gotten lost in the mail," Benny says, not missing a beat.

"It's a rigorous process to be approved," Rae says.

"I'm gay and like rosé," he says.

"You're approved!" Rae shouts. "So what do you two want? What are you doing tonight?"

"That's kinda why I was calling," I say.

"We need to get out," Benny interjects. "I'm withering away in here!"

She laughs. "Not sure if y'all are interested, but there's a concert on campus for Laurene students," she says. "Years & Years. Not sure if either of you have heard of them."

"I think you mispronounced A-ri-a-na Gran-de," Benny says.

Rae bursts out laughing.

"I know them. They're a queer pop band with, like, an electronic rock vibe," I say, remembering the poster of the band tacked on Jack's wall. "If it's just for Laurene students, how're we getting in?"

"If you'd let me finish, slore, I would've told you I was legit just about to call you because a group of us were gonna go, but at the last minute, Harry and his friends decided to—wait for it—*study*."

"Ew," Benny says.

"Right?" she scoffs. "So I have three extra tickets. You hotties in?"

Benny grabs my shoulder and jerks me sideways. "Yes, please, god! I can't stay here while Xavier and Aaron parade around shirtless. I mean, the gall of these hot men with their . . . exposed . . . nips!" He fans himself.

"I guess we're in," I say. "And I'm going to bring another friend."

Rae squeals. "I'm so excited I get to caress you after two whole weeks apart!"

"Wait, I want in on this caressituation," Benny says.

"I have a lot of love to give," Rae says.

With a glint in his eye, Benny says, "I've been found."

When I hang up, I turn to Benny. "You down to casually run into Jack?"

"Ohmygod, a gay *Mission: Impossible*!" he shouts. "But first, I gotta get cute."

Benny and I have exactly one hour to casually run into Jack, convince him to come with us to Laurene for the free Years & Years show, and get our asses on a bus so we have time to meet up with Rae.

"So what's the Jack Plan?" Benny asks. When I say nothing, he stops just as we reach Jack's dorm. "You have no plan, do you?"

"I was thinking maybe we can walk by Jack's window a few times until he notices. It worked for me the other day."

Someone pushes open the door on the side of the building, and without thinking, Benny bolts toward it and has just enough time to wedge his foot in before it slams shut.

"Or you can just go knock on his door," Benny says, ushering me inside. "But, uh, I'll wait in the hallway."

"Don't want to see Rhett?" I ask.

Benny's nose scrunches like he's smelling something terrible.

"I mean, you do look cute today. And you're going to a show at Laurene. You're kind of a big deal," I say. "If you act aloof, I bet he'd be super jealous."

"I do like the sound of that." Benny boops me on the nose.

When we reach Jack and Rhett's dorm room, I freeze. My entire body feels sticky and gross, and I battle the urge to run away screaming.

"Ohmygod." With a serious eye roll, Benny steamrolls me out of the way and pounds on the door before darting back down the hall and out of sight.

"I hate you!" I whisper.

Jack opens the door, and a smile brightens his cheeks. He's wearing a tank top that shows off the musculature of his arms.

I try not to stare, but damn. I glance quickly around his room, and Rhett is nowhere to be seen. His side of the room looks just as pristine and untouched as it did when I was here last weekend.

"Chase! I was wondering when I'd see you again."

Ohmygod, he's been thinking about me?

Jack nods for me to come in and pulls up the chair at his desk. The only place I can sit is on his bed, but I'm frozen because he it's his *bed*. The place where he possibly sleeps naked, or at least semi-naked and, great, now I can't stop imagining his body. Under the covers. With me. Must. Stop. Thinking. About. Jack's . . . *HOLY FUCK*, CHASE, STOP!

My cheeks heat in embarrassment.

"I realized *after* I saw you Monday I didn't have your number," Jack continues, not missing a beat. "I waited here for you to show up so we could go to dinner."

I bury my face in my hands. "Fuck. Sorry. I went to the Garden Dining Hall and waited for you there. For a while. When I didn't see you, I figured you forgot, or I don't know. Clearly, I suck."

"Yeah, you do." He winks.

Jesus, take the wheel.

"So what's up?"

"Two things." I hand him two books I carried with me under my arm. "Thought you'd like these"

As he studies the covers of Elizabeth Acevedo's *The Poet X* and Dean Atta's *The Black Flamingo*, I continue, "I really loved them. And I'm not a big poetry person, but I thought of you. They're gorgeous."

Jack opens the cover of *The Black Flamingo* and reads the first two pages, leaving me in silence to study his face: the way his forehead creases and his smile twitches, his pupils dilating. When he looks up, his eyes are wet.

"Thank you," he says, like I just gave him the greatest gift on planet Earth.

My chest pangs with a longing to reach out for him.

"Wanna grab dinner with me?" Jack asks. "Rhett's not around. I think he's wooing some girl he met, and I haven't really connected with anybody else, so I'm on my own tonight. I'd rather not spend another night FaceTiming Callum as he plays *Fortnite*. I think he's sick of me." He laughs nervously as he goes on about his best friend from back home.

My first thought: *Poor Benny*. My second thought: "I have an idea." I point toward his Years & Years poster. "Wanna go to a free show at Laurene tonight?"

"You kidding? They're my favorite band." He hops to his feet and does an adorable little jig, the way a child might at a toy store.

"My roommate Benny and I are meeting my best friend who goes to Laurene."

"Eggs Benny?" Jack looks to Rhett's empty side of the room like he's piecing together a puzzle.

"Did you know Benny and Rhett went to high school together?"

"Yeah, I've, um, seen him around. Small world." He knows something.

"Yep." I do my best not to let on. "He's in the hall now. He's not, uh, really a fan of Rhett at the moment. No offense."

"None taken," Jack says. "Rhett Febrezes my side of the room every morning. Sometimes I wake up to a cloud of linen-scented chemical dust floating onto my face."

"Shut up."

Jack's eyes widen. "No joke. He hovers over me like a serial killer. He's got wild eyes, that one. He definitely hates me." Jack grabs a black tee and throws it over his head. "How do I look?"

Fucking beautiful, I think, but say, "Good."

"Let's go!" he says, throwing open the door and bumping head-first into Benny.

"It's about time!" he shouts, looking over Jack's shoulders into his room for Rhett.

"Rhett isn't here," I say.

"Like I care," Benny says. "The bus should be here in like, five minutes. Andiamo!"

"Is he always like this?" Jack whispers.

"Pretty much," I say.

Jack knocks his shoulder into mine. "I like him."

Benny speed walks outside and abruptly stops on the path, just so he can tap his foot impatiently. "I swear!"

The three of us hop off the bus onto Laurene's sprawling campus. Seriously, it dwarfs CIA's, making it look like a cute little compound in comparison to Laurene's rolling hills lined with turn-of-the-century stone classrooms and dormitories. It feels stately but in an overwhelming way. It's definitely not a place where I could flourish. I'd much rather be a big fish in a small pond than the other way around.

When Rae sees us, she hurtles toward me like a bowling ball at full force. I swear, if this were a scene in a movie, she'd be blasting people out of the way. She throws her body at me, flinging her arms around me, and you'd think we were long-lost lovers or something, the way she screams.

"I am so happy to see this stupid face!" She plants a wet smooch on my cheek.

"Your face is stupider!" I shout back.

"I hate your face!" she yells.

"Are they okay?" Jack asks, genuinely concerned.

"I'm not sure. I think they're doing a skit," Benny says.

"Looks very dysfunctional," Jack adds.

"You're damn right it's dysfunctional!" Rae shouts. "Benny, get in here!" They're basically the same height, two six-foot giants, all limbs like giant redwood trees.

Benny purses his lips and hops over like Tinkerbell doused him with pixie dust, flinging himself into our sandwich.

When Rae pulls back, she looks at Jack. "Who is this? I don't know him."

"*That* is *Jack*," Benny whispers into her ear, making his eyebrows dance suggestively.

"Oh," Rae says, picking up what he's putting down. "I see."

Jack extends his hand for a firm handshake.

Rae puts on her serious face. "Nice to meet you. I've heard *a lot* of good things."

"You have?" He looks to me, and I shrug, embarrassment heating my face.

"Yeah, but coming from Chase, they're probably all lies," Rae says.

"Sounds right," Jack says.

"Wow," I say.

Rae gives Jack a sly wink. "We should move," she says. "The show is about to start."

There are a few hundred students at the bottom of what Rae calls Laurene's Slope, a grassy area surrounding a pavilion situated in front of a small, sparkling lake. The sun is an incandescent orange and, as it sets, leaves a streak of pink that stretches to the remaining blue—a gorgeous late-summer painting. The band has already started their set, making Jack twitch with excitement and Benny tweak with FOMO.

Benny hooks his arm onto Jack's, and they take a running start toward the stage. Jack's beaming like an excited child, bouncing up and down, feeding off the electric energy.

"Coming," Rae says, sashaying at her own pace, her arm linked with mine.

I laugh, and Rae catches me staring at Jack as he runs.

"You're hopeless," she says.

"What?"

"*Jack*." She nudges me.

"I've known him five minutes. There's nothing. I mean, he's . . ." Gorgeous, funny, smart, ambitious, cute. "Cute, I guess. But we're not sure he's even gay-*adjacent*," I say coolly.

"Sweetie," she begins. "I wish Harry would look at me the way Jack looks at you."

"Stop."

"Seriously. Who knows if he's gay or gay-adjacent or bi or pan or whatever, but he's definitely into *you*." She stops me and looks deep into my eyes. "Girls know these things."

"Teach me your ways."

"Sadly, I cannot. I am a wise sage. I love you," she says earnestly.

I nudge her with my shoulder. "Love you too."

As we reach Benny and Jack, she shoves me toward Jack, and I bump into him.

He grabs my arm. "Let's get close to the stage!"

I look back toward Rae.

"Go. Benny and I will stay here." Benny looks at her sideways. She flashes him a flask, and his eyes go wide.

He ushers us off. "We love a good back-of-the-crowd moment!"

Jack and I weave through the crowd of sweaty bodies. It's musky. The stench of wet hair and weed permeates the air. When we reach the stage, Jack starts jumping up and down, matching the frantic energy of the band. I admire his carefree way of wholly embracing the moment.

"Get into it!" he encourages, though nobody else seems to be jumping.

Everyone is staring at Jack, scrunching their faces and rolling their eyes and barely listening to the band. He's bouncing and mouthing random words that don't match up with the lyrics; his smiling face is bright red as he flails his animated limbs, like he's totally free and doesn't care how he looks.

Olly Alexander, the face of the band, starts the next song. "This one is called 'Shine.'"

Jack stops jumping when the first few notes play over the speakers. "I think you'll like this one. It's my favorite," he says as lightning streaks across the sky.

I join Jack's solitary mosh pit, and we're jumping in tandem, shouting random words, and haphazardly throwing our hands in the air.

The sky is growing dark, and ominous gray clouds tuck the night sky beneath a false security blanket. It starts to drizzle. I can't take my eyes off Jack as he sings the words to a song called "King," and when it crescendos during the last chorus, he turns and grabs me and shouts, "Ooooh-oooooh-oooooooh!"

The muscles in my cheeks ache from laughing, and I can't remember the last time I've felt like this. Actually, I don't know if I've ever felt like this before. There's a strange calm, a happy excitement washing over me; I want to never leave this moment with Jack.

The rain picks up harder, moving from a light mist to a torrential downpour. The band, tucked under a white canopy, keeps playing as Jack spreads his arms, sticks his chest out, and peers toward the sky, letting the water cleanse him.

"I love the rain!" he exclaims.

The band wails, telling us to let go of everything.

It's coming down harder now, and small puddles form in the uneven grassy plain.

Jack turns to me and kicks water from a small puddle in my direction, drenching my legs. He rests his arm on top of my shoulder and says, "I love the rain."

Without warming, he sprints through the grass, and it looks like he's headed toward the sheltered pavilion where everybody else seems to have gone, but he's really just running in circles, splashing through puddles and yelling, "Woooooo!"

Cool rainwater snakes into the collar of my shirt, sliding down my back, making me shiver. *Let go of everything* repeats over and over again in my mind.

I stretch my arms and feel every single drop of rain hit my body.

The grass squishes beneath me, and I sink into the mud.

I close my eyes and feel the world move around me.

When I open them, the floodlights on the stage streak across the crowd, and for a second, it looks like lightning; Jack's face is lit up, like he's holding a bolt of light in his hands. The strobe light moves, hitting me—and Jack, not missing a beat, "tosses" the lightning toward me. I pretend to grab it, hold it in my hands, feel its imaginary power flow through me.

I push it up toward the sky as the rain pours down on us.

On Jack and me.

Like we're the only two people left on the entire slope.

In the world.

At least for the length of the song, I experience true magic.

7

I shut the door to my room after putting Benny to bed.

No joke, he's like a toddler needing to be tucked in after being tuckered out by a concert in the rain. Granted, he drank whatever was in Rae's flask, so by the time the show was over, he was gone.

The suite is pretty quiet. The rest of the guys must still be out at parties. The only person here is Jack, who lounges on one of the chairs in the common room.

"This is not a bad setup," he says.

"It serves its purpose." I teeter on my heels a bit, not really sure what happens now. Jack helped me get Benny back, and I figured once that was done, he'd leave.

But he's still here.

And neither of us is saying anything.

"I want to do something. I'm not ready to go back to my dorm," Jack says, finally cutting through the awkward silence.

I want to say, "I'll do anything with you." What I actually say is, "What do you have in mind?"

Looking out the window, he stands and says, "It's stopped raining. Come on!"

He doesn't tell me where we're going, but I follow him as we make our way across the dark campus. A few streetlamps along the walkways shine little spotlights for us, and when he walks under one, I study the way the golden-blond hairs on the back of his head swirl into a cowlick. I live for it every time we emerge from the darkness.

Without warning, he strays from the concrete onto a small grassy hill and plops dead center. He motions for me to join him. "We're already soaked from the show."

My sneakers squish. I lift one shoe. "Well, these are probably trash anyway."

"Lose 'em." He pops his off one at a time and pulls at his socks until they peel away with a schlocky sound, and I follow suit. He must notice my horrified face when my bare feet dig into the muddy grass. "Not a nature person?"

"Oh, me? I love nature." I offer a pained smile. "It's textures I take issue with."

Jack grins as he looks up toward the night sky. The clouds have started to dissipate like someone is pulling back a curtain to reveal the stars shining so bright above us.

"You know what I love?" he asks, and I hum, intently waiting on his answer. "That no matter what is happening on this planet, rain, storms, whatever"—he points up—"*that* is always there on the other side of the clouds."

"Ahh, you're a stargazer," I say.

"Aren't *you*?"

"What do you mean?"

"You're an artist. So you always see beyond what's right in front of you. Thinking about possibility. The unknown," he says. "I know that when I write, I'm constantly thinking about the infinite ways a story can go."

I lie back on the grass and shiver. Fuck, it feels like the temperature is dropping by the minute. I'll probably wake up tomorrow with a cold or something. But I don't care. I don't want this to end. "Sometimes that trips me up. If there are so many possibilities when I create something, how do I know if I'm choosing the right story line?"

Jack lies back until we're elbow to elbow. "I like that I can talk about this stuff with someone. Callum doesn't get it."

"People who aren't artists don't," I say, a little annoyed that he's bringing up his friend right now.

"Yeah." He turns to face me. "You're thinking too much. Good stories let their characters show their creators who they are."

I can't help but think about Professor McPherson's assignment and how much is riding on getting that mentorship at the end of the semester. Yet I have zero ideas.

"Remember at the show earlier when the strobe lights were streaming over the crowd, and it looked like lightning?" he asks. "And I grabbed it and tossed it to you, and you just went along with it?"

"Yeah," I say.

"How'd you know what to do?"

"Instinct, I guess."

When Jack smiles, it's heavy, and the edges around his eyes crinkle. I could drown in the moonlight-blue pools of his irises. "There's your answer."

We let that sit in the air between us for a while.

"The stars are so bright here," I say, finally, my voice airy like a gentle whisper.

"Yeah, you can really see the dippers when the sky is clear."

"Where?" I ask. "I don't think I've ever seen them."

"See that bright star straight ahead?" He sits up, and I follow. He moves in impossibly close. His hot cheek grazes mine. I smell him, an earthly mix of sweat and cologne, and my entire body aches. "Follow my hand to the tip of my finger. See that star? Trace it with me." His finger outlines the geometric ladle.

"That's it?" I ask excitedly. "That's the Big Dipper?"

He laughs. "Sure is." For a moment, everything is suspended, like the stars in the endless void above us. If I wanted to, I could reach out and grab the Big Dipper and pull it close, hold it to my chest, carry it with me everywhere I go. Or climb inside its basin and peer out at the world below, at this, us, right now. Then he turns, and we're close, so close that our noses almost touch.

I hold my breath, and my heartbeat increases as his eyes search mine.

Then he pulls back, returns to his position in the grass, and I release a ragged breath, missing my chance. I guess that's the thing about stars: they might always be there, stuck in the same fabric that lines the sky, but they will always be out of reach.

Jack reminds me of a star—no, Apollo, Greek god of the sun. How the world seems brighter, lighter with him in it, the way his words flow like poetry. Gods, like stars, are untouchable. If Jack is Apollo, I guess that makes me Icarus, who flies too close to the sun.

"What do you think comes first?" Jack asks. "Thunder or lightning?"

Without thinking, I say, "Lightning. Always."

I've spent many stormy nights with Taylor outside watching and listening to the cracks in the sky during storms. The way the air goes silent always enraptured me like somehow all the people and all the cars and all the noise just stopped, and there was this swell of silence, the breath just before the downpour.

"Actually," Jack says. "Thunder and lightning happen at the same time. But light travels faster than sound. That's why we see lightning before we hear thunder."

"The thunder chases the lightning," I say. "Mom always told me to hold my breath and count after the lightning strike and however many seconds it took to hear the thunder, that's how far away the storm was."

I hold my breath and count. Jack does the same.

We move closer, wrapped in a sudden squall, so close that I can hear Jack's heartbeat. Or maybe it's my own.

Jack talks first, and I exhale. "Sounds like an old-school fable." He sits upright and gets crossed-legged as if he's readying himself to tell a story. "Lightning and Thunder, who live high in the clouds, chasing each other, longing to find one another. Every so often, they collide. That's when the *booms* happen." He smiles his crinkly smile, and his one dimple creases.

"What if Thunder and Lightning are lovers?" I suggest. "And the booms happen because Thunder cries when he realizes he's missed catching Lightning again." I pause and look up at the sky, remembering the way Jack captured lightning in his hands and passed it to me at the show, the way the ground shook and the earth moved, and we became something else entirely. "Ever wonder why we see something before we hear it?" I ask, not entirely sure we're still talking about lightning or thunder or something else.

He shrugs. "Or feel something before we see it. Like Lichtenberg figures."

"Huh?" My face crinkles in confusion.

He holds out both hands. With his right, his fingers brush his left palm and spider out. "Lichtenberg figures are the tattooed marks that appear on the skin after being struck . . ." His voice shifts mid-thought to something brighter. "By lightning." He takes out his phone, pulls up the Notes app, and starts furiously typing away. I try to peer at the screen, but he tilts it out of view. When he's done, Jack holds the phone to his chest. "Sorry, I was inspired."

"Can I read it?"

"Really? You'd want to?"

"Of course I would."

He nods slowly. "Okay. I . . . trust you. It's short," he says, almost apologizing. "Give me your number, and I'll text it. But you have to wait until you're in your dorm to read it."

I do the "cross my heart and hope to die" sign across my chest as I give him my number. Immediately, my phone vibrates. It takes every ounce of strength not to look at it.

When I'm home, I don't even peel off my wet clothes before pulling up Jack's message.

JACK:

> Everyone says it's
> lucky
> to be struck by lightning

No one tells you how
to live
once you've been struck

All I know is that it is
impossible
to harness

The bright phone screen is a beacon in my hands. Jack's message is the light that spreads through my body like . . .

Lightning.

I sit down at my desk, turn on my lamp—which causes Benny to stir but not wake up—and I draw until my muscles cramp.

The Prince Who Captured Lightning

PART I

The skies were once ruled by two titans, Thunder and Lightning, who also happened to be lovers. Together, they controlled the rains that gave life to the two Kingdoms Below the Skies, the clouds that allowed sunlight to nourish the trees, grasses, and flowers, and the winds that spread seeds and cooled the People Below the Skies on hot days. To maintain balance, Thunder and Lightning often created dangerous but beautiful electrical storms where light and sound would meet. Sometimes this caused chaos and destruction on the lands, but it was a fair price to pay for bountiful harvests and the steady change in seasons that kept the kingdoms in perfect balance.

For generations, the People Below the Skies respected and gave thanks to Thunder and Lightning, revered their love, and thought them to be gods. But there were a few who grew jealous and fearful of the titans' love and combined power. Soon the few corrupted the minds of the many and sought to destroy the titans' reign. A war broke out between the two kingdoms, and the people within each became divided, mistrusting all who seemed different, including an old, gnarled Witch who only ever minded her own business.

Scorned, the Witch took to the skies and cursed Thunder and Lightning, casting them apart. No longer would they rule the skies together. Lightning lost his charge and disappeared, leaving Thunder resigned to search for him alone until the Witch's spell was broken. No one knew why the Witch did this; some say she was jealous of their love while others say she was angry at the kingdoms who hated her. All reviled her as darkness fell across the land.

Violent storms brewed as Thunder scoured the skies, his anger and doubts turning into hurricanes, his tears into tsunamis, and his heartbreak into earthquakes. The People Below the Skies no longer revered him as a god but saw him as something to be destroyed. And so, the two Kingdoms Below the Skies continued their war. Eventually, when the storms ebbed and the lands dried up, the People Below the Skies stopped telling stories of the titans, outlawing even a mention of the forbidden, unnatural love that tore them, the two warring kingdoms, and the lands apart.

Until one day, many years later, a Prince was journeying home after a quest for a new water source. He happened upon a lone Knight from the rival kingdom in the woods. The Prince was curious about this Knight, captivated by his handsome beauty in a way he hadn't been by any maiden or princess before, and stopped to talk to him.

Hours passed, and he found the Knight to be beguiling, mesmerizing. Before long, night fell, and the Prince had to return home. Upon his arrival, he was supposed to marry a princess. As the Prince and the Knight parted, the two shook hands, and a jolt traveled between them.

As the Prince walked away, he looked down at his hand and gasped. For in his palm, there was but a tiny spark dancing around his fingers.

8

On the day of the flip-book presentations, the class is held in our new, state-of-the-art animation studio. We are surrounded by a group of twenty junior animation majors. By the end of class today, I'll be paired with two of them.

Of course, Leila volunteers to go first. She is poised and polished in her business-ready blazer, the one she always wears when she wants people to take her seriously. She plays her flip animation for the third time, and the characters she created come to life. Sort of.

Here's the thing. I'm not being judgy—I swear—but they're literally two eggs in a carton inside a refrigerator, personified with googly eyes and wiggly mouths. They're having a conversation where one egg is saying how it can't wait to be chosen for the Great Scrambling, while the other talks about how it feels the weight of its yolky dream that there's something more to life than waiting to be eaten. This egg wants to hatch and become a chick, so it devises a plan to escape the clutches of the carton.

"So," Professor McPherson says. Her hand rests on her temple as she leans back in her chair. "Explain to us what's happening here?"

"Food as sustenance," Leila begins. "I've named him Eggbért. And Eggbért and all the other eggs in the fridge are, like, *so* conditioned to believe that The Great Scrambling, which represents our collective gluttony and consumerism, is all there is to their lives. So this is a story of Eggbért rejecting that predetermined path and choosing the one of most resistance. I'm thinking a *grand* journey to a city-like farm, you know, like in *A Bug's Life*—it's a metaphor, *obviously*. There, all his notions about his sense of self will be challenged . . . and end in flames. I call it *Unscramblé a Flambé*."

I . . . have no words.

"So he's gonna end up eaten anyway?" someone behind me shouts, and I giggle.

Leila rolls her eyes. "It's a metaphor. A hard truth."

"That's certainly . . . interesting." Professor McPherson offers an exaggerated nod.

"Thank you *so* much!" Leila beams before bowing.

"What's the trope you chose?" one of the juniors asks.

Leila moves strands of her wavy brown hair behind her ear. "I was thinking the *Eat Pray Love* journey. The whole, like, journey in search of the self. Very existential. Very representative of our modern culture and collective unhappiness."

She doesn't seem to notice that's not really a trope and more of a cliché.

Professor McPherson eyes her and makes a note in her pad.

The juniors lead the class in applauding her.

I swear I'm not bitter.

"Who's next?" Professor asks. "How about you, Gray?" When people laugh, she adds. "Relax, I know his name is Chase. Can I joke?"

My legs wobble as I rise to my feet and move to the front of the room, passing Leila, who offers a tight-lipped smile.

I take a deep breath. "Have you ever had one of those electricity charged moments that changes your entire life, even if it looks like something small from the outside? One of those moments that forever alters your body chemistry? That's something I tried to capture with this." I pause so I don't trip over my words. I try to make eye contact with each of the juniors so they can feel my sincerity. "My flip animation is called 'The Prince Who Captured Lightning.' It's a fairy tale. I'd like to read the intro to you first, if that's okay, Professor."

I look for her approval, and she gives a terse nod. I clear my throat and launch into it. I wrote the intro yesterday after I animated my flip-book—when I couldn't stop thinking about Jack and rereading the poem he texted me.

My flip starts with a bird's-eye view of the Prince, looking down at his cupped hands. As the pages turn, it zooms in on a close-up of his hands until the only image on the page is that of a personified lightning bolt with dotted black eyes and a zigzag smile.

Sparks shoot from the Prince's fingers.

The insides of his fingers are tattooed with Lichtenberg figures.

"Wow," one of the juniors says. She has light-brown skin and long, pin-straight black hair that shines under the fluorescent lighting. "I love the shading you did there to represent the glow of the spark."

"And the story was beautiful," adds another junior with rich dark skin and piercing green eyes. She gives me a thumbs-up.

Leila's hand shoots in the air. "I mean, I can obviously see the trope. Or trope*sssss*." She lingers on the *s*, and I squirm. "You got a prince meeting his true love, a wicked witch, a fabled once-upon-a-time beginning, star-crossed lovers. Like, pick a struggle."

Professor McPherson bites the inside of her cheek and narrows her eyes at Leila before moving her gaze to focus on me. "What say you to that?"

That's the thing: I have nothing to say. I love fairy tales. Always have. Leila knows this. I grew up on them and consume them the way some binge-watch Netflix shows. I've always loved the whole happily ever after thing, so why shouldn't I explore it?

But I don't say any of that.

The junior who "wowed" me earlier shoots her hand up. She turns to address me and only me. "I saw, or heard, all those tropes in what you wrote, and sure, some of that is overdone and overused, but the assignment was to take a trope and turn it on its head. What's more head-turning than a gay love story in a fairy tale."

The girl sitting next to her, who commented on my story, chimes in, "Tropes are a luxury of the majority. And LGBTQ-plus and Black, brown, and Indigenous folks should get to use these tropes because, for people like us, they're not tropes. They're just never-told stories or stories told over and over again by the majority."

"The white majority," her friend next to her adds.

Professor McPherson crouches forward and props her chin on her hands. "Points have been made. If I didn't take tropes that had been done before, I never would have created *Crumbs*. Nice job, Gray."

I shake like an old person, my bones rickety and unbalanced, and move slowly toward my desk, tipping an invisible hat to her.

I avoid Leila like the plague, but I'd bet anything she's pouting. Maybe not outwardly, but inside she's likely about to explode.

"Touché," the professor says with a wink.

All ten of us wait while Professor McPherson confers with the twenty juniors to create animation teams that will bring our shorts to life. And, of course, ultimately win the mentorship. No biggie.

As we wait, Leila saunters up to me. "Hey."

I nod. I mean, I can't totally ignore her—try as I might.

"Just wanted to say I really did love your flip," she says.

I guffaw. "Right."

"Even if it wasn't the most original. Then again, what idea is, amiright?" she says, hiding a jab inside a joke. "Look, I don't know what happened between us, but we're in college now, Chase. I think we should act like adults." Her hand is on her hip.

"I, uh, what?"

Is she really trying to pretend she has no idea what happened? Like she didn't talk shit about me and put me down and lie to me?

"I'm just saying, it really hurts that you just dropped me. I know you were going through something, but I did nothing wrong," she says.

"What do you mean I was 'going through something'?"

If blood really did boil, I'd be a hard-boiled egg right now.

"Well, I didn't want to say anything, but when you came out as nonbinary, you changed. It felt like you were reinventing yourself, and then *you* just stopped talking to *me*."

My head is about to explode. Guts on the wall. Everything.

Is she using my gender identity as a scapegoat for being a terrible friend?

That is *not* happening. Not today. Not ever.

But I don't even know if it's worth it to bring all this up.

Is this a friendship worth salvaging?

Is there a friendship even *left* to salvage?

She continues, "And it just feels like you were never really supportive of me. Like you never took my art seriously, and I just felt like you let your own jealousy get in the way of us. And I know you can't be happy that we're in the same program, but that's on you. I just wanted you to be happy, with me and for me, but also with yourself. I just feel like you're not happy with yourself . . ." Her words leak out at half speed. "And *that's* on you, too."

My eyes are wide.

I'm not breathing.

I'm legitimately in shock.

She's twisting *everything*.

I shouldn't be surprised. This is what she does. I've witnessed it with other friends back when we were in high school. Anyone who has ever challenged Leila has been knocked off their feet and out of her life. But somehow, I'm the one at fault?

I want to ask her if she's talking about herself, but if I do, I know I'll cry.

And that is not happening.

Luckily Professor McPherson pops back into the room with the juniors in tow.

Leila rolls her eyes. "You don't have to say anything. I know." She puts her hand on my arm, and it burns my skin. "I'd be happy to let you sit in on my mentorship with Linda, and I'd love to invite you to the *Vanity Fair* Oscar party after I win Best Animated Film," she says straight-faced, without a hint of irony or malice, which is quite possibly the worst part of it all, before quickly scurrying back to her drafting desk.

I stare straight ahead, fixating on a spot on the wall as the professor talks, pairing everyone up. But her voice is far away, replaced by Leila's, who blames *me* for the downfall of our friendship in her Academy Award acceptance speech.

Sure, I cared about the scholarship. But I also cared about her.

I don't have many friends. I can count them on less than one hand. In high school, Rae and I spent most weekends watching movies in her parents' basement and going to the Cheesecake Factory, where she made sure I ate like a normal human and didn't take laxatives afterward. Sometimes it worked. Still, Rae and I weren't exactly the cool kids. And other than her, Leila was the only person I trusted.

But that was a lifetime ago.

"And Chase," Professor McPherson intrudes into my swirling thought storm, "will be paired with Sofía Rivera and Chloe Thomas. Hear that, Gray?"

I snap out of my stupor and see the two girls who defended me earlier waving at me, and I can't help but smile.

It's heavy, but it's there.

And I'm so grateful to have two people who get me on my team.

They make their way over to me and introduce themselves.

"I really loved your story," Sofía says. "Reminds me of the bedtime stories my mom used to tell me."

"But real gay," Chloe adds, tossing her curly hair. "And I mean that in, like, the best way possible. Period. Just so you know who we are, Sofía is the brains, and I'm the brawn."

"Which makes you the talent," Sofía interjects. "I'm a story-board artist. And Chloe is director extraordinaire, tech genius."

Chloe does a confident half bow.

"She'll be the first Black woman to win Best Animated Film Director at the Oscars," Sofía says.

"First, we have to convince the Academy to create such a category," Chloe says. "But yes, that's the plan." She narrows her eyes as if she's examining me. Then she turns to Sofía. "They look so scared, such a baby froshie."

I pause at her unexpected use of *they*. It feels . . . nice. Like wearing somebody else's well-worn hoodie. Comfy and warm and maybe I could steal it and make it mine. But could it ever *truly* be mine?

"Was that okay?" Chloe asks. "I watched that interview you did with *The BuzzWord* before class today, and you used they/them pronouns. But I heard Professor McPherson use he/him. I wasn't sure if I had to have a word with her."

I love how protective she is over pronouns. "Yeah, no, totally."

She raises her brow.

I chuckle nervously. "Sorry, I mean, I've been using he/him lately. I did use they/them for a while. I'm just . . . not sure. But you can use either. I like either." Oh my god, I'm rambling now. "Sorry, I swear I'm not this scattered. I'm beyond excited to work with you both. I just had a really shitty run-in with"—I nod toward Leila—"so I'm kinda out of it."

"She rubs me the wrong way," Sofía says.

Chloe tilts her head. "We know her type. The overconfident ones who think they're changing the world with some grand statement. They're always the first to burn out. What happened between you? Not-so-friendly competition?"

"Because that happens in this program," Sofía adds.

"I used to hate Sofía," Chloe whispers. "Now she's like my left tit. Without her, I'd be lost."

"Why the left?" Sofía asks. "And how would you be lost without one boob?"

Chloe shrugs. "I dunno. It's an analogy or something. Leave me alone."

That elicits a smile. "Leila and I used to be like you two. Now, not so much."

We're all silent for a few seconds.

"Shit happens," Chloe says. "Now you roll with us."

Her words make me feel a tiny bit better. There's something incredibly genuine in her voice, about both of them, that makes me feel like they'll have my back. And not just for a class project.

"I like that," I say.

"Good, but we'll also kick your ass this semester," Sofía says.

"I need that. Please," I say, thinking about Mom and how she's often saying similar phrases to me. Mom would love them.

"You're cool, kid," Chloe says. "You got one week to get us a rough storyboard. Next week, we'll meet and discuss. A hive mind, if you will." She hands me her phone. "Give us your number, but don't abuse ours. This is your one warning."

I nod quickly. She means business.

As I pack up my supplies, Sofía asks, "You busy? Have you had a chance to try the paninis at the Watering Hole?"

"What's the Watering Hole?"

Chloe buries her head in her hands. "You haven't been to the Hole? It's the hub underneath the Campus Center. Filled with cafés and places to grab food." She grabs on to my arm. "Come, we must educate you."

And educate me they do.

The Watering Hole is a carousel of food vendors from Middle Eastern to Mexican to French—I already plan to wait in line for a strawberry Nutella crepe—to your standard-issue deep-fried American fare. Chloe and Sofía don't hold back, either. They order me to find us a table, and I watch them navigate the frenzy with ease. It seems like everyone there knows them, and they're easily able to cut through the crowds to grab platters of falafel and hummus, enchiladas and citrus guacamole, paninis with melty cheeses and caramelized onions sticking out, and an actual mountain of boneless chicken wings smothered in a tangy honey lime sauce.

Sofía loses herself in uncontrollable laughter when they return, trays piled high with food. "You should see your face," she says. "Priceless."

I can't exactly tell them that all that food scares me or how much I want it all—and that it might lead me to the bookstore to find a box of laxatives.

"Dig in," Chloe says, but it's more like order. "Better be fast, or you won't get any."

"You know what would make this better?" Sofía holds her fingers up to her lips and sucks in a quick breath.

"You're gonna corrupt this baby." Chloe smacks Sofía's arm. Then she lowers her voice and leans in closer to the table. "You smoke?"

"Totally," I lie.

Chloe pout-smiles. "This one's adorable. With a terrible poker face. It's okay," she reassures me. "We just thought we'd offer. Nothing like spreading the love."

"I've always wanted to try it," I admit.

"It really heightens my creativity," Sofía says.

Chloe mumbles, "Lucky."

"I'm down," I say earnestly.

"Look at us, corrupting young minds," Chloe says. "An-y-way, where you from?"

"New York, just outside the city," I say, tooling with the food on my plate. "What about y'all?"

"Y'all?" Chloe says. "What's a Southern word doing in your mouth?"

"Gender-inclusive," I say.

"Nice." Chloe smiles. "I'm from New Orleans." The way she pronounces *Nawlins* is friendly, comforting. "Sofía is a Masshole from Bahston."

Sofía elbows her. "You *love* Boston."

"I love the legal weed dispensaries," Chloe says. "Much easier to get product than New York. And the variety! And the amount of shops. It's the only win over New York. Sorry, Sof."

"How'd y'all meet?" I ask.

"In the same seminar our freshman year," Sofía says in between bites of falafel. "We competed for the arts endowment with our respective shorts before realizing we could be unstoppable together."

"She's just saying that because I beat her ass." Chloe takes a swig of Coca-Cola.

Sofía rolls her eyes. "We've been inseparable ever since."

"We're planning to study abroad for the spring and summer

semesters in Los Angeles. A certain animation studio has been wooing us after seeing a film we worked on all last year," Chloe says.

"Really? I'd love to see it. If that's okay, I mean; sorry if that's, like, inappropriate or whatever."

The excitement builds in my chest. Not only do I have two new friends and mentors, but they're also up-and-coming animators!

"You are the cutest," Sofía says. "You should come to our house on Friday. We're having a little soiree. You can see what we're working on, and we can have fun times."

Friday just so happens to be my birthday. Should I mention it? That's weird, right?

"Actually . . ." I'm about to answer, but it's as if the world stops because I see Jack. He's wandering around, talking to somebody on the phone, looking all sorts of lost. My mouth goes dry, and my heart races.

Then Chloe's hand is in front of my face, snapping. "Hello, earth to Chase."

"Sorry, I—"

Jack sees me, and his hand shoots up. And I obviously have no chill, so my hand does this awkward wiggle thing that makes me look like a T. rex doing the "shopping cart," and my cheeks get insanely hot.

"Did we break him?" Chloe whispers, but Sofía had already swiveled to follow my line of sight and manually turns Chloe's head in the direction of Jack. "Oop!"

Both Sofía and Chloe follow Jack as he winds his way through the scattered mess of tables to get to us. Neither one takes their eyes off him. I don't blame them. He's beautiful.

"Callum, I gotta go. Talk later, bro. Tell my dad I'll call him tonight." Jack clicks off then shouts over the noise. "Chase!"

Stay calm. Keep cool. Collect yourself. Make a mental note to inquire more about this Callum fellow later. "'Sup."

Chloe busts out in a guttural giggle.

"Hi, I'm Jack." He extends his hand to them.

"Yes, you are," Chloe says, leaning back to get a better look.

"You eating lunch?" he asks then winces because *obviously*.

I nod, and he shifts his weight from leg to leg.

"Cool, cool. How'd your flip-book thing go?"

"Good—"

Sofía interrupts. "It was fabulous. Beautiful, actually. We're working with him."

His eyes widen, and he smiles, the balls of his cheeks shining. "Oh, wow, that's amazing. Congrats." He hikes his backpack on his shoulder. "I gotta get to class, but you wanna grab dinner at the Garden Dining Hall tonight?"

"Yeah, sounds good."

"Nice to meet you all," he says, offering a chin nod before turning on his heels and heading out.

I exhale and look down to see my hands shaking. I hadn't seen him since the night of the Years & Years show, which, granted, was barely thirty-six hours ago, but still.

Snapping back to attention, I realize Chloe and Sofía are fanning themselves with folded napkins.

"What?" I ask.

Chloe glares. "You could cut the sexual tension with a machete."

"No way," I say. "Really?"

"Um. Ya," Sofía says.

"I mean, he's obvs gorgeous—" I start, but it feels strange saying it out loud. Sure, I've thought about Jack nearly every minute of every day since we met, but it feels like a betrayal to reduce him to one surface-level word when he's so much more than that. More than I could ever put into words. I'm such a cliché.

"But?" Chloe asks.

"I don't know if he's gay or what."

Sofía and Chloe exchange knowing glances.

"Bring him to our place Friday," Sofía says. "We'll scope out the situation. Observe you two in the wild."

"Oh god, that sounds . . . like so much pressure," I say.

"No, not at all," Chloe says, her voice becoming super serious. "I can sit here from an outsider's perspective and say that judging from the way Jack looked at you. At only you. The way he smiled. His eyes—"

"Those eyes." Sofía swoons.

"I can tell you I think he's interested," Chloe continues. "But sometimes people need a little push. And, no offense, but you look like you need to be dragged to make a move."

"Ouch," I say. "But also accurate."

"Also, not to be that girl," Chloe says. "But I've been where you are. I know that look on your face right now, and if he's not into you and he's just one of those friendly bros, it's better you know sooner rather than later. So you can move on."

Well, that was sobering. "Fine. I'll see if he's down to come. But, um."

If Chloe were wearing glasses, she'd totally be Meryl Streep in *The Devil Wears Prada* right now, peering at me over the top of her frames, pursed lips, waiting for me to stop taking up oxygen in the room. Or just, you know, saying what I need to say.

"Friday is actually my birthday," I mumble.

"Shut up!" Sofía shouts. "That's perfect! Now we have a reason to party. Not that we ever need a reason. Time to celebrate our new friend. Bring a couple people."

"But don't get wild, now," Chloe adds.

"Um, maybe my roommate Benny. He's a gay chaos tornado. You'd love him. And maybe my friend Rae from Laurene."

"Oh, he's got a friend that goes to Laurene." Sofía brings her fingers to her chin and mimes like a mustachioed villain playing with her beard. "What? I'm just saying. Those nerds have a good time over there."

"It's settled," Chloe says. "Bring your friends; we'll have some adult beverages. You'll get my invoice at the end of the semester."

I laugh, but she doesn't.

"Not kidding," she deadpans.

Silence.

A smile stretches across her face. "Relax. Of course, I'm kidding." She turns to Sofía. "Looks like we're taking in another stray."

Then Chloe's gaze settles on me. "Welcome to the crew."

9

JACK: Hey! You around?

Shit. What do I say? Be cool, Chase.

Jack and I have been hanging out *casually* the past two days, grabbing dinner at the dining halls. Super breezy AF. No more stawkward (stalker + awkward) run-ins.

It shouldn't be a *whole thing* to . . .

Breathe.

ME: Yeah. Wanna chill?

I hate myself! Who even says that anymore?

JACK: No.

Not to be dramatic or anything, but my hand goes numb, and I resist the urge to scream and throw my phone like it's a ticking bomb because oh. My. G—

JACK: Hahaha just kidding. Be outside your dorm in five.

I have a quest for us

Never mind.

Jack is waiting just beyond the entrance to my dorm, donning his Red Sox baseball cap and a tight plain white tee that hugs his chest.

He smiles, and my entire body aches for him. I don't know why, but all of a sudden, I hear Chloe's words in the back of my head: *If he's not into you it's, better you know sooner rather than later. So you can move on.* The flustered butterflies followed by all the questions about him and the potential of us nag at me. Because the reality is he hasn't made a move of any kind, despite how close we're getting.

"What's this quest?" I ask.

"Ah, good sir—err, what's a gender-neutral term for *sir*?"

"Uh."

That's a good question. I've never really been called a "sir," and it's never crossed my mind that I would, so fuck if I know. I hold up my hand, take out my phone, and do a quick Google search.

"Boss? Ew. Gentleperson? Friend?"

"Ahh, good friend," Jack says, with a knightly bow, and my stomach drops at the use of *friend*.

To be fair, I did walk right into that, and maybe I'm reading too much into it, but maybe I'm not, and he just friend-zoned me?

"I hath been bequeathed a quest."

"Are you high?"

"I ameth not." Jack's trying so hard not to smile, to maintain a stately composure. "Dost thou not enjoy the words that are forthcoming from mine mouth?"

Honestly, just watching his lips move is enough to sustain me for life, but I can't say that because it's wildly creeptastic. So I go with it. Hand on stomach, I bow back. "Thou hast tickled mine fancy with thine quest."

He straightens his back like a Buckingham Palace guard and motions for me to walk first, a gentlemanly move. I could be Jack's princess. Hell, I'd settle for the damsel in distress if it meant he would sweep me off my feet. But he doesn't tell me what his quest is about or where we're going, and I don't question it until we get on the bus that takes us off campus and down into the small college town square that sits at the shore of a lake, resting between CIA's and Laurene's campuses.

The bus is empty, but he still sits right next to me. Straight guys don't do that. They always leave the obligatory eight-foot distance.

"Are you kidnapping me?"

He shoots me a dastardly glare. "You've found me out. I remember you said you hate busses, so I had to be stealthy."

He remembered that? Damn.

Digging into his pocket, he pulls out a handout for me. "My creative writing professor has us dissecting the Hero's Journey."

Your Task: In order to better understand the characters you've created in your first short story, you will act as that character and go on a quest of your own making. Traditionally, a quest is something a hero must accomplish in order to find something of importance that restores order to their world. Using the Five Stages of the Hero's Journey below, develop a quest for your main character and actually go on that quest. Use your imagination (and the questions below) to transform CIA's campus, the college town, or the surrounding areas into a new, exciting land that you'll write about.

"I figure who better to help me visualize a new world and go on a quest than another storyteller," Jack says. "Plus, quests are always better with friends."

There's that word again. *Friend.* Color me defeated. Slightly. The magnetic allure to Jack is still there, but perhaps Chloe was right. I do need to protect myself a bit more.

"You okay?" he asks, swiveling his body so he's facing me.

"Yeah, why?" I do my best monotone straight-bro voice.

"No reason. You just look a little . . . I don't know." He settles back into the seat.

"Who's your character?" I ask, doing my best to perk up.

"That's the thing," he says as the bus brakes at our stop.

I follow him out. He hops off the bus, and once he's at a safe distance, he turns around to face me. "I'm not entirely sure yet, and I was hoping you'd help me figure that out."

"How?"

Jack's right eyebrow arches, and he smirks. "The place where all great quests start: a sweet old bookstore. I've been dying to visit this place, and I saw online that they have a whole section of art books dedicated to animation."

"Oh. Cool."

Again, I hate myself for being so monosyllabic, but honestly, who does that unless they're interested? Right? No, I refuse to keep overthinking.

I'm just going to go with the flow.

Or at least pretend to.

As problematic fave RuPaul might say, "Your inner saboteur needs to STFU."

Jack leads us along a cobblestone street that leads through the center of the small town. The street is lined with brick and stone buildings and is closed off to cars. Most of the businesses are bars and restaurants. There's the organic smoothie and waffle bar, which I've heard is owned and operated by a local commune, and the outside looks carved out of a weirwood tree, and cute antique boutiques and specialty soap shops. Along the pathway are informational signs about how every building in town is one-hundred-percent green-energy efficient thanks to solar panels.

It doesn't take long to get to The Pagemaster, a sprawling storefront that looks like an old apothecary shop from the outside, except instead of old potions and herbs and magical artifacts, its windows are filled with books.

Jack looks like he's in love, his pupils dilating as a calm washes over him. That's just not fair when I'm pretending to be unbothered by his beauty.

"Can I just say?" I begin. "I love that this place is called The Pagemaster."

"It's punny," he says.

"Yes, which, by the way, is a great word," I say, and he looks almost surprised that I stole his line. "But no, haven't you ever seen the 1994 film *The Pagemaster* starring Macaulay Culkin?"

When Jack shakes his head, I teach him a thing or two. "It's about this boy who takes refuge in a library during a storm, and he slips and falls and passes out, and when he wakes up, he's literally inside an animated world full of personified books."

"Sounds like a dream. As in, that's what I want for my life," Jack says with a chuckle. "I've never heard of that movie. I never watched that kind of stuff growing up. I was always doing something outside with Cal. You'll have to show it to me sometime."

He's always name-dropping his friend Callum, and every time, it makes my chest tighten with jealousy. *Push through, Chase. Don't let your instability show.* "My mom loved it, so she passed it down to my sister and me," I say, sliding past him to open the door for us.

Chimes above the door jingle. The sweet, musky scent of used books hits me immediately; it's a delicate mix of ink and mothballs with notes of roasted almonds and dry coffee beans. Books take up nearly every square inch of the long shop, and in the spots without are book-related artifacts. There are swords and dragon eggs from *Game of Thrones*, the One Ring and various armor replicas from *The Lord of the Rings*, talismans from *The Chronicles of Narnia*, and other nondescript bookish tchotchkes.

There are also glass cases containing old, tattered first editions with thick red and blue hardcovers embossed with gold lettering and covered in a fine layer of dust.

"I'm home," Jack says. His hands graze the tops of book-lined counters and shelves, and he wanders the aisles like he's looking for nothing and everything all at once. I guess that's the nature of a quest. He's been sent by his professor in search of inspiration. Least I can do is let him find it on his own.

I don't want to hover, so I quietly browse, searching for a section on classic fairy tales. While I'm here, I might as well do some research for "The Prince Who Captured Lightning." Immediately, I gravitate toward a collection by the Brothers Grimm. It's an older edition, with no illustration on its navy-blue cover aside from scrolly silver gilding around its edges.

Flipping through the musty, yellowing pages, I read stories I've read dozens of times, and the one thing I keep taking away is how straightforward they are. There's not a whole lot of gray area. There's "right" and "wrong" woven into the magical tales in slightly fantastical but mostly historical settings that don't really map onto the world that exists today yet somehow still act as moral guideposts.

I don't know how long I've been reading when Jack comes up behind me carrying an eco-friendly bag filled with stuff.

"That was quick. What'd you get?"

"Quick? We've been here an hour already," Jack says, and my eyes widen. "You looked really deeply involved in that book, so I didn't want to interrupt you." He tips up the cover of the book. "Fairy tales, huh? That makes sense."

"What does that mean?"

He shrugs. "You strike me as the fairy tale type. And not just because of your *Beauty and the Beast* shirt." He smirks.

My face heats thinking about that shirt with Prince Adam half-naked on Grindr and how I was wearing it the first time I met him. And that he noticed it. *And* he knew it was a *Beauty and the Beast* reference.

"I take it you're not a fan?"

He offers me a very "meh" face. "I love them as story blueprints. We've been reading a bunch in creative writing to prep for this Hero's Journey assignment. And I think they're succinct, and I love how they've become these modes of storytelling for contemporary writers to imprint their own stories upon. Like the ones that really dig into the characters and twist them around and expand them into full-length novels."

"But?"

"I'm not really into abrupt, forced endings that sugarcoat," he explains.

"What do you mean?"

"The focus on the 'and they lived happily ever after' is super damaging. I mean, look."

He moves in closer to me, his shoulder brushing against mine, and static electricity passes between the hairs on our arms. He flips the pages until he lands on "Rapunzel."

"Obviously, all these fairy tales are translations, and the exact wording varies from publication to publication. Some have it, but the most well-known fairy tales don't. Yet *that's* the thing we take away: 'And they lived happily ever after.' And we stop there. As if that's all there is to it. But look at this. This one is my favorite." Together, we flip past the ends of "Snow White," "Rapunzel," and "Cinderella," which all end the same way: *And they lived happily ever after.* Then Jack directs us to the ending of "Hansel and Gretel":

> Then all anxiety was at an end, and they lived
> together in perfect happiness. My tale is done, there
> runs a mouse; whosoever catches it may make
> himself a big fur cap out of it.

"The 'happily ever after' stuff is a construct," he continues. "Hansel, Gretel, Cindy, Snow? These characters never really deal with the trauma they endured. I mean, these are dark-ass stories. It's all so messed up. But Disney said, 'Every fairy tale must be this linear story and end with a tidy heteronormative bow,' and we bought into it! That's become what we're supposed to want, but it's so marginalizing and restrictive! What gets me is that 'happily ever after' is not even the important part of that line. The important part is ignored."

"Which is what?" I ask, a bit breathless.

He pauses and points to three words on the page: *And they lived*.

I look at him.

His smile crinkles his nose. "Because the point isn't that they were happy forever but that they lived. They took a chance and lived." He pauses before shaking his head. "Sorry, I get intense sometimes."

"No, I like it . . . I mean, I admire people who are passionate about stories." I wince, quickly correcting myself so I don't come off like I'm saying I like him, which would be the truth, but what he said is making me think about the whole point of stories in the first place; how they end, where they end, and why.

I reread the last line of "Hansel and Gretel" before placing the Brothers Grimm book back on the shelf:

My tale is done, there runs a mouse; whosoever
catches it may make himself a big fur cap out of it.

What the actual fuck does that mean? My mind dwells on everything: that last line, what Jack said, and those three words— *and they lived*—tumble around my brain as we walk out of The Pagemaster.

"I'm not ready to go back to campus," he says. "You wanna walk to the lake?"

I nod, and we walk in a comfortable silence out of the confines of the small town and toward the park by the water.

"What're you thinking about?" he asks. "You look deep in thought."

"This story I'm trying to tell in my animation seminar," I say, not quite sure I'm ready to tell him the details. Uncooked ideas are too fragile to be shared and consumed.

"If you need a story person, I'm your guy," Jack says, rather confidently. "I've always wanted to dip into script writing."

I'm your guy.

We perch on a wooden bridge that stretches across a small inlet, lean on the ledge, and stare at the lake. There's a soft trickle of water rushing over the rocks below, the faint tweets of birds in trees, insects buzzing, all creating a peaceful symphony around us.

"I like your presumptuousness, thinking I need help." I wink. Or try to. When I wink, my face gets all twitchy, which is probably why he's smirking. "Actually, help *would* be nice."

"I like that word," he says. "*Presumptuousness.*"

It's luxurious and pompous, nothing at all like Jack.

"It'd be cool to write a script one day, like a great romantic tragedy," he says. "We'd be a good team, I think."

We'd be a good team.

"How do you know?" I ask softly.

He shrugs and goes silent, and I want more than anything to know what's going on in his head. His left arm moves close to mine, and I can feel him even though he's not touching me. Should I move closer? Slide my fingers across the invisible airstream between us that keeps pulling us closer together, like a vacuum? What if my pinky finger touches his? What would he do? Would he wince? Pull away? React by coiling his fingers around mine? Am I making this entire thing up in my head? Am I creating this attraction out of nothing? Maybe he's just a smiley person? Like a celebrity with Vaseline on his teeth.

This is totally the part of the animated film where the lovesick main character sings a cinematic ballad about how much they want love. How it's so close, yet so far. It's the song that gets the Oscar nod and a remix by Beyoncé.

"Sooo . . ." I clear my throat and draw out the *o* for far too long like the awkward goose I am. "What'd you buy in there?"

He doesn't waste a beat, positioning his bag on the railing. "Glad you asked." He reaches in. "There are three items, so I'll give you four guesses."

"How very Rumpelstiltskin of you," I say, and he glares at me. A smile spreads across my face because it's so obvious, I can't even deal. "Fine. Okay. Um. A book."

"I have to confer with the judges on that." Jack turns his head and whispers to himself like a play actor on stage. "It's vague, but given the nature of the shop from whence it came, we'll give it to you. But that's your one pass."

He pulls out a leather-bound journal with a metallic pen that looks carved from stone. "It's a magic journal, or so the shop owner claims. It's basically a regular journal but with a special pen that has disappearing ink." He waves the pen. "Seems like the kind of thing that would spark a quest of some kind. Or at least secrets."

"We love main characters with secrets," I say.

He shifts his weight from leg to leg. "Next item," he says, rather quickly.

"Uh, a book on that Hemingway dude you like."

He makes a noise like a buzzer. "Wrong! And I'll ignore your dudeifying of Ernie Hem for now. You have two guesses and two items left."

"This game is rigged."

What the hell could be in his bag? I could say, "Another book," but that's no fun. I did see a specialty candy rack in the store, and who doesn't like candy? A monster, that's who. "A candy bar."

"Are you even trying?" Jack accuses playfully. "One more guess. Give up?"

"To the likes of you, never!"

Okay, Chase, focus. The hell is in this boy's bag? I've already lost, but I could potentially get one more if I just think.

Of course, there are no thoughts in my head.

"Fine, white flag."

He lights up. "I *always* win this game." He pulls out a small pink bottle that looks like a witch's brew of some kind.

"Seriously? How the hell would I ever have guessed that?"

"I don't know. I figured it was in keeping with the whole quest theme," he says. "My best friend back home would dunk on me so hard if he saw this."

I take the bottle and read the label:

Clarity: For the traveler who seeks clarity of mind and love

"Interesting choice."

Jack snort-laughs. "I was thinking about what you said that day we met. About how every story is a love story. It's true, I think. I feel like ever since move-in day, I've been in my own version of the

Inmost Cave, and I'm just trying to clear my head a bit to see what my story is." He looks away, out toward the lake. "For my character, I mean."

Right.

"What's the last item?"

He hesitates. "I wasn't sure if this was it or not, but I think it is."

He's rambling and still not looking at me as he digs through the bag, which, the way he's rummaging with his whole arm inside the flaps, must be Mary Poppins's bag. He's stalling. When he finally does pull it out, his hand is shaking.

It's *The Art of Crumbs* by Linda McPherson.

"I saw it as soon as we walked in, and I don't know, I was drawn to it and wanted to check it out. The art is . . . stunning. I had to get it."

I don't realize that I'm holding my breath until he tells me I look pale. Or paler than usual. Everything seems to have led to this one moment, right here, and I don't know what the hell is going on in Jack's head, but he's clearly thinking about me. Whether it's the same way my thoughts dwell on him, I don't know. He's hesitant but forward. He's holding back, yet he's putting something out there for me: the journal, the potion, the *Crumbs* book. It has to mean something, right? I think I've been holding back because I didn't want to push him or seem needy, but this feels like a sign that maybe he could like me?

Though my entire being tells me that someone like him could never love a soft, genderless cub like me, I take a leap: "Friday's my birthday. Wanna come to a party?"

For a few seconds, he doesn't say anything. And then, "No."

My face falls.

The sun is almost completely gone, a sliver of hot orange still glows beyond the mountains in the distance, and it's considerably cooler now as September grows closer.

"Kidding." He punches my arm softly. "Yeah, sounds good."

10

Mom says I suffer from restless leg syndrome. She claims it's because she always shook her leg when she was pregnant with me, and after I was born, bouncing me was the only action that soothed me.

It's sort of become a major problem for everyone around me.

If I'm sitting upright, my leg shakes. Doesn't matter where I am—on a bench, at a table, in the car, at my desk, as I'm lying awake in bed. And it's worse when I'm nervous, sort of like a rocket about to launch into space. Violent. This is what's happening right now as I wait for Jack to text me.

Because it's my nineteenth birthday and he's coming up to my suite to hang out. And though this is definitely not a date—even Benny agrees because, according to him, "No self-respecting gay would say, 'Yeah, sounds good' when asked out"—my leg doesn't know that. I'm pretty sure our entire dorm room is rumbling, and it's gotten to the point where Benny is hypnotized.

He's been silently staring at my legs, face blank, for the past five minutes.

It's unnerving. Which makes me shake harder.

When my phone buzzes, Benny actually screams.

"It's not Jack," I say, which elicits a groan from Benny.

RAE: You're lucky I love you because my ass is on the bus on my way to your loving arms so you better be ready for your birthday surprise 😘

"What is life right now?" Benny says. "You're actually making me feel like I need to throw up." He comes over and kneels beside me. "Do we need to have a 'come to Oprah' moment?" He closes his eyes and takes a deep, cleansing breath and motions with his hands as if he's pushing out the bad toxins, like some sort of gay guru—a gayru.

"Maybe."

He holds out his hands, and I take them as he prompts me to close my eyes and do as he does. He makes a wild grunting breath thing with hissing noises. It's oddly calming.

Eyes still closed, I whisper, "Why am I such a mess?"

"I don't know, but it's tragic," he says. "Luckily for you, I, too, am tragic."

"I said *mess*, not *tragic*."

"Same thing," he says, all zenned out.

"Any advice?"

"Nope."

"How is that lucky then?" I ask.

Benny shrugs. "Misery and company and all that."

My phone buzzes again, and he paws at it, sliding it off my desk and into his hands. "Oh, it's my wife!" He slides it open and puts Rae on speaker. "Hi, gorgeous!"

"I'm on this godforsaken campus. What do I do now?"

"Rude!" I shout.

"You're right. Your campus is actually beautiful," Rae says. "But you won't be if I'm stuck out here for too long. Makeup is melting off my face."

The camera tilts, and Harry's face enters the frame. He waves awkwardly like the bubbeh he is. But his zayde-aesthetic is strong tonight, from the way he styled his hair, all slicked back like a member of the Rat Pack, to his ill-fitting Argyle sweater and khakis. I hope it's okay with Chloe and Sofía that we're bringing an extra body to their house.

"Oh, clown realness," Benny says, and Rae gasps. "Ohmygod, I'm such a binch. Okay, listen, sweetie, I see where you're at, so I'll come down to get you because Chase is waiting for his maybe-straight crush boy. I think he might have a stroke if we ask one more thing of him."

As Benny goes to leave, there's a knock on the door. He stops and turns, like a victim in a horror movie about to face his demon. "What do I do?" he whisper-screams.

"Open it?" I shout, peeking my head out from our room and glancing down the hallway because it could be Jack.

And it is.

Except it's not just Jack.

He's with Rhett.

Benny immediately freezes up, and Rhett offers a head nod. Then, in a move worthy of a late-'90s sitcom, Benny slams the door in both of their faces.

"Ohmygod, what is happening?" he whines. "Did you know he was coming?"

121

"You guys are so loud!" Xavier says. He walks out of his room shirtless, abs all exposed, which shuts Benny up.

Xavier's carrying one of his cameras, which I noticed fairly early on is something he always has at the ready. He says he doesn't look for inspiration in his photographs, inspiration finds him, and he has to be ready. He doesn't spend much time in our suite, choosing instead to wander around town, searching for something that speaks to him. From the few interactions we've had, I really admire his dedication to his craft.

"Sorry, X," I say. "This guy Benny is hooking up with randomly showed up, and he's freaking out."

Benny shoots me a "really, binch?" glare.

"What's the problem? Let him in," Xavier says.

"The problem is he denies our sweet Benny," I explain. "Plays with Benny's delicate emotions and then pretends he doesn't exist."

"Ahh, the self-hating type. Got it. Is that why Benny cries in the bathroom at night?" Xavier asks.

"Hi, I'm right here!" Benny says sharply.

There's another knock at the door. I hear Jack's voice calling, "Uh, hello?"

"Pretty much," I say.

"Wow," Benny says. "If I wanted to be invisible, I'd go to Italy and visit my homophobic nonno who once looked right past me and said, 'I thought I heard something, but it was only a fairy,' in Italian. Have you *ever*?"

"Brutal." Xavier purses his lips. "Open the door. I have an idea."

Benny does as he's told.

Jack's arms are folded. "What the hell, man?"

Rhett still won't look at Benny, but by the look plastered across his face, he's hovering somewhere between pissed and guilty.

"Sorry," Xavier says, his hand caressing his own bare stomach as he saunters toward them. "That was my fault. I didn't know we were expecting company, baby."

He wraps his strong, muscular arms around Benny and gently tips Benny's chin up toward his mouth, kissing him delicately. I don't have to be on the receiving end to feel the power of that kiss.

When he's done, he boops Benny on the nose then extends a hand to Jack and Rhett. "Xavier. Nice to meet you."

Both Jack and Rhett stand stunned, but neither is as stunned as Benny, who wobbles and sways like he's been put under a magic love spell. He takes a few seconds to snap back to his quippy self, and without missing another beat, says, "You really tuckered me out, babe."

Then Benny glares at Rhett, whose cheeks are candy-apple red.

"You have a bathroom?" Rhett asks Xavier coldly.

"Right there, killer." Xavier points the way.

"That was dee-licious," Benny says once Rhett is out of earshot. "I gotta go find Rae and regain feeling in my legs. Ohmygod, you should totally come out with us tonight!"

"That was *my* pleasure." Xavier licks his lips. "Maybe I will." He looks to me for permission, and I give it.

"The more, the merrier," I say, hoping three new bodies— Harry, Rhett, and now Xavier—are welcome at Chloe and Sofía's.

Benny dashes out of the suite, and Xavier makes his way back to his room to get dressed—most likely throwing on whatever shirt is lying around and making it look New York Fashion Week runway-level effortless—leaving Jack standing alone in the hallway just outside my room.

"Hey," I say softly.

"Happy birthday," he says, his voice buttery and rich, making me shiver. He stands in my doorway, propping himself casually against the frame. "Nice room. Who's Tim?"

I turn toward the Once Upon a Tim sign above my bed. I never did get around to peeling it off, but I kind of like it.

Should I be a little bold and say, "Why? Jealous?" or should I shrug it off and leave him to wonder about the mystery of Tim?

But I don't get a chance because Jack talks first. "I got you something." He hands me a rectangular package shoddily wrapped in a plastic bag from the CIA bookstore.

"Should I open it now?"

"Sure," he says. "If you want."

I sit at my desk and delicately unwrap the white plastic. I pull out a picture frame with Cayuga Institute of the Arts up and down its plastic border.

"Sorry, it's all they had in the bookstore."

But I'm not listening to him. The frame doesn't matter. Inside is a painting Jack took from *The Art of Crumbs*. It's one I know well because it's early concept art from my favorite scene in the movie, where the witch sings a "Defying Gravity"–style song. The sprawling painting, almost abstract in its brush strokes, shows the two faces of the witch. Her shadow is cast against the ground from bolts of jagged lightning.

It would be enough that Jack chose this picture to share with me, that he thought I would love it, but overlaid on top of the picture is a poem I don't recognize.

LICHTENBERG FIGURES, YOU

Trees shed leaves
the way I shed faces,
collectively
holding our breaths
until we can flower
once harsher weather
ebbs.

The last leaf
clings to its limb,
to seasons gone,
the way I cling to a mask
that no longer fits.
Maybe it never did.

Naked trunks sprout
from scorched earth
branches feather out like
jagged bolts of
lightning
waiting for the rain

to learn how to breathe again.

I point to it. "Did you write this?"

Jack nods. "I saw that picture in the book and, I don't know, it inspired me and reminded me of you and that night after the Years & Years show. I know it was probably nothing to you, but those kinds of nights don't happen to me often. Or . . . ever."

"Small moments last," I say.

He nods and smiles. "I hope you like it."

A tear rolls down my hot cheek, and I turn quickly to wipe it away. I pick my head up, and he's looking away, purposely avoiding me. Then he turns to meet me, and it's sheepish with a hint of a smile, and I'm about to say something when Benny bursts through the suite door with Rae and Harry pulling up his rear.

"Happy birthday, you big giant whore!" Rae shouts behind Jack.

"Excuse me?" Xavier pops back into the common room.

"You must be Xavier! I've heard so much about you. I'm Rae, Chase's best friend in the entire world—sorry, Benny, but it's true—" she says, and Benny pretends she stabbed him in the chest. As she's introducing herself, Rhett emerges. "Hi! Who are you?"

"Rhett."

"I don't know a Rhett," Rae says, obviously going through the Rolodex of my roommates in her mind.

"Makes two of us," Benny mumbles.

"I'm Jack's roommate," he says.

"Oh, we *love* Jack." Rae yanks Harry forward. "This is Harry, my boyfriend—" She babbles on a little more, making small talk as she usually does.

I'm not listening.

Jack and I are locked into each other's eyes.

Hard-core.

We only break our gaze when Rae barrels fully inside my room. He blinks, looks down, and turns to meet Rae, who throws her arms around him.

Once she pulls away, she sets her sights on me. "There's my birthday whore!"

Her loud voice pierces my brain. She hops onto my lap and straddles me, hugging me so tight that I almost can't take the pressure. I watch, helplessly, as Jack walks out of my room and into the common room to meet up with Benny. When she tries to pull away, I keep her close.

"You okay, boo?" she whispers, and I nod. "You sure?" she asks.

"Absolutely."

Which is partially true. I haven't processed the poem and what it means, but it does mean something. Is this gift a message? A sign? That's what Rae had said after Jack's first poem. Maybe he feels about me the way I feel about him. To be fair, I'm not sure how I feel about Jack because this is entirely new territory for me. All I know is that I want to be near him all the time. I want to stare at his beautiful face just to wait for the moments he smiles. When I'm not with him, my body screams at me to go find him, even if we're just sitting in the library together, not talking as we study. I've had crushes before, but this? This feels bigger. More important. Terrifying.

Xavier's head peeks into my room. "Who's down for pregaming? I got tequila."

"You're speaking my language," Rae says. She reaches into her bag and pulls out a handle of cheap vodka. "I brought this."

"Shots for everyone!" Benny shouts as he wraps his arms around Xavier's waist.

I look for Jack, but he's disappeared into the common room. Something tells me I'll forever be chasing Jack.

The group sticks close together as we walk off campus in the pitch-black darkness toward Chloe and Sofía's house. Benny leads the way with the help of Google Maps, while the light from Xavier's phone serves as a beacon to light our path.

Everyone is buzzed-on-the-verge-of-drunk except for me and Jack, who told me he doesn't drink because he doesn't like the taste. I'm too nervous I'll say something to him I'll regret, so it's better to be sober. I shot off texts to Chloe and Sofía warning them that I might be bringing a few extra people, but they haven't gotten back to me, and the closer we get, the more my stomach curdles.

I listen intently as Jack talks to Harry. "I went to a charter school in Vermont," he says. "I want to be a writer, but I could also see myself going into teaching, like my brother. Maybe I'll start my own charter school, or I don't know. I could probably just work at my brother's, but I don't want to go into the family business. I have my own ambitions."

I make a mental note to ask Jack more about his family. And his future. But there's a pinch in my gut because I want his future to include me, and that seems like a wild thing to think. Right?

"Ambition is a good thing," Harry says.

"Says the Laurene guy," Jack quips.

"Gotta go big and be bold to make it, you know," Harry says, not at all sounding the dad he dresses as. "Charter schools are great alternatives. All you need is one big donor, and I know there are plenty of rich assholes who feign philanthropic interest."

"The one I went to relies on donations. It was the best experience I ever had." Jack pauses, his eyes traveling to me. "So far, anyway." He smiles, and it's filled with hope. "They were always planning trips to Europe and Canada and stuff. We went to Iceland to see the northern lights during my senior year and learn how Icelanders utilize the land to harness green energy and about all the environmental protections in place there."

As Jack dazzles with his knowledge of green energy, Rae leans in and whispers in my ear, "*Love* him."

Same, girl.

He continues, "The school also offered electives like kayaking and white water rafting. I'd love to teach there and write books during the summer months. That's the plan." Jack is now beaming.

"You're a writer?" Harry asks.

"Yes, I told you this!" Rae yells, slurring a bit. "Remember the poem he wrote Chase?"

My heart plummets to the floor.

"Babe, I think you're drunk," Harry says exaggeratedly. But he can't delete what she said. It's out there now.

"No, remember I showed you the text?" Rae trips over her heels and tumbles into Harry, who struggles to hold her upright since he's a full foot shorter than her.

Jack's head whips fast toward me.

Harry, quick to notice the tension, takes Rae's arm, and they break away from the group until they're at the back. "How about we go over here, huh, babe?"

Worry lines crack the glass of Jack's face. Betrayal pulses through his clenched jaw.

I don't know what to say.

He speeds up to Rhett, who sulk-walks behind Benny and Xavier.

Shit.

This is not how I pictured tonight going. At all.

"Apparently, we're here?" Benny says.

The only house in the thick woods looks dark. Empty. Save for one hot-pink neon sign in the front window that blinks, You Wish You Were Here! There's a faint hum of music, an electronic beat that pulses far away. Like pretty much all the off-campus houses around CIA, it's dingy and small and looks like the set of some C-rated horror flick, complete with a broken concrete path to the front door sprouting dead weeds in the cracks.

Everyone except for Jack turns to me.

I guess I'm expected to lead the way.

I knock on the door, but nobody answers.

"Just go in," Benny says, and when I turn to give him a "get up with me, you coward" look, he shrinks away and hides behind Xavier.

The door is unlocked, and I mumble, "I hope this is the right place," before pushing it open. Immediately, the sound of the bass knocks into me, reverberating off the walls and escaping through the door. The house may be small, but it's wall-to-wall bodies, and I breathe a sigh of relief that I brought so many extra people. The hazy air inside reeks of skunky pot and sweat, and the lights are low, giving the living room a distinct club vibe. It's beautiful chaos.

I recognize a few people from class and others from having passed them in the hallway of the visual arts building. CIA is not that big, after all, and the animation program is even smaller. I turn around and look for Jack, but he's gone, disappeared into the sea of people, along with Rhett, Benny, and Xavier. Rae and Harry stick close by, and she grabs a fistful of fabric from the back of my shirt to not lose me.

"There you are, birthday kid!" Chloe exclaims, literally appearing out of thin air. She's wearing a bright-orange skintight dress that hugs her curves. She throws her arms around my neck and kisses my cheek. It's wet and sloppy but nice. I introduce her to Rae and Harry. Her eyes have trouble focusing, but she gives them equally enthusiastic hugs. "It's time for y'all to get drunk! Go into the kitchen! We have jungle juice in the big Gatorade cooler, beer in the fridge, and some harder stuff on the counter. I think Sofía is there, but who knows." With that, she jumps back into the crowd, dancing her way to the center of the room, red Solo cup in hand.

Jack's in the corner leaning against the wall like James Dean. He's talking to some girl who looks straight from the cast of *Riverdale*. He laughs, and it's so over-the-top that my fists clench.

I need a drink.

Rae, Harry, and I snake our way to the kitchen, and we almost make it unscathed.

Almost.

I see her before I hear her, but it takes my brain a few seconds to process Leila leaning against the counter nursing a cup of jungle juice, talking to Benny, Rhett, and Xavier of all people, before she screams, "Rae!"

My whole body goes numb.

Rae screams, too, and they barrel toward each other.

"What're you doing here, you tall drink of water?" Leila says, practically squealing.

Rae turns to me, and suddenly her eyes sober up. "It's Chase's birthday. His friends live here," she says in a "Chase was invited, what's your excuse?" tone.

Leila turns to me and offers a polite wave but doesn't say, "Happy birthday."

"You haven't really answered any of my texts, R. Are you mad at me?"

"Sorry, I've been busy with sch—"

"I see," Leila says, nodding toward me. "So busy."

Benny slowly walks over to me and hands me a cup of jungle juice. I down it in one gulp and shiver from the horrible, bitter taste. It tastes like straight kerosene and feeds the fire in my belly. He quickly takes it and refills it.

"It was really *great* to see you." Leila grabs Rae's hand and swings it like they're young kids on the playground. "I would love it if we could reconnect. There's no reason why *we* can't be friends."

Rae nods, but I can tell she's not sure what to say.

I can't listen to this anymore. I grab my cup from Benny, take another swig that goes down much easier, and push my way past people until I reach the center of the dance floor. Suddenly, someone grabs my waist, and I turn to see Sofía in a short neon-yellow bob wig and a paint-splattered white dress.

"I thought that was you!" She hugs me, and our bodies press together.

Everything blurs as our hips sway and grind to the beat of a song I don't know. I tip the cup to my lips and drain it. I have no idea how much time has passed, but we cycle through songs, and suddenly Chloe is behind me and Rae is to my side as Harry watches us from afar, eyes wide. A hard-techno remix of Miley

Cyrus's "Party in the USA," a song Rae and I used to love when we were kids, crashes through the speakers, and we're both infected by its *snap, crackle, pop* confection. I start scream-singing the lyrics, and Rae follows suit until the entire party is backing us as we mosh. For a while, at least the length of one song, I forget about Leila and Jack.

It's hard to focus, but I think Benny and Xavier are making out in a dark hallway. I can only tell because aside from Rae, they're the two tallest people here. I want to enjoy this because it's fun and something I don't normally do, but my thoughts return to Jack.

Each 808 beat reminds me of the way my chest flutters when I'm around him.

The way our bodies entwine makes me yearn for his.

If I keep my eyes closed, I can pretend it's him I'm holding instead of Chloe or Sofía or Rae; that's the magic of imagination. But when I open them, I see he's just out of arm's reach. Touching him would be a different kind of magic.

Sweat trickles down my back, and everything overwhelms me: the heat of the party and the bodies and the jungle juice and Leila's unexpected presence and the look of betrayal on Jack's face that replays in my mind like the chorus of a shitty song.

"Excuse me," I say.

"You okay?" Rae asks.

"I just need some air. I'm good."

Keeping my head down, I push toward the front door, which hisses open. Thumping music streams into the dead night air before it slams behind me.

Leaving me in silence.

It's so dark that I can only make out what's vaguely lit by the blinking neon sign.

It's so still that my thudding heart shakes my entire body.

I tilt my head back and stare at the millions of stars strewn across the endless sky, some brighter than others, some fading into black.

Something rustles in the dark on the other side of the house, sending a chill down my spine.

I turn, expecting a bear because, of course, that'd be my luck while drunk on my birthday. It takes a second for my eyes to adjust to the dark, and it's Jack, sitting in a camping chair, phone in hand. I expect him to stand up and brush past me, to leave me alone under the blinking fluorescent light, but he doesn't.

"Sorry. I just needed some air."

"You looked like you were having fun in there," he says.

"You too."

He snorts. "Not really my scene."

"What about that girl?"

"Who?" He crinkles his brows. "Oh. Her? She's in my creative writing class."

I mosey over to one of the empty camping chairs and plop down.

He's tapping at his phone screen.

"I'm sorry about showing Rae your writing. I—"

"It's fine." His face isn't peppered with a smile or a promise of something else.

"It's not, though. I shouldn't have broken your trust like that. I was just—" It feels like one of those "do or die" moments, where I take a chance and tell him how I feel to see if maybe he feels the same way about me.

"Just what?" he asks softly.

My palms are sweaty, and my mind whirrs trying to find The Perfect Thing to say.

"Forget it," he says, rising to his feet. "I'm heading back to campus."

He makes it to the edge of the road when my feet kick into gear, and I run after him.

"Go back to the party, Chase," he says coldly.

"What's wrong, Jack?" I ask, grabbing hold of him. "I said I was sorry."

He's breathing rapidly, his chest rising and falling in quick succession. Moonlight shines softly on his pale face, and I can see just how wet and cloudy his eyes are.

"Talk to me," I ask gently.

"I need to sit." He squats on the curb and brings his knees to his chest.

"What's wrong?" I ask again.

"Everything," he confesses. He's shaking, and I inch closer, wanting desperately to wrap my arm around him and pull him into me, to protect him from whatever he's going through, even if that thing is me.

His foot tentatively slides across the concrete and meets mine, lingering for a brief second, but retracts quickly, as if it were probing new territory and found something scary.

I don't want to play these games anymore.

I move closer until our bare legs rest gently against each other. The soft hairs on his leg send jolts of electricity up both of our bodies. He shivers and tenses up, and I think he's going to move it away, but then he presses his leg into mine deliberately. He leans closer, and I'm drawn to his lips like a powerful magnet.

I hold my breath, afraid to move, to break the connection.

But he looks away. "I'm scared." He's so quiet, I barely hear him.

"Of what?"

"You."

I suck in a breath and hold it.

Jack looks at the sky, which feels impossibly clear, the constellations closer than ever before. He doesn't look at me when he continues; it must be easier not to. "It's not just about the poem. I mean, it is, but it's not." He's got clouds in his eyes.

"You're talking in riddles," I say. "Look at me."

"I can't."

"Why?"

"Because." Then he does something I wasn't expecting.

He grabs my hand.

Did that really just happen? Or did I fall, hit my head, and slip into a fever dream? I look down and, nope, there it is. His fingers intertwine with mine. His palms are sweaty, but his grip is strong, really strong, and I squeeze back to match it. His thumb starts to gently stroke mine. I've never had someone hold my hand like this, tender and sweet.

"I'm good with words," he says. "But some stuff is impossible to say out loud."

I need him to say what he means. "Like what?"

"What I only think about in the dark when I'm alone." It trickles out slowly at first, like water through a hairpin crack in a glass. "It's not that I don't have accepting parents, but . . ." His voice trails off. "But it's always, '*Those people* can have whatever rights they want, just so long as they don't force it on me.' That sort of thing. My dad is a guy's guy, you know? God-fearing and all that. He has certain . . . expectations for his sons, you know . . ."

Jack doesn't have to finish. I know the story. It's the same one every person faces when they realize they're not straight.

"That's why I came here, so I could figure out who I am. I didn't expect *you*."

He looks at me, his beautiful face, and I'm done. I want to kiss him. To hold him and never let him go. He moves closer, and I feel his warm breath on my face.

"What are you saying, Jack?"

I don't need him to come out and label himself. Not for me. But I do want to know how he feels about me. I lock eyes with him again and decide it's time to take the plunge: "Because I've never felt like this before. You're the first thing I think about when I wake up, and you make me smile as I fall asleep. I read that poem every single day, and the spark I held in my hand that night is still burned into my skin."

His jaw clenches, but his gaze never breaks. "When we got home from our quest the other day, I sat down to write in that journal with the invisible ink pen. I thought that if I could just write down how I felt, put the words on the page, knowing they'd fade away once the ink dried, it'd make me feel better. It's like I started this journey here at CIA feeling a bit lost, but when I met you, it all started to come together. My Inmost Cave is admitting it out loud. That I'm . . ." He pauses.

"You don't have to say anything," I try to assure him, knowing what he's about to admit. There's determination etched onto his face but also fear. I wish I could take away, but that's impossible.

He shakes his head. "I'm gay." He lets out a breath, and the tension in his shoulders melts.

I pull him closer, making sure he knows I won't let him go. Then he hands me his phone, his hand still trembling.

"I never said that out loud, even though I've always known."

I let his confession settle in for a few moments. "How does it feel?"

He shrugs. "I wrote this tonight. Well, technically, I started it after our quest, but watching you inside dancing, I don't know. I felt like I needed to be next to you, too." He shakes his head. "I wasn't mad that you showed Rae the poem. I just didn't realize until now that I never really had a chance to figure out what it meant first."

I pick up his phone and read the words in his Notes app:

Bedtime stories start,
"Once upon a time"
but nobody says the
quiet part out loud:
that happily ever after
is a lie
and the real story begins
long after the end
once the reluctant hero
learns love is complicated
and easy to admit in the dark
once the lights go out

and nobody can hear
the sounds of your heart
beating

"Jack—" I lean in and trace the outline of his face.

His heartbeat is a *quick-quick-thump, quick-quick-thump.*

Our noses nuzzle, his mouth hovering above mine, our lips two magnets just within range, pulling toward each other but held back.

"I've never done this before." His breathing is shallow. "I've kissed girls, but—"

"That's okay, we don't have to. We can take our time," I shift away from him, but he grabs the collar of my tee and yanks me toward him, kissing me.

It's soft, tender, and grows in intensity the longer we stay entwined. His mouth opens, and mine does the same until his tongue brushes mine. I pull back just enough to nibble on his bottom lip, which elicits a primal moan, and he moves his hand from my shirt to my face, caressing my cheeks, then to the back of my head, pulling me toward him, chasing me, making my body shudder.

His lips are the spark, my body the thunder that follows, shaking the earth.

When he pulls away, he looks as punch-drunk as I feel drunk-drunk. The clouds in his eyes are less stormy, hazier.

My first kiss.

"Can we get out of here?" he asks, standing up and thrusting his hands in his pockets. He wavers, his feet unsteady, looking a lot like he did that evening in the rain on Laurene's slope.

"Yeah, let me go say goodbye to Rae." I don't know where Jack wants to go or what he wants to do, but I'd go anywhere with him. He nods tersely, and I dash inside, finding Rae almost immediately.

"Are you okay?" she asks.

I smile. "He kissed me. And he wants to get out of here."

She screams and wraps her arms around me. "We'll be fine. Momma Rae will take care of the masses. Go!"

With her blessing, I'm practically skipping toward the door.

But when I throw it open, Jack is gone.

The Prince Who Captured Lightning

PART II

For many days, too many to count, the Prince held the spark in his hands, wondering how it came to be and what he was meant to do with it. No one had ever dealt with such a problem, though he was not sure it *was* a problem. All the Prince knew was that every time he held it in his hand, he thought of the Knight in the woods, and it would zap his body, and visions of their day spent together revisited him. It made him feel more alive than he ever had before.

Upon return to the Kingdom, the Prince had to choose between eligible maidens for his bride, but what would he do with the spark? The Prince knew harboring something so powerful was forbidden, so he was resigned to keep it hidden. He buried it in his dressing chambers, but the glow crept out of the gap between floor and door. He hid it under his bed, but when he slept, its energy seeped into the Prince's dreams, evoking the Knight and restless slumber. So he sewed the spark into his pocket, keeping it close but out of sight. Though the spark was not visible during the bride selection ceremony, the Prince could still feel its intense heat. It distracted him, preventing him from connecting with any of the maidens, for none gave him the same jolt as the Knight when their hands touched.

Once alone, the Prince decided to let it dance upon the wick of a candle so that it looked like a burning flame. He kept it under a brilliant glass orb on a shelf in his living quarters. For a time, it seemed to fool everyone, even the Prince, who pretended to forget that it was anything but a candle. Until one night, the spark grew even brighter, cracking the orb's glass. The spark's power and energy were growing.

Not wanting the King, Queen, or any servants to become suspicious, the Prince decided he could not contain this phenomenon any longer, not when it meant possibly endangering his Kingdom.

The Prince had heard tales of a banished, scorned Witch, well-learned in the magic arts, who lived deep in the same woods in which he met the Knight. As it was also forbidden to seek the counsel of a Witch, he took leave at twilight, when all the kingdom was asleep. He traveled by horse until the morning sun peeked over the mountains and through the dense forest canopy, the spark held tightly in his hands guiding his way.

But it was not the Witch he found in the forest.

Once again, the Prince came upon the Knight, who had made camp just beyond the edge of the woods.

For a while, they stood in silence, staring at each other, the Prince unsure what to say out of fear. After all, how could he tell the Knight about the spark and that ever since their first meeting, his thoughts had dwelled on the handsome Knight? The Knight might think him mad, or worse. In all the history of the Kingdoms Below the Skies, a prince had never been allowed to love a knight.

Love. Is that what this is? thought the Prince to himself. *This cannot be.* The spark in his hands glowed, and its electricity flowed through him until his entire body was illuminated.

But the Knight did not cower, nor did he seem surprised at all.

For when the Knight stepped forward and extended his hand, the Prince saw that in the Knight's palm was a twin spark that glowed brighter the closer the two became.

"I have been searching for you," said the Knight. "I see you every time I close my eyes."

All at once, the Prince understood that these twin sparks had been calling out to each other, and so he reached out a hand to the Knight's. As their fingers intertwined, a bolt of lightning shot up into the skies, its brilliant flashes stretching across the blue. Moments later, a thunderous boom shook the earth

143

as if a giant stomped across the clouds. The force ripped the Prince and the Knight apart, and the bolt of lightning retreated from the skies back into their hands.

Suddenly, dark storm clouds grew, blanketing the skies as hard, tear-shaped droplets of rain poured down across the earth.

"What does this mean?" asked the Knight.

"I don't know, but I was on my way to see the fabled Witch of the woods to rid myself of this curse," said the Prince.

"Is that what this is? A curse?" asked the Knight.

"If it isn't, then what explanation is there?" asked the Prince.

"If it's a witch you seek, a witch you'll find," said the Witch, appearing suddenly before them. "I can help you, but you'll pay a price."

"How much?" asked the Prince. "To break this curse?"

"A small sacrifice, one gold coin cannot buy." The Witch grinned, manifesting a knife in her hands. Running the blade across the Prince's chest, she said, "You must each carve out a morsel of your own hearts."

11

I always thought that after my first kiss, the clouds would part and the sun would shine down on us, and the world would become this wondrous Technicolor cartoon landscape where little forest critters and birds would break out into a thumping song about how lovely love is, and we'd dance off into the sunset. Or something.

For a second, it kind of was like that.

Then Jack disa-fucking-ppeared, and the cheesy song came to a screeching halt.

Yet I can't stop thinking about it. The kiss. His lips, the stubble on his cheeks, the way his heart beat so erratically until I kissed him back and then slowed to a steady rhythm in time with mine.

I think about it on the walk back to my dorm that night, alone. I think about it when I text Jack in the days that follow, and he leaves me on read every time. When I call him, but it goes to voice mail. I think about that kiss when I wake up and trudge to class, hoping I'll run into him because I memorized his schedule. When I wait outside our favorite dining hall, expecting him to show up for dinner.

He never shows.

It's almost as if he never existed at all.

A few days after, I stop by his dorm, but when Rhett opens the door, he says Jack has hardly been around and that he only shows up to shower and sleep. Benny assures me that Rhett has no idea about Jack and me, but the way Rhett looks at me with pity swelling in his eyes makes me feel like he knows *something*.

I loop the night of the kiss and every minute I've spent with Jack over and over again in my head. The thing I keep coming back to is that he admitted, out loud, to himself and to me that he was gay for the very first time. Then he kissed me. And then he evaporated into the night sky.

Was it because I'm chubby and undesirable? Did I somehow make him feel pressured? Should I have been more resolute about pulling away from him? Of all people, I should know that coming out is a major fucking deal. Your head spins with uncertainty right before the plunge, but then once you say it out loud to another person and it's real and not just an idea in your mind, there's an immense, weight-lifting relief *and* niggling fears that you won't be met with love every time you come out. Because you'll be coming out in small ways every fucking day of the rest of your life.

Leila was the first person I came out to as gay freshman year in high school, even though Rae and I were closer. It was easier because she always called herself "a gay man in a woman's body" and boasted about how "all the Instagays love my Insta content, yaaasss queen!" At the time, it made me think she would be accepting, and I just ignored the gross discomfort I felt when she said that. Because the fact is, she's not a gay man, so she's appropriating what doesn't belong to her. Granted, this isn't something only Leila does—many straight white girls co-opt queer culture like fashion accessories when it suits them but stay silent when we talk about the actual struggles of being queer. It's like we're only worth our meme value and only when it fits into a binary: Acceptable versus Everything Else.

When I finally worked up enough nerve to come out, I slipped a note in her locker in between classes.

> **ME:** I left something in your locker. A note. Plz don't say anything.
> **LEILA:** omg please don't tell me you're in love with me 🙏
> **LEILA:** you're in love with me, aren't you?
> **LEILA:** I have that effect on boys
> **ME:** LOL

When she finally saw the note, she texted:

> **LEILA:** OMG CHASE! I knew it! I totally called it. It was so obvious.
> **ME:** Thanks?
> **LEILA:** You're welcome! And btw, I love you, hope you know that!
> **LEILA:** This is literally the best thing that's ever happened to me btw 🤩

The response was typical Leila, centered on herself, making me sound like a shiny gay bauble to be collected. I think that's why I told her first. I liked the idea that it wouldn't be about me, but then her reaction soured my stomach because I realized it really *should be* about me. I wanted more. More than just a "yeah, I knew," like my identity was some sort of running bet.

Rae was entirely different. Like, worlds apart. Aside from being slightly peeved that I'd told Leila first, she hugged me and told me she loved me just the same. She asked me how I was feeling, and she sat with me in silence as I processed. She even held my hand as I came out to Mom and Taylor, who were unsurprisingly amazing. Dad was kind of emotionless but made sure to tell me he still loved me. He still doesn't know I'm nonbinary. At least, not from me directly. I'm sure he's seen the article on *The BuzzWord* and chooses to ignore it; he still says shit like, "Be a man!" if I'm having a tough day.

A few years later, when we were seniors, and I started mining my gender identity, exploring terms like nonbinary or genderqueer or genderfluid, and rejecting heteronormative gender labels, I didn't feel the need to pronounce that to anyone. Especially not Leila. It was—and *is*—nobody's business but mine. Period.

Instead, I spent months animating a black-and-white short about a knight who always felt uncomfortable being forced into rigid male-appropriate armor, so one day when the queen was throwing out old garments, he snuck them back to his chambers and tried them on. I set it to Lady Gaga's "Chromatica II" transition into her song "911," and the second the knight tries on an opulent, gemstone-studded ball gown, he transforms into a fabulous medieval drag queen who ignites the entire kingdom in glorious color. It was fun, silly. I never expected another video to go viral when I uploaded it to YouTube, but it exploded.

Suddenly I was being interviewed by *The BuzzWord* and having to talk about what it meant to be nonbinary, even though I didn't understand it myself. It felt easier to just let people find out that way, so I wouldn't have to come out to them.

That was when Leila started distancing herself and making passive-aggressive digs at me: "That Lady Gaga song transition was so 2020 and unoriginal," and "Anyone can animate a short, but it takes real talent to sculpt with your hands." Then it morphed into "you've *changed*." Coded bullshit that I knew was about *me*, not my art.

So I regretted ever letting myself get too close to her in the first place. I'd given her a piece of myself when I trusted her and let her into my inner circle. But I should have listened to my gut when she Yaaasss Queen'd everything and then turned her back when I seemed to no longer fit the GBF box for her.

Now I have a hard time trusting people.

Which is why I didn't want to force Jack to come out.

I've cycled through these thoughts every time I see Leila on campus in *my* classes, making art with *my* medium, trying to befriend *my* friends like Chloe and Sofía. Now it's blending into what happened between Jack and me, because I let Jack in, too, and he ghosted me, but this one is probably my fault. Did I misinterpret his intentions? Did I ruin everything with him? My brain is a constant maelstrom, and it's becoming hard to separate my stories and anxieties.

I miss him, and it tugs at my chest.

The long days without him stretch into one week, then two.

Classes drone on, and I feel bad when I zone out, gazing out windows and hoping beyond hope that I'll see Jack walking across campus. Today is no different.

But what would I even do if I spotted him? Grab my shit, run outside after him, and force him to talk to me?

"Gray, any thoughts?" Professor McPherson interrupts, arms folded, glaring at me as someone flicks on the lights.

"What?" My eyes focus on Leila in the center of the room.

"Any feedback for Leila about her short?" Professor McPherson asks sternly, annoyed. She's always like this on days when the juniors aren't here. Probably because they balance our freshman greenness.

Leila huffs. "Chase wasn't paying attention." She folds her arms to mirror our professor's. "You know, I, for one, am paying for an education at this fine, upstanding institution, and I believe I'm owed the baseline respect of my fellow peers. Chase clearly doesn't value the feedback process."

Tears sting the corners of my eyes as I remember long nights in the "art studio" (her parent's two-car garage) where I pored over her work. Leila somehow managed to capture the feminine form in clay, the bodies of her subjects expressing such fluid movements that it felt like they were flying through the air, ballerinas in mid-pirouettes. Her hands were always caked in brownish gray, and her hair was tied into messy buns. I spent hours with my sketch pads, drawing her, studying her motions.

Back then, her art had a purpose, a fervor, an energy that felt like a lyrical dance, and I told her that as often as I could. I told her when I thought her work was too restrained or not truthful, when it lacked power, and we would talk about why. We always spoke about her work. But she never did the same for my art.

"I just think Chase believes they're too good for this class," Leila continues. "We've all seen 'Drag the Knight,' amiright? Just because two animations went viral *last year*, by the way, doesn't mean Chase is above participating."

I roll my eyes to stop the tears from falling. "Christ, give it up, Ley." The class takes a collective breath and holds it. "I watched your storyboard. Eggbért leaves his egg friend behind and travels to a big farm that looks like New York City. Tries to settle into a chicken coop and watches as all the baby chicks hatch from the other eggs, just to be told he's never going to be anything more than a yolk. And it ends with him as a smiling omelet on the farmer's breakfast table, as if he's resigned to his fate. I get it. It's just . . . What is it even saying? I'm sorry, Professor McPherson, but we've been storyboarding and critiquing those boards for like three weeks now, and I just don't see any movement in terms of character development. Eggbért has these big dreams and then just returns to where he was at the start. There's zero growth."

I look around as I word vomit. My chest flutters as I struggle not to appear angry. "Also, Professor, you know that I'm the first to start the critique circle, and I stay quiet when it's my turn in the hot seat, but I just don't see the point of offering feedback when it's clearly not being taken."

My hands tremble as I glance at the clock on the wall above Leila's head. Class ended mid-rant, but nobody is moving. Or breathing. Neither am I, so I make the first move, shoving my shit into my bag and slinging it onto my shoulder as I barrel past Leila— who is frozen in place—and out of the classroom, letting the door slam behind me.

I don't stop until I reach the academic quad.

The hot midafternoon sun beats on my face as a cool Finger Lakes breeze whips past.

My chest is so tight.

My body crumples until my hands are on my knees.

I can't believe I did that. I eviscerated Leila in front of the entire class. She didn't deserve that, even if it's a taste of what she's done to me.

My phone vibrates as texts pour in. First from Rae:

RAE: Uh. Random, but got a message from Leila. Did you really do that? 👀

Then Chloe and Sofía in our group chat:

CHLOE: Prof McPherson just called. WTF did you do boo?
SOFÍA: What Chloe means is, are you ok?
CHLOE: That too
CHLOE: (ngl, Leila is mad annoying)
CHLOE: BUT. You cant just pop off like that in class.
SOFÍA: What Chloe means is, we're here if you need to talk
CHLOE: 👆

The ding for my email goes off, and I'm certain it's from Professor McPherson, probably scolding me or kicking me out of the program. I stash my phone away because I just *cannot* right now. The only person I wish I could talk to won't answer my texts or calls, and I'm not entirely sure he hasn't just disappeared off the face of the earth entirely. If Rhett is to be believed, anyway.

Jack kissed me and then ran away.

He trusted me, and I let him down.

He opened up to me, and I wasn't enough.

I'm never enough.

Not for Leila, not for Jack, not even for this damn animation program.

My legs carry me across campus. I don't have a destination, though my stomach is grumbling, and technically, the campus center is straight ahead, so maybe a mountain of chicken tendies and an assortment of dipping sauces from The Watering Hole is exactly what the temper tantrum caused by a broken heart ordered.

I happen to glance at the library as I reach the campus center, and there he is in that damn Red Sox cap, looking like a blond god sculpted from lumps of Leila's forgotten clay.

Jack.

Every single bone in my body aches for him and hates him all at once. What does that even mean? I didn't know that was possible until I saw him, just walking casually, face blank, holding a stack of fliers in his hand. I want to follow him into the library, but that's creepy, right?

My hand is frozen on the door handle to the campus center, debating whether to follow him instead of my rumbling stomach.

But Jack isn't inside for more than a few short minutes. He stays just behind the doors, and from my vantage point, it looks like he's tacking something to the corkboard in the entryway.

I wait until he walks back out before dashing across the quad and into the library. It doesn't take me long to spot what he put up.

It's a flyer for the Creative Writing Freshman Class's Open Mic, and it's happening tomorrow night in the Watering Hole.

He might be able to ignore my texts and calls, but he can't stop me from going to a free college event.

This is a horrible idea.

12

Ever since my birthday, Benny and Xavier have become inseparable. Well, technically, Benny is the one who won't leave Xavier's side, and Benny is the one who has started to dress like Xavier, right down to the muscle tees that his skinny-ass frame cannot pull off. X's slick 1980s acid-wash jeans-and-open-button-downs vibe look hot as hell on X, but not so much on Benny—bless his heart.

Luckily, I only walked in on them having sex in our room *once*. One time is more than enough to scar a person, though. Imagine coming home after a particularly long day of hating a stupid boy in a stupid Red Sox cap, and there's Xavier, all glistening and sweaty and abs, mid-thrusting as Benny moans like a banshee.

Some images—and sounds—never leave the mind.

Benny and Xavier have, however, called a "fashion-tervention" for open mic night. I wish this were a nightmare, but it's real life. Because apparently, my super cute graphic tees with cartoon characters don't scream "Fuck me!"

It doesn't matter that I've told both of them I'm not trying to wear anything that would scream "Fuck me!"

"You need to send a message," Xavier says, holding up a black turtleneck.

"What's that?" I ask. "That I have horrible taste in clothes and hate my own neck? Or that I'm a beat poet from the 1960s?"

"She is feisty," Xavier says.

"She's always feisty, ever since Jack pulled a *Gone Girl*," Benny says.

"What?" I ask.

"*Gone Girl*? Ben Affleck? Based on the bestselling novel of the same name?" Benny says. "I literally can't even be your friend right now. Neil Patrick Harris peen!"

Xavier looks at me, concerned. We've learned Benny has a tendency to just scream random things sometimes, so neither of us is sure if NPH peen is connected to *Gone Girl*, but Benny doesn't wait for us to figure it out.

"Whatever. Basically, Chase has been a moody binch for weeks," he says.

I grind my teeth. "Sorry, I know I've been awful."

"Leave 'em alone, Ben," Xavier says. "Jack really tore 'em up. Have some compassion." X tosses the shirt at me. "You want to be incognito tonight, right? That'll make you blend into the background."

"Now all I need is a beret," I say. "And circular sunglasses."

Xavier's eyes light up. "I have—if you want."

I close my eyes. "This is a bad idea, guys. Seriously bad. Epically bad."

"Why do you think that?" Xavier asks.

"Because he clearly doesn't want to have anything to do with me, and I'm basically chasing him down. Stalking him. It doesn't feel right."

Xavier sits down on the bed next to me and wraps his arm around me. "How about this? Let's just act like we're going for dinner at the Hole, and we'll sit far away, and it'll be like we're not there for him at all."

"Maybe we can just do a drive-by," I suggest. "Grab food and go eat outside in the quad or something?"

"Will that make you feel better?" Xavier asks.

"No," I say. "But I don't think anything will."

Benny walks over. "Whatever you want to do, we got your back. But honestly, you do need to work on your fashion, and we're long overdue for a makeover montage set to a Lil Nas X song."

I exhale and groan all at once. "Why do I feel like I'm going to regret this?"

Xavier smirks, and they get to work.

On the walk to the center of campus, Benny and Xavier are bantering about something related to Ariana Grande, but they're just background noise to the swell of doubt screaming in my head, telling me to turn around.

I want to see Jack, but I'm petrified that he'll take one look at me and run. Again. Or worse, pretend like I don't exist.

My palms sweat through the pockets of my skinny jeans, and I feel super self-conscious in the shirt I ended up picking from Xavier's carefully curated collection, a slick black button-down that

X insists I leave undone basically to my navel because "chest hair is sexy."

To be real, I feel like my moobs are practically pouring out of this neckline, like J.Lo's infamous Grammy dress. I'm deeply uncomfortable, but Xavier *and* Benny tell me to push through because I "look hot." I want to believe them, but sweat is now also dripping down my back, and I'm trying not to focus on my body.

I stop just before the entrance to the Watering Hole. "I can't do this."

Benny narrows his eyes. "Girl, *I* can't." He takes a deep, stabilizing breath like the YouTube influencers he watches when he thinks I'm not paying attention and forces his frustration off his face. "It'll be okay. We're just three hot gays on the hunt for chicken tendies, and if we happen upon a certain Gus Kenworthy–looking binch, then the power of our coven shall protect you. But honestly—" Benny leans toward the door and listens. "It sounds intense and busy in there, so we probably won't run into *him* at all."

The second we throw open the double doors, I literally run headfirst into Jack. If there is a god, she hates me.

Panic smacks his face. His cheeks redden, and he does everything he can to avoid eye contact, but I still feel this incredible pull toward him. "Oh. Hey."

"'Sup." Why is this my go-to? Am I an early 2000s straight-bro?

Insert: awkward AF silence.

Benny steps forward. "Chase, the line for tendies is ridiculous. Let's go so we can get out of here!" He sizes Jack up. "Because we're only here for the tendies."

I sigh and resist the urge to bury my face in my hands.

Jack clears his throat. "I, um, if you all are interested, the freshman creative writing majors are doing an open mic." He points to the far end of the Hole toward a small, dimly lit stage with a singular microphone stand and stool, flanked by speakers and surrounded by already full café tables.

"If we have time," Xavier says. "We got a thing after we eat."

Jack nods as he chews the inside of his cheek, and I'm drawn to his lips. I feel them, soft and faint, like an afterimage. "Okay, well."

Neither one of us walks away.

My fingers twitch, wanting to reach out and grab his hand, feel his strong fingers.

But I don't.

And then it's too late because Jack turns his back and leaves us behind.

"Holy shit, I felt that," Benny says sympathetically. "I'm sorry." His tone tells me he didn't get it until just now.

Maybe I didn't either.

As we walk out of the Hole, food in hand, one of the creative writing professors steps to the mic to introduce the freshman class. He does the usual excited teacher bit about how brave they all are for organizing and signing up and how much talent is present. I've stopped walking and find the nearest open seat at an empty table. It's far enough from the stage that maybe Jack won't see me.

Benny and Xavier join me, and we listen as student after student gets up to read. Some read short stories, others read poems. One dude with a ginger beard and a knitted beanie brings his acoustic guitar and sings a love song about environmental waste. I'm moved to tears by a Black girl who artfully turns classic lullabies like "Twinkle, Twinkle, Little Star" into a spoken word eulogy for her mother who died of cancer.

And then Jack steps to the mic, his hand shaking and holding a crumpled piece of paper. "Hi, everyone. I'm Jack Reid, freshman from Vermont. I've been writing a lot of poetry lately, which I never used to do. I've heard that's what CIA does. You come in wanting to be the next Hemingway, and then one night, everything changes."

His voice cracks as he looks out into the crowd, and our eyes meet. His jaw sets. "This is called 'Disappointment.'"

He reads from his paper like a slam poet, and I hold my breath.

I drink whiskey with my father
It doesn't matter that I'm not legal
or that the church would frown
to spite the blood of Christ
"You're a man, a guy's guy"
as he pours me a glass
in a snifter
and tells me it's smooth
like velvet,
and it'll give me hair
on my chest
*like a real man, like **him**,*
the son he wants me to be
He teaches me to sip,
how to hold it in my hands
and I pretend to like the taste

I listen as mom sips wine,
talks about how her
friend's son came out and
went to Pride
She doesn't realize the curl of her lips
as she sighs and says
"There's nothing to be proud of."
The liquid stains her teeth
as she asks me when I will
bring home a Christian girl
"How about Courtney
from down the road?
She seems nice"
and I nod because mom is right

I take Courtney to the movies
to the Italian joint
in the center of our small town
She's nice. We laugh over calzones
and she grabs my hand and says,
"Your fingers are so big,
and mine are so small and
fit into yours
like the pieces of a puzzle."
Except one of the pieces
doesn't fit
so I smile—it's what I do—
and tell my best friend I'll marry her one day.
I convince my reflection.

Then there's you
with eyes like a mirror
full of divine conviction
your irises undiscovered galaxies
shards of broken glass
distorted by tears
mine and yours
you don't demand anything from me
*but **me***
And I run away
because I fear what I see
when I look at you,
the endless possibilities
and your inevitable
disappointment . . .

Jack looks up at me, tears swelling his eyes.

Applause thunders around him.

He bows his head and makes a dash for the door.

I leave my plate of now-cold chicken nuggets on the table and find him outside on the stone patio, leaning against the railing overlooking a patch of grass between the campus center and the glass-enclosed fitness center.

It's eerily empty out here tonight.

Jack's shoulders hunch like a vulture. His back rises and falls. He's either crying or breathing heavily.

My sneakers scrape the pavers, and he tilts his head toward me.

"There's a reason I don't let people read my writing. It's fucking brutal. Like ripping open my own chest."

"Jack—" I don't even know what I'm going to say.

"I know what you're going to say," he says. "I screwed up, Chase. I should never have kissed you."

Oh. Yeah, that's *not* what I would have said. But good to know where he's at.

He waits for me to say something—anything—but the hurt and whatever gooey feelings I have for him are being blocked by an anger I've been letting slowly build.

My fists clench as I move toward him. I'm a volcano at the point of eruption. "You are so fucking frustrating, Jack! You have some fucking nerve, weaseling your way into my head. Holding me in the water like that, smiling like you know you got me hooked, writing poems for me, holding my hand, kissing me." I don't hold back. "I don't know where your head is at. You tell me you regret kissing me but then, that poem in there, and . . ."

Jack stands straight and faces me, a single tear trickling down his cheek.

"I'm sorry I kissed you back that night and maybe scared you. I should've thought about what you were telling me. But fuck, Jack—" I walk closer to him, but not too close, because the kinetic energy firing between us is like a bomb ready to explode. "You are all I think about, and I probably would've done anything to be with you, and you just ghosted. You know what? Fuck y—"

He grabs my face and kisses me, shutting me up.

Which, okay.

Because those lips! His body presses against mine as his arms wrap around my back and pull me closer. I feel the heat radiating off his hard chest. His mouth moves with a hungry fervor, and I lose my breath trying to match it.

A group of passersby cheer for us, and I immediately stop, expecting Jack to pull away and run again.

But he doesn't. At least, not yet.

The onlookers scream out for us again, and I flash a quick wave, still holding on to Jack's strong back, which tenses. He looks away, his cheeks red. He's breathing heavily, so I let him go. But he doesn't want to be let go of. He pulls me around the side of the campus center so we're shielded by bushes and trees, and our voices are muffled by the hum of a giant air vent. He's breathing heavily, like I do when I'm on the verge of a panic attack.

"I don't understand you," I say, panting.

"I'm messed up."

"A true writer." I offer a nervous laugh. To lighten the mood. Or something.

His body is shaking.

"Are you going to run again?" I ask.

"I don't want to," he says softly into my ear, the heat from his breath sending chills down my back. He hugs me so tightly that I'm afraid of what I'll do if he lets go. "I don't want to disappoint you, but—" He looks back toward where the onlookers cheered for us. "I'm afraid."

"Of me?"

"Of how I feel when I'm with you. Like I'm alive. For the first time. I don't want you to think that you're the reason why I up and left that night. When I came out to you, it's because I . . . was starting to feel things for you, and I felt comfortable because, well, with you, I feel more like me than I ever have. But I have issues with . . . stuff."

Okay, vague.

Also, same? Does he think I don't have issues too?

His blue eyes stare me down. His grip loosens, then his hands travel to my sides, and suddenly I'm very aware of my body, the extra padding around my midsection, and I squirm a bit under the weight of his touch.

"What's wrong?" he asks.

I shake my head, but suddenly all I can hear is his comment from the day we met about me being thicker, my thighs filling out his shorts, the way I compared my fuller, curvier body to his, and now I'm fully aware that Jack is touching me deliberately. My mind goes blank, and my thoughts are replaced with what I think he must be thinking about me: *Wow, Chase is bigger than I thought. Squishy. Nothing like my body. Insert vomit noise. I can't do this.*

I wriggle out from under him and turn away.

He comes up behind me, doesn't touch me, but I feel him. "I won't disappear again."

"No, it's not that," I say, perhaps too quickly as I look down at myself and cover my stomach with my hands.

He must notice, because his arms snake around my body and rest on my hands. "You're self-conscious. Why?"

Jack's already disappeared once, so why not just lay it out all there, right? As these thoughts tumble dry on low in my head, I realize I have a shit ton to lose, but c'est la vie.

"What if I'm not . . . what you expected?"

"You're not," he says matter-of-factly. His mouth hovers above my ear, and he kisses the lobe. He presses into me from behind. "You're more."

"Stop," I say, half because I might melt if he says stuff like that and half because maybe he's just saying what he thinks I want to hear to make up for his disappearing act.

Then he lets go.

As predicted.

I brace myself for rejection, but instead, he slides around me and looks me right in the eyes. It's so fucking intense that my knees buckle. He backs me up against the stone façade of the campus center.

At first, his voice is shaky. "You drive me crazy, Chase." His fingers, matching the tremble of his voice, snake up the hem of my shirt, and I gasp. He leans his forehead against mine and exhales, his breath traveling down my face. When his hands leave my stomach, my body bucks, yearning for more. "You're so goddamn sexy, you have to know that I . . ." His voice is low, grumbly, but steadying now as he moves to undo the last of the buttons on Xavier's shirt. He starts kissing my neck, and I close my eyes and tilt my head back hard against the stone, which must knock some sense into me because suddenly, I'm very aware of where we are and what he's doing.

I push him back hesitantly. "Jack . . ."

His eyes are sultry and hungry like something is possessing him.

Which is kind of the problem.

It's as if he's a different person.

"Don't get me wrong," I say, trying to catch my breath. "I want you so badly, but I don't want you to get scared again, and I, just, is this too fast?"

"Would it be weird if I told you that every night since I kissed you, I've gone to sleep dreaming about you and what I would do to you if I ever got up the nerve to apologize and you gave me a second chance?" His fingers hook onto the belt loops on my jeans. "I've waited my entire life for you, and yeah, it seems like I'm moving at Mach 5, but in my head, in the fairy tale I've told myself to help me sleep, I've been with you this whole time."

That makes logical gay sense. "You're more fucked up than me. But also, same."

He smiles so wide, and it's unencumbered, freer than I've ever seen it. The balls of his cheeks are so cute I might actually die. I want to kiss each one.

He licks his lips. "I have to get back inside to wrap up the open mic. They're probably wondering where I went, but Rhett books a private studio to practice on Thursday nights in the music school, so my room is free until one a.m." Jack kisses the tip of my nose then squeezes my hand before smoothing the wrinkles in his shirt and adjusting his dick so it's not visibly hard; I do the same. "Should be done in an hour. See you at nine?"

I have no idea what I'm doing.

13

Back in our suite, Benny and Xavier find me frantically typing "I have exactly fifty minutes to learn everything about the mechanics of gay sex because our education system failed me, and gay porn is overproduced, help" into Google. They shut the door and take turns Vanna White-ing an assortment of lubes, dildos, and condoms. Xavier busts open a shoebox filled with more elaborate sex toys, silicone prostate massagers, and now my head is too airy. I'm going to pass out from the combo pack of the information deluge and my embarrassment at being woefully unprepared.

Even though I've been jerking off to gay porn for forever and have seen many a thread on Reddit about prepping for anal, I'm overwhelmed by the possibility of actually participating in "getting dicked down," as Benny keeps saying.

Isthisreallyhappening?

Noticing my hyperventilation, Benny says, "You're such a little virg. Don't worry, you don't have to go penny; there's lots of other stuff you can do."

"Penny?" I ask.

"Penetrative," he says incredulously.

Xavier sits down beside me. His presence is a comfort. "You'll be fine. You might wanna shower."

"Do I smell?"

He sniffs me. "No, but a little freshness goes a long way. And, uh, you trim the hedges, right?"

Ohmygod. "Yes," I mutter.

"You'll be fine," he says. "Benny's right. Take it slow. You like him, and from everything you said, he likes you. Sex, especially penny, is worth the wait." He winks.

My friends are right. We don't actually have to do anything. I just want to be with Jack.

I feel slightly better, but every ounce of confidence vanishes when I get to Jack's room five minutes early and he doesn't answer his door.

Maybe I'm not knocking loud enough.

Maybe he got scared and bolted back to Vermont. Packed up and submitted a transfer application.

I debate getting on my knees and trying to peer under the crack in the door to see if the light is even on. What do I have to lose at this point, right?

Humiliation rattles me when I realize dorm room doors are designed so that you cannot peer under them—and at the exact moment, one of Jack's neighbors rounds the corner.

"Lost a contact," I say so loudly that the guy jumps back before offering me the flashlight from his phone. "Nah, I'm good. Found it." I grab what I'm pretty sure is a fingernail and flash it quickly so he moves on. "Thanks!"

The clock on my phone says it's 9:03 p.m. Utterly embarrassed and feeling like quite the failure, I dip out.

As I throw open the building's front door, I see Jack. Because of course I do.

"Hey!" he yells. "Sorry I'm late. I wanted to get some provisions. Apparently, the bookstore on a Thursday night at nine is the place to be. I shut it down."

He holds up a plastic bag from the school bookshop, and my heart drops because he's clearly expecting sex—what else could be in the bag except for condoms?

"You're a deviant."

"I wish," he says.

He waits until we're inside his cramped dorm room before leaning in for a kiss. He smells like sweat and cologne and laundry detergent.

"Were you waiting long?"

"Nope. Just got here."

"You're a terrible liar."

He shuts the door and toes off his sneakers. I do the same; as Mom would say, "Mind your manners; you're not an animal."

"Close your eyes," he says.

"Are you planning to kill me?" I deadpan and do as he says.

I'm tempted to peek as I hear manic rustling and shuffling, but I'm too nervous. My heart is pounding so loudly, it sounds like it's in my ears.

"Okay, open."

The room is dimly lit. There's a tee thrown over Jack's lamp for some makeshift mood lighting, and a battery-operated tea light candle in a glass CIA holder "burning" on Jack's desk.

"They don't sell real candles in the bookstore, for obvious reasons." He mimes an explosion with his hands. "But they had this, and I wanted our time together to be perfect. Oh, and obviously, they don't sell wine or champagne either on campus, but they did have Mountain Dew and these cool plastic mason jars with handles, which are just practical. And in case you wanted a snack . . ."

He holds up a package of Ferrero Rocher hazelnut chocolates.

"Setting the mood? Nice. But, um . . ."

"What?" His face falls. "Do you not like Mountain Dew? There's a vending machine down the hall. I think they have Dr Pepper or something."

I laugh. "No, it's just. I don't know that I'm ready to have sex."

His eyes go wide. "Whoa. Chase. Neither am I."

"Right. Of course." Wow. Completely misread that one. I'm so dense. My cheeks are red-hot, and I can't look directly at him, or I'll collapse into a pile of ashes.

He moves in closer, grabbing my waist. He stares at me until I turn to face him. He's smiling like a goofball. "I want to take our time. This is new for me, and I think . . . I don't know. It's like I've been running my entire life, but then I met you, and I finally stopped. And these past two weeks have been so brutal. I couldn't even shower. Rhett had to stop me from wearing my bathrobe to class."

"You brought a robe with you. To college?"

Jack nods toward his open closet, and sure enough, there it is. "Don't knock it till you've tried it."

I laugh, but it's kind of forced because my mind is spinning thinking about how fast Jack switched from running scared to inviting me back to his dorm for Netflix and . . . Mountain Dew.

"I made the decision that if I'm going to stop running, I need to be all in. With you. And not in that way, like sex, I mean," he stammers. "I just wanted to be near you tonight. Make it a little romantic. And maybe"—he kisses me—"do some more"—he kisses me again, his tongue wedging between my lips—"of this." He nibbles my bottom lip. "Did you shower since the open mic?"

"Maybe."

He smirks and raises his eyebrows. "You really went all out, huh?"

"Shut up." I shove him away lightly.

"You mind if I change?" he asks. "Open mic clothes smell like the Hole." His brows crinkle. "You know, that's truly a terrible name for a place where people eat. They didn't workshop that one, huh?"

I shrug. "I dunno, sounds delicious to me."

He whips his head. "Oh."

I try not to look, but he subtly adjusts himself. Actually, it's better if I turn away entirely as he changes into basketball shorts and a ribbed tank. I hear the mattress springs boing, and when I turn around, he's flopped on the bed, legs crossed, looking like a snack underwear advertisement. Not so coincidentally, it reminds me of one of my "I'm very, obviously, obscenely gay" moments as a kid. There is nothing like being in the underwear aisle of Target while Mom yelled at me to come and try on a pair of cheap, oversize khakis.

"You look nice," he says.

"Xavier dressed me. Too much?"

Jack bends over and reaches under his bed. He grabs a pair of basketball shorts and tosses them at me. "Seriously, those jeans look restrictive."

He's not wrong, given my ever-growing boner.

"I won't peek," he says, noticing my hesitation.

"I'll be fine," I say.

"Oh, come on."

I sigh. "I'm not wearing underwear."

A hunger brews in his eyes, transforms his face, but he bites it back. "That's kinda hot. Not gonna lie." Then he covers his face and turns away. "I'm not looking. Just change. Be free." His voice is steady, reassuring.

"Okayyyyyyy." I peel off the skintight jeans, fold them nicely, and neatly hang them on the far end of Jack's bed frame. Sliding into Jack's shorts knowing my dick is now pressing into the same place his does instantly gets me even harder. I try to hide it, but it's not working. At. All. I guess I have no choice but to pounce into his bed and keep the leg closest to him bent so he can't see. "How do I look?"

Instead of answering, he reaches over and cups my chin and brings my face closer to his. I will never, ever get tired of feeling his soft lips. The muscles in his arms flex, and I melt into him, pulling him closer. "This shirt is so stiff and scratchy." He sits up and pulls his arm out from between us, and his skin is red. "Damn."

"Also Xavier's. Must be the detergent or something."

Jack shakes his head. "I like *your* style. And I prefer to live hive-free."

"You have a tee I can wear?"

"Just take it off."

My body stiffens at the suggestion, and I can't look at him. "Nah, it's fine."

He shimmies to his knees. "Stand up."

The place between my eyes throbs, but I don't want to make a scene. Jack always exudes such confidence, and I wish I could bottle it and drink it every day of my life.

My body shudders, and I want to crawl out of my own skin.

"Hey," he says softly. "Don't be scared of me." I'm still not looking at him when he grabs my hands. "Can I tell you what I see when I look at you?"

"Oh god."

Swerving right past that, he says, "I see someone whose passion radiates from their fingers"—he plays with each fingertip—"to their toes." He moves closer. "You didn't see me, but I saw you last week in the academic quad. You were sitting with Sofía, drawing something. I couldn't see what, but I stopped dead in my tracks and just watched you."

"Creepy."

"Don't ruin the moment," he says, his thumbs gently stroking mine. "Anyway, I saw how your hands moved, the way the veins in your forearm pulsed as you swept across the page, the way your calves tightened to steady your sketchbook. The way your eyes twitched when you stopped to consider your next move but then would brighten when you knew you already had it all figured out."

I remember that day. I was working on a scene with the Prince and the Knight, whose combined spark created lightning. I couldn't get the lines of the Prince's face down, and it was because I was thinking about Jack. I kept closing my eyes to clear my head, but my chest would pang, and I had to keep sketching in order to focus.

Jack straightens his back and inches forward, and I want to ask him how he knows all that just by looking at me. "I also see someone completely unaware of just how mind-blowingly hot they are."

That makes me snicker.

"Seriously, Chase."

His gaze travels to my chest then to my stomach. The way he looks at my body makes me feel completely naked. He moves our hands to the bottom of my belly.

"Can I?" he asks.

I want him to touch me, but what if I'm not enough? What if he thinks I'm just a misshapen potato not worthy of the peel?

Pushing aside the negative thoughts, I nod quickly.

He lifts the bottom of my shirt, exposing my flesh.

His warm hand grazes my skin, fingertips dancing lightly across the layer of hair that covers my belly, and I tremble, slowly loosening the muscles in my back.

"Can I?" he asks again, motioning to the buttons.

I barely get out a breathless *yes*.

Taking his time, he slowly undoes each one, pausing to look up at me and make sure I'm comfortable. When he gets to the center of my chest, he presses his palm in the space between my pectorals and lets out a measured breath. We maintain eye contact as he finishes the last button, and his hand moves gently to my collarbone. His touch lingers, lightly tracing the bone as the side of his hand pushes the fabric to the cliff of my shoulder.

As the shirt falls to the floor, his eyes travel the length of my body with something more than just hunger in his eyes. I'm breathing heavily as he bites his bottom lip, and his hands travel down to my nipples, then around my midsection, finally wrapping around my back. I brace myself for his inevitable disgust, but it doesn't come.

"You . . . are a work of art." He hums low.

In the moment, I believe him.

He cranes his neck to kiss me soft and quick, but the second our lips mesh, he grabs me and pulls me close. His lips eagerly attack mine.

We fall back onto his bed, and suddenly I'm on top of him, wedging his legs open with my thighs. He pulls me down, chest on hard chest, and his fingers run through strands of my hair.

I'm impossibly hard, and there's no way to conceal it, but so is Jack. I feel him poking into my stomach, and I instinctively buck my hips into him.

He hooks both legs around my back, and his fingers paw at my shorts. I want him to go further, but it's like we both realize at the same time that we're about to enter unexplored territory. We're both breathing heavily. My mouth hovers in the space between his lips and nose, his hot breath making me weak and heightening every one of my senses at once. His strong grip in my hair loosens, and I roll off him, falling back onto his pillow.

My skin is so hot, I think I might pass out.

Jack is just as red-faced as I feel.

We look at each other and burst out laughing.

"Fuck," he gasps. "I really didn't mean for that." He lingers on the word. "But I get lost in you."

"Are you wired? Is there some suave dude feeding you lines somewhere?"

"You had to go and ruin it, huh?" he says, playfully punching my arm.

I glance down, and he's tenting. "Yeah, I really ruined it."

He immediately covers his dick, pressing it down. His body strains as he tries to temper it, but clearly, it's not going anywhere. "I haven't jerked off since the night of the Years & Years show."

"You jerked off that night?" I ask.

I didn't think it was possible for Jack to blush on top of his already reddened sex cheeks, but I'm learning a lot tonight.

"The truth shall set you free," I add.

"I was so charged," he starts. "I really wanted to kiss you, but, you know, I was too scared. And I couldn't stop thinking of you when I got back to my dorm, and Rhett was out practicing in the music school. Dickful thinking."

"That's kinda hot."

He looks at me expectantly.

But I don't give him what he wants. Which drives him crazy.

"What else did I miss when you vanished on me?" I ask, hoping to drive the conversation away from his dick, which looked perfect and delicious through his mesh shorts.

He lets out a pained groan. "Oh, actually, a lot. I joined the crew team."

I sit up. "Wait. We have a crew team? At CIA?"

"Technically CIA has a deal with Laurene where CIA students can join Laurene's crew team, but yeah. I mean, we are on the Finger Lakes."

My eyes travel to Jack's chest, still sheathed in a tank top. His pecs look bigger now, up close, than I remember. *Fuck.*

"I'm intrigued."

He sighs. "*Intrigue* is a great word. Full of mystery and excitement."

"Kind of feels like a detective of a word," I say. "Like, if the word were a person, it'd be a noir detective from a black-and-white film."

"*Noir*," he repeats. "Another one."

"My seminar professor uses that word every. Single. Class," I say. "It's lost all meaning. So tell me about this crew sports thing."

"I have to be up at four a.m. to get the first bus to Laurene," he says. "We practice rowing in a giant tank. I'm dead by the time I get back." He flexes his shoulders.

"Every morning?"

"Five times a week. Got one tomorrow."

"Shit, I can go if you need to sleep," I offer, shifting my weight on the mattress.

"No," he says quickly, gripping my thigh so I don't leave.

I snuggle up next to him, wanting to be closer than physically possible.

"How's your creative writing assignment? The Hero's Journey thing?" I ask.

"Ahhh." His head rolls back and bangs the headboard. "A turning point has been made. I had a conference with my professor, and I think we got to a mutually beneficial place through some artful bartering."

I narrow my eyes at Jack. "Sounds like you made a deal with the devil."

He laughs. "Depends on who the devil is. I realized I was getting stuck on the prose, probably because I was being pulled toward writing in verse."

"Make sense."

Ever so slightly, Jack turns away. "Right? So even though it's a creative writing fiction class, not a poetry class, my professor agreed that I could write my story in verse, assuming I still hit the same word count as everyone else. I'm not ready to give away any spoilers because, well, I have no idea how it ends, but that poem I read earlier tonight is sort of the basis. It's about a kid who journeys his way out of the closet. I know coming out stories are passé—"

"Coming out stories matter," I assure him. "They're so important. If I didn't have stories like *Love, Simon* and *Love, Victor* and *Moonlight*, and all the books I read and shows I watched in middle and high school, I think I might have had a really shitty time. Even though my mom is cool and my sister is everything. I don't know. Coming out is *one* moment in our lives, but it's a pretty big one. And I've been out for a couple years, but it's not as if it gets easier when you go to a new place." I pause, and he nods, deep in thought, concern creasing his brows. "*Easier* might not be the right word, though it does get easier. But there's always this tiny peach pit of nerves in my stomach when I meet new people. How do I know if they're cool or if they're MAGA hat–wearing bigots? Or worse, secret MAGA hat collectors."

He doesn't say anything.

"That's why I was worried I may have scared you off that night when you kissed me and I kissed you back," I say. "Too much, too soon."

Jack exhales. "Not enough, at just the right moment." His words are gentle whispers that waver as he utters them—deep, dark, threatening secrets.

Though Jack hasn't ever really talked about his family, what he has told me implies that they might not accept him. But that poem he recited. I don't want to assume anything, but maybe that's why he came to CIA, to live a life he's always wanted but had been too afraid to pursue. There's a pinch in my stomach that grows into a sharp pang, telling me that maybe I'm part of something he's trying out, a sample in a store he never shops in, and though he might buy it, he'll never actually use it.

At that moment, I become overly aware of how shirtless I am. The constant, phantom voice in my head screams at me to cover up, to keep myself hidden. But I don't want to hide anymore. Not from Jack.

I grab his hand. "I suffer from body dysmorphia. I had an eating disorder in high school. I look in the mirror and see—" I shudder. "Makes it hard to get close, because what if you saw what I see?" Now it's my turn to shrug and look away. "Combine that with trying to figure out how I fit into the nonbinary spectrum, because some days I feel very genderless and fluid and unmoored, and others like a bear of a man, and I don't know." I go quiet for a few minutes. "I don't talk about this stuff with anyone. Even Rae. I've been meaning to see one of the campus therapists, but I'm not sure I'm ready."

"Really?" he asks, and I nod. "I'm glad you feel safe enough with me."

"You're the first person who has ever made me feel whole." I pause. "And like my body is something . . ." I don't know what to say because I don't know how to talk about myself without using words like *ogre* or *blob*.

"Desirable?" he offers. "Sexy?" His hand rests in the center of my chest. His fingers comb through my chest hair gingerly. "Let me show you," he grumbles as he buries his face in the crook of my neck. He turns his body and koala bears my side, resting his top leg over mine and his head where his hand used to be on my chest.

I lay my head back and feel him breathing, his chest rising and falling, and I want to stay like this forever. For the first time, I feel safe enough to just be here, now, with him. I don't hear anything in my head telling me that I'm inadequate because his heartbeat and my heartbeat drown them out.

He starts humming, and I immediately recognize the song as the one we splashed in the puddles to at the Years & Years show. I can't remember the name, but I know the melody. It's the soundtrack to my dreams.

I shift down on the bed to get a little pillow action, which makes Jack stir. He moves, and I feel him hardening against my leg. I push against him, causing him to press his pelvis into me until he's rocking back and forth. He looks up from my chest and into my eyes, and my breath hitches as his fingers walk down my stomach, hovering at my waist, tooling at the elastic band of my shorts.

"Wait," I stammer.

He picks his head up, almost reading my mind, our gazes never breaking.

"I want to make *you* cum," I say.

"Are you sure?" His breathing is shallow, and his whole body shivers as I kiss him to steady his lips.

I pivot so my body faces his, and I reach under the band of his shorts. His hair is coarse and untamed. I hesitate at the base—once I grab it, there's no turning back.

Jack reaches down and quickly shucks his shorts then nestles back beside me. My breath snags as I stare at it, so long and girthy. It dances as his chest rises and falls. It's soft and strong, a strained muscle that throbs in my loose grip. I grab the lotion on his bed-side dresser and warm it up in my other hand before I continue. His body bucks as I bring him closer and closer to the edge. His toes curl, and he presses the back of his head into his pillow before clawing at my chest. As his moaning increases, his lips find their way to mine, and he's kissing me, his tongue lapping at mine, which sends him over the edge, and he explodes on his chest.

Panting, he looks down at me, hooks his finger into the elastic band of the shorts he gave me to wear, and commands, "Take off *my* shorts."

I love the forcefulness of his voice, and I don't hesitate to obey.

He reaches for me and starts, slow at first, appreciating its form the way a sculptor might a marble statue. I let out a moan so loud, he laughs.

He lulls me to ecstasy, staring into my eyes.

On the brink, I hear a faint whisper: "I love you."

14

"So, Chase, what happens next with our short?" Chloe asks as Professor McPherson makes the rounds to each group in class.

"Huh?" My mind is elsewhere. I'm across campus, in Jack's bed, shuddering as he holds me and tells me he loves me.

It's been nearly four days since he uttered those words, and though we've spent nearly every day together since, he hasn't said them again, not once, and I haven't said them back because he caught me off guard. We've fallen into a rhythm of dining hall meals, library study sessions that are actually for studying, and making out when we're alone, which has become extremely difficult because I live with three other guys and, all of a sudden, Rhett never wants to leave Jack's dorm; Jack and I think he's afraid of running into Benny. I get it.

Chloe clears her throat, and I blink to find her borderline enraged.

"Sorry, I'm—"

"In another solar system?" Chloe huffs. "We've noticed. But Sof and I are trying to help you pull this short together, and we love you and are so happy for you and Jack, and I know he's the source of that stupid-ass goofball smile, so don't try to play me. But get your house in order."

I swallow hard. "Sorry."

"Don't say sorry. Just tell me what happens next," Chloe says. "We've spent the past two weeks storyboarding and gearing up to engineer and rig these scenes with the Prince trying to conceal his spark, and now this Witch comes in and tells them they have to cut out pieces of their hearts."

She looks to Sofía, who snaps her gum.

"What's the Witch's motivation?" Sofía finishes. "What's her role in the story?"

"Well," I begin. "She's the one who cursed Thunder and Lightning, obviously."

"Obviously," Chloe repeats in frustration.

"I was thinking the Witch represents all the obstacles that they face," I say. "You know, the idea that the spark they share is amazing and confusing and scary, and when they reunite, it creates a bolt of lightning, something these kingdoms haven't seen since the Witch cursed the titans. It's like they're willing to do whatever they can for things to go back to normal. Because the alternative is the unknown."

"So they just cut out their hearts?" Sofía asks. "Sounds extreme. Even for the gays."

"Well, it's part of their trials. What are they willing to give up?" Truth be told, I haven't thought much past the Witch's ask, but I know from my knowledge of the fairy tale structure that this is their moment of great trial.

"And?" Chloe asks, drumming her nails on the desk.

"I haven't gotten there yet. But I know the Witch plays a larger role. Right?"

"Why?" Chloe's nails clink harder and louder, and Leila clears her throat, a signal for us to be quieter.

"What if," Sofía starts, "you remove the Witch physically from this stretch of the story? She can still loom overhead in the background, but it would let the Prince and the Knight actually explore their shared spark. What happens to the story then? Does it change the ending or make it stronger?"

I haven't gotten that far yet, either. I don't know what becomes of them. Is this a cautionary tale? One of romance and trusting your heart? A moral fable? Do they end up together just as the credits roll? Or are they fated by design to fall apart, to give in to the Witch's manipulation, knowing their kingdoms wouldn't accept them?

"I'd like to challenge you on the inclusion of a witch, in general," Chloe adds trepidatiously and flips through my sketches. "Witches can be extremely powerful feminist symbols, but it does feel as if you're relying a bit on sexist, puritanical stereotypes, at least in your renderings here."

My face heats. She's right. "Damn. I can't believe I didn't realize that."

"Don't beat yourself up," Chloe says. "Instead, ask, 'What can I do about it?'"

I've been thinking about the Witch in a very one-dimensional, Rumpelstiltskin-y villain sort of way—the frustrating pot-stirrer who visually represents evil, but why? Is she actually evil?

I glance up and find myself staring at Leila for longer than I should.

There's always more than what's on the surface.

It's time to let go and redesign my thoughts about her. The Witch, I mean. *Obviously.*

"What if she's a drag queen?" The suggestion tumbles off my tongue.

"Ooooh," Sofía says. "Talk to us about *that.*"

"Thinking about why she sought to destroy Thunder and Lightning . . . maybe it's not because she's jealous of what they have, but rather she longs to be seen and revered the way they are." I think about how I feel when I look in the mirror some days. "The People Below the Skies see her as less than because she exists outside gender norms. It's not exactly where my head was at when I came up with the idea, but it could work."

Chloe and Sofía exchange a knowing, satisfied smile.

"What?"

Chloe hands me her phone, and I immediately recognize what's on her screen: my *Knight* short from high school. "Sof and I were watching this last night. Have you thought about making the Knight in the short we're working on the same character? Sort of a continuation of this video?"

I sit back, considering. The old animation is pretty good, but I've grown so much in the past year that it feels like a lifetime removed.

"They have a point," Professor McPherson says, appearing from nowhere. I hate when teachers do that.

"Think about it," Sofía adds.

"Also of note," Professor McPherson continues. "I see some improvement in the way you draw the human form. But I've been conferring with your figure drawing professor, and we both agree that you need to log some extra hours in that department. Especially with your proportions, the posture, and hands specifically."

"Yeah, fingers have always been my personal kryptonite," I say.

"Be sure to work on that. Add it to your task list. You have incredible potential, Gray, but I need you to push yourself," she says before sashaying to the next group.

My head swells with the ever-expanding list of shit I need to do for this short.

"She's right . . ." Chloe begins, launching into another lecture.

Rapid-fire texts blow up my phone:

JACK: We did this activity in class where we had to turn our twenty-minute prose freewrite into a traditional haiku.
JACK: I had to send it to you. Hang later?
JACK: I wake up alone
　　　phantom fingertips and lips
　　　ghosts of you I keep

He's determined to destroy me.

Sofía snaps her fingers in my face. "Chase, boo, come on."

"Sorry."

Another text from Jack.

JACK: Or this one (which I can't share with the class.
Or . . . can I?)

JACK: six inches, a bomb
      in my hand. licked lips trip
      wires. disarm me.

Yep. Definitely trying to give me a heart attack. Or at least a hard-on in the middle of class. I shove my phone back into my pocket, but my head is super fuzzy and warm.

Chloe is talking, and I'm not listening at all, but I catch the tail end: "So, basically, Sof and I want you to figure out what the point of this twin spark is and where the Prince and Knight's story is going."

"So you think I should have the Prince and the Knight explore each other, uh, I mean, um," I stutter, still flustered from Jack's haiku sext. "Their sparks."

"Keep it PG now," Chloe says with a laugh. "But yes."

"Should I scrap the Witch altogether?" I ask. "Make it just about the Prince and Knight then? Tell me what to do!"

I knew this program would challenge me, but I didn't expect so much pressure right off the bat. The mentorship with Professor McPherson would mean everything for my career. It would make the loans Mom took out for me worth it. I can't disappoint her, or Chloe and Sofía, who also count on me doing well. Or myself. But I've never been good at loving myself.

Chloe shakes her head. "This is *your* story. *You* need to figure that out."

"We're just here to guide you, boo," Sofía adds, leaving me no closer to figuring out where to go next.

At the end of class, Professor McPherson makes an announcement. "Real quick before you all go on your merry ways. This is a reminder that we're nearing the end of September, which means story workshopping should be wrapping up and full renderings underway. Time moves quickly, so if you're not paying attention, it'll slip away. I expect to see fully animated storyboards and fleshed out scenes starting to be colorized by midterms." She leans coolly against her desk in a multicolored paisley frock over 1960s Woodstock patchwork mom jeans. "Also, in mid-October, we have an exciting exhibit by a recent graduate in the college's art gallery. I expect all of you to attend. Bring whomever you'd like."

I immediately think of Jack. He'd love it.

Leila's hand shoots up, and Chloe, Sofía, and I groan at once. "Professor, will this be an extra credit opportunity, perhaps?"

If looks could kill, Professor McPherson's would laser the shit out of Leila. "No."

"I was just wondering because some of us are extremely busy. I, myself, am double-majoring." Leila looks around, expecting a round of applause or some shit. "And—"

"Ms. Casablanca, *this* is important. One day, you could be the freshly graduated CIA student putting their entire heart and soul into an exhibit on this very campus that nurtured your talents, so being engaged and supportive members of the art *and* CIA communities is not just expected. It's good karma. Of course, I can't force your attendance, but . . ."

She leaves it there, dismissing us.

Leila and I are the last to clean up our spaces. She's lingering and stealing quick glances my way. This time she seems different. Hesitant.

I mirror the slow pace of her movements to see what she does next.

She takes a deep breath and whisper-counts to ten, psyching herself up to talk to me. I haven't seen her do that in a long, long time. Leila is always so fearless.

Suddenly I'm struck by a longing for the way things used to be between us back when we used to laugh and cry together, for a Leila-Chase dance party to bad 2000s pop music together. When our friendship was good, it was amazing. But our breakup destroyed me.

A part of me wants to talk first, but I *always* spoke up and apologized first.

"How's the short coming?" My voice shakes. Old habits die hard.

She bites the inside of her cheeks. "It's coming."

Typical Leila answer. She wouldn't tell me if she were struggling, not *really*, not after everything that's happened. The real fears, the stuff that spreads like mold in the dark, she'll keep to herself, locked in a vault I no longer have the code to.

"Chloe and Sofía seem really great," she adds. "I'm not so sure my junior partners get what I'm trying to do."

"What *are* you trying to do?" I wince because I know that sounded bitchy as hell.

Her body stiffens. I steady my voice, put on my Concerned Former Friend hat. "I mean, like, what do you want them to see?"

"You know, the rejection of our capitalistic society and how anyone who dreams they can escape the predetermined plans will always fail and end up a victim of that society," she says, and I half expect her to add something petty and patronizing, but all she says is, "I don't know," and rummages through her overflowing backpack.

I want to ask if this is about her double-majoring, which is practically unheard of for animation majors. I wouldn't be surprised if she is struggling with pursuing art, especially animation, a medium she derided until I gained a modicum of success and notoriety, however small and fleeting. Sure, she's talented. I mean, her portfolio was good enough to be selected for one of the most competitive animation programs in the country. But a few decent ideas and the ability to mimic people who actually love the art form is nothing without drive, passion, or willingness to learn and grow and take risks. Especially as an artist, a career I've been told (by my father) is not guaranteed. Knowing Leila, her parents probably pressured her to declare a dual business major as a backup, and I know firsthand how art imitates life . . .

"Do you ever question what you're doing?" she asks unexpectedly. She's let her guard down, putting away her fake theatricality for a moment.

"All the time," I say, then add, "and not at all. I think it's unrealistic to not question your own choices as you create. But I have to make mistakes in order to figure out how to correct them."

"Yeah, right, total same," she says. "It's a good thing I don't make mistakes." She winks, and just like that, the wall is back up. "I can't wait to share Eggbért and *Unscramblé a Flambé* with the world. It truly will be my magnum opus. I can hear the announcers at the Academy Awards now. 'And the winner is . . .'"

She doesn't have to finish the sentence. I know her well enough to realize she's masking a pain she won't share with me. I want to ask her to drop the act, to talk to me, because deep down, even after everything that happened, I can't erase the fact I cared about her. Maybe a part of me still does.

She gathers the rest of her belongings and breezes straight out of the classroom before I can find out.

15

My interaction with Leila is a ghost that haunts me.

It hovers over every moment with Jack and makes me want to know every part of him, especially the parts he keeps to himself. I think about what my old therapist might say if I told her I felt possessed by memories of a phantom friendship. She'd probably tell me not to project my fears onto Jack, but, yeah, that doesn't work.

I want all of him. And it kills me that he still hides pieces of his life from me. I should probably find a new therapist to help me deal, but obsessing in my head feels easier.

So I have a plan: I'm going to ask him to come home with me for Taylor's birthday in a couple weeks. It's a big step for us, but maybe if I show him more of my life, he'll be prompted to show me more of his.

Now, to find the perfect moment. Obviously, I want like, some big rom-com-level backdrop, and the fear of rejection kind of prevents me from just gritting my teeth at every other perfect opportunity that comes our way.

Since Jack and I have spent most of the cool autumn days wandering aimlessly around campus, watching leaves slowly change from greens to yellows to oranges and reds, this afternoon, like many others, we're seated beneath our favorite maple tree.

A giant red leaf falls into Jack's lap. It's hard and crispy, but his touch is gentle, careful not to let it disintegrate under his touch as he picks it up by its stem. He twirls it between his thumb and pointer finger like a pinwheel. Then he holds it up toward the setting sun. Dark veins thread through its blade; a blood-orange glow outlines the shape. Bringing it down to eye level, he says, "Place your hand against it."

I stretch out my fingers and hold them up to its surface, spreading each one out to match each apex of the leaf.

"You feel that?" he asks.

"What?"

"Keep steady. You'll sense it. The heartbeat." He smirks.

"You playing me, Reid? It's dead—"

Then he places his hand on the opposite side, and though I can't feel his flesh, I feel him, his heartbeat, the skin of the leaf as it pulses between us.

Hand to leaf to hand, he bends forward, does a quick glance around to make sure there aren't any onlookers, and kisses me. "Fall is my favorite season, but not for the reasons everyone else loves it. I mean, sure, the leaves on the trees are beautiful, but it's so much more than that." He gestures in front of us toward the peaks and valleys of the mountains, a rainbow tapestry set against a hazy gray sky, and a setting sun hidden behind a thin gauze of clouds. "Something about shedding the past and going through the harshness of winter appeals to me. It's almost religious."

I shiver, and he cozies up next to me. He's still a touch reticent about PDA, but little by little, he's casting aside his fears.

"Is that something you want? To shed the past?" I ask.

He shrugs.

Maybe this is my moment to dig a little deeper. "If you could, what would you leave behind?"

He turns to me and tilts his head. His eyes, though, stare beyond me, his thoughts clearly dwelling somewhere else. "You know, Callum used to say all the time that he would never leave Vermont or my parents' farm because all he ever needed was right there."

And there it is: Callum. His parents. They're Jack's ghosts. We haven't really gone deep about his family or Callum and coming out to them, because every time I bring it up, he changes the subject. It goes something like this:

Jack: "Callum was just telling me about this ridiculous thing my dad did at work today, and I'm dying, it's so funny. I really miss them."

Me: "I'd love to meet them. Tell me more about Callum."

Jack: "Do you like Skittles? I love Skittles."

He's told me that Callum is the only person who has ever *gotten* him, is an important relationship, yet he says coming out to him would be "complicated."

"What do you think?" I ask. "Can everything you need be in one place, the only real place you've ever known?"

He sucks in a sharp breath.

Fuck. I've pushed too far.

Jack's story revolves around his parents and siblings and Callum, how they're his best friends, yet he writes poems about his family not understanding him and brings them up in reflective moments like these when I challenge him.

Is it possible for both of those things to be true at once? Rae tells me, "That just means he's a writer," and as an artist, I get it. Sort of. I think about my own father and how I've never been able to call him a best friend or a friend at all, but at least he's cool with who I am. It makes me wonder what space I occupy in Jack's mind. Maybe I'm just a way for Jack to help prepare himself for the winter ahead. Am I the skin he'll have to shed, the warmth he'll seek during hibernation, or his spring awakening?

"I don't know," he says.

"Sorry, didn't mean to pry." Guilt rattles in my chest.

"You didn't," he says. "It's just a bit difficult for me to talk about my life back home. It's not that it's bad or anything, it's just . . . hard to describe, and it shouldn't be, but it is."

"You don't have to say anything."

"For now, I want to just keep you here," he adds, and it sort of feels like a deliberate separation of church and state, but I don't challenge him on that. "You're something sacred, like a hymn."

Our hands are still joined, and I make a joke about him writing a hymn about us for his church back home. He lets go of the leaf and digs into his pocket for his phone, making a comment about loving the word *hymn*.

He hasn't shaved in a few days, and it's adorable because his light, patchy facial hair has barely grown in, just enough to feel scratchy when I peck his cheeks.

My temples throb a bit, and this isn't exactly a perfect moment, but I figure now is as good a time as any. Just because he wants to keep me and his family life separate doesn't mean I have to keep him away from mine. Maybe it'll show him he can trust me. "Question."

"Answer," he says, not looking up from his Notes app.

The intensity with which he writes makes me smile, especially the way his eyebrows crinkle and his tongue sticks out slightly as he pulls from his arsenal of words.

"Next weekend is my sister's birthday, and I was wondering if you'd want to come. Home with me. Rae is driving."

He looks up. "As your . . ." He still can't say the word *boyfriend*.

I shrug. "Not if you don't want to be."

"I didn't say that," he says playfully.

"I know it's weird timing because midterms are the week after, and then it's Halloween, and the weekend after that is Parents' Weekend, and if you'd rather chill on campus and go to parties and stuff, that's totally cool. Oh, and this weekend there's an exhibit in the gallery I wanted to check out. Someone who graduated in May from my program. It'll be cool if you want to go with me, but I know I'm asking a lot of you, so . . ."

He kisses me quickly, and I didn't realize I wasn't breathing until his lips touch mine and my whole body relaxes. I inhale, breathing him in.

"I love when you ramble," he says.

"So is that a yes?" I ask.

He shrugs with a smirk. Then his face changes. "Ugh, Parents' Weekend. I forgot about that."

"Your family is coming, right?"

I want him to say, "Yes, and I'd love for you to meet them!" But I know he won't.

"They've had it marked on the calendar since I got my acceptance email," he says. "Just here for one night, though, Saturday into Sunday, so, you know, I'll be busy showing them around and stuff." Subtext: *Not a chance in hell are you meeting them, Chase.* He might as well do the sign of the cross: Father, Son, and Holy gay Ghost.

"Gotcha." I clear my throat. "So, what do you think about coming home with me for my sister's b-day?"

He smiles and holds out his phone.

> you dance on my tongue
> all notes and chants and heavenly praise
> our bodies pressed together
> in prayer
> i see capital g god
> when i sit at your altar
> and take in the body
> of christ
> father son and holy ghost
> screaming names in vain
> and asking for-giveness
> of my sins
> to stay on your lips
> like a hymn

At the bottom of the screen:
I'd go anywhere with you 🙏

16

"Ladies, are we decent?" Benny's voice echoes through our door.

Definitely not. My dick is totally in Jack's hand when Benny follows up with a knock on our door. Jack shoots up off my bed in a panic, like he got caught watching gay porn by his mom right before church.

"They're so not decent. Door's been shut for two hours," Aaron shouts from the couch.

"Spicy," Benny says as Jack lets him into the room. "Hi, sweetheart, you look flush."

"Benny, always a pleasure." Jack keeps his head down so nobody sees his face. As it turns out, he is a tad prudish when he's not horny. "Chase, dinner at the Garden Dining Hall tonight?"

I stand and move toward him. Aaron and his gym bro João are playing PS5, legs strewn haphazardly over the arms of the couch, remote controls in hand. It's clear they do not give a shit about what's going on in my doorway.

I grab a fistful of Jack's shirt, pull him back inside, and kiss him softly, sweetly. "Stay. It's okay. Everyone knows about us."

"Yeah, but I gotta go write," he says, trying his best to smooth out his voice. He kisses the tip of my nose, nods to Benny, and slips out.

"That boy," Benny says, tossing his bag on the floor and flopping onto his bed, "will be the death of you."

I don't answer because I'm distracted by the very loud, headboard-banging sex sounds emanating through the wall from Xavier's room.

"Wait. Are you not in there?" I point to the source of the screams.

"If I am, I'm really talented at throwing my voice," he says.

"I'm confused." I shut our door. "Is X cheating on you?"

Benny sits up and pouts. "Babe, *ohmygod*, you're so cute! No! We're not *together*. I figured you knew that."

"When did that happen?"

"Always? We were never together. We're friends with bennys. Get it?" He winks.

"How does that even work? Like, how do you not catch feelings?" I ask.

He purses his lips. "Well, I mean, feelings are weird." He props his body against the wall and kicks his feet over the ledge of the bed. "Let's put it this way: If X were to propose marriage tomorrow, I would *probably* say yes because, *hello*, have you *seen* him? But yeah, no, we're just having fun. We're both on the same page with that."

"You're still into Rhett, aren't you?"

"The heart wants what it wants. And in my case, it desperately craves a toxic, masc-for-masc straight-bro who denies me in public, and now also in private," Benny says. "At least you and Jack are on the same page."

"Are we?"

Benny's brows arch, and he barks like Scooby-Doo. "Ruh-roh. Trouble in paradise? Already?"

I shake my head. "I mean, he's come a long way, and superfast from running away to kissing me in the quad. Granted, he always does a three-sixty to make sure nobody can see before he does, but I get that. It's like he's grappling with us and wanting us while trying to battle the internal shit gifted to him by his family and supersecretive best friend, which he never talks about. It's a lot. And I get it."

"A tale as old as time," Benny quips.

"Beyond that, we still haven't done anything more than handies."

Benny's face drops. "Blowies?"

"Nope. Not even close."

"Shower? A suds-and-tug?"

"We've never been, like, fully"—I smoosh my hands together—"yet."

He hums, clearly surprised. Then his face gets all serious, a look I've never seen on him before. "Sex isn't everything."

"You okay?"

Shrugging, he says, "Last week I was feeling, I don't know, kinda sad about Rhett and how I'm cursed to live inside my own head. I came back here and saw you and Jack asleep in your bed." Benny's eyes got a little wet. "I wish you could've seen the peace on Jack's face as he held you. It was gross." He smiles. "I still retch."

His smile twitches and fades. "I wish I had that: a boy who looks at me the way Jack looks at you. I'd trade all the dick in the world for that." He hops off the bed, walks to my desk, and picks up the frame Jack gave me for my birthday. "This binch writes you poetry and whispers rogue 'I love yous' as he makes you cum with those strong hands. You're living a gay fairy tale. Who cares if he has demons? We all do. We're gay."

Benny's right.

"I know I'm right when you go all quiet like that," he reads me like a book.

Damn. Two months ago, I never thought I'd meet a guy like Jack, a veritable Prince Charming. Even though it's not perfect, it's the only thing I want.

Because I love him.

Which begs the question: Do I tell him?

"You love him, don't you?" Benny asks, his voice a quiet echo.

"Stop reading me!" I toss my pillow at him.

He clutches it. "This smells like your man, you dirty slut."

My face heats.

"Ohmygod, you really have it bad, don't you? Okay . . ." He rolls his eyes and pulls something out from a drawer. "I got this at the school's clinic a few days after X and I found you googling 'how to have sex.'"

In a grand flourish, he reveals a series of pamphlets that say:

So You Want to Bottom?: Tips to Receiving Anal Sex Safely

How to Be a Thoughtful, Safe Top.

But the one that catches my eye is:

When You're Ready to Have Sex.

"You go to the clinic?" I ask.

"Girl." Benny's glare pierces me. "X and I go all the time. I got tested for STDs before I came here, post-Rhett, and I hadn't hooked up with anyone until X. But he still insisted we get tested before we fucked. Now that we're hooking up with other people, we go together, like, every other week."

"Wait, who are you hooking up with?"

"You are nosy," Benny says, patting my head like I'm a puppy. "One day, little grasshopper, one day."

I flip through the pamphlet about bottoming, but it's so sterile.

"Do you think Jack and I should get tested? I'm a virgin. Jack is the only person I've ever . . . done anything with."

"Peace of mind is not just the headline of a very poignant article from *O Magazine* that I read when I'm about to spiral," Benny says. "You haven't been with anyone, but what about Jack?"

"I have no idea. We haven't talked about stuff like that. His past. I know he hasn't even kissed a guy before, but girls?"

Benny purses his lips and stares impatiently, waiting for me to come to the conclusion he's already made.

"This feels awkward," I admit.

"Sweetie, if you can't talk to me about sex after you saw me fully splayed out like a Thanksgiving turkey getting stuffed, how are *you* going to *have* it?"

"No," I say quickly. "Not that. Thanks for that image, by the way. I thought I'd scrubbed it from my brain, but nope."

"You're welcome!" he cheeses.

"I mean, like, bringing all this up to Jack."

"Wait, so you fondle each other but don't talk about it?"

"When you put it like *that*, it sounds, you know, bad," I say. "Okay, this stays between us, but the other day, we were hanging out in his dorm, and when he went to the bathroom, I might've done a little snooping—"

Benny grabs at his chest. "Ugh, I'm so proud."

Ignoring him, I continue, "And I found a box of brand-new condoms, lube, and a fancy anal douching kit in a toiletry bag right in the top drawer of his desk. It was just, like, *right there*."

"What size were the condoms?" Benny asks, eyes wide.

"You're a pig."

"Oink, binch."

I'm still thumbing through the pamphlet about bottoming when he puts on "7 Rings" by Ariana Grande and starts voguing across the room.

"What's going on?" I ask.

"This is the part in the movie of our lives where a certifiable queen like Ariana triggers a montage wherein I learn you some things about bottoming and topping." He grabs my hands and pulls me to my feet.

"I really want to know what being inside your head feels like," I say.

"No you don't. Now shut up and give in to the montage."

For the next two hours, Benny gives me the whole extensive rundown that includes safe douching, which foods to eat and which to stay away from, maintaining proper hydration, PrEP and different lubes, poppers, and dildos, breathing techniques, and explicit descriptions of rimming and fingering. He sing-talks about how and says it's important to "*see it, like it, want it,* and *get it*, but also prep for it."

I walk out when he gets on his bed and mimics various positions.

★ ★ ★ ★

Images of Benny dance in my head as I meet Jack at the dining hall and load my plate with high-fiber foods.

Jack is staring at my tray with a funny look in his eye. "Your dinner looks bland as hell, babe."

Do I tell him, "I want to bottom for you. I'm starting to prepare mentally because this feels like a monumental undertaking, no pun intended, but I'm ready for the dick"?

Probably not.

But I have to start somewhere. "I'm trying something new."

He grabs my hand once we're seated away from people. "Are you sure this isn't, like, something I should be worried about?" Concern reflects in his irises, and I realize he's worried about my eating disorder.

"No, this isn't about that." I chuckle. Nerves shake my hands. "Can I ask you something kinda weird?"

"What's up?" He leans back and folds his arms, something he does when he's intent on listening.

"I don't know where you're at, but we've been together for a few weeks, and obviously no pressure at all because you make me so happy and . . . I wanted to let you know that when you're ready to, uh, you know, take things to the next step, that I'm ready. To talk about it, I mean," I add quickly. I hold back the three words that always dangle at the tip of my tongue when we're together.

"You're shaking." His voice is so calm and steady, and his thumb strokes the fleshy part between my thumb and pointer finger. "I've been thinking about it, too. I didn't know how to bring it up. Didn't want to seem pushy. Whenever we decided to go for it, I wanted it to be perfect." Jack looks down. "Should we get tested? I've only ever been with one girl. And not even full-on sex. Just fingers—"

"I don't need to know," I say quickly, imploring him to stop.

He smirks.

"You're the only person I've ever . . . even . . . kissed, let alone, you know," I say. "But yes, let's get tested. Tomorrow?"

His eyes crinkle like he wants to say something, but he doesn't. There's so much in those beautiful blues that I don't know but want to—stories and dreams and night terrors that paralyze him. There's a depth to his constellations that stretch light-years, and I get the sense that I may never know all the bits and pieces that make up Jack Reid. It's like he's in a constant battle with himself, between what he says and does and what he holds close. I watch him tear into a plate of French toast sticks and wonder which part of him will win out.

All I know is that the rest of it doesn't matter because *I love him, I love him, I love him.*

17

I'm waiting outside the CIA Art Gallery for Jack. He hasn't really spoken to me since we went to the school clinic earlier today, which was relatively painless. The STD and HIV rapid tests were the easy part. The questions they asked about sexual activity were the hard part because, holy shit, it's so embarrassing to tell a relative stranger that you've only jerked off your boyfriend and haven't done anything more. When everything came back negative, and the doctor gave me the "safe sex" tutorial, I sat down outside to wait for Jack. At that point, I was missing my last class of the day, but at least I got to ask the nurse about on-campus therapist recommendations.

The minutes ticked by, and still, I waited. And waited. And waited.

By the time the sun started to set, and the nurse asked me why I was still there, I realized Jack had booked it out of the clinic before I was done. Without so much as a text.

And now, I'm waiting for him again. I have no idea if he's even going to show up for the exhibit.

My leg shakes, so I pace. When pacing doesn't help, I text Rae.

ME: He's still not here.

RAE: I'll kill him.

RAE: But seriously, wtf?

RAE: If you want, I'll get in my car and be right over. I'm a very hot +1

RAE: Actually, question about next weekend. What exactly is going down for Tay's bday? My mom is asking if I'm going to be staying with you or going home, and the Jewish guilt is REAL.

ME: My parents rented three hotel rooms in that fancy new indoor waterpark place. One for my mom, one for Tay and her friends, and one for us, if you wanna stay. I assumed you would, but you don't need to.

RAE: . . . because Jack will be there 😘

ME: We'll see. He's still not here. Did I say that already?

RAE: Would you kill me if I spent the night at home? I'll come back in the am for breakfast.

ME: Yea ofc np. Who can resist a continental breakfast?

RAE: You know me so well. What time do we need to leave next weekend?

ME: As early as you can wake up?

RAE: You're asking a lot of me now Chase Arthur. But I know how important seeing Tay is to you, so I'll let you live. How's 8am?

RAE: BTW I just involuntarily projectile vomited thinking about waking that early.

RAE: THE HORROR!

RAE: You owe me

ME: You love me.

RAE: Ugh I hate when you're right.

ME: OMG HE'S HERE.

RAE: 🙌🙌🙌🙌

Jack saunters up in fitted light acid-washed jeans and a tucked-in white button-down shirt embroidered with tiny red roses. He even gelled his sun-kissed blond hair, so it's kind of messy and flips up in the front. His gray boat shoes really do me in, though.

"Wow," I say. "I didn't think you'd come, let alone looking like . . ." I swallow. "A damn snack!"

"Jack the Snack." He licks his lips and does this thing where his head dips and his arm reaches behind his neck. He massages it sensually until he slowly looks up at me, all hazy bedroom eyes and soft lips and pink cheeks. "You look cute, too," he says, reaching for my black-and-white geometric poncho with fervor.

I can tell he wants to kiss me, but he won't—not so out in the open.

"Sorry I bolted earlier. My head was kinda fuzzy. Being in the clinic was a lot for some reason." With his other hand, he pulls out his phone and shows me his test results. "Negative, across the board."

I do the same. "Me too." I want to be openly mad at him for ditching me, but this thing between us feels so delicate that even though I'm holding it in my hand, there's a chance it could break with just a little bit of added pressure.

"I'm okay now. I just needed a breather," he says. "You ready to go in?"

The waiting area of the exhibit is pitch-black, save for a string of dotted lights along the perimeter of the room and a bowl of neon fluorescent bracelets.

"Welcome to 'Mirror.'" An attendant in a white mask immediately emerges next to us and asks us to take two bracelets, one for each wrist. "You're the first visitors, so you have the space to yourselves. Follow the white lights on the floor," he starts. "They'll take you around the exhibit. It's interactive, so the artist encourages you to touch if you'd like. It was designed with the objective that you become the focal point of each section. You are both spectator and subject of the gaze. How you interact with the space is meant to be a mirror to how you interact with the world outside. Do you engage, move within it, shy away from it, observe from the outside, all the above? Will you regret it if you just sit back and do nothing, or are you content to watch? These are questions the artist wishes you to consider. Are you ready to travel through the looking glass?"

Jack's fingers intertwine in mine, and he bounces on the balls of his toes. "This is beyond cool. I'm so ready."

Double doors swing open slowly, and we exchange quick glances. Jack's blue eyes guide us forward, beacons in the dark.

The first room's perimeter is lined with what looks like one long flower box along three of the four walls, separated into three distinct sections. The first is cascading valleys of thick, clay-like sand illuminated by blue overhead spotlights. There's a sign that says, Touch Me, and Jack rolls up his sleeves and dives in. The moment his fingers make contact, the sands change color to a deep red, the light rippling out beneath his touch like water. I watch him recoil at first then smile as he gets to work molding a makeshift sandcastle.

When he's done, he steps back, and the light effects color it with various shades of green as if it were topography on a map.

I pull him toward the section of the box filled with aqua-blue slime. I poke at it, and the lights projecting from above make cartoon bubbles.

Jack stops to smell actual rows of flowers in another part of the box, and he gasps. "Chase, holy shit, come here! Start at the beginning, and when the petals change color, sniff. My brain is melting!"

I do as he says, and the first line of flowers, stalks of lavender, smell like, well, lavender, but the second row of pink chrysanthemums give off a burst of cotton candy. As I move to the sunburst-yellow sunflowers, I smell rich, buttery popcorn. White roses smell like piña coladas and sunscreen at the beach. At the end of the row, a series of bouquets with sapphire-blue and bright-orange orchids carry the scent of freshly baked brownies. It's safe to say we're both disoriented.

"What do you think the point of that was?" he asks. "Because I'm questioning literally everything ever."

"I don't know." I resist the urge to race back and do it all over again. "I think that's the point. Our brains are wired to expect certain things—flowers to smell like flowers. But when they don't . . ."

"It triggers an existential crisis," Jack finishes, and I nod.

The next room has us stepping into a series of famous paintings, like Mary Poppins into Bert's sidewalk chalk drawings. The usually stark-white walls are now moving projections of re-rendered landscapes and images that I've been studying for years. We immediately step into *The Birth of Venus* by Sandro Botticelli and onto the seashell Venus is standing on, so we become the Venus as pink flowers whirl around us and waves ripple behind us. Jack grabs hold of me as if he's going to fall overboard.

He wobbles as we move into the next live painting, *The Persistence of Memory* by Salvador Dalí, where clocks melt over barren tree limbs, falling limp over a stalk landscape as Madonna's "Hung Up" plays in the background.

"Shit, this place is playing with me." His grip tightens.

"I feel high," I say.

"Is the name of this exhibit 'Give Jack a Panic Attack'?"

"Yes, yes it is," I say, kissing the soft spot of his cheek, just above the line of stubble. "Did I not tell you?"

"What's next? Dante's *Inferno*?"

I smirk because, god, I love him so much. "Only one way to know." I lead the way, pulling him by the hand around the corner.

But I stop short.

My breath catches.

We're inside Vincent van Gogh's *Starry Night*, swirls of heavy brushstrokes moving like clouds across the dark sky, illuminated by pricks of yellow starlight that ripple out. Lush green hills move with the same fluidity, and as we stare at the walls around us, the paint begins to dissolve into an actual scene of hills beneath a starry sky, clearly taken with a high-res camera lens because I forget that we're inside.

We are the hills and the city. We're the stars. We're the spectators and the subjects.

I'm mesmerized.

"Wow." Jack's breathing becomes shallow, too. "This reminds me of that night."

I know what he's talking about, but I pretend I don't. "Which one?"

He doesn't seem to catch on. "The night I realized I lo—liked you."

Okay, now I'm really not breathing. "You like me?" *Or do you love me?*

Say it.

He moves to face me and places his hands around my waist. His nose grazes mine.

We hear people shuffling behind us, so we move to the final room of the exhibit, which is accessible by a crawl-through hole in the wall. The floor of the gallery has been transformed by synthetic grass, and there are giant beanbag chairs around the perimeter. We're still on our knees when I look up and see vines of icicle lights hanging from the ceiling, and in the center of the room is a giant plasma globe with pink and purple electricity emanating from its nucleus.

"I think we're meant to sit and look up," I whisper.

Jack flips over and lies flat on his back, hands behind his head as if we're outside on the grass under the stars.

Suddenly speakers play the sound of rain, and a machine puffs out air that smells of freshly cut grass and wet earth. The plasma globe zaps high-voltage charges toward the surface of the globe, and it looks like lightning.

Jack reaches to touch it, concentrating all the electric discharge to his fingers as if he's holding lightning.

I turn to him, eyes closed, and whisper, "Everyone always says it is lucky to be struck by lightning. Nobody ever tells you how to live once you've been struck. All I know is that it is impossible to harness."

His hand slowly drifts down to his side, and he turns to face me. "My poem. You—"

"Memorized it, yeah." My voice is shaking.

"Why?"

"Because you wrote it."

"Damn it, Chase." He reaches around me and pulls me close.

"You inspire me," I breathe into his chest, against the fabric of his shirt. "Come with me. I want to show you something."

I pull him to his feet and don't tell him where we're going until we get to the visual arts building.

It's late, so the building is empty; all the classrooms are dark. They keep the studios accessible for students who want to work well into the night.

"Hey, isn't that your not-friend?" Jack points into one of the only lit rooms, and I spot Leila in a dirty smock, hair tied up into a messy bun as sweat drips off her brow. Her arms and hands are caked in a layer of gray clay as she molds something shapeless that, once it's done, I'm certain will be breathtaking.

I yank Jack out of view, not wanting to stop and make small talk. I'm on a mission.

"Where are we going?" he asks.

"Patience," I say, rounding a corner to a windowless studio for solitary work, sort of like those soundless Do Not Disturb rooms on the fifth floor of the library where students work and never know what time of day it is. It houses our portfolios, the big stuff we don't want to cart around campus.

I punch in the security code they gave us on the first week of school. Once he's in, I close the door behind him.

"Being in that exhibit was beyond, and I realized a couple things. First, you've been writing me poems, and I haven't shown you any of my art."

He nods slowly. "I figured you'd show me when you're ready. I know how it is, showing your stuff."

"Trust," I say, repeating what he told me the day we met. "You know I've been working on this short with Chloe and Sofía since the start of the semester. It's still a work in progress."

"Can I wait until it's done to see it?" he asks sincerely. Then, he adds for good measure, "I want to see your complete vision, if that's okay."

And I get it; it's harder to get a sense for something when it's piecemeal.

"Yeah, of course, but that's not why we're here."

His brow arcs in confusion.

"You know that feeling when you're inspired by something, and it consumes you? And so all other parts of your brain shut down except for that one part that says, 'You have to draw or write or whatever'? And there's like this nervous twitch until you can sit down and tune everything out and the world falls away for hours and hours?"

He holds up his phone. "That's the only reason I carry this hellish thing with me. It fits better than a notebook in the pocket." He slaps his thigh.

"I knew you'd get it." I sigh in relief. "That's what that exhibit did. And you. Seeing you, touching that globe, and I thought maybe you could help me."

"Help you? You don't want to see me draw. Stick figures are an understatement."

I laugh. "No, I mean, okay, don't freak out, but . . ." I pull out my portfolio, which is housed in a designated cubby against the wall. "The main character in my short is kinda based on you, and I was kinda hoping I could sketch your face? More of a . . . life drawing instead of my usual overly exaggerated Disney style. If that's cool with you?" I add quickly.

"I'm your inspiration?" He blushes. "Really?"

"Does that surprise you?"

He shrugs and chews the inside of his cheek. "Where do you want me?"

I point to a chair facing me but slightly angled away. "Just sit there and try not to move so that I can capture you."

The clean, crisp smell of untouched paper, edge to edge with endless possibility, pulls at me. Every nerve ending in my body is alive, pulsating, brimming with kinetic energy as the tip of my pencil grazes the surface of the page. Romantic sweeps around the top of his head marry the hard, sharp lines of his jawline. I don't really need him here because I see his face every time I close my eyes, but having him right in front of me, blue eyes all longing and brooding, forehead full of frown lines, I see him more clearly. The freckle beneath his right eye, the one I kiss when we're lounging lazily in bed, his small ears and ball of his nose, the way the muscles of his face tense when he's lost in thought and relax when he feels like he can let his guard down.

When we're in public, I feel like he never breathes, but here, now, alone without anyone to happen upon us, he seems at ease. Peaceful.

A lone tear drops onto the page, and I wipe it away, but my hands are coated in pencil dust, and it smears across the paper, giving Jack's portrait a darkness I didn't intend. Yet it works. I draw bolts of lightning spreading out from his irises.

When I'm done, I twirl the pad around and show him, keeping my arm outstretched across the table.

"You did this?"

"Something quick, nothing crazy," I say.

"He looks so confident. Strong. This is what I look like?" his voice is soft.

"To me," I say. "That's how I see you."

His fingers move toward mine, resting atop them. "I like the way you see me." He licks his lips and wipes his wet eyes. When he clears his throat, which is kinds of mucusy, he says, "I'd love to see more of your drawings."

I give him permission to flip through my sketchbook, and this time, I look away.

"I didn't realize my boyfriend was so talented; it's sexy."

I make the mistake of sneaking a peek at the page he's on, and it's one from my figure drawing class of a middle-aged woman who modeled for us a few weeks back.

"Eh, I'm not the best at life drawings. My professor says I need to work on limbs and proportions."

"Are you kidding?" he gasps. "These are perfect. They look so real. The lines in the musculature, the way her back curves to show her posture, the creases in the skinfolds. Chase, your professor is batshit!"

"She expects perfection, which I'm happy she does because I

want to be her." I grab the pad and try to see it through Jack's eyes, and I guess he has a point. Maybe. "It sucks because I feel like I never have time to really focus on life drawing. It's hard enough for the art department to find models willing to be naked in front of a room full of artists."

He immediately stands. "Why didn't you ask?"

I swallow hard. "Huh?"

Unbuttoning his shirt, he reveals his chest.

"Are you sure?"

"Shut up and draw me." He unzips his jeans and, with one quick motion, shoves both jeans and boxer briefs down to his ankles.

Immediately, I snap into student mode, and Jack is just another model.

Jack is just another model.

Jack is just another model.

I take to readying my station as Jack strips completely naked and moves the chair to the center of the room. My hands shake as I place my supplies neatly around my sketch pad.

"How do you want me?"

What a loaded question!

"Uh." I look up, and there he is, completely naked, waiting for direction. I exhale. "You know Michelangelo's *David*? The contrapposto pose?" I demonstrate it for him, shifting all my weight to one foot and twisting my upper body slightly in a relaxed manner. "Face me, and—"

"Like this?" he asks, and I try not to stare at him.

"Perfect. Just hold that for the next hour or so."

"What the . . . ?"

I snicker. "You offered."

"You're lucky I lo . . ." He hesitates and rewinds, again. *"Like your art."*

I crack my knuckles systematically before leaning into the page. I feel the weight of my arm against the desk, the arch of my back, my feet on the ground. Professor McPherson says it's crucial to feel your own muscles and bones; the way you're positioned determines your openness to the work. Right now, I feel loose but steady. Firm but aware of where I am and the vulnerability of the model in front of me. Suddenly, he's not Jack anymore but a fellow artist, a subject to learn from, to respect, and treat with the utmost care. My chest stops fluttering, and I get to work.

Dark lines spread across the page, taking the shape of his body. I glance up every so often, my eyes taking snapshots of his form to transpose over the page. My eyeline traces the muscles of his thighs down to his calves. Using a tortillon, I shade in the dimples where skin ripples over his abdomen and chest. Something about knowing in the back of my mind that it's Jack and not just another model makes me want to get this right. For it to be as lifelike as possible, I study his posture, the curve of his back, the plump definition of his chest which has gotten slightly bigger from rowing, the weight of his arms at his side, the way his fingers are loose but carry with them the secrets of the universe. With those fingers, he's written epic poems that make me want to cry. His body tells me stories about his life—the summers spent white water rafting in the rapids behind his house in Vermont, the winters spent skiing.

Since he kissed me, I noticed a small twitch in the curve of his lips that only ebbs when I kiss him back. He's doing that now, and the more I take in bits and pieces of him, the more his mind drifts away from me. Until he catches me staring, and he smiles that crinkly smile that made me fall in love with him.

My pencil sculpts my own version of *David*, Jack's smile a focal point.

Because Jack deserves to smile all the time.

When I'm done, I sit back and can't help but be in awe of my work. But it's not me—it's Jack. "What do you think?"

Relaxing his body and shifting his weight to his other leg, he stretches out before walking over. He doesn't bother to cover his body. I swivel in my chair to meet him as he walks around the table to stand directly in front of me. My eyeline is on the part of Jack I've only ever had my hands around.

"You caught me smiling," he says, trembling.

"I love it when you smile."

Jack gazes down at me, and all the moody brooding and crinkly smiles are replaced with a hungry determination. His fingers graze the underside of my chin as he wedges his bare legs in between mine. He's breathing heavily, his chest and stomach rising and falling into rhythm with mine, neither of us looking at my sketch.

He's already incredibly hard, and when I reach for him, he pulls back and smirks. "Not yet." He's on his knees and unbuttoning my jeans, then he's tugging at them with a ferociousness I've not seen yet from him. Once I help him shimmy them down my ankles, Jack gets to his feet and straddles me, settling on top of me with his sturdy thighs. His arms brace themselves against the back of my chair, and he grinds against me as he leans in for a kiss so wet and forceful, it sends shock waves through my body, like if he pulls away, I'll stop breathing entirely.

When he does pull away, my head dips into his shoulders by his armpits, which smell of his cologne. I kiss and nuzzle the soft fleshy spot between his pecs, and he pulls me to his body with one hand as the other snakes underneath to the strain in my briefs. I run my hands through his spiky blond hair, grabbing a handful of it, making him grunt.

His upper lip curls into something more than a smile. He's in full control, a titan or a god with the power to destroy and reshape me. Dismounting, he lifts my shirt up over my hair and tosses it to the ground, and then his lips are on my neck and then my chest, following the trail of dark hair down to my stomach, where his soft lips linger, kissing in a circle around my belly button.

Then he looks up at me expectantly.

Maintaining eye contact, his fingers hook around the elastic of my briefs, and he pulls the fabric down slowly until I spring up.

He takes a deep breath and grabs the base, and I close my eyes as his tongue gently closes the gap between us. Then his mouth encircles me, and he goes down, but it's a mess of scraping teeth and hoovering.

"Babe, slow down, don't suck, watch your tee—*ow*!" I remember everything Benny told me. I relay Benny's instructions, and Jack's a fast learner because—"Holy fuck . . . yes!"

I brace myself on the chair as my hips buck beneath him.

My breathing increases rapidly as my body tenses. My legs straighten, and he grabs hold of them, now comfortable with only his lips and a glint of determination in his eyes.

In one quick motion, he ventures down to the base, and my toes curl. He gags and starts laughing, mouth still full, cheeks beet red as sweat beads his brow. I don't want to cum quick, but all I can focus on is Jack, the most beautiful man I've ever seen.

One of his slick hands travels farther down, and he applies a light pressure as his lips do something new that makes me feel like putty in his hands.

I grab the arm of the chair. "Babe, I'm gonna—I'm gonna—"

But Jack doesn't pull up, and his resolve gets stronger. He works his neck, which sends me over the edge. I let out a loud moan I hope doesn't echo into the empty halls.

He licks his full lips, which look plump and red, and kisses me hungrily as he straddles me again. We press into each other, and I taste myself on his lips.

"My turn," I whisper, pushing him off me and onto the desk, legs splayed out before me like some sort of religious painting, all hard brushstrokes and bursting colors and golden rays of heaven, the artist's hand heavy on the canvas.

Grabbing hold of him, feeling every hard inch of him between my lips, I am both spectator and subject, artist and patron, worshipping at the altar of the divine.

18

With duffel bags slung across our shoulders, Jack and I wait as Rae cautiously pulls up to my dorm to pick us up for Taylor's thirteenth birthday road trip home. I had a momentary freak-out earlier because as I packed it hit me that her birthday is at a water park. Squeezing into a bathing suit—*in public!*—just to stand alongside my perfect Captain America boyfriend in front of a bunch of judgmental middle school girls is basically asking for a body dysmorphic episode of epic proportions. Benny calmed me down before Jack arrived, but I can't get it out of my head. No matter how much Jack loves my body, I can't stop comparing mine to his and feeling . . . inadequate. And I just know Dad will do the same. I don't tell Jack any of this. I just swallow it down.

"Is she for real?" Jack whispers, jolting me alert. He takes his Red Sox cap off and puts it back on again, pressing down on its visor.

I love Rae deeply, but she drives in slow motion, so leisurely that I can feel the gravity around me and the planet rotating on its axis. It'll probably take us ten hours to get to the hotel/water park combo when it should only take us three and a half, four hours, max.

The window slides down as she slams on the brakes next to us. "Get in, loser, we're going shopping!"

Jack eyes me, clearly having no point of reference for *Mean Girls*, which somehow makes him irresistibly cuter and infuriating because how!?

I move to hop in the front seat, but Rae throws herself across the armrest.

"Uh-uh. Get in the back," she says. "Jack, get up here."

"Rude," I say.

Jack dips his head beneath the doorframe. "You sure?"

"Yes!" she exclaims. "One, because I want to get to know you better, and two, because Chase is a notorious car napper."

"Weak," Jack says with a smirk.

"Again, rude," I say.

"Twenty bucks says you'll be asleep before we hit the highway," Rae says. "Now shut up and get in the back." She blows me a million air kisses as I climb in behind them.

"Joke's on you because I can stretch out now." I prop my legs up across the seat.

"Jack, prepare to blast off into the wonderful world of Rae and Chase with my carefully curated playlist of all our favorite sing-along songs," Rae says, hitting play on an epic mix of Disney songs, which causes Jack to bury his face in his palms.

He resists the urge to sing, eyeing both of us with indignity as it cycles through *Moana* to *Aladdin* to *Beauty and the Beast*, but then "I'll Make a Man Out of You" from *Mulan* comes on, and all of a sudden, Jack busts out his best Broadway persona, his voice booming as he matches the lyrics word for word.

"Okay, he passes the test," Rae says, turning onto the highway. "We can keep him."

"By the way, you owe me twenty bucks," I say with a yawn.

Five minutes later, I'm out cold.

I dream in charcoal sketches of Jack in the rain, his face shadowed by heavy lines of black lightning as it veins across a dirty white page. He doesn't flinch as it strikes the ground around him. I hear his voice in the background. I hear Rae's voice, too, but they're far away and laughing like they're old friends, and it blends with the sounds of obscure Disney songs and tires whizzing over concrete highways.

The car jerks to a stop, and I nearly fall off the seat.

"We're here, Sleeping Beauty," Rae says, smacking my leg.

"He really is a beaut when he sleeps, huh?" Jack says. "Drool and all."

"Oh my god, you are the worst." Rae slaps him, and they burst into laughter.

I wipe the dribble down the side of my mouth. "The hell has gotten into you two?"

"Inside joke," Rae says. "You missed a lot, and now we've bonded and are best friends. Sorry. You've been replaced."

They do this weird secret handshake where they slap each other's palms like some nerd version of Miss Mary Mack.

"Did I fall through a wormhole in my dreams?" My head is still fuzzy as I text Taylor to tell her we're at the hotel.

"Oooh, that's good," Jack says. "I need to write that down."

"I do not give you permission to steal my intellectual property, traitor," I say.

"Calm your tits," Rae says. "It's not his fault I like him better."

Wedging myself back up onto the seat, I pout and do my best big-eyed Puss in Boots impression, which never fails to guilt Rae.

"You are pure evil," she says.

"But so cute." Jack pecks my lips quickly.

"Okay, I'm going to vomit. This cuteness will not stand in my car," Rae says.

"She wants a kiss, too." I pucker my lips, and she kisses me then turns to Jack, who shrugs and kisses her, too.

"Do anything for you?" she asks.

"Meh." Jack smirks.

"You have a boyfriend!" I snap.

Rae sucks her teeth. "Meh." She kicks open her car door before I can ask a follow-up.

As I make a mental note to pull her aside later, Taylor emerges from the hotel's entrance and books it toward the car, flinging her arms around Rae. How is it possible that in two months, my sister's shot up a few inches? Her hair is longer, and Mom must've let her dye it because it's a brilliant shade of strawberry pink with white-blond highlights. She's not even wearing her glasses anymore.

The second I get out, Taylor screams, eyes wet, and hugs me so tight, I have trouble breathing.

"Are you crying?" I ask.

Taylor holds me tighter. "Shut up, am not. *You* are!"

"Solid burn," I retort.

Then she whispers, "Is that really Jack?"

"Yep." I pull away, and my brows dance. "I know, right?"

"He's too hot for you," she says, loud enough for Jack to hear.

"Ouch."

Jack holds out his hand, but Taylor pulls him into a hug.

"Come on, I have to show you off to Mom and Dad before all my friends get here," she says, pulling Jack by the hand toward the hotel.

I exhale hard.

Rae locks her arms with mine. "You ready to see your dad?"

"Nope," I say. "And even less ready to introduce him to Jack."

"Why? Your dad is cool like that." She squeezes my arm.

"Yeah, but Jack has these perfect parents."

"I thought you said his parents are kinda homophobic?"

"Well, that's the impression Jack gives me. But that's a whole other thing. I don't know much, except that his dad is like one of his *best friends* and that relationship is the most important thing to him. He kind of acts weird when I tell him about me and my dad and how things are tense between us. I don't know. I don't want that to work against me." Suddenly the world seems a whole lot bigger and harder to navigate than it does at CIA, where Jack and I can easily visit the stars and splash in puddles and explore each other in the in-between.

"Booboo, stop waiting for Jack to disappoint you," she says. "I spent the last three and a half hours talking to that boy, and I know two things. The first is that he really likes you. No, *loves* you. He would not shut up about you to the point where it kind of made me super jealous because it's like there's this whole side of you that I'll never know in that way."

That's how I felt when she started dating Harry. The way she would talk about him and all the shit they had in common, like playing Dungeons & Dragons, which, gross. It's a weird feeling when you realize your best friend has a whole other life outside of you.

"You think he loves me?" I ask.

"Big. Time."

Warmth fills my chest despite the chilly October air. "Can I tell you a secret? I think tonight might be the night we, you know."

She squeals.

"He sort of implied yesterday that he was ready, and I am too. Anyway, what's the second thing you learned?"

She smirks devilishly. "That you and Jack had a very Jack and Rose from *Titanic* moment last week that you didn't tell me about! You kinky slut!"

"Ohmygod. He told you that?"

"In his defense, he thought I already knew since you tell me everything. And—" She starts laughing. "His face became such a shade of purple that he couldn't look at me for a good half hour. We just drove in silence."

"How'd you get him to talk again?" I'm *dying* to know.

"I played a weird country cover of Cardi B's 'WAP.'" She snort-laughs so loud, it rings in my ear.

"Shut. Up." I can't breathe. "You. Did. Not!"

"I did! I did!"

"You know what Benny said when I told him what happened? He said, and I quote, 'Draw me like one of your French twinks!'"

I'm crying actual tears of laughter when I see Mom. "Oh shit, be cool."

"Why?" Rae mutters. "You don't want to swap blow job tales with your mom? Uh—hi, Momma Arthur!" Rae unlatches to hug her.

"I'm so happy you came!" Mom says. "I was wondering when the hell you'd get here. I just met Jack!" She has her judgy "is he good enough for my baby?" face on.

"We love him," Rae says.

"Do we now?" Mom says, glaring at me. "In that case, we better get back inside because your father has a hold of him now."

"Oh god," I say.

"Relax," Mom says. "He's on his best behavior today." She stares me down. "You look like you're wasting away."

Which is not true. I guess I did lose weight, even though I haven't been trying. Especially when trying for me has historically been destructive. But Mom is used to me with a lot of extra padding.

"Are you eating okay? Have you found a new therapist yet? We haven't talked about that in a while."

"Mom, I'm good."

"All right, all right," she says. "I'll third-degree you later."

We head inside and find Jack and Dad sitting in the gigantic lobby on a couch talking about baseball, of all things. Like a couple of straight-bros bonding or something. They're laughing too. Jack is slapping his knee as Dad tells what I can only assume is a sexist joke because all his jokes are. Jack even crosses his legs like Dad, ankle resting on the knee, legs spread apart to show the entire world how utterly massive their balls are. It's unsettling how quickly Jack slips into this role, and it's equally unsettling how jealous I am of Jack right now.

Then the thought hits me: Am I attracted to Jack because he's that traditionally masculine guy? He rows crew, likes to play

Frisbee for fun(?), broods over his poetry, and reads a bunch of masc books from dead authors only straight dudes read, and he wears a baseball cap and watches sports. We couldn't be more in opposition. Part of me is drawn to exactly that: a secure man comfortable enough with himself to know who he is within the binary.

"I don't know about this Jack guy," Dad says, eyeing me. "He's a Red Sox fan. We're squarely a Yankees family."

"Are we?" I ask.

"Chase doesn't like sports," Dad whisper-yells. "Never liked anything that made 'em sweaty, right, Taters?"

"Don't call me that," I mutter under my breath.

Rae smirks at the sweaty comment, and I know her so well, I can hear her thoughts: *Chase loves to naked wrestle with boys! That's a sport! Full-body contact and everything.*

I bite my lips back, and so does she.

Dad propels himself off the couch to give me a handshake-hug. "How's college life, Taters?"

I cringe at that fucking nickname. Not even Rae knows why he calls me that, and I don't want to think about it because it makes me want to purge. I tug at the bottom of my shirt so it makes my front look flatter.

"You look good, managing to stave off that freshman fifteen." He smiles like he's expecting me to laugh, but my jaw clenches. He knows about my eating disorder. Mom told him about it when he came to pick up Taylor and me for one of his weekends, and he had said, "That doesn't sound like *that* big a deal. He needed to lose weight anyway."

So yeah.

"Food's pretty good, actually," I say, covering my stomach with my arms.

"Good, good." He pulls back and opens his arms wide, like this place is his castle and he's the fucking king. It's one of those hotels with glass elevators and an internal courtyard that's open all the way up to the roof. Each floor has balconies overlooking the marble lobby with lush couches and real palm trees they maintain well during winter in New York.

"Isn't this place great? Only the best for my little girl. Little woman, I should say." Dad looks to Taylor, who blushes because she eats up everything he says. "Can you believe your baby sister is old enough to have a hotel party?"

Hotel parties are a status symbol in our small town. The elite, rich assholes I grew up with would book a block of rooms in the Times Square Marriott Marquis—if they were "poor"—or the Plaza at Central Park. I never got invited to any of them. But Dad always wanted us to seem like we were in that class. Even when he lost his job, and we had to go on SNAP (the Supplemental Nutrition Assistance Program), he went out of his way to spend money as if we had it. This is just another show, and he doesn't miss a moment to act like our family is well-off, which was always the source of late-night fights. One of the sources, anyway.

"Can we afford this?" I look past him to Mom, and she offers a tight-lipped smile.

Mom rolls her eyes. "Your father's doing well at his job . . ."

He tips his head toward her as if she did him a favor. It's funny because, usually, they can't be within six feet of each other without fighting. The exception apparently being Taylor's birthday.

"Have a little faith in your old man, huh?"

"Mm-hmm," I hum.

Mom moves toward me and grabs my arm. "Try to be good. For your sister's sake."

I catch Jack staring at me, and I cringe, wondering what he's thinking about my father—the showman and the bullshitter. His face is blank, which is somehow worse than any other potential reaction. I've learned his faraway stares mean he's thinking about his family and the weight of his relationships with them. His crinkly smiles mean he's genuinely happy and light. When he clenches his jaw and closes one eye, he's deep in thought about something existential. But his blank stares? They scare me because they're unreadable.

"Is *she* here, too?" I whisper.

"Krissy'll be coming later," she says, and I groan. "Be on your best behavior."

"Hey, Jack," Dad says. "Come help me set some stuff up. I'm sure Chase and Rae want some time to gossip, and I got a bottle of whiskey we can crack open. You're twenty-one, right? No? Eh, it's okay . . ." He puts his arm around Jack's shoulders, and they make their way toward the entrance to the indoor water park. Dad doesn't give me another glance.

"Thank you for being here," I say to Rae, who hugs me tighter. I think about a few years back when Taylor was hospitalized with appendicitis, and Rae spent hours with me in the hospital waiting room while Taylor was in surgery. And when Dad up and decided to stop loving Mom, Rae dropped everything to bake me my favorite Funfetti cake with rainbow sprinkles mixed into the frosting. She sat with me and watched Disney movies all night. It's nice to know there are some people you can always count on, no matter what.

"Come help me set up the hotel room!" Taylor wedges herself in between Rae and me. "I need this to be perfect. We have a manicure station and hair station all set up for after we're done at the water park. We got a suite! It's so exciting!"

She's brimming with energy, and I see a lot of Dad in her. Or, at the very least, the excitement of the promises he always makes but rarely follows through on. But it looks like, for once, he's pulled through. I have to try to mask my disdain for Taylor's sake.

And for Jack's.

Rae and I get to work ensuring Taylor's party is a success, decorating the suite, stuffing goody bags—cheap makeup bags from the dollar store full of free samples of concealers and eye shadow and perfumes because Mom is quite thrifty—and making sure everything looks like a scene from a CW teen drama on a budget. But, to be fair, Mom has most of it done already. She seems in control. Almost like she didn't need me around at all and had been getting on fine without me. That's sobering, but I have to admit that I'm happy to see it. Like a tiny bit of the weight I carry has been lifted off me.

The second Tay's friends show up, Rae and I become second-class citizens, relegated to the background as Taylor fights for her spot in the social hierarchy.

"I do not miss this," Rae says, emerging from the bathroom in a cute 1950s-style one-piece bathing suit. "Remember Leila's hotel party at the Plaza?"

"Yeah, I wasn't invited, remember?" I usher us out of the room to make our way to the indoor water park. From the balcony, I spot Jack sitting with Dad at the bar.

"Oh, right. What was her excuse?"

"Girls only," I say in Leila's lilt. "You understand, don't you? You're such a good friend, my best friend, the bestest I've ever had!" The back of my hand wilts against my forehead, and when I'm done, I bow.

"Brilliant." Rae claps all daintily like she's at the opera. "What's crap about that is Hunter Thomas and Nick Vivianno came, and she ended up hooking up with both of them."

"Wait. What?"

"You didn't know?"

I take a deep breath. In and out. "Nope, but I shouldn't be surprised."

"Shit. I'm sorry. I didn't know you didn't know!"

"Rae, it's fine. Leila's not in my life anymore for a reason. Even though I see her every single day."

"Yeah, how's that going?" Rae asks as we walk out of the elevator. "I think Leila's given up texting me because I never respond."

"I think she's going through something—I don't know. She's been slacking in our seminar, but I've seen her sculpting again late at night. I'm trying not to care, but . . ."

"But you're you," Rae says as we reach the bar.

"Look at you," Dad says, eyeballing Rae. "You going in the park?"

"I can't resist a waterslide," Rae says.

"Maybe you can get Chase to go," Dad says, and my stomach turns because I anticipate the train wreck ahead. "Remember the time you got stuck, Taters?" He chuckles. "He was a *big* kid." He makes a pizza pie with his hands out in front of him.

"Dad, come on," I beg. "There wasn't enough water."

"Lighten up, pal. It's a joke."

233

I look to Jack, but he looks away, slouching toward the bar.

"At my expense," I say sharply.

"Watch your tone," Dad says.

"Watch your asshole instincts," I mumble.

Everything goes silent.

"What'd you say?" Dad's chair skids back behind him, and he puffs out his chest.

I want to repeat what I said, but my temples are throbbing, and my fists are clenched, and I feel like if I open my mouth, I won't be able to breathe, and I'll go off. I don't want that for Taylor. So I grab Rae and pull her away.

Jack doesn't move. He's frozen in place.

Rae and I don't stop until we reach the party room, sectioned off inside the park, where Mom is busying her hands doing god knows what because everything is perfect, and Taylor and her friends don't even care because they're all huddled together gawking at a pair of skinny-ass boys who look slightly older than them.

Then Jack is running after me, calling my name. I feel his hand on my shoulder, and I turn to face him. "What the hell was that about?"

"Did you not hear him?"

"He was joking," Jack says. "You were kind of rude . . . to your dad."

I have to literally bite my tongue. "It was his face. You didn't see it because you weren't paying attention."

"What's going on?" Mom starts.

But I don't have the bandwidth to explain how I'm feeling right now. I don't want to cause a scene, and Mom would absolutely take the match I'd be giving her and douse it with kerosene before lighting up the entire hotel. I already feel like I've somehow set myself on fire just by being here with him.

Jack and Rae wait for me to say something.

Then Rae answers for me. "Chase doesn't want to go on the waterslides with me."

Mom can read between the lines, because she looks at me with pity in her eyes. She knows how Dad can be, but she also knows not to call it out in front of my friends. "Oh, well, you know how *I* feel about water parks. Half of it is urine. Let's just enjoy Taylor's birthday," she says.

"God, I hate him," I say.

Jack says nothing.

We make it through most of the party, not speaking.

Jack talks to Mom, Dad, even Taylor and her friends, who fawn over him and drag him into the water, which is adorable because he indulges their drool-laden stares (can't really blame them, to be fair). But not to me. He won't even look at me. Luckily, I have Rae, but she leaves after we sing "Happy Birthday" and eat cake so she can spend time with her own family.

So now I have no choice but to push through alone since Jack is no help. I hate that his family life is so supposedly perfect that he can judge mine.

At some point, Mom ushers the girls upstairs to the suite, mouthing, "Help me!" as Dad's new girlfriend, Krissy, pulls up the rear. It's so obviously fake when they try to get along, but we all tell ourselves it's for Taylor's sake. Still, I don't have to fake it if Krissy doesn't see me, so I duck out of sight.

I find Jack—body still dewy from the water—with a towel draped around his shoulders, talking to Dad. Again.

As I debate whether or not to approach, Dad sees me and waves me over.

"Jack here was just telling me about his family's farm in Vermont," Dad says in a tone that says, "You better watch what you say, but I'm trying to make nice."

I can't think of anything I'd rather do less than be near Dad. But I have to make the best out of it so that maybe Jack will talk to me again.

"You didn't tell me that his father is the Reid of Reid's Whiskey."

I didn't know. Not that I pay attention to whiskey since I can't even legally drink.

"I can't believe you know it," Jack says. "I thought it was an indie Vermont thing."

"Well, I'm sure you know that I'm a big skier," Dad boasts. "I spend most of my winters up there in Vermont, skiing Stratton and Killington with my kids."

"Yeah, Chase told me," Jack says, flashing me a smile.

"You'll have to come skiing with us," Dad says.

"I always go with my pops, too," Jack says. "Me and my sister, Claire. She's about Taylor's age. They'd probably get along well."

"You grew up on the mountains, huh?" Dad sits back and puts his hands behind his head. "Sounds like the dream. What made you want to leave that for Upstate New York?"

Jack looks to me. "Had to get out of my comfort zone and figure out who I am away from all that. My best friend, Callum, is apprenticing with my dad at the distillery and the farm, and he tried to get me in there, too. Callum's two years older than me. After my older brother went into teaching, my dad was pretty disappointed I wanted to study writing."

"Writing," Dad scoffs. "What do you even do with a writing degree?" Then his eyes widen, realizing he put his foot into his mouth again, and he slams forward. "I didn't mean it like that—"

But Jack just laughs it off. "No, my pops says the same thing. I get it."

"Can't deny the heart," I add.

"Right," Jack agrees. "Exactly. And he gets that, too. I hope."

"You sound like you're trying to convince yourself," Dad says.

"Dad!"

"What?" Dad throws his hands up. "He does."

"Nah," Jack says. "I love writing, and I love it at CIA. My brother wants me to teach, like him, so there's that. I get a lot of pressure to follow in footsteps that aren't mine." His cheeks go red. "I *do* miss my family, though. Especially my dad and bro. And Callum."

It's strange how little I know about Jack's best friend, yet he felt comfortable sharing intimate shit about our sex life with mine.

"This is nice, though, you having me here for Taylor's birthday. I appreciate it, Mr. Arthur."

"Ah, call me Frank," Dad says. "We're happy to have you, right, Chase?"

"Absolutely." I reach for Jack's thigh, but he shakes me off, his leg moving as restlessly as mine do.

"Maybe over the holidays, our families can meet up at Killington."

As much as Dad frustrates me, it is nice that he's genuinely interested in my boyfriend. I'll give him that.

Jack nods erratically, and I know it must be because Jack isn't out to his parents, so the chance of all of us spending any time together like that is about zero percent.

"But I'll have to warn you, if the conditions aren't perfect, Chase'll have a fit," Dad says with a belly laugh.

Jack and I exchange glances.

"I don't like ungroomed snow," I say.

"You'd hate Callum, then," Jack says. "He's a tree skier. All about moguls, freshly fallen snow."

Right. Because I care what Callum thinks. Who the hell even *is* Callum?

"A real prima donna, my kid is," Dad continues. "You haven't even gone in the water at all today, Taters."

"Not feeling it," I say through gritted teeth.

He reaches over and slaps my stomach so hard it jiggles. "I take it back about that freshman fifteen. Is that why you won't go in the water?"

Oh god, no. Please don't.

He leans closer to Jack. "He's always been ashamed of his baby fat. Wears a shirt in the pool. Will you tell him there's nothing wrong with putting on a little weight? It's probably that happy relationship weight, am I right? As long as it doesn't get bad again. He used to look like a potato when he was a baby."

He laughs, and it's the worst sound in the entire world.

Jack pivots his body uncomfortably away from him.

"Did he tell you he had an"—he uses air quotes for extra douchey impact— "'eating disorder'? I thought college dining halls put laxatives in their food to avoid food poisoning. I read that on Facebook once."

"Dad, please, stop." My voice is shaking.

"Oh, come on, I'm joking."

"That's not a joke."

"Laxatives, Chase? Give it up already. That's not an eating disorder. That's a really shitty decision." He starts laughing. "Get it, *shitty*?"

I hold my breath as a tear spills down my cheek. This always happens. It starts as a joke and then spirals because he thinks he can just say whatever he wants.

"That's not right, Mr. Arthur." Jack rises to his feet. "With all due respect, I've sat and listened to you dig at Chase all day, and this is really harmful." He's trembling, clearly not used to speaking like this to a father figure.

Dad looks like he was slapped. "I—I—"

Jack's chest rises and falls rapidly. All he says is a stern, clear, "You would be lucky to know the Chase I do," before hesitantly placing a hand on my back, urging me to walk away—to be the bigger person. I want to add more to what Jack said, but it'd probably get us kicked out of the hotel if I open *that* Pandora's box. Plus, I'm tired. So fucking tired.

We turn and leave my dad behind.

Jack stands on the other side of the elevator, his eyes not focusing on anything. I can almost hear his thoughts—my fears—tumbling around his head: *I can't believe I just spoke like that to Chase's father*, and *I touched Chase's back in such a public space*, and *This family is fucked up, I can't do this.*

I don't look at him as he slides the key card into the slot and pushes open our hotel room door.

I collapse onto the bed and curl into a fetal position, hugging one of the billion bed pillows to my body.

Jack slides in behind me and holds me. "I'm sorry about that."

If I say anything, I'll cry, and I really don't want Dad to have that power over me.

"When he was joking earlier, I thought it was normal guy stuff. That's how my dad and brother and Callum act. I didn't even realize what was going on, and I thought maybe you just had it out for your dad. But what he said . . ." Jack starts to stroke my hair, fingers like a comb, and it soothes me. "I didn't think parents could say that kind of stuff to their kids."

"Does it make you think differently of me?" I roll over to face him, but I can't look him in the eyes, so I bury my face in his chest. "I know how you feel about your family, and now you've seen mine. We're not these perfect people who live on a farm and sing kumbaya over campfires."

He doesn't say anything, but he holds me tight and steadily rubs my head until I fall into a restless sleep.

The next morning, as I ravage the hotel's free continental breakfast buffet before Jack wakes up (he does *not* deserve to see me stress-eat butter-and-whipped cream–soaked waffles), Mom badgers me about Parents' Weekend.

"You don't have to come," I say between bites.

"Are you sure?" she asks, a mix of sadness and relief on her face. I know she doesn't really have the money, but she would give every last penny to support me. "Your father actually paid child support, so I have a little extra money. If you want."

"Wow, he's a big spender. First this"—I gesture all around us to the lavish hotel—"now doing what he's court-ordered to do. A real hero."

"I heard what happened yesterday," she says. "Your father told me. Do you want to talk about it?"

"He told you?" Color me shocked.

"He was pretty upset."

"Aaaaand there it is. It's always about him," I say with an exhaustive eye roll. "What'd you say?"

"I told him if he doesn't get his shit together, he's going to lose you." She takes a long swig of pulpy orange juice then reaches across the table to grab my hand. "Your father and I have our . . . *differences.*" She tries not to smile. "But I want you two to have a real relationship." I jump to say that it's all on him, but she speaks over me. "And I told him that the shit he says is hurtful and misinformed and—"

Good on you, mom. "Misogynist and sexist and fat-shame-y," I add, pushing food around my plate. I shove my towering plate of waffles to the side, suddenly feeling gross with my urge to comfort eat every last crumb on the buffet line. "So what? Are you going to make us have some heart-to-heart moment or something? Is that supposed to make up for all the hurt he's caused by leaving and constantly making digs at me?"

She takes a bite of a cheese-filled Danish. "I wish it could. And I'm not sure it ever would. You're an adult now, and that means having to figure out your own path, which you've always done. I admire that in you. I don't know where you got that bravery from, but it's not from your father or me. That's for sure. Part of that path means having to figure out what's important to you and what will help you grow versus hold you back. What your father says is not reflective of you but of him. What other people want from you is more about them than you. Don't let anyone hold power over you. You're a beautiful person, inside and out, and you deserve to hear *that*."

19

On Monday, CIA's campus center is flagged with giant PARENTS' WEEKEND banners. They are delightfully decked with tiny gourds and jack-o'-lanterns and goofy-looking spiders with little blue hats stamped with CIA's mascot, a cartoonish river otter. Most of the conversation on campus revolves around how Parents' Weekend falls on Halloween and "how am I going to ditch my 'rents to get wasted?" Since I convinced Mom to save the money and not come, and Dad wouldn't dare after yet another awkward encounter, I get to enjoy the cheesy decor of the Hole with a side of loneliness.

"You're super spacey, binch," Benny says, waving a chicken finger in my face. "Meanwhile, Chloe and Sof and I have been discussing Halloween costume ideas on a budge for the last fifteen and have yet to hear your thoughts."

"A budge?" I ask.

"Budget," Benny says matter-of-factly.

Chloe and Sofía await my suggestions, but I've got nothing. I'm notoriously bad at coming up with costume ideas. Last year, Rae, Leila, and I wanted to do a group costume idea that was punny, and all I could come up with was Deviled Eggs. As in, let's dress up as eggs with devil horns. I was nearly kicked out of the friend group for that, which, fair.

"Halloween is ruined this year," Sofía says. "Parents' Weekend is cockblocking my fun times. The usual parties aren't happening. But I wanna do *something*."

"Have another party?" I suggest.

"Can't," Chloe says. "Sof's parents are staying with us." She glares at her.

"Don't look at me like that when your grandma is flying here from *Nola*," Sofía says.

"My grams can hang," Chloe says, and Sofía waves her off.

"Ladies," Benny says. "I have no parents coming this weekend, so I'd really love to find a man on this holiest of weekends."

"You have more men than the Republican party," Chloe says.

"Allow me to translate," I offer. "When Benny says he wants to find a man, what he's really saying is, 'I'm picturing a costume-themed wedding that will take place immediately upon meeting my future husband, and we will marry beneath the full moon.'"

Benny holds up his phone with the "I'm in this picture and I don't like it" meme on the screen.

"You're ridiculous," Sofía says, laughing.

I'm also laughing. "You think I'm joking?"

"Marriage?" Chloe scoffs. "Girl."

"Here's a secret," Benny says. He pulls up Grindr on his phone. "When I meet someone hot, I'm mentally planning the wedding in my head. The trick is after the hookup because if he's all, 'let's cuddle, I love you,' I'm immediately like, 'Okay, this was nice, don't call me, gotta go, bye.' But if he's emotionally distant and plays hard to get, I'm a goner, lost somewhere in a daydream where I'm at our beautiful country kitchen whipping up biscuits while he watches football in the living room."

"Wow," Sofía says. "You're fucked up."

"You just sent women and gays back, like, a hundred years," Chloe adds.

"What're we talking about?" Jack says, emerging from the masses with a tray of food for us to share.

"Nothing productive," I say, and Benny scowls. "Unless you have any tea on Rhett?"

Benny leans forward, elbows on the table.

"What is a *Rhett*?" Sofía says.

"My straight roommate Benny is in love with," Jack says.

"Are we sure he's straight?" I ask.

"Can confirm he's done some very not-totally-straight things to me," Benny says.

"Oop—" Chloe shouts.

Then Benny practically throws his body across the table. "I just want him to love me! Is that too much to ask?"

"Have you actually talked to him?" Jack asks. "Had an honest conversation?"

Benny stares at him blankly. "Does not compute."

I hold my tongue because Jack and I haven't talked at all about what happened last weekend, and I haven't brought it up. There's been this strange tension as if he's gotten a peek inside my world outside of him, and maybe he didn't like what he saw. Or maybe that's just the story I'm telling myself. All I know is that his parents are coming up this weekend, and every time I bring them up, he avoids the topic.

So. Yeah.

"You could talk to Rhett for me, maybe?" Benny asks.

Jack's eyes widen. "Rhett and I don't exactly talk. He makes it a point not to be in the room when I'm there. I haven't said much to him since the first week. All he does when we're there together is huff and puff and spray the entire room with Febreze."

"He's such a nervous bunny," Benny says, lovesick.

"Where did you even come from?" Chloe deadpans.

"Born of Bravo TV and anxiety by way of Italy. *An-y-way*," Benny says. "I want to dress like a slut, so I need man-baiting costume ideas. And slutty Carole Baskin is not an option because that was my costume two years ago, and I simply cannot repeat. Then we can figure out where to go."

"Actually, I have an idea. Benny, why don't *we* throw a little gathering at our suite Friday? We're gonna be the only ones there since everyone either has parents coming and staying with them in their various Airbnbs or are going home for the weekend. It'd have to be small because we don't want to get written up, and we'd have to check that it's okay with the other suitemates, but why not?"

"I like how you think," Benny says. "But only if we can invite Rhett."

"Hopeless," I say. Then I turn to Chloe, Sofía, and Jack. "Y'all in?"

"Benny, are you finished yet? I have to shower!" I yell through the bathroom door.

"You cannot rush perfection, binch!" he screams back.

He's been in there for damn near an hour putting on his

costume, which he's successfully kept a secret after we took a bus to the nearest mall, and he managed to conceal everything he bought. All I know is that he spent an obscene amount of time in the Christmas Tree Shop.

When he emerges, he's dressed in a skimpy nutcracker soldier outfit, but instead of pants, he is wearing black heels and a bikini bottom that barely contains him. He's got a long white Santa Claus beard and a top hat but also a giant drag queen–style breastplate. Makeup lines are drawn around his mouth, which opens and closes mechanically.

I can't look away. "What. Is. Happening. Here?"

Using his best feminine porn star voice, he coos, "I'm a nutcracker, daddy. Do you want your nuts cracked?"

"I'm confused and aroused," I say.

He tilts his head. "Aww, sweetie. Thank you. You think this is enough to get me laid tonight?" He rubs his plastic breasts, which makes me very uncomfortable.

"I think you need to stop doing that."

"Feel them. They're so real."

"Ignoring you. Is Rhett coming?"

"I do not know. I'm assuming Jack will, though, right?"

"Yeah . . ."

"What's wrong, sugar?"

"We've been *off* all week, and I think maybe it's his parents. They're coming tomorrow, and I can't shake this feeling that their presence is going to send him back into the closet. That sounds selfish and awful and insensitive, doesn't it?"

"Yes." Benny touches my arm. "Sorry to hear that. I guess that means no sex?"

"Well, that's the thing. We pretty much blow each other every chance we get. Yesterday, he pulled me into the campus center bathroom in the middle of the day, and he's been dropping hints that he's been *practicing* for the Big Stuff."

"Oh." Benny's eyes go wide. "And we all know *you've* been practicing. No, wait, scratch that. You're practic*ed* judging by the vibrations inside our room when the door is locked, and I'm waiting outside."

"*Binch*. You can hear me?"

He smirks at my use of *binch*. "The whole suite can. But it's *fiiiine*. Get yours, prostate massager!"

"I feel like I'm *always* ready these days."

"Same," Benny says as a knock on the door jostles me.

"Get that. I'm hopping in the shower."

"I love when you talk dirty to me!" he says, then shouts, "Coming!"

In charge of using his connections to get alcohol, Benny lines our coffee table and TV stand with handles of cheap vodka and gin. Cases of warm Natty Ice line the room.

Benny makes Chloe, Sofía, and me take a zillion pictures together. Chloe is dressed like Ursula from *The Little Mermaid*. Well, sexy Ursula, and it works, especially side by side with Sofía's Ariel costume, complete with a luxurious red wig and purple seashell bra. They roped me into being Prince Eric. I couldn't afford a complete costume, so I'm shipwrecked Eric, with a ripped white button-down and ripped navy-blue pants, no shoes, my hair wild like I just washed ashore. Luckily, even though it's ripped, I'm still fairly covered, so you can't really see my body. Baby steps, right?

Sofía put on bright-red lipstick and kissed my cheek, so I've been branded by Ariel, and for good measure, they both make me hold a fork I stole from the dining hall. Chloe roped two other freshman animation majors into being Flotsam and Jetsam, so she had minions to boss around. We really do stand out.

The suite is wall-to-wall people, and I have no clue who any of them are. And that's not just because most of them are costumed to the gods.

But one person isn't here.

"Where the hell is Jack?" Sofía slurs, gulping down whatever is in her Solo cup that has turned her teeth a Smurf blue. "I love that hot piece of ass. Sorry, can I say that?"

"Yes, he is hot," I say. "I'm kinda pissed. He was supposed to be here an hour ago."

Benny comes up from behind and flings an arm around both of us. "Listen, I'm really upset Rhett isn't here."

"You two and your boy drama," Sofía says. "You shouldn't have to take this!"

"We *don't* have to take this." The words slosh around Benny's mouth. "I'm a strong, confident woman!"

"Hell yes, you are!" Sofía screams.

"Let's go down to their room and, I dunno, storm 'em or something," I shout.

"Oh," Benny says, shrinking down. "Idunnoaboutallthat. Maybe a text? To channel every senator in Congress, send a Strongly Worded Text full of Strongly Worded Concern."

"That traitor," Sofía mutters as Benny furiously types something and hits send before conferring with us.

"What'd you say?" I ask.

Benny flashes us his phone: You coming tonight? Free booooooooze

"Really?" I say. "That's what you said?"

"We can't all be as strong as you, Chase Arthur!" Benny cries.

Chloe comes over with a bottle of vodka and tips it into Benny's mouth, then Sof's, then mine, giving me more than the others. It bubbles out; I try my best to swallow, but it burns like fire.

"That's . . . awful!" My entire body convulses.

"You need to relax," Chloe says.

My face is so hot. "No, I need re-Jacks."

"Oh, she's got jokes now?" Benny golf claps.

"I'm going to his room."

"Chase, I don't think—" Chloe starts.

"No, that's exactly what you need to do." Benny cheers me on.

"Yeah, Chase, are you sure?" Sofía asks.

"Absolutely!" I declare. "I'm just gonna be like, 'Hey, man, the fuck is up with you?' and demand he figure his shit out."

But the second I get to Jack's dorm, the momentary buzz I felt dissipates, and my hands are all sweat. I try to turn around, but there he is, in a towel(!) emerging from the shared floor bathroom, shower caddy in hand, dripping wet like an Olympic swimmer, looking every bit as delicious as he did the day we met. Except his eyes are red and puffy. He's been crying.

"Chase?" His face brightens but just a bit. He wipes his cheeks. "Sorry I'm late, I was writing, and my phone was on airplane mode, and then I had to shower, and . . . wow, you look." He walks toward me and puts his free hand at the dip of my waist. "Hot." He clears his throat, and all the worry in his face disappears.

"You like me all shipwrecked?" I ask as his fingers hook into the tears of my shirt, grazing against my chest hair.

"*Shipwrecked*," he repeats, lips and tongue playing with the syllables and hard consonants. "That's a word I don't think of too often." He bites his bottom lip, and his eyes squint as he studies my face. "What's wrong?"

I'm still a teeny bit buzzed, and I don't want to pick a fight, but . . . "I had a feeling you might blow me off, and I can't shake it. I feel like, I don't know, I'm so sure of you and us and how I feel about you, but . . ." I pause. "You're so distant lately and . . ."

I'm trying not to cry, but loose liquored lips and all make it increasingly hard.

Tension pulls at his jaw. "Come inside. We'll talk."

That's never good.

Breakups on TV shows and movies and books always start with some variation of *Let's talk*. Is this that?

I stand by his window overlooking the dark courtyard. A lesbian couple in knit hats and North Face jackets kisses beneath the lamplight and dashes into an adjacent dormitory.

Jack shuts the door behind him.

He doesn't come up behind me, but I hear a dull thud.

When I turn around, he's slumped on the floor against the door, head in hands.

I immediately drop in front of him, arms on his bare knees, hands on his. "Hey, talk to me."

He lifts his head like it weighs a million pounds. "I don't know what I'm doing."

"With me?"

"No." His head shakes. "You're the one thing I'm sure of, and that scares me because what happens when I'm not enough for you? What happens when I come out to my parents, and they reject me, or what if I can't come out to them, now or ever? Would you still want to be with me? I wasn't supposed to fall in love with you, but I did. I love you so much that my body aches when I think about it. My whole life, I've felt like I've been struggling to keep my head above water, and then you showed up out of nowhere and fucking jumped into that river with me, and I've been drowning ever since." He exhales, and his chest shudders.

"You love me?"

He laughs as my thumbs wipe away his tears. "Yes, dumbass."

"How eloquent, Mr. Poet."

"Is that all you have to say?" He stares at me with those big, dumb, beautiful eyes.

I should let him squirm like he did after he told me he loved me weeks ago during peak orgasm and never even acknowledged it. But my entire body feels like it's on fire, and if I don't say it back, I'll burn to death.

"I've been disgustingly in love with you since you touched me in that river, and you drive me wild because I'm in this, Jack."

"Really?" he asks softly.

"I need to know that you're in this with me, even if you're scared." I grab his hand. "Because I'm scared, too."

"What if . . . I'm not worth it?"

I wedge myself in between his legs, and the towel falls to the side. My forehead rests against his, and I close my eyes. "You are."

"Even if I hurt you?" Jack keeps saying that, and it's making the pit in my stomach harder to ignore.

But I do, because I love him and need him to know that. "You won't."

His lips gently brush mine. "I love you." He repeats it over and over again, a prayer on his lips, a hymn he sings under his breath, at first as if trying to convince himself that it's okay to love me and then growing stronger and more resolute with each refrain until his worship is loud.

He kisses me softly, so impossibly soft that it feels like I'm dreaming.

Then he pulls back, and we stare into each other's eyes, both of us afraid to blink out of fear that if we do, the moment will pass us by.

"I'm ready," he whispers. "I want you."

"Is Rhett around?"

"I think he went to your party, actually," Jack says.

I rise to my feet and pull him with me. I drink in his body, the dip of his waist, the way his Adonis belt is more pronounced on the left side, the tiny freckles splattered like paint across his chest. He's a masterpiece, a rare work of art to be revered, but one that I actually get to touch, to experience.

He undresses me slowly, never breaking our gaze.

He lays me down on his extra-long twin and wedges himself between my legs, lifting the bottom half of my body. My legs wrap around him as he dips to kiss me. It's not aching and hungry but slow and deep and passionate. As our lips and tongues move together in a choreographed dance, his hand moves downward. Spit and fingers spread me open, slowly, little by little, one by one until

253

I'm gasping for air in between kisses. Sliding down, he uses his tongue for the first time. My back arches.

He reaches for the lube and a condom. As he towers over me, body slick with sweat already, I close my eyes.

"Go slow," I whisper, sucking in a breath.

He pushes against me, shoving the tip inside with a pop.

I let out a yelp. "Slow!"

"Sorry! Are you okay?" He leans down to kiss me softly, and my body relaxes.

I exhale, and he slides deeper inside me, enough so that I convulse, a confusing swirl of pain and unbridled pleasure.

"Should I stop?"

"No," I beg. "Just hold steady for a sec."

Breathe in.

Relax.

Feel him, his weight, his power, his control.

Breathe out.

I open my eyes, and the soft lines of Jack's face are all I see, and it's enough for me to let go and let him in. I nod, and he goes deeper, and my eyes roll.

"I love you so much," he groans.

He's so close, closer than he's ever been before, sharing my body in ways I never dreamed were possible, and the faster he goes, the more I hope this never ends. After this, I can't go back to living and breathing and walking around without him inside me.

I don't have to ask him to hold me, to kiss me, because he does, and we move together as one, twisted up in his bedsheets, Jack a veritable god as he moves his hips with assured precision. I scream in ecstasy, my body shivering with a fullness I've never felt before, and it's almost too much to bear as I bite down on my bottom lip and my head gets light. He grunts as his brows furrow. I clutch his back as he finishes then collapses onto me, shaking, his arms jellied as they try to prop him up and fail.

He picks his head up and kisses the tip of my nose. "My turn."

"Really?"

He barely smirks before I roll over on top of him and pin his arms to the headboard. I gently kiss the space between his ear and his neck.

His legs open for me, and at first, I do what Jack did, but an animal fervor leads me down farther, using my tongue to get him ready. Instantly, he moans, and it's so primal that it makes me go harder.

"I need you, please," he begs. "Fuck me."

There's something about the way he bites his bottom lip, the same lip I've kissed maybe hundreds of times now, that makes me want to know every square inch of him, mind, body, and soul. I thought before, when he was on top, that I could never feel closer to him, but now, as I stare into the ocean of his eyes as I enter him and his body trembles as his fingers grip my arms, this is a whole different level of intimacy.

As I find my rhythm, I can't help but whisper everything that's in my heart, exquisite paintings I can't verbalize as anything but "I love you, I love you, I love you."

Afterward, when we're both spent, sweaty messes, and neither one of us wants to go back to my suite for the party, Jack puts on my shredded Prince Eric shirt and picks up James Baldwin's

Giovanni's Room. It's so achingly hot how the fabric that touched my body is now draped around his. I watch the muscles in his forearm pulse as he turns to a new page. I haven't the strength to get dressed. All I want to do is watch him read.

His Moleskine notebook is open on the nightstand.

"What's this? A new poem?"

"Just some ideas I scribbled when you went to the bathroom," he says.

"Can I?"

"You don't have to ask," he says.

The wind carries seeds
like your name on my breath
So why is there ground
where flowers never grow?

Why do some things never settle
and root like trees?
Then I realized what
my garden lacked

You

I'm in bloom

"I was thinking of something involving the word *shipwrecked*," he says. "But my mind took me to weird, sexual places where I focused on being wrecked."

I bend down to kiss him. "Did I wreck you?"

"Mm-hmm," he hums. "I—"

Muffled voices outside Jack's door freeze us in place. A key card clicks, unlocking the door. Rhett says, "I think Jack's in. If not, you can wait for him with us."

There's no time to cover myself before Rhett and Benny walk in with a guy I've never seen before. Jack jumps to his feet, Rhett shouts like he's seen a ghost, and the new guy just stands in the doorway, face completely drained of all color.

"Callum?" Jack shouts.

"What the fuck!" Callum says before turning on his heels and walking straight out.

Jack is shaking, and Rhett apologizes before slowly backing out and grabbing Benny, who looks at me with fear in his hazy, drunk eyes, not wanting to leave.

And then we're alone in a room full of naked fucking elephants.

"Callum? As in . . ." I start.

Jack's throwing on shorts and flip-flops even though it's borderline freezing outside.

"What's he doing here?"

"I don't fucking know, Chase, but you need to go." Jack won't look at me. Or can't. Either way, it makes me want to cry.

"Jack, I—" I reach for him.

Slipping away, he roars so loudly it rattles my bones, "Get the fuck out!"

20

I'm shaking.

What just happened?

This isn't how it's supposed to go.

Losing my virginity should've been the most magical moment of my life. But instead, I'm walking through Jack's dorm in a state of absolute shock, and I can't seem to find the exit.

Somehow, I end up in Jack's community bathroom, bracing myself against the sink.

Benny appears behind me. "Babe, you okay?"

I shake my head.

Rhett stands a few feet behind us.

Then I hear Jack's voice screaming in the hallway, "Cal, just come in. Please, please, I can explain. It's not what it looked like!"

Callum yells back, "You were naked with another dude. You gay or something?"

"Just come in, please."

I know that tone. Jack doesn't want to have this conversation in public. He never does. Everything he's ever done with me has been when he's sure nobody is looking.

Jack stops in front of the bathroom entrance. He quickly glances our way, and he reaches for the handle to shut the door so Callum doesn't see us.

Benny moves to the other side of the door. I don't know how long he's been there, but eventually, he says, "I think they went inside Jack's room." He looks to Rhett. "Can you help me bring Chase back to our room?"

"Not like *I* can go back," Rhett says.

Benny hisses.

"I want to hear what they're talking about," I say.

"I don't think that's a good idea," Benny says, but I'm already out the door, barreling toward Jack and Rhett's room.

Pressing my ear against the door, I don't hear anything. At first. Then:

Callum: "So you're a fucking fag?"

Jack: "Come on, Cal. That's messed up." [crying sounds]

Callum: "Do your parents know?"

Jack: "No, please don't tell them."

Callum: "For fuck's sake, Jack, you're hooking up with that *fat* kid and, what, I'm supposed to pretend like it's no big deal."

My heart sinks so deep in my chest, it might as well fall out the bottom. *Jack will defend me, right? He has to. He loves me.*

Callum: "I don't even know you, bro. But I can't lie to your parents. I won't."

Jack: "You're my best friend. Please."

Callum: "Am I?"

Jack: "What does that mean?"

Callum: "I told you when you were fifteen and you tried to kiss me that if you ever pulled that shit again, I would seriously . . ." [unintelligible words]

Jack: "Cal, come on, we were kids!"

Callum: "Your dad is like my dad. If I didn't think it'd destroy him to know his son takes it up the ass, I would tell him right now."

Neither of them says anything for a few minutes. I don't realize I'm weeping until Benny puts his hand on my shoulder to steady me.

Jack: "I'm the same goddamn person, Cal."

Callum: "You love him or something?"

That's when I peel myself away. I can't listen anymore.

Neither Benny nor Rhett says anything as we walk down the hall.

Rounding the corner toward the exit, we run right into Leila.

I can't catch a break tonight.

"Chase, oh my god, are you okay?" she says, rushing to me. She looks to Benny and Rhett. "What happened?"

I can't say it out loud.

"Shit, you're shook." She looks me up and down. I want to leave, but there's something comforting about her being here that I can't put my finger on. She takes out her phone and holds up a finger in dramatic Leila fashion.

"Hey, girl, yeah, I know it's been a minute. Listen, I'm not calling for me. It's Chase. Something happened. I don't know, but how fast can you get here? Okay. Thanks." Hanging up, she turns to Benny. "Rae is gonna meet you at your dorm."

I can't even thank her because if I do, I may lose it.

It's so cold out that it's snowing. And I'm shirtless, but I don't feel a thing. I'd make an Elsa-from-*Frozen* joke if I weren't completely numb.

Benny and Rhett walk me up to our room, where the party is still raging. Benny creates a barrier around me that not even Chloe or Sofía can penetrate as I slip into my room and shut the door.

"Do you—" Benny starts.

"Leave me alone," I say.

He nods. "I'll be out there if you need."

My mind is buzzing, and I try to lie down and close my eyes, but all I can see is Jack's face, the shame splashed across it when he saw his best friend.

No.

It was me.

I'm the reason Jack was ashamed and afraid.

He couldn't even look at me, and when he did, there was such hate in his eyes.

I grab the nearest sketch pad and the charcoal pencil on my desk and rip into the nearest blank page.

Charcoal blobs start in the empty corners of the paper, becoming hard, dark swirls obscuring the white like a curse spreading across a kingdom. Out of the thick ash of pencil shavings, two figures emerge, large and looming, with sad eyes sunken like shadows. The tip of my pencil shreds through the page. The minuscule fraying threads make thick black lines like bolts of lightning.

Tears swirl into the mess until I can no longer see what I'm doing.

I fling it across the room, and it smashes into Benny's TV.

My chest heaves, in and out, in and out, rapidly.

There's a knock on the door. I try to tell whoever it is to go away, but they ignore me.

I look up and see Rae.

"Baby, what happened?"

I fly up and into her arms. "I wasn't enough . . ."

She wraps her arms around me, holding me until I can't cry anymore.

21

Jack won't respond to any of my text messages, and at some point during the course of the night, he blocks me, because they no longer say *Delivered* and have turned from blue to green.

"What's he doing?" Benny whispers.

"Staring at his phone again," Rae says.

"He blocked me."

"Oh, he's giving us full monotone," Benny says. "It's an improvement from the silence." He groans as he slides off his bed and waddles across the floor like a Disney witch with a bad back. "I'm hungover after last night's massacre."

Rae flings a pillow at him. "Insensitive bitch!"

"He's right," I say. "It was a complete and total massacre. Of my heart."

"Oh my god, that was the most dramatically gay sentence ever uttered," Benny says. "And I've uttered at least four of the top five."

"I actually feel like the world is ending." My stomach gurgles.

Rae and Benny stare at me.

"You need to eat," Rae says, rubbing her own belly. "As do I. Do you CIA people have food on this campus?"

I flop around the bed, pulling the blankets over my head. "Bring me back something."

"You know it's against policy to take food out," Benny says. "And a little sunlight would do you good."

"I hate the sun."

"It's beautiful out," Rae says, pulling back the blinds.

"I hate beauty."

"Put clothes on, binch," Benny says.

"I hate clothes."

Ignoring me, he says, "Rae, I'll use one of my dining hall swipes on you. Consider it an early Hanukkah present!"

"Thanks to you, kind sir," Rae says. She catches a glimpse of herself in the mirror. "I look like I'm doing the walk of shame."

"Nope, that'd be me." I stretch, but it hurts.

Rae winces. "Mazel, you've somehow gone darker than I thought possible." She slaps me. "Get up. Don't make me call your mother, because I will."

"All right, all right, I'm up. But I'm *not* going to the Garden Dining Hall." That place reeks of Jack.

Rae ties her hair into a messy bun. "Sweetie, brush your teeth. You smell ugly. I'm gonna call Harry and . . ." She hesitates. I can tell something is wrong when she says his name, and I want to ask her about that look in her eyes, but I don't. "I'll tell him I'll probably be here for a looooooooooooong time. I'm sure he won't mind."

She throws me air kisses, and I feel a pang in my chest. I thought she's been happy with Harry, but I've been so wrapped up in Jack, I haven't asked her about *her*. I usually clue into her patterns, like when she dated Matt Moskowitz in high school and constantly dropped plans with him to hang out with me. Is she doing that again with Harry?

The least I can do is brush my damn teeth and be a better friend to make sure Rae doesn't blow it with Harry for me.

"Hey, you don't have to stay here, you know," I say.

"Shut up. Of course, I do," she says.

"No, seriously." I hold my breath, not really wanting to bring up her dating history because she tends to get a bit defensive. She crinkles her eyes and tilts her head. "Are you and Harry okay?"

Her face softens. She shrugs. "Yeah, sure, whatever."

"I don't want to be the reason you . . ."

"What?" she asks. "Break up?"

"Matt Moskowitz."

She sits on the edge of the bed, palms gripping her thighs. "I'm scared, Chase."

"Of what?"

"Harry is one of those guys who wants to be married by the time we graduate. That's what his parents did. And I *know* that's what *he* wants."

"What do *you* want?" I almost add, "Isn't that what we've always talked about . . . finding our Prince Charmings and riding off into the sunset?"

"I don't know. I feel there's so much I haven't experienced yet. We've been together for like, five, six months? His mother includes me in her biweekly family newsletter."

"Shut up. She does not!"

Rae pulls up the Trash folder in the email app on her phone. "This was last week's." She points to one line in particular that says,

"We can't wait to see what the future brings for our Harry and his love, Rae. We're not saying wedding bells yet, but ding-dong!"

My eyes get so wide they might as well pop out of their sockets.

"Yeah," she says. "Exactly my reaction. It's just . . . a lot."

"Do you love him?"

She avoids my gaze. "I don't know." Her voice is small. "How did you know that you loved, you know . . ."

She won't say Jack's name, which I sort of appreciate, but it just makes me so deeply, devastatingly sad all over again. I don't want to tiptoe around Jack's name; I'd rather forget him entirely so that I can breathe again.

"This feeling in my bones. The safety I felt. The way he looked at me as if I were the only one who mattered. His smile. The poems he wrote me. I didn't care about anything or anyone as long as he was around. Something like that doesn't just happen. And it doesn't just vanish, either." I don't realize I'm crying until she wipes away my tears.

"I don't feel that with Harry," she says. "Does that mean something?"

We both sit in silence for a long, long time, neither one of us knowing the answer. Or at least not wanting to admit it out loud.

★ ★ ★

The campus center dining hall is so crowded that I breathe a sigh of relief. So many parents are dining here that I feel like I can slip under the radar, completely unnoticed.

Rae, Benny, and I slog through the buffet lines and snake our way around bumbling parents and screaming kids, and holy shit, I hate absolutely everyone right now!

"There're no open spots. I wanna set this place on fire," Benny says, clearly irritated. "Oh, wait, there's Rhett." Benny's hand shoots up, and he immediately beelines toward him. Rae and I follow, but the closer we get, the more scared Rhett looks, his head twitching, eyeballs darting side to side.

Suddenly I see why.

Rhett's at a table with Jack, Callum, and who I presume to be Jack's mom and dad. I didn't get a good look at Callum last night, but he sort of looks like Jack's breed of boy; he's a clear foot taller than me and more broad-shouldered, like a linebacker, one of those corn-fed white football players on TV who somehow get endorsements to pose shirtless for Nike. Jack's dad looks like the kind of man who drinks whiskey and chops wood, a Ron Swanson clad in flannel with a full salt-and-pepper beard and Jack's blue eyes. His mom has long brown hair and high cheekbones with Jack's cute button nose. She looks like she's ready to go skiing, all cozied up in a baby-pink pilled sweater and thick gray yoga pants, which are appropriate given how damn cold it got this weekend.

"Are these your friends?" Jack's mom says, her eyes bright.

"Sorry, we didn't mean to intrude," Benny says. "We should—"

"Nonsense!" Jack's dad shouts. "Please, sit."

Jack and Callum are seated next to each other, across from Jack's dad, mom, and Rhett. Jack's dad motions for me to sit right next to him, and Rae and Benny sit across from me, next to Jack. I try not to look at Rae, who is seething, so my eyes find Benny, who looks like a frightened bunny in the woods during hunting season.

"We were almost finished, but we were just telling Jack how we'd love to meet his friends."

Jack's dad holds out a hand for me to shake, and it's strong as hell and reminds me of Jack's hands, the hands that just last night made me tremble and feel like they were the safest place in the world.

"You must be Chase. I can tell by the gray hair. You know Jack, ever the writer. We get descriptions of all his friends." He laughs, short but hearty.

"Nice to meet you," I say. Callum is staring at me, clenched jaw and dagger eyes. Jack won't even look at me, which is fine because if he does, I'll probably burst into tears.

"This is awkward," Jack's dad says, and I freeze, afraid to breathe. "I'm just realizing that Chase is the only one he's told us about, besides Rhett, of course."

Rhett gives an awkward salute with his fork.

"I'm Rae, Chase's *best* friend." She extends a hand and gives Jack the dirtiest glare.

"Benny." He offers nothing but a curt wave.

Jack's dad shifts a bit uncomfortably in his seat because Benny is so obviously gay, it practically radiates off him in glittery waves.

Jack's mom clears her throat. "I was just telling Jack and Callum that I met Jack's father at college. Boston College, class of 2000. Maybe Jack will meet The One, too." She looks to Callum, nods, and flashes a toothy grin.

"It's a bit too crunchy granola here," his dad says.

"Aren't you from Vermont?" Rae asks, and I love her for that. "It's like, an entire state of crunchy granolas. No offense. I'm a *huuuge* fan of Vermont."

"Yeah, you got the Bernie Sanders libs, and they're probably the majority, but there are pockets of *real* Vermonters like us," Jack's dad says, and his mom smacks his arm. "As long as he doesn't come back a lib. Or a queer."

The way he says *queer* is not how I use it. His is malicious, a slur meant to make me feel unworthy, targeted. I want to stand up and claim my queerness in front of him, make him feel just as small as he's trying to make me feel. But then I notice Jack, all color drained from his face, clenching his teeth, and I feel like I have to reserve myself.

"Simon!" his mom hisses.

"What?" he says. "There's a lot of queers in this town."

Rae mouths, *We should go*, and I nod. I don't feel safe.

"He's being an idiot. Don't listen to him. We're happy Jack is here and that he's making a *ton* of friends," she says. "It would've been nice if he stayed closer to home, but Cal has stepped up to help run the family businesses. Our other son, Jack's older brother, is a teacher, you know. Our youngest is with him for the weekend."

"I got one son who insists on being a teacher, another who wants to be a writer, and a daughter too young to get involved in whiskey-making," his dad says. "But we got the next best thing, right, Cal? Maybe Cal will inherit the whole kit and caboodle."

"Right, sir," Cal says. "It'd be an honor. You know, it's funny you should bring up girls because Jack was just telling me last night that he *did* meet someone."

I hold my breath.

Rae and Benny exchange glances then look at me.

Rhett stares at his plate.

"Really?" his mom says. "Do we get to meet her?"

"Atta boy, son," his dad says.

"Leave it alone, Cal," Jack says.

"What's her name?" his dad asks.

"He's clearly uncomfortable, Simon. Look at him," his mom says. "It's okay, honey. You don't have to tell us anything."

"No, it's fine," Jack says, clearing his throat. His eyes meet mine, but he quickly looks away. "There isn't a girl." Then he adds quickly, "There isn't anyone. I'm too busy focusing on my writing, which . . ."

I don't care what he's telling them now.

I don't care how it looks to his family or to Callum.

I'm gone.

I leave my tray, completely untouched, full of food, on the table and walk out.

I think his father shouts something fake like, "Nice to meet you!" in a way that makes it clear he doesn't give a shit about meeting me.

Rae, Benny, and Rhett find me outside in the cold.

"That was rough," Benny says, cuddling into Rhett for warmth. I want to ask them when exactly they started cuddling together in public, or at all, but I don't have the strength to hear about their potential happiness. I need everyone to be equally as miserable as I am right now. At least in my head.

I shrug.

"You should eat something," Rae says, but I push her away.

"It's over, huh?" I ask.

"You know I don't want to lie to you," Rae says, but something catches her attention, and her body tenses up. When she continues, her voice is exponentially louder. "Hopefully, *he'll* be a decent person so that I don't have to." She looks at me and urges me to look behind me. I don't have to turn to know Jack is there.

"Can I talk to him?" Jack asks. "Alone?"

Rae walks right up to him and chest-bumps him. Using her pointer and middle finger, she gestures from her eyes to his. "I'm watching you. From over there."

Do I walk toward him?

Let him come to me?

Neither of us moves. It feels like there's this delicate glass bubble separating us, and if either of us moves, it'll shatter.

"Just say it," I say.

"Chase—"

"Tell me, you fucking coward." I'm breathing heavily. "Tell me you didn't love me. Tell me that I'm just a fat kid you're hooking up with. Tell me I meant nothing to you. Because if you say anything else, I'll know you're lying."

"It's not that simple, Chase."

"So was I just an experiment? A way to get over whatever weird crush you have on your childhood best friend? A way to rebel against your shitty dad?"

"That's not fair." His voice deepens, his back straightens.

"You know what's not fair? You telling me you love me. Because here am I, loving you back so much, I'm willing to do whatever you need me to do. I'll wait forever with you, for you to be comfortable to come out to your parents. I'll help you work through all that shit. I'll stand by you. But I need you to stand by me, too. If you love me." I wait for him to say something, but he doesn't.

"What do you want me to say?"

That's when I realize he can't—or *won't*—say it out loud again. He's going to let his parents and that asshole Callum ruin us.

I bite back on my bottom lip to stop myself from completely losing it. "If you're not gonna let me fight for you, then end it. Because I'm losing myself in you, and I can't." My temples are pounding, and it feels as if time is stopping. As his eyes well, all the time we spent together floods me. All those moments replay in my head like it's the last time I'll ever get to hold on to our memories. "You're ending it, aren't you?"

His face drops to the floor. "I'm sorry, Chase."

He shrugs and slowly turns around to walk back inside.

I wait for him to hesitate.

To turn back.

To run toward me and into my arms.

To tell me he can't be without me.

But the last of him I get is the back of his stupid Red Sox cap.

The Prince Who Captured Lightning

PART III

The Witch had seen many things, lived a thousand lives, and carried with her much wisdom that the Kingdoms Below the Skies did not recognize. She had lived long enough to foretell the changing tides, and she had seen how the People feared Thunder and Lightning's love simply because they didn't understand it.

The Sky Titans were not the only ones at risk, the Witch foresaw. The People also feared magic, especially from her. For the Witch could take on many forms and identities, and the People were mistrustful of a truth they could not see.

To protect herself and the titans, the Witch *had* to separate Thunder and Lightning, cursed to remain apart until twin male souls brought back the titans and the People Below the Skies were ready to heal.

The Witch's curse would only be broken for True Love, and the twin souls would have to pass three trials to ensure that they were worthy of the task: sacrificing a piece of their hearts, convincing their kingdoms to accept their love, and finally, accepting their own destiny.

"How much," asked the Prince, "to break this curse?"

"A small sacrifice, one gold coin cannot buy." The Witch grinned, manifesting a knife in her hands. "A willingness to give of yourselves." Running the knife across the Prince's chest, she said, "You must each carve out a morsel of your hearts."

"Are we fated, then, to break this curse?" the Prince asked the Witch.

"Curse?" scoffed the Witch. "Perhaps. What do I know? I am but a Witch, scorned by your People. What I do know is that this is a question only you two can answer," the Witch said. "You must journey to the Temple of the Sky Titans. There you will find your answers, and ever more questions, should the answers not be satisfactory."

"The Temple of the Sky Titans?" the Knight asked.

"It is but ruins. And to get there, we will have to travel through both our kingdoms," the Prince said, looking at the Knight.

"This should not be of any worry," the Knight said. "For my rulers have seen the spark and will provide us safe passage."

"Your kingdom," the Witch pointed to the Prince, "will prove more treacherous, as old traditions and fears reside there."

"We will have to be cunning because the King and Queen have eyes on every road," the Prince added. "We will have to conceal it well, and if they catch us together, we face certain death. Can't we just return the spark to you and be on our way?"

"This is not something that can simply be *returned*. It is not a trinket," the Witch explained. "It is sacred. It is yours."

Suddenly, a great cloud of smoke rose from the ground, and in an instant, the Witch vanished, leaving the Prince and Knight to contemplate their journey.

Together, the Prince and the Knight set off to the Temple of the Sky Titans. As they rode on horseback, they spoke of things they loved about their kingdoms, their dreams of living beyond the borders, out of the shadows of royal expectations, much as they did the first day they met. Unbeknownst to them, their sparks grew in power and size the more they laughed.

The Prince found himself growing very fond of the Knight, and their sparks glowed brightly, announcing their arrival to the Knight's kingdom. The Knight's watchmen trotted up on horseback, surrounding them.

"Your spark has grown," the commander said. "And now it has a twin, belonging to a rival prince?"

275

"We have been tasked with traveling to the Temple of the Sky Titans," the Knight said. "And this Prince is not a foe."

"We shall let you pass," the commander said. "But first, you must share with us stories of how you came to be joined."

As day stretched into night, the Prince and the Knight regaled the ranks with tales of their spark, and the more they shared, the stronger still their sparks grew.

The next morning, as the pair rode toward the Prince's kingdom, the Prince said, "I did not expect your kingdom to be so accommodating."

"We are an open and friendly people," the Knight said.

"I do not believe my mother and father will be so welcoming." The Prince held his spark in his hand, and it danced, firing off tiny lightning bolts that made him smile.

It wasn't long before he realized that it was not the spark that made him smile but the Knight.

On the outskirts of the Prince's kingdom, the Prince said sternly, "We should find a way around."

"The quickest way is through," the Knight insisted.

They did not have time to debate because their sparks had grown so large, bright, and loud that the King and Queen had seen them from miles away. Soon, they were surrounded by the King's Guard, demanding answers. The Prince was overwhelmed by the fate that confronted him: Risk his heart—and ostracism by his family—and tell the truth, or betray the Knight. Either way, his heart is at stake.

"This Knight is my prisoner. I have captured him and the sparks he carries," the Prince lied.

The King's Guard seized the Knight and both sparks, locking them away deep under the castle. In the morning, the Knight would be put to death, and the sparks snuffed out.

"You cannot do this!" the Knight wailed. "Tell them who I am to you. Tell them of my character, Prince."

With all eyes on him, the Prince could do no such thing.

As the Knight wept behind bars and the Prince sat in his ivory tower overlooking the dark, dreary domain, both of them considered the ease with which they would cut out their own hearts if it meant it would quell the pain.

That night, the Witch appeared to the Prince with a sharp blade and a riddle: "If saving the Knight is what you desire, pure of heart, then you know what you must offer, as it was forecast in the past. But take it, I cannot; it must be given of yours, willingly, without future forecast."

22

The first week without Jack doesn't feel real.

Here's the thing with all the Disney films and various rom-coms Rae and I grew up watching in her parents' basement: They didn't prepare me for the hollowness that comes with a broken heart. I always imagined that if I was ever in love, my heart would literally break open if it ended. But that doesn't happen. The deep hurt I feel is not something that can be mended with bandages or surgery. I can't see the wound, but I feel every square inch of it as it rips across my body. I want to cry, and I do, but the tears spill out unpredictably—never when I'm in my dorm, alone, and almost always when I'm walking across campus or standing in line at the vending machine for Flamin' Hot Cheetos. One second, I forget Jack exists, but then I remember him and everything that happened between us—from our first meeting at the river to our final showdown at the dining hall and all the lightning-striking moments in between—inundates me, and I can't even think.

I float from class to class.

I replay my last twenty-four hours with Jack, dissecting every scene, looking for things I did wrong, that he did wrong, reasons that would mend me.

I skip lunch and dinner and go straight to bed. Sleeping is the only way anything makes sense. I am sleeping so much, Benny genuinely asks if I need an at-home nurse to change my sheets and flip me over so I don't get bedsores.

I work on "The Prince Who Captured Lightning," but only on the parts that have already been workshopped and approved. I can't seem to muster the energy to figure out an ending. Chloe and Sofía and Professor McPherson love the dimensionality I gave the Witch, but there's still the question of how it all gets tied up, and for that, I have no answers. How can I, when any ending feels too raw to process?

Every day I struggle with the urge to shred every sketchbook, burn every drawing, and completely delete my project altogether because when I work on the Prince, all I see is Jack's awe-full, beautiful face.

It takes two weeks before I see Jack roaming across campus, but I keep my distance. I try not to pass by his dorm if I can avoid it, but sometimes my feet just take me places, and I have no control over where I spot him, and when I do, I duck behind a barren tree. He's completely unshaven, his hair has grown and pokes out beneath his dirty Red Sox cap, and he's in a bathrobe, something Rhett told me Jack never seems to take off. I didn't believe him until I saw it for myself. He's wearing shorts and flip-flops despite the cold.

Do I say something?

Chase after him?

Pretend to run into him at the campus center?

Once upon a time, that might have seemed appealing or even endearing (in a desperate rom-com sort of way). Now, it just feels like twisting the knife he left in my chest.

Not long after that, I make the decision to start using the campus gym. Hard. I spend *hours* doing cardio and lifting until I feel like I'm about to pass out. I stop skipping meals at the dining hall, instead opting to binge-eat after working out.

Chicken fingers, waffles, French toast sticks, tacos, mashed potatoes, french fries. Anything I can get my hands on. And when my stomach feels about ready to burst, I find an empty bathroom, stick my fingers down my throat, and purge it all. Then, I wander into the bookstore and toward the pharmacy section to pick up a box of laxatives. Depending on the day and how easy it is to conceal from Xavier, Aaron, and Benny, I oscillate between purges.

It's a routine I know well, and it's scary how quickly I find my rhythm. But the more I purge, the less I think about Jack. It doesn't matter that all this—spending hours a day at the gym, purging my meals, taking laxatives—increases the hate I have for my body exponentially. Because, really, the one thing I've learned from all this is that my body isn't enough. I'm ugly and fat and misshapen, and I'll never be desirable. Not for Jack. Not for anyone. I'll never be enough. I'm useless and miserable, and I hate every square inch of the skin I wear. I want to rip it off and start over, slip into anything else, be anyone else as long as I'm not me.

Because I am nothing.

I'm not beautiful or handsome.

I'm not skinny.

I'm not someone worthy of love.

I am nothing.

I pop a laxative.

Because I am disgusting and disgusted with myself

I overeat.

Because what's the point? I'm fat, a word that grows teeth and bites me every time I stuff my face with carbs.

I just want the pain to go away.

Every day is a week, a roller coaster that never ends, just loops and curves around the same bends, over and over. I'm not strapped down, but I'm also unable to exit the moving cart. I'm screaming for help, but nobody can hear me.

Because I don't actually speak up.

When I look in the mirror, I see something hideous, something so deformed that I don't recognize it, and it haunts me. It lives in my shadows and stalks me in the reflections of windows I walk past, taunting me. Wherever I go, It follows. It swallows me. Whole.

I float across campus like a ghost.

Even if I'm around friends, I feel alone. Hollow. A void that can only be filled with food, which slides into more depression and more laxatives, more chronic exercise, more, more, more just to feel more, more, more than nothing.

At dinner with Benny and Rhett, who have quietly become a thing, Benny looks at me with serious eyes.

"Chase, you need to get help." He grabs my hand. "I'm worried about you. We both are. What's going on?"

"I'm fine," I say through a smile so forced, it hurts my cheeks.

Benny and Rhett exchange glances. Then Benny says, "I hear you. I saw the laxatives. Rae told me—"

"Rae told you?" I wish I were shocked or that I can at least pretend to be mad, but I'm not. I didn't know Benny and Rae talked, but like everything else, I don't care.

"I was worried. So is she. You're like a zombie and—"

"I wish. Being dead wouldn't be so bad."

The statement shakes me to my core. I haven't had that thought since high school, maybe when I was fifteen, but saying it out loud makes it real. Terrifyingly real. Like it's been hiding in my mind all these years. My breathing becomes ragged, shallow, and all the sound in the room is muffled. I'm floating above the scene, looking across the table at both of them as their faces go slack.

When I settle back into myself, I decide I can't do this alone anymore. Benny says nothing, but he goes with me to make an appointment with one of the therapists on campus.

The next day, I'm in the waiting room, my leg restless. Twitch-twitch-jump. When I'm called in, it's all the same questions I've heard before from my previous therapist: "How are you feeling?" and "What brings you here?"

It starts off slow, a leaky faucet, and before I know it, I'm spilling my guts about Jack and the whole sordid soap-operatic tale to this relatively young-looking man with glasses and a sweater-vest.

"So this is about a guy?" Dr. Sweatervest asks.

I'm not particularly fond of his dismissive tone. My eyes scan the room for his credentials. My old therapist, from back home, knew me well. She knew my ticks and tells. She knew how to coddle and challenge me when I needed it. And she would never reduce my feelings to one guy. "No. Yes. No. I don't know."

"Which is it?"

"It is about him, yes, because I lost my virginity to him, and I loved him. *Love*, present tense. And I hate that I love him because I don't think he ever really loved me. But what's hurt the most is that he made me feel safe and beautiful and wanted. But only when the doors were closed. And the second his friend from home caught him, us, he disregarded me. His friend called me fat. I heard it. And Jack said nothing. After I told him about my body dysmorphia." My leg twitches so violently, I have to steady it with my hand.

"Body dysmorphia?" Sweatervest scribbles in his pad.

I nod. "Jack's parents said such awful things, and when his friend alluded to Jack dating someone, he flat-out denied me. Said there was nobody. *In front of me*."

"How'd that make you feel?" Sweatervest shows zero emotion. Damn! Come on, Sweatervest, give me something.

"Like I'm not worth anything." I take a deep breath and lick my dry lips. When I can exhale, I tell him about the scene in the dining hall with Benny and how he confronted me about purging. "I had this, like, really quick thought that scared the fuck outta me." I look at him, and he leans forward, waiting. "I wished I were . . . dead."

He doesn't react. Like, at all. But he says, "Is that a thought you often have?"

I sit with that for a second. "No. Not in a realistic, substantial way."

"Have you ever come up with plans or done research on how to—"

I don't let him finish. "No, never. I don't want to take my own life." As I say the words, I know them to be the truth. "I was just overwhelmed by my eating disorder and all the stuff happening with Jack, and it was like I couldn't breathe. I can't even have a moment where I'm not consumed by food or the pain I'm in, and I just . . ."

He takes a deep breath. "Oftentimes, those thoughts are your body wanting to experience relief. It doesn't mean you actually want to die."

"I don't." I barely choke that out as my bottom lip trembles. "I just don't want to be in pain anymore. From Jack, from the eating disorder I've had on and off since high school, and the body dysmorphia I've pretty much always had. I just want to feel . . . me. Not that I know what that even feels like."

He narrows his eyes. "And how does Jack tie into your feelings about your body?"

"If Jack, the person I loved, can't even defend or claim me, how can I claim myself?"

"So," he starts, "your emotions in regards to your body are connected to Jack?"

"No, but I'd had everything under control until things with us fell apart."

"Is that true?" Sweatervest puts the pad on his desk and leans forward. "In my experience, it's a lifelong battle learning to cope with body dysmorphia, especially when it's tied to eating disorders, and while this experience with Jack might have triggered a relapse, I'd be interested to know if you had those compulsions before what happened between you?"

"Your experience? What are you? Twenty? You don't look much older than me."

He leans back. "Is my age important to you?"

I shrug. Because, of course, it's not. I'm being an asshole, and I know it.

"It seems like you're avoiding my question."

I fall into silence, which feels like it's crushing me with everything left unsaid. "It's like the monster under my bed at night. I know it's there when I turn off the lights, so I can never sleep. And the lights are always off."

"That's interesting." Dr. Sweatervest bites the corner of his lips as he thinks. "Let's work with that, the monster under the bed. Oftentimes, I find it may be helpful to personify your feelings. I want you to think about your body dysmorphia as a physical being. What does it look like to you? Close your eyes, and what do you see?"

I sigh, and though I hesitate, I do as he instructs. "I don't know." I pause. Then I see it. "It's kind of amorphous. No, not really amorphous so much as a giant flesh-colored blob peppered with trash." But as I describe it, it changes shape. "No, wait, it's large and hairy and . . ." I stop because it mutates into a form that takes my breath away. "It looks like my dad."

"What would you say to this being?"

"I'd tell him that I'm so fucking mad at him. For all the times he said I was too chubby then ditched the word *chubby* for *fat*. Said I needed to lose weight when I was ten because I looked like a potato. He started calling me *Taters* in public because it was the only way he could make sure I wouldn't reach for an extra slice of cake. When I heard him tell Mom that I'd never find anyone to love me because of how I looked, I cried myself to sleep. He said the way I chewed when I ate made me look like a garbage truck. Then, when I started to take laxatives and purge, he told me I looked good, and I thought he was proud of me, so maybe I was finally doing something right. But I was destroying my body to make him love me."

I don't realize that I'm crying until I open my eyes and my vision is blurry and my cheeks are wet.

"How do you feel?" Sweatervest asks.

"Like shit." I pause. "But a tiny bit better."

"Have you ever thought of writing your father a letter? You don't have to send it, but it could be a way to say everything you might not be able to in person."

His suggestion makes sense. My old therapist told me something similar. I've started one a zillion times but always gave up and deleted it because it feels like nothing will ever change.

"It's something to consider. Also, it may help to think of your body dysmorphia as a separate personified being or creature. It could allow you to identify and separate it from yourself so that you can identify some of the compulsions to act on the way you feel and instead develop healthy coping mechanisms."

"What do you mean?"

"How do you cope with how you feel about yourself and your body?"

"Now, or before?"

"How about before your recent relapse?"

"My old therapist tried to get me to work on changing the language I used. She had me stand in front of a mirror and describe my body."

"How did that make you feel?"

"Sometimes, I was lying so she would think I was making progress. Other times it felt good because I could see my weight loss and I looked less like a monster." I cover my stomach with a pillow from his couch. "But most of the time, it really hurt to just have to look in the mirror at all because I never saw what I wanted.

There's also the added layer of me trying to figure out if I'm nonbinary or genderqueer or whatever, and sometimes it felt hard to breathe."

"So you also question your gender identity? Talk to me about that."

"It's not like something that's always on my mind, but yeah. I reject the gender binary. And I don't know if I like the terms *nonbinary* or *genderfluid*. *Genderqueer* seems to fit best, but that also feels very nebulous, especially because, like, some people think *genderqueer* means *transgender* because those terms get lumped together. Some genderqueer people are trans, and some aren't. Sometimes because of this I just feel very . . . invisible, you know? Like technically *genderqueer* and *nonbinary* fall under the trans umbrella, but I'm not trans. I know that much for sure. But we don't have language for that nuance, really, and I spent a lot of time trying to define myself: If I'm questioning my place within the binary, does that mean I'm not necessarily cis? Maybe. But maybe not. Is it an either/or thing? Is it just another binary?"

Dr. Sweatervest nods. "What do you think?"

I shake my head. "When I came out as nonbinary, even though I wasn't ready to do so—something I created went viral, and it just sort of happened—I ended up losing a best friend who started talking about me behind my back. It made me feel like I wasn't valid at all as myself. Even though I knew who I was without all the terms and labels. But then came the expectations from others to define me based on what they saw or thought. It felt like I was attacked from all angles—internal and external, you know? I just want it to be okay that I am who I am. Gay. Nonbinary. Queer. He, maybe they, but always Chase Arthur." I brace myself for his judgment.

"Why do you feel there's a need to define yourself in that way?" he asks.

"Because it feels like something I *should* do. Put a name to the feelings I have that don't fit into any boxes. Right?"

"*Who* said you should do that?"

I sit with that for a few moments.

"I'm not going to make you look into the mirror because of your body dysmorphia. But I remember you mentioning having sex with Jack and the way he made you feel about yourself and your body. Was his validation important to you?"

"Yeah, of course," I say, and Sweatervest nods, prompting me to elaborate. "Because if the guy you're having sex with says you're sexy, that's a boost to the ego."

"Did you believe him?"

"At the time, yes."

"But not now?"

I don't know the answer to that.

"Did he ever invalidate your gender identity?"

"No, he wouldn't. I told him that I was trying to figure things out, and he didn't bat an eyelash. That meant a lot because he made me feel like my feelings mattered and that I wasn't just . . . I don't know, abnormal."

"I bet that was affirming."

"It was. It's like, why shouldn't it be normal to wonder where you fall on the gender spectrum, right? I don't know. I don't want to change anything about me. He sort of made me feel like I was sexy and desirable, and through his eyes, I looked at myself differently. I used to hate my hairy chest, but he loved it. He worshipped other parts of my body, too, and it made me feel like there was nothing wrong with me."

Sweatervest's smiling, and it's weird.

"What?"

"As you're talking, do you want me to tell you what I'm hearing?" he asks, and I nod. "I'm hearing things you might actually like about your body."

Huh. Is he right? "I don't know."

"We're almost out of time, but I'd like for you to continue working on your coping mechanisms until our session next week. Take a look at how you're coping currently and how you might be avoiding your feelings. Don't push them away. Confront them. What I heard from you today is that there's a lot of uncertainty, but there's also a lot of love for yourself. Perhaps it's easier to rationalize your emotions as something you can't change or as things that are wrong with you because you think you can control a situation by overeating or purging. But what that does is prevent you from dealing with the root causes."

"Which are . . ."

He smiles, but it's caring. "This is just our first session, so I can't say, but I suspect, based on what you said, that confronting your issues with your dad may help you get to the root. You seem to place a lot of value in your weight, and you've let shame and fear override your rational decision-making, which perpetuates the cycle of believing the fictional monster you see in the mirror is reality, which then allows you to rationalize your eating disorder. This may also play a role in your gender identity. Though your eating disorder and relationship with gender are not connected, maybe you're conflating the two because one—the eating disorder—is controllable, while the other—gender identity—is not. You don't have to do this, and hopefully, through our sessions, you can begin to see that for yourself. There is nothing wrong with questioning your identity. And maybe there doesn't have to be an answer, despite what people like your former friend may lead you to believe based on their actions."

No answer? That seems to fly in the face of literally everything I've ever known. Everybody rushes to label every little part of themselves.

"Isn't that how we make sense of the world?"

"Who is *we*?" he asks. "I'm talking about *you*. Sometimes, there isn't any way all of you can be wrapped up in one pretty package with a shiny bow. And that's okay." He lets me sit with that for a minute before continuing, "This is a process. This will not happen overnight. But this starts with you. Not your father or your former best friend or Jack. You cannot change your father's past actions. You cannot control how Jack acted or what your former friend believes about you. But you can control how you cope with the stressors associated with each of them that connect to your identity and disorder. How do you feel about that?"

I feel like he just read the hell out of me. But it makes sense. I can't control how other people treat me or see me. But maybe I can change the way I see myself.

Maybe.

I'm not there yet, and I don't know when I will be, which sucks, but I do feel a bit lighter walking out.

And then I see Jack in the waiting room. He doesn't notice me at first, and I think about ducking into an open room, but why should I? He takes off his hat, and his hair is a disaster. He's not wearing his dirty bathrobe anymore, so that's an improvement, but he looks like he hasn't showered. At least he's in the counseling center, though. Maybe he's finally working on his issues. A little twinge of hope warms my chest, but it's dangerous because I can't control how Jack processes his feelings, so I have to let that go.

He looks up and catches my gaze.

For a second, we're connecting again, and I want him to be that person I thought he was. I remember what Dr. Sweatervest said, and I think I need to be the one to walk away this time. I have to be strong for myself. It starts here, now, with Jack because I can control that, even if it means I may never have closure with him. Leila and Dad are going to prove much harder, but I'll figure that out when the time is right.

The weight of walking away from Jack without a word nearly crushes me.

But I do it.

And when I get back to my dorm, I sit down and pour every ounce of anger I'm feeling into an email to Dad. Everything I said to Dr. Sweatervest finds its way into a draft, and it feels a lot like putting aloe on a sunburn. It doesn't make it go away, but it lessens the sting. I stare at the carefully worded monsters until my eyes cross and I fall asleep.

23

Classes are intense, but none as much as the seminar.

We're in the final stages of rendering our shorts. Basically, we're bringing this shit to life, pulling it all together, making sure what we're transitioning from hand to computer matches our visions, storyboards, and color boards. The hardest part is generating the look, which is based on Van Gogh's *Starry Night*. It's painterly, heavy on the brushstrokes, and it's been a bit of a battle between making the landscape look abstract and dreamy while being deliberate in grounding the Prince, the Knight, and the Witch in a more Disney style of character animation.

It's fucking hard—and I barely sleep—but it's been helping me cope with everything Dr. Sweatervest said. I'm trying my best to channel my energy into the things I can control. Getting lost in the world I'm creating has been the best medicine, even if staring at the Prince all day reminds me of Jack. I try to separate the two, but meeting him inspired the story, and Chloe and Sofía are quick to point out that art is pain, and pain is art. Or something.

Professor McPherson perches atop her desk, unwrapping a Twix from a bag she sent around the room. "Happy Thanksgiving, everyone. Have a free sugar rush."

Everyone is already packing up, and I glance around the room. We all look smacked, a huddled mass of dark circles and slumped shoulders—all of us except for Leila, who is conspicuously absent and has been for the past week.

"Remember," the professor continues. "When classes resume next Monday, you'll have two weeks until the final showcase. Invitations are going out to all your parents, but for those whose families live far, it will be broadcasted live on CIA's website. I'll email you all with the information. Most of you are in great shape, but everyone still has much to do to finalize their shorts, so make sure you utilize your breaks well."

"Hear that?" Chloe asks. "That means you." She winks.

"I'm not going home," I say.

I don't need to tell them about how I don't want to be obligated to see Dad because I'm not ready to tell him how I feel yet. There are still so many feelings I have to work out. Every time I practice what I might say to him, I end up screaming incoherently at my reflection in the bathroom mirror, and Benny has to make sure I'm okay. I can't seem to untangle the mess Dad's made. Plus, Thanksgiving is a horrible holiday for someone suffering from an eating disorder and weight shame.

"So I'll be here, working my ass off to figure out the end of this short. By this time next week, once I get your approvals, of course, we'll be in the home stretch."

I hope.

Sofia drums her fingers together. "Interesting." She narrows her eyes. "Chlo and I will also be sticking around. I believe that means we *have* to hang."

"Why aren't y'all going home?" I ask.

"My family and I boycott the colonizer holiday," Sofía explains. "We usually visit family in Colombia, but I have *way* too much work to do. This semester is killing me softly."

"I'm trying to save money so that when we're studying abroad in Los Angeles next semester, we're not living solely off ramen," Chloe says, looking to Sofía.

"That too," Sofía adds. "So we might as well be alone together because this place is a literal ghost town over breaks."

"Buuuuut," Chloe interjects. "The cool thing is that Aguyack Mountain opens this week to kick off the annual ski season, and CIA always organizes a bus for students who stay on campus to go enjoy the first, usually manmade, snow."

"You ski?" I ask.

"Coming from Nola, you wouldn't think," Chloe says. "But I've had to learn to tough out the conditions up here. And what better way than to go hurtling down a mountain at a billion miles an hour?"

I laugh. "A billion?"

She nods sharply. "Sure feels like it."

"So?" Sofía nudges. "What do ya say? Thanksgiving at our place? We'll do a mass Uber Eats takeout from all the best places in town and binge-watch movies all night in our pajamas. Maybe dabble in a little weed. You in?"

Though I'm definitely worried about being surrounded by what will probably be mounds of starchy, bready, deep-fried fast foods,

I'd be lying if I said being with my new friends didn't sound like the best kind of Thanksgiving.

Plus, get me high AF. Maybe I'll finally forget about Jack.

I'm on my way to Dr. Sweatervest's office for my second session when I see Jack walking out of the campus center.

He stops.

Maybe he's about to wave. Or do that pathetic head nod boys do. Or even speak something resembling words. I don't need a poem, just a hello, a five-letter word that may not mean anything to him but would mean everything to me.

But I recognize the faraway look in his eyes; it's one I've caught when he didn't think I was watching, and he would travel someplace in his mind closed off to me. Yet, at the same time, the way his body is turned toward me, the stillness of his movements tell me that he's just as rooted as I am.

I can't break this connection. I want to go to him and grab him and hold him and tell him that I love him but also hate him.

A loud group of people bursts out from the campus center double doors and breaks my concentration. I look away for one second.

But that's enough time for Jack to dart out of sight.

My second session with Dr. Sweatervest wastes no time diving into the muck.

"How did you feel about our last session?"

I ignore his question. "I just saw Jack."

Sweatervest waits for me to continue.

"He didn't even acknowledge me."

"Is that important to you? To be acknowledged by him?"

"Yeah, I mean . . ." I grind my teeth and go silent. "Never mind."

"You don't have to censor yourself in this office." He smiles, and it's reassuring.

I take a deep breath. "Of course Jack has to acknowledge me! Just a few weeks ago, he told me he loved me. He was inside of me, for crying out loud!"

Okay, calm down, Chase.

"Sorry for the overshare, but it's just . . . I don't understand how he can treat love like a switch that can be flipped so quick. Is that normal?"

I think of Dad and his quick exit from our home and his marriage, and I get hot with anger.

"One day, you just wake up and think, *I don't love this person.* Because, fuck. I don't know much, but I know how I feel about Jack is so complicated I could cry at any minute then smile because of how he made me feel. If I could turn off my love for Jack . . ." My voice trails off.

"Would you?" Sweatervest asks.

"No," I say quickly, and he motions for me to continue. "Yeah, it kills me to love him, but loving him was the best thing that's ever happened to me, even though I wasn't enough for him. Big surprise," I mutter. "The hating him part sucks, even though I don't actually hate him. But I have to because if I don't hate him, I wouldn't be able to focus on anything but how I wasn't enough. But even if I could turn off the love part, it wouldn't negate the pain. Right?"

When I finish, he nods, and his eyes narrow in on me. Before he can say anything, I add, "So how come he gets to turn it off?"

Dr. Sweatervest clears his throat. "I'd like to focus on you, not Jack. You can't control what Jack does and how he thinks or what he's really thinking."

What he's *really* thinking? "So you think Jack might love me?" I interrupt.

"I don't think that's a question anyone but Jack can answer. And that might not be an answer you ever get."

Suddenly I can't breathe. I want to cry and scream and curse out Dr. Sweatervest. But that's not helpful. I avoid looking at him, opting instead to study the pattern of the carpet in his office.

He continues, "So I'd like us to focus on you. Because loving somebody is a wonderful thing, and being loved by somebody is a beautiful feeling, and you should be allowed to feel joy among the pain. So one thing I'd like us to work on is how these feelings are tied to your self-esteem and self-worth—your weight, your relationship with your father, and Jack—and how you can get to the point where *you* are *enough* for *you*."

Oof. That hits hard. I stare at him, not sure what to say. Then I ask, "How do I get to that place?"

"That's the hard part," he says. "And it's going to take a lot of mindfulness, time, and the recognition that it won't happen overnight. It's like climbing a mountain. You have to be aware of the terrain while also listening to your body and mind."

"That hardly seems fair."

He smirks. "It doesn't, does it? But it will happen. I'll help you get to the top of that mountain." He waits for me to agree, and when I do, he says, "Let's begin."

Benny, Rhett, and Xavier are hanging out in my room when I get back to the dorm. Benny and Rhett are all over each other right in front of Xavier, which has become pretty standard practice. It's always a bit weird because even though both Benny and Xavier insist they were never really a thing, they sort of were? I don't know, maybe I'm not an enlightened gay yet, but it would be damn near impossible for me to just casually hang out with Jack and another person he might be dating. The thought alone is damn near over-whelming, and I have to fight the monsters in my head who seek to draw me further toward my fears.

Luckily, Benny is quick to distract. "Chase, settle something for me. Who is the better kisser, X or Rhett?"

"Uh."

"Pucker up, buttercup," Xavier says, holding out his arms toward me.

I shove him away. Not because I don't want to kiss Xavier because hello, he's gorgeous, but this is way too uncomfortable.

"See, I told you that would get his attention," Benny says.

"You're an ass," I deadpan.

Benny smiles sweetly. "I know. But we're all about to head out soon and wanted to make sure you're okay. And you can still change your mind and come home with me for a Big Fat Italian Thanks-giving at the Gorgas'."

I resist the urge to make a *Real Housewives of New Jersey* joke.

"Me too," Xavier says. "Invitation still stands."

"Same," Rhett offers in a vaguely Southern twang. "Though Turkey Day at my house generally consists of boxed mac and cheese in front of the TV while watching football."

There's a bit of sadness in his eyes, and I'm realizing now that in all the times I passed him on my way to his and Jack's dorm or casually hanging out with Benny while he's there, I don't actually know anything about Rhett other than his penchant for Febreze and that Benny tells me Rhett sometimes cries after sex. Which is more information than I needed, frankly.

"Why are you even going home?" Benny asks. "Just come to my house."

Rhett shrugs. "I'll probably end up there after I come out to my parents."

My brows raise. "You're doing that *this* weekend?"

"It's a bit cliché, isn't it?" Benny says.

Rhett elbows him. "Shut up. Not everyone is like you three. It took me a while to not hate myself enough to admit that I liked Benny." He's looking right at me. "Benny's been out for as long as I can remember, and our school never cared, but just because it seems like the outside world is cool doesn't actually mean that it is behind closed doors."

"You know," Benny adds. "There's a reason why I didn't come out to you two"—he looks to Xavier and me—"and Aaron on the group chat over the summer. Even though this is a queer liberal paradise of a college, you just never know."

"Side note, I barely see Aaron," I add.

"Same, and I live with the guy," Xavier says. "Aaron's always at his girlfriend's. I think she's a sophomore and lives off campus. He can stay there. I like the privacy." X shrugs, and his phone goes off. "Ahh, that's my ride." He wraps his arms around me and squeezes.

"You need help with your bags?" Benny asks. When Xavier nods, Benny's face falls. "Oh, I was only being polite. I didn't mean— ugh, *fine*."

Benny slings one of Xavier's bags over his shoulders, and you would think he's being forced to lift a car with his bare hands by the way he moans and grunts and whines as they trudge out the door, leaving Rhett and me alone.

Well, this is awkward. We've never been alone together. Ever.

And all I want to do is ask him about Jack. The thought pulls at me.

"So," Rhett starts. "How are you?"

Oh. Small talk. Cute. "I'm, you know. Living. Two weeks ago, I don't know what the answer would have been. But two sessions of Dr. Sweatervest and tossing myself into my schoolwork sure does keep the mind occupied."

Rhett nods and dry swallows. Then his voice gets low. "He's not doing so well."

I don't have to ask who he's talking about.

"Sorry, Benny told me not to say anything, but . . ." Rhett looks around the room because, yeah, this feels uncomfortable. He's giving off a weird energy, from his stance to his tone. "Jack doesn't talk to me really, but I see it in his face. Doesn't go to class much. Or even crew practice. And a couple days ago, I caught him crying. When I asked what was wrong, he just turned over in his bed."

I don't really know what to do with this information. Am I supposed to be grateful for a small window into Jack? Am I supposed to go all scorched earth and shit-talk Jack to Rhett, saying he deserves to cry alone in his room? Because he doesn't, and all I want to do is go find him and hug him and tell him it'll be okay. That I love him. That I'll wait for him to love me back. And if that never happens, then all I want for him is to be happy. Then I hear Dr. Sweatervest in my head telling me that I should prioritize myself, that I need to love myself before somebody else can love me, and theorizing what I think Jack is thinking does nothing to help me move forward.

Benny barrels back in like a hurricane and sweeps Rhett up in a storm of "we have to go, our ride's here, 'bye Chase, love you, happy Thanksgiving!" and before I can say anything, they're gone.

I'm alone.

Again.

But this time, it feels different. Sure, I'm physically alone, and I don't have Jack anymore. Rae is probably grandma-driving down the highway toward our hometown, and she won't pick up the phone because she's got her hands firmly at ten and two. But I think that, for the first time, I can be okay with the quiet. If I can allow my mind to stop spinning and overthinking.

I have a lot of work to do on myself and *for* myself, to *love* myself, and maybe this is the perfect time to start.

24

Yeah, all that loneliness and "working on myself" stuff? Screw that.

It's not that I want to ignore the mountain of bullshit I have to climb, but have you ever climbed a mountain? You need the proper footwear and outdoor gear and have to remember shit like hydrating and not wearing underwear that'll chafe. Honestly, it's easier to just drive to the top and stand at the lookout point. You get the same level of awe, I'd imagine, without all the physical and mental exertion of actually climbing.

Knowing that I won't run into Jack this week does help because at least I know the terrain. I can wander through the campus center without fear of bumping into him. It's freeing to be able to dip into the art building and lose hours to "The Prince Who Captured Lightning," even though I still can't figure out how to end the damn thing. I'm too hung up on Jack to separate him and our story from the Prince and his spark with the Knight. So I'm ignoring *that* part for now.

But I'm at least following Dr. Sweatervest's advice of being mindful of my body. I'm logging everything I eat so that I don't overeat, and though I do go to the gym every day, I'm not killing myself. I'm still not looking into mirrors, but I'm trying my best to give voice to all the things I love about myself and my body.

In our last session, we came up with a mantra where I focused on a few things I admire about myself and read them until I believed them. My homework is to add to the list as much as I can. So far, I have:

1. Grapefruit calves
2. Thick thighs, the good kind
3. Cool gray, wavy hair
4. Good artist
5. Great friend.

Technically, Rae insisted I add that last one, but I'm counting it as something I came up with if Dr. Sweatervest asks.

One of the other things Sweatervest suggested was asking my friends to check in on me. Opening up to them. Being vulnerable. It's an exercise in building trust, even though I think it could end horribly. But I'm trying my best. So I spend an inordinate amount of time at Sofía and Chloe's off-campus house. The more I get to know them, the safer I feel around them, and the more comfortable I feel baring my soul. With a little help from some pot, of course.

On Thanksgiving Day, I'm not over their house for five minutes before Sofía dangles a ziplock bag of mossy weed and a small handblown glass bowl with pink and yellow swirls. "No shoptalk tonight. Only mellow fun times. You down?" she asks, and I nod. "Chlo, load him up." She gently tosses the bag and the bowl at Chloe.

I run a hand through my unkempt hair. "What is that thing?"

Chloe blinks at me. "You've never seen a bowl?"

"A what now?" I ask. "I'm used to the pens."

"Oh, the shit that kills you?" Chloe sucks her teeth. "This is the only way to smoke unless you have a joint, but that takes too long. This is way healthier."

Sofía chuckles. "Just don't pull too hard. We've seen many a rookie pull so deep, they end up violently coughing and blowing all the pot onto the ground."

Chloe instructs me on how to place my lips on the mouthpiece while holding one finger over the vent, lighting with my free hand, and sucking in the smoke from the embers. "You're gonna cough, so hand the bowl over gently. If you drop it, I drop you."

"She's not kidding," Sofía adds. "Here, I'll help you." She holds it and lights it for me. The lighter flicks and ignites the grass for me, and I pull too gently.

"I didn't get anything," I say as a tiny wisp of vapor escapes my lips.

"Don't be shy. Suck harder," Sofía commands.

"That's what he said," I say with a smirk, and they laugh. She places the bowl to my lips again, and I inhale deeply like I'm gasping for oxygen. It burns as I trap it in my lungs.

"Hold it," Sofía says, ripping the bowl away from me and sucking down any remaining smoke from the embers.

I can't hold it any longer; I feel like my lungs are about to explode. I gag as an endless white cloud streams from my mouth, and I cough uncontrollably.

"You're gonna feel that," Chloe says, grabbing it from Sofía once she gets a hit. She holds the smoke inside and slowly lets it seep from her nostrils. She lies back on the couch across from the one Sof and I are on, wholly unburdened, and closes her eyes.

We pass around the bowl until it's kicked, and I don't really feel anything aside from my lungs burning.

Until I super feel it.

I'm transfixed on the two couches, and a memory of Taylor and me as kids swells.

"We should push these couches together and lie in the middle. My sister and I used to do that. We pretended it was a ship and—"

"Say no more," Chloe says, eyes still closed, body rising slowly and unsteady like the undead. "I love this idea. This idea is life. Batten down the hatches, mates. We're setting sails on the high seas." She stands up.

"The fuck are you saying?" Sofía asks. "Are you having a stroke?"

Chloe places her hand over her heart for no reason at all. "Perhaps, yes."

Have you ever moved furniture completely blazed out of your mind? I wouldn't recommend it. My arms are Jell-O, and I'm utterly useless, stopping every three inches to laugh and fall on the floor with Chloe as Sofía stares at us from where she sits cross-legged. But eventually, we somehow push the two open ends of the couch together so that we have to crawl up and over the arms to get inside. Chloe gathers blankets and tosses them in before diving on top of them, arms splayed.

"We have to order the Hangry Cookie," Sofía says. "Perfect Thanksgiving dinner."

"What the hell is the Hangry Cookie?" I ask.

"Shut up!" Sofía says. "You don't know?!" Quickly, she pulls up the menu on her phone. "Custom cookies freshly baked. They are literally the size of a personal pizza. You can get any dough base they have blended with any of their mix-ins. I'm a peanut butter cookie with crushed Oreos and chocolate sprinkles kinda girl. And they come warm and gooey, and I swear it's better than dick."

Chloe's eyes go wide. "I see no lies."

I hear my therapist's voice in my head telling me to be vulnerable and open up to my new friends in ways I'm too afraid to about my eating disorder, but I'm high, so that voice is drowned out by: *Get a giant-ass cookie.* Which I do. Birthday cake dough. Rainbow sprinkles. White chocolate chips. Pink candy glitter. It's so gay, I have to pose with it as they take turns snapping pictures.

Then it comes time to actually eat it, and all I can think is I'm wrestling with the urge to shovel it all in my mouth, which will most certainly lead to me running to the bathroom to purge, or to not even touch it at all.

"You look green," Sofía says. "What's wrong? Is it undercooked?"

"Nah, he doesn't eat," Chloe says. "Ever notice how he just pushes food around?"

I don't say anything. My jaw goes slack. It takes me gnawing on my nails before their faces soften, and each of them reaches out a hand.

"What's wrong?" Chloe says. "Talk to us."

I take a deep breath. This is the part where I have to get a bit vulnerable. "I have a fucked-up relationship with food." I don't look at either of them as I tell them about my eating disorder and body dysmorphia and how much I've struggled over the past month. Neither of them takes their hands away until I'm done, but they only do so to move in closer and wrap me in a three-way hug.

Chloe is the first to pull away. "I'm sorry for what I said."

"You didn't know," I say, picking at my cuticles. "It's totally fine."

For a while, neither of them says anything. Probably from weed inertia or a warm-cookie–induced coma.

Chloe squints her eyes. "I don't know if this is a horrible thing to say, but for what it's worth, I never got the sense you had body issues."

Sofía smacks her arm. "Chlo!"

"I don't mean it in a bad way," Chloe says quickly. "But, like, take the Knight character in your short. We never mentioned it because we figured it was intentional, but his face looks just like yours. And he's got this hot dad-bod, but you always animate him with such"—she gestures with her hands like Benny when he tries to act super Italian/masculine—"confidence."

Sofía's lips thin into a thoughtful grin. "She's right. Take Disney movies. Usually, the heroes are slim and cut and muscular. Totally disproportionate to real bodies. And it's the villains who are on the bigger side."

"Fat," I say. "You can say it. Fat is almost always an 'evil' characteristic."

She nods. "But the Knight feels so realistic. It's refreshing. I agree with Chlo. I thought you were making a statement about your own body with him. It's empowering, actually."

I never thought of it like that. It definitely wasn't something I was consciously thinking about, but when I did the original animation last year that went viral, I guess I was animating myself.

Or, rather, a version of me that I wanted people to see. I never meant to make a statement, but it's heartening to hear that Chloe and Sofía see a certain level of empowerment there.

It's strange, actually, because I remember being younger and signing up for Instagram and searching out hashtags like *body positivity* or spending hours cruising Reddit forums praising cubs and chubs in the gay community. But for every twenty positive comments on a picture some brave soul posted, there was always one truly awful, viscerally disgusting one that stuck with me. Never mind the guys who were basically ripped bodybuilders complaining about hating their bodies. It was a bombardment of mixed messages telling me that even if I were Michelangelo's *David*, I'd still hate myself, still wouldn't be enough. Then I'd inevitably end up down a scrolling rabbit hole where I'd click over to some hot guy's profile and find a whole manifesto decrying the body positivity movement as unhealthy, fat people as lazy, and it'd reinforce every horrible belief I held about my own body.

All I've ever wanted was to feel comfortable, whole, *normal* in my skin.

Maybe that's why the Knight feels confident. I gave him what I wish I had.

I tell Chloe and Sofía this, and when I'm done, I feel breathless and want to cry.

"Can I tell you something?" Sofía asks. "I was drawn to you that first day of McPherson's seminar because I saw something in your eyes and the way you spoke. It was earnest and real. And I remembered your viral short when I saw your flip. It shouldn't be revolutionary to see a curvaceous, cute character as a hero in animation, but it felt like working with you would be. I had to be part of whatever you were creating." She bites her lip. "I've struggled with my weight for years, too. Hated myself. Tried, like, every diet. It's bad enough having to combat constant racism for being a brown Colombian, but add body image standards to that, and oof."

"Same, just sub Black for Colombian," Chloe says.

My cheeks heat with a mix of embarrassment and anger because I never really stopped to think about how much the world judges and hates anyone who isn't thin, cisgender, straight, male, abled, and white; I've had my own struggles, but I will never understand what Chloe and Sofía have experienced, and they're such beautiful souls, inside and out. I wish I could take all their pain away.

"Sometimes, I just didn't want to give people more reasons to look at me. So I went hard at the gym to keep myself tight. My ass even dropped money on those Insta ads for that tea that supposedly makes you lose weight. Scam," Chloe says.

I raise my hand. "Same. My mom and I did Atkins when I was ten. I've never heard a doctor yell so loudly as mine did when he found out I was eating a pound of bacon a day but stayed away from apples."

"I do Weight Watchers every spring because of my mom," Sofía adds.

"Oh, see, my dad used to say Weight Watchers was for women," I say. "And the way he said *women* was so gross. Like he was disgusted by the thought that I would do something designated for women. So that was a fun additional layer of subtle trauma, which I've definitely had to work through. Still am. I don't know."

I remember what Dr. Sweatervest said about not needing to nail down my identity with a label, but I can't help feeling an itch to define myself. Chloe and Sofía seem unfazed, and I realize it really is just me pressuring myself.

"Fuck that guy. Ugh. You know my dad threatened to send me to fat camp over the summer? Literal fat camp if I didn't join a sport to lose weight. Because that's manly."

"Shiiiiiit." Chloe, still high as a kite, struggles to rise to her feet inside the couch ship. "Look at us. We are three beautiful people. Thick and curvy and delicious. Black, Colombian, and queer queens who have let this shitty world take power from us."

Sofía leans in. "I think I know what's coming."

"You're damn right," Chloe responds. "Let's take it back." She dives across the ship and grabs her phone. Cookie platters bounce, and crumbs fly everywhere, but she doesn't care. "Sof, get the scarves."

"Scarves?" I ask.

Chloe scrambles out of the ship and disappears down the hall into her room. When she emerges, she's carrying a bundle of colorful fabric and tosses it at our feet. Sofía grabs a cerulean one with sequins in varying shades of blue and wraps it around her shoulders like an old Hollywood starlet. Chloe goes for a blood-orange-and-yellow one with specks of gold and wraps it around her hair, completing the look with a pair of gold aviator sunglasses.

I spot a white, sheer one with silver and opal teardrop sparkles that looks like an ethereal wedding gown dream. My fingertips graze the fabric. It's so soft, almost like silk.

"Go for it." Chloe presses play on a Lady Gaga song called "Hair Body Face."

Following Sofía's lead, I wrap it around my shoulders and start to shimmy with the beat of the song. Chloe hops aboard the ship, and the three of us dance until we can't breathe, scream-singing that we're perfect in each other's eyes and about how much we love ourselves. Sofía whips her long, straight black hair over her shoulders in a display of fierce hairography. Chloe gives Naomi Campbell a run for her money with her supermodel face, and me? I am hand-on-hips, flaunting my curves.

For the first time since Jack, I feel powerful.

But this time, it's on my own terms.

25

A plume of gray smoke billows from the exhaust of the idling CIA bus the next morning. After a phone call with Mom where I get the rundown on Turkey Day at home—Taylor spent the morning with Dad and Krissy before going with Mom to see our grandparents, who of course asked if I'd gained the freshman fifteen—I meet Chloe and Sofía outside the campus center, decked in my best ski outfit.

Chloe snaps her fingers at my hot-pink ski pants and snow-white jacket with pink, yellow, and black splatter paint design. "Work! If I'd known this was a fashion show extravaganza, I would've worn my ball gown."

She's in a full one-piece tan snowsuit with a subtle camouflage print that looks like leopard spots. Sofía also has a one-piece suit, but hers is jet black with silver accents in the seams.

"My sister picked this out for me," I say, modeling best as I can, though I probably look like a penguin waddling and flailing its flippers.

"Your sister has impeccable taste," Sofía says.

"She's excited to meet my friends," I say.

"Is she coming up for the showcase?" Chloe asks, and I nod.

The bus driver peeks his head out. "Last call for Aguyack Mountain." He stares directly at us, the last three standing.

We trudge on board and find our seats, which is easy since there aren't that many other students on campus. As the bus is about to take off, the driver slams on the brakes to pick up some random student barreling toward the bus. He's carrying a pair of skis and has a boot bag slung over his shoulders.

Nope, *not* a random.

"Is that . . ." Sofía begins.

Jack. "Yep," I say.

He's panting as he grips the metal handrails and propels himself up. His cheeks are pink, and his eyes sparkle and, fuck, I hate him and hate that I love him. My chest heaves, and I feel a bit breathless, so I look away, pull the wool hat low over my eyes and slump against the window so he doesn't see me. Sofía, who is next to me, does the same, almost acting like a shield, and Chloe, who sits in the row across from us, turns toward the window, so her back is facing the aisle. Thankfully, he plops down in the front row toward the door, and I hold my breath for what feels like the entire drive.

When we get to the mountain, we wait until Jack is off the bus and heading into the lodge before we bother getting up. The girls defer to me, and I tell them to be cool, act naturally, and we'll try our best to avoid him. But inside, I'm literally dying a thousand deaths a minute.

Since neither Chloe, Sofía, nor I have ski or snowboard equipment, we head to the rental area of the lodge, which means I don't have to worry about running into Jack for a solid thirty minutes.

By the time we make it out onto the mountain and up to one of the only two chairlifts, I'm finally able to breathe.

As the tips of my skis graze the ramp at the top of the lift and I glide down the snowy slope, I'm alive in a way I only am when skiing. Dad was an avid skier, and Taylor and I grew up in the mountains every winter. No matter how much our family struggled, we somehow always found a way to get on skis, and I started when I was five. Dad insisted it was too late and made Taylor start when she was three, much to Mom's chagrin.

There aren't many things I give Dad credit for, but I'll admit I'm happy he stuck me in ski school and forced me out of the safety of the pizza wedge, because as I skate under snowmaking machines and down the few open trails, I'm able to disconnect my mind from Jack. I feel the mountain beneath my blades and the crisp, clean, pine-scented air that envelops me and whooshes past.

Sofía, daredevil on a snowboard that she is, skids to a halt at the opening of an ungroomed tree trail. "Last one to the bottom buys hot cocoa!"

Chloe looks to me, and she registers the hesitation on my face. The last time I was on an ungroomed tree trail was with Dad when he tried to teach me how to do what he did on skis. Except Dad is an expert. Skilled like an Olympic skier. And I know I'm extra as fuck, but that's not an exaggeration. He floats on top of powder with a beautiful fluidity that's an art in and of itself. Me? I don't move like that. I'm calculated. Careful. Risk-averse. Precise to a fault. So when Dad tried to teach me to be like him, I spent most of the day on my ass, holding back tears, floundering beneath mounds of snow, and close to having a panic attack.

"You coming?" Chloe asks. "You don't have to, you know. You can cut through the terrain park and meet us at the bottom. Sof won't know." I can see her wink through her rose-tinted goggles.

Do I take the shortcut here? Or do I do the thing that scares me? I hear Taylor's voice in my head, telling me to go find my adventure. Maybe it was never about finding a love to fulfill me but rather taking the risk and loving myself?

It's time to turn my back on the Chase that floundered in the snow. The one who only dreamed of adventure. And actually go on one.

Using my poles as leverage, I slide past Chloe and let out a howling *woo!*

With quick turns and sharp zigzags, we dart around trees and over barely covered rocks. There hasn't been a decent enough snowfall yet, and I'm thanking the gods that I'm using rental skis because Mom would kill me if I scratched the bottom of mine, which she scrimped and saved to buy a few years back. Either way, it doesn't matter because, right now, I'm living in a way I've been too afraid to, for far too long.

I'm fearless.

Okay, maybe not fearless, but I'm not focusing on what makes me afraid. Instead, I'm just enjoying the trail. The right now.

Chloe zips past me, but I don't care because I make it down all the same, unscathed.

I breathe a sigh of relief, and though I don't tell either of them, I'm proud of myself.

After three runs, Chloe is winded and heads into the lodge for hot chocolate. Good thing Sofía is game for more because I'm just getting started.

I lose myself on every new trail. Skiing has always been a place to clear my head, to dream up new animation scenes or ideas, where unformed characters wander into my mind and stir shit up, cause some chaos, or burrow into my subconscious and beg for me to tell their stories.

Today, the Witch from "The Prince Who Captured Lightning" calls to me, paws at me, asking me to tell her story next. An outcast from the Kingdoms Below the Skies, the drag queen sorceress only wanted to find her people, those who would love her, and she strove to protect others like her from ridicule. It's why she cast a spell to hide Thunder from Lightning. Not because she was a vindictive, power-hungry stereotype, but because she knew that the People Below the Skies would come for the male titans because they were lovers.

Her story is one of pain and humility and queer magic. And I can't wait to flesh her out. Perhaps if I win the mentorship, it'll be something I can work on under Professor McPherson's tutelage.

My thoughts drift to Leila and how there once was a time when I would've gone to her to gush about my new idea, so excited to work on it. I think about how she instinctively knew to call Rae the night everything fell apart with Jack and how much that meant to me, and I wonder what she's doing now. She hasn't been in our animation classes for a while. I'd be lying if I said I'm not worried about her. Residual love, I guess. Is that what happens after a breakup, friend or lover? Will there always be a residue of what was? I try to push the thought out of my head and instead focus on the rhythm of steady turns down a slope.

I don't think about Jack until our fifth run of the day, when

Sofía decides she, too, needs a hot chocolate break and leaves me alone. I remember how Jack and I made plans to go skiing together. I was so naive, dreaming that he would invite me to his parents' house in Vermont, and we'd somehow be able to be open in front of them. With each turn, my stomach winces as flashes of memories we never got to make fill my mind.

Jack and I by the fireside in the ski lodge, his head on my shoulders.

Jack writing my thoughts in a poem as I sip hot chocolate.

Jack studying me as I sketch the mountain.

Jack and I exploring forbidden or closed trails.

Jack and I.

Jack.

Jack.

Jack.

By midafternoon, visibility on the mountain is shit. A rogue snowstorm that didn't appear on the weather app I checked this morning is roaring through the area, and I barely make it inside before what looks like a blizzard engulfs the mountain.

Chloe and Sofía are sprawled out over the comfiest-looking couches near a crackling fire. As I strip off my ice-encrusted wool hat and wet gloves, I make my way over to them. I use my sweat-slick palm to wipe my eyes and absentmindedly walk into someone.

"Sorry, I wasn't look—"

I stop walking, moving, breathing.

Because, *of course*, it's Jack.

He swallows hard. "Hey." His face, red from the storm, goes slack. His eyes are a vicious storm themselves, swirling vortexes that pull me into their centers.

I don't know what to say. So I walk past him to get to my friends. They see me, and Chloe starts to wave me over before she sees him, too, which just makes his presence realer and more inescapable.

"I came out to my parents yesterday morning," he shouts.

The entire lodge goes silent. All heads turn toward us like we're the eye of the storm.

My feet are rooted to the weatherproof vinyl floor, but I don't turn around.

"I wanted to tell you, but I didn't know how. That's why I'm here. Back. On campus. Well, not on campus *now*, but you know." He's rambling. "I thought you'd be happy."

"Happy? Why would I be happy about that?"

I don't turn around. My gaze is transfixed on the fire in front of Chloe and Sofía, who both slowly rise to their feet and tiptoe toward me.

"I just thought . . ." He goes silent. I'm perched on the edge of his words, dangling off a cliff, suspended midair. Then I realize he's not going to say anything. He's going to leave me hanging. Again.

"No, you *didn't* think. Not about me," I say, turning around to face him, not willing to let him have the final word and walk away. Not this time. "I'm happy you came out to your parents, and I hope it was for *you*, *not me*. Because I never needed you to come out to them. I needed you to fight for me. Not to toss me away in the trash like words that don't fit your poems. I understand why you didn't say anything in front of your parents because, believe me, I know it's so fucking hard to come out. And I know how much it ate at you. You let Callum say that awful shit about me, and I still would've stood by you while you figured everything out, in private. But you didn't even give me a chance. You walked away from me."

I'm screaming now, and Chloe and Sofía each grab an arm. "I deserve better than that. I'm not asking for grand romantic gestures and a knight in shining armor because you were already all those things on your own."

I'm shaking. My head is hot and heavy on my shoulders.

Jack's eyes are wide and wet.

People have gathered around us. Chloe says something that sounds like my name, but I shake her off.

"I *was* all those things?" His face scrunches like he's about to cry. "Past tense?"

I shake my head no, but my mouth says, "Yeah."

He moves closer, but I back away.

He starts to say something, but before he can, an announcement booms over the lodge's loudspeaker. "Attention Aguyack Mountain skiers. Due to hazardous conditions on the roads and highways, we're temporarily asking all patrons to remain at the mountain until the storm passes. Please use caution when skiing or snowboarding, as many trails are still closed, and visibility is poor."

The CIA faculty supervisors round us up. They tell us that we're going to be here for a while and to get comfortable. I use the opportunity to snake through the crowd, away from Jack.

"Are you okay?" Chloe asks. "That was . . . intense."

I shake my head. "I don't know what I was expecting from him, but it wasn't that."

Sofía drapes her arm around me. "How do you feel?"

I shrug. "I really wish I didn't love him, but I think I'm starting to realize that if he can't love me the way I need him to, then it's better that he leave me alone."

She looks like she wants to say something to contradict me, but instead, she settles in beside me. Am I overreacting? Am I wrong? Taylor would probably tell me I'm too stubborn like she always used to. That thought rattles me.

Chloe orders me a hot chocolate with extra marshmallows and a shot of Kahlúa, and though the waitress must know we're not old enough, she also must've witnessed the show I put on, and she doesn't question it.

The lodge is spacious for such a small mountain but not large enough for one person to get lost in the crowd. Jack plops down on the couches in front of the other fireplace, slumps forward, and buries his face in his hands.

I watch him for a long time in between sips of cocoa.

Should I go over to him? Ask him how he's doing? Maybe he needs a friend, someone to lean on, to comfort him. He looks like he's hurting, and I can only imagine how his parents reacted. That's probably why he came back to campus early. Did he sit his mother and father down at their breakfast counter and say, "I have something to tell you," as they clutched each other and cried? Did they throw him out? Did he already have a bag packed and an escape route planned? I study the lines in his face, in particular a new crease on his forehead that wasn't there before; it's a crack in his impeccable marble statue.

He realizes I'm staring and doesn't look away.

We stay like this, him on one side, me on the other, hoping our stares can bridge the gap until the storm outside ebbs.

26

The sun yawns over snowcapped mountains in the distance as golden early evening rays peek into the studio I've set up camp in. The building is emptying as I mentally prepare for another all-nighter with "The Prince Who Captured Lightning."

The thing is, I still can't figure out how I want to end it.

Do the Prince and the Knight end up together?

Is that their destiny?

If art mirrors life, then the answer would be no. Jack and Chase do not end up together and live happily ever after. Not after the showdown at the mountain.

Yet the thought of these two characters who decidedly look an awful lot like Jack and me not ending up together makes me undeniably, overwhelmingly sad. So sad that my body feels numb.

I stare out the window until the sun disappears and darkness sets in. I watch clusters of people walk and laugh together across campus, all bundled up in their jackets as they brave salted paths for dinner in the dining halls. I wonder what Benny and Rhett are doing. At least their saga ended happily.

My chest pangs, yearning for that.

For Jack.

For something I can't have.

A fairy tale that was never meant to have a happy ending.

I try to shake it off because closure happened at the ski mountain. Even Dr. Sweatervest agrees it's time to work on letting go. But for me, love doesn't die so quickly.

Or does it?

Rae has gotten distant lately. She's trying to work through her feelings about her current boyfriend. Last we spoke, she told me Harry resented me and our friendship because apparently I "gave her things he couldn't," and that she always dropped whatever she was doing to talk to me or come see me. She wanted to snap his fingers back when he told her that. But then he pointed out that she never even told him she was going home with me for Taylor's birthday. And one night, a few weeks back, they were having sex and I called her, and she literally got up off his dick to talk to me. I had no idea.

"I need to figure out how I feel about him," she said.

I told her, "Rae, please don't think you have to choose one of us over the other. I don't want to come between you two."

She told me to shut up, that I was her best friend-sibling. But after that conversation, she went dark, and I know it's because she's trying to figure out if she loves him.

I wonder if those moments of clarity truly exist.

When I get like this, Dr. Sweatervest suggests I take a walk to clear my head, to see if I can process my feelings. Might as well try it.

I don't get far when I spot Leila alone in one of the sculpting classrooms, nose buried in a book, sitting on the ledge of the window overlooking the snowy campus.

Freezing in place, I contemplate my options: turn around slowly, tiptoe quickly out of sight, or say something. She hasn't been in class in weeks, and I haven't seen her around, so I could easily book it down the hall. But I'd be lying if I said I'm not worried about her.

"I realized I never thanked you for that night a few weeks back," I say loudly, even though I don't need to because it's eerily quiet. "When you called Rae for me. So, thanks." I smile and mean it.

Leila looks up, a bit startled, and then her eyes widen, giving me a window in. She nods slowly and offers a terse smile back. "I knew she needed to be there for you. That you'd want *her* there."

There's a hint of jealousy—because it's Leila—but it's earnest. Say what I will about her; she'll always have a piece of me. Or she did, once, and we share a history that allows us to know pieces of the other.

"Are you okay? You looked pretty shaken up that night. I would've checked in on you, but . . ." She doesn't finish. She doesn't have to.

"I've been better," I say.

"I hadn't realized you and Jack Reid were a thing. The girls in our dorm have been trying to figure him out for months, but it makes sense." She pauses for a few beats then says, "I heard what happened at the ski mountain. Dorm chatter. His roommate, Rhett, has a big mouth."

Leila always did immerse herself in idle gossip.

"We were." Part of me wants to walk farther into the room, pull up a chair, and talk the way we used to in high school. But we're not there anymore, and opening up about Jack with her feels wrong in a way I can't quite place. So I evade. "What're you reading?" I lean against the doorframe.

She looks up, a momentary smile flashing on her lips. "*A Midsummer Night's Dream*." She holds the spine with dried clay molded to her fingers. "The freshman drama majors are putting it on in the spring. Thought I'd audition. Branch out, or return to my roots, or . . . something." It's easy to forget how much Leila used to love acting, especially when she's cycled through so many dreams: acting, sculpting, being a high-powered CEO, now animating.

I nod, unsure if she wants to talk to me or not. I take a chance because the thing about having pieces of each other is that no matter what happens between the two of us, we'll always care about the other. "You were in that . . . freshman year, right?"

She smirks. "Good memory."

"How could I forget?" I ask. "You made a big deal about not getting to play that fairy queen."

"Titania," she corrects. "I was the *most* talented. I should've gotten the part over that skinny blond wench Katie Novak." She tries to joke, but I can tell all the acting is taking a toll on her. Her eyes are sunken. She gnaws at her lip. "I *want* to change," she admits, handing the play to me and pointing to a passage by Lysander.

As I begin to read, she recites it word for word.

"*Ay me*," she says solemnly. "*For aught that I could ever read, could ever hear by tale or history, the course of true love never did run smooth.*" Her eyes swell with tears. "*Swift as a shadow, short as any dream, brief as the lightning in the collied night, that, in a spleen, unfolds both heaven and earth, and, ere a man hath power to say, 'Behold!' The jaws of darkness do devour it up. So quick bright things come to confusion.*" She stops and pulls the book back. "I made a mess of us, didn't I?" She lowers her voice.

There's nothing to say, so I nod.

"Do you think things would've been different if . . ." She never finishes the thought. "You know, I decided I'm leaving the animation program. It's not that I can't rock it because, obviously, I can."

"Obviously."

She clears her throat and avoids making eye contact. "I don't think Professor McPherson gets me. I don't know. You think you want something, and then it's like, 'Wait, why? Why do I want this?' I mean, I was making a fucking macabre animation about eggs that could only end with the realization that the dreams we have never actually come to fruition. I was really trying to sell myself something with that one, huh?"

"There's nothing wrong with trying, Ley."

"Try living inside my head." She folds the book between her legs.

I know it's because she feels the pressure from her doctor parents, who supported her art and acting "hobbies" yet still expected she'd pursue a more guaranteed, "respectable" career path. I guess they were right.

"But," I continue, "pushing for something you think you should want or have but don't actually have any desire for? That could only leave you . . ."

"Scrambled? Like an omelet?" She tries to laugh, but it's so sad, it hurts my heart. "My dad was happy when I told him," she adds. "I just keep asking myself, 'Will *I* be okay?'"

I realize she's just as fragile as I am. Maybe more so.

"Of all people in the world, Ley, you will be okay," I say. "More than okay. You can scramble shit up and still figure out how to rule the world. You're no unfertilized egg, and you're sure as hell not an omelet." I force a chuckle. "That sounded awkward as fuck."

"Maybe eggs benedict with fresh lobster," she says with a wink. "We speak the same language, remember?"

I want to laugh, but I also want answers. "Why'd you do it all, Ley? Why'd you go after *my* dream when I know for a fact that it was never yours? Why did you talk about me behind my back, shit on my viral shorts, and make me feel like I was nothing? I told you at the beginning of senior year that I needed that scholarship to come here. You *knew* because I called you crying the night my dad told me he couldn't help pay for college, and you came over and stayed with me all night. I didn't even tell Rae because she's not an artist and her family has money, but you, you knew what animation meant to me. What CIA and this program meant to me. I was the one who even told you CIA existed, remember? That night, when you were comforting me, it was *you* who did the research for me into CIA's animation scholarship and told *me* about it. Said it was my way in. Then you went behind my back and applied for it when your parents had money saved for you?"

Her eyes are wet. "I wanted what you had, Chase." She raises both of her hands level with her chin. "We started off together, and all of a sudden, you got the recognition and . . . and I wanted that praise. Is that so bad?" She doesn't give me time to respond, which is probably a good thing because I could go *off*. "Then my father got on my case and was like, 'How can you make a career out of sculpting? You should do what Chase did. At least that's a direct career path,' and I don't know. I wanted to prove to the world that I could do it, and do it better, without the theatrics."

"What does that mean?"

I *know* what it means. Out of everything, that's what hurt the most: that she thought I was putting on a show when all I was doing was trying to live authentically and find my way through my art as a nonbinary person. But hearing her question suddenly makes something click for me.

I *am* nonbinary. I'm not trying to find my way. I've been there all along. It's been other people who have made me question myself. Made me think I wasn't exactly who I am. Others' expectations and perceptions became my own. Well, fuck that. I just needed to realize that the journey *is* the destination.

That doesn't mean I won't feel masculine and refer to myself with masculine terms if they fit me at any given time. I am exactly who I am, someone who rejects binary labels because they simply don't fit, like too-tight clothes that were never made for me. I let out an easy breath because Leila inadvertently made me realize that I don't have to rationalize who I am. Not to her. Or anyone. Maybe not even to myself because I'm allowed to be a living, breathing contradiction, if that's who I am.

She sighs. "It doesn't matter."

She's right. It doesn't matter . . . *to her.* It never will. And that has to be okay. I can't make other people care. I'm not surprised she doesn't want to know me beyond who she *thinks* I am. Once upon a time, I wanted more from her, but now I don't. I'm done justifying my identity. I don't owe her—or anyone—that conversation. Nobody is entitled to more of me than I want to give.

"So quick bright things come to confusion," she says again. "And before you know it, the world you thought you knew is gone."

"It feels like the end of the world—and I get that feeling because we're both very dramatic people, and everything is our apocalypse. But it's not the end of the world. You're going to be fine, regardless of what *I* do or what your father says is 'acceptable.' You're going to live."

She doesn't say anything at first. Then, she adds, "I wish I knew how it ends for *us*."

It's not an apology, nowhere near one. But I'm starting to think that I don't need one.

"I don't think the ending is important," I say. "It's what we do on the way there."

She gazes out the window. "I think between the spring play, focusing on my one major—business—and now a minor in sculpting, I'll be okay."

"You will." I teeter on my heels, ready to leave.

"So will you," she says. "Are we good?" The way she looks at me with puppy-dog eyes, makes me think she wants more, something beyond an ending. A new page, another story. It's the Leila Casablanca Method of indirectly asking if there's a future for our friendship. In true Leila fashion, she'll never just come out and say she misses me.

The truth is, I *do* miss who we used to be, who I thought we were. And we're different people now. Or, at least, I am. After everything I've been through with Jack and busting my ass to better my art and follow my dreams, healing from the underhanded shit she did, I'm *different*. Maybe she is, too. But I think it can be okay for us to just *be*. We don't have to be friends, but we don't have to be enemies, either.

I smile because it feels good to be able to finally let go of the anger I've held inside. It doesn't do me any good to carry around all that toxicity because it's clear that she's working through her own demons. We're all doing the same thing—even Jack.

This isn't the end. It's *one* ending.

Suddenly, the last line of "Hansel and Gretel" fills my head:

My tale is done, there runs a mouse; whosoever
catches it may make himself a big fur cap out of it.

It finally hits me: Each story is a mouse, a small creature in a
much larger world, and if I catch that mouse, I can do with it what
I want. I can view it as a meaningless rodent, or I can make beautiful meaning from a seemingly small moment, to interpret *us* how
I see fit.

I can take this interaction with Leila and heal. It's not an
ending but a path forward for me, having let go of the pain.

I can live without Jack just fine. I've been doing it for weeks,
sans the "fine" part. Do I want to? No. But I don't have a choice,
and while that's painful, I will live beyond this realization. But the
Knight? He doesn't have to live without his Prince. He can live out
the happy ending that I can't. I can't believe something so obvious
and easy was staring me in the face the whole time.

I get to create the ending I want for *my* story.

"You have that look on your face," she says. "Like you got an
idea. Or clarity."

A comforting nod confirms her suspicions. "I'll see you around,
Ley?" I let the question linger for the sake of possibility.

She swings her legs off the windowsill and looks like she wants
in on my idea the way we used to share that kind of stuff with each
other once upon a time, but she stops herself from asking and lifts
her legs back up onto the sill.

"See ya, Chase."

The Prince Who Captured Lightning

PART IV

When the Witch appeared to the Knight in his dungeon cell, the Knight willingly offered his whole heart to the Witch in order to save the Prince, but she declined.

"Your readiness to offer your heart is all that was needed," she said. "You must keep what you have left intact if you're to change the hearts and minds of the rest of the People Below the Skies."

"I do not wish to change hearts and minds," the Knight said. "I only wish to be happy. A fool's errand, I know."

"Your mind dwells on your Prince." The Witch held out her hands, and in her palms, the sparks danced.

The Knight wondered how she was able to get them from the Prince's Calvary, but he dared not ask.

The Witch explained, "Once upon a time, there were two titans who ruled the skies, Thunder and Lightning. During their reign, gods and magic were not outcasts nor traitors but celebrated, revered. Until one day, the hearts and minds of the People were corrupted by those who did not understand us, who feared and hated us. So I did what was necessary. I cast a spell that would hide Thunder and Lightning from each other in order to keep them safe and preserve their love. A love so pure, it kept our world balanced."

She circled the Knight, and the sparks glowed brighter in her hand. "Like all spells, the curse can be broken, but . . ."

"What?" the Knight asked.

The Witch smiled, weary and haggard. "Only when the hearts of all the Kingdoms Below the Skies are ready to accept those they deem outcasts, and welcome the true love sparked from twin male souls, will the spell be broken." She gestured with her hands.

"You were protecting them?" the Knight asked, though it was not so much a question as a statement.

As his gaze fell upon the Witch, he saw neither evil nor a monster but a kindred spirit. He saw himself reflected in her eyes.

His eyes traveled to the sparks.

"The Prince and I . . ." He did not finish his thought, for even though he knew in his heart of hearts that he loved the Prince, he also knew such a love was forbidden.

How can such a pure feeling be so wrong? he thought.

"It is *not*," the Witch said, banging her cane on the stone floor. "It is the purest of loves, one not bound by privilege, the duty of marriage, or gendered obligations. It is but a primal spark that if allowed to grow and tenderly tended to has the power to light the skies like the sun and the moon and the stars."

A tear spilled down his cheek. "But I do not think the Prince feels about me the same way I feel about him."

"Think again," the Prince called out from the other side of the locked cell. "I apologize if it took me a bit too long to realize what you knew all along."

"You dare to unlock me? But why risk your whole heart, your safety?" the Knight asked.

The Witch shrugged and offered a sassy pout. "I asked him what he was willing to sacrifice," the Witch said.

"I was not willing to sacrifice my heart to those who seek to persecute me any longer." The Prince unlocked the cell and took the Knight in his arms. "But I am willing to sacrifice all *this*. The throne. The crown. The kingdom that I am promised. Because a promised kingdom without you by my side is no kingdom of mine."

"What of the rivalry between our lands?" the Knight said.

"Perhaps we can mend old wounds," the Prince said, holding his love in his hands. "Wounds that seem to have no point of infliction aside from hate or unreason."

The twin sparks flew upward from the Witch's palms and swirled around the two souls, fusing and imbuing them with a golden light.

As the Prince and the Knight were about to kiss, the sounds of galloping hooves and boots marching on stone slabs echoed through the dungeons.

"We must go quickly," the Prince said.

The Knight turned to the Witch, but she was gone.

"I know the way to the Temple," the Prince said as if he could read the mind of his love. "There's a secret passage through these dungeons that leads out beyond my kingdom."

As they took off under the guise of darkness, their paths lit only by their love, the Prince told the Knight about how he would sneak away as a child to lands beyond his parent's borders. He would wish for only three things: a warm hearth, a small plot of land for sustenance, and happiness. He held the hand of his love as they climbed hills and slid into valleys.

They made their way across the lands, eventually reaching the Temple of the Sky Titans, at the border of both kingdoms. It was a grand stone sanctuary with towering marble pillars carved from lightning bolts and the hammer of thunder, weathered by rains that once breathed life into a landscape now dried by a centuries-long drought in the absence of the titans.

"What do we do now?" the Knight asked, holding tight to his Prince.

In the center of the temple stood a stone slab in the shape of a heart, broken down the middle. Beyond that stood the Witch.

"Mend the heart," she instructed.

The Prince stood on one side and the Knight on the other. On the count of three, they pushed the stone slab together until the two ends fit neatly into each other.

As they waited for a sign that the curse had been broken, soldiers from the two rival kingdoms flanked the temple mountainside, ready to wage war. The two armies hurtled unintelligible and nonsensical insults back and forth. The Prince and Knight looked at each other in confusion because none of it made any sense. It was never clearer that neither kingdom knew why they hated the other.

Frustrated, the Prince hopped up on the slab and pulled his love to his side.

Both armies grew silent; for the first time, they could *see* love. It radiated out, spreading across both armadas.

"You know not why you fight," the Prince said. "But both kingdoms waste resources and time hating the other. To what end? Isn't it better to love than punish those who love?" He brought the Knight's hand to his lips and kissed it.

Just then, the Prince's father, the King, stepped up and into the temple. "He's right," he said. "This fighting is senseless."

The Queen from the Knight's kingdom did the same. "I agree, though I suspect it will take some time to get used to new ideas."

The King looked at the two men then to his army. "What I see here is True Love."

With his words, the heavens opened, and a bolt of lightning shot up from the Prince and the Knight into the clouds, illuminating the dark night sky. They watched with awe as a figure made of electricity formed above them, Lightning. A rumbling roared across the skies as Thunder emerged to greet his long-lost love.

"Only when the hearts of both Kingdoms Below the Skies are ready to accept those they deem outcasts, and welcome the true love sparked from twin male souls, will the spell be broken," the Witch repeated. "It doesn't mean all hearts have changed or *will* change, but change starts small."

She swirled into the sky. Her haggard appearance melted away, revealing a brilliant sorceress dripping in diamonds and gemstones of many colors. With a wave of her wand, the night sky disappeared like a drawn curtain that revealed the sun. The two armies ceased their fighting, and a year-long celebration reigned across both kingdoms, who welcomed the Sky Titans back with open arms. Though there were many who opposed those once considered outcasts, the kingdoms were, for the first time in centuries, peaceful and prosperous, reveling the rains and seasons the Titans brought back to the lands.

The Prince and the Knight were married at the temple, with Thunder and Lightning presiding over the ceremony.

Somewhere between the two kingdoms, they continued their adventures, together, and weathered the inevitable storms.

And they lived.

27

"Where are they?" My hands shake as I crane my neck looking out into the crowd. Taughannock Gallery, the lecture hall on the second floor of the campus center, is filling quickly. Five hundred seats plus standing room. That's at least one thousand eyeballs on "The Prince Who Captured Lightning." At once.

When my shorts went viral last year, I wasn't in the same room as the millions of viewers who ended up watching and sharing it at their own paces, on their own solitary devices. There's something wildly different about this setting where *everything* is shared, including facial reactions. At least from behind the screen, I can pretend everyone likes it. Here, there will be no escaping tepid applause and upturned noses.

"They'll be here," Rae says, grabbing hold of my shoulders. "But I need you to calm down because I'm absorbing your anxiety like a ShamWow."

"Ohmygod," Benny gasps. "A ShamWow! Are you eighty?"

"I watch infomercials at two in the morning to help me sleep," she says.

"If I were straight, or you were a straight-adjacent, emotionally unavailable man, we'd be perfect for each other," Benny says.

"Speaking of." Rae points into the crowd at the front row, where Rhett looks like a nervous bird. His head darts around as he tries to save way too many seats. "He's adorable, but we should help him hold down the fort."

Benny waves her off. "Oh, he's fine."

"Please don't leave me," I beg.

"Why are you such a wreck?" Chloe says from behind, with Sofía in tow. "Your short is amazing. You've poured literally your entire soul into this, and it's perfect."

"It's not cliché?" I ask. "They're not gonna become an angry *Beauty and the Beast*–style mob and pitchfork me to death?"

"If you ask that one more time," Sofía chimes, hand raised to eye level and balled into a fist. "We've been where you are, and trust me, not only will you live, you're gonna be a legend." Her confidence in me is both a blessing and a curse. It's inspiring to know that ridiculously talented people like her and Chloe believe in me, but talk about pressure!

"Your work is always amazing," Rae says. "I wish you believed that."

I do, I say to myself.

Benny bites his lip, and his eyes well up.

"Are you . . . crying?" I ask.

"No!" he shouts quickly. "Chaos Italian gays don't cry. Shut up!" He yanks me into a hug then whispers, "You're, like, the best friend I've ever had, and I'm just so proud."

And folks, that's what does me in.

"Alrighty, loved ones." Professor McPherson bounds across the

338

staging area. "It's time for us to get. This. Party. Started!" She does a little jig with her hips, and I have to bite my lip to stop myself from laughing. "You'll have plenty of time to celebrate after the showcase." She claps twice to shoo everyone off.

"Love you, Chase," Rae says. "You're gonna be amazing."

"Please make sure to—" I start, but Rae cuts me off.

"Save seats for your parents and Taylor, got it. Taylor has been texting me all day. She's gonna let me know when they're here." Rae takes a deep breath and implores me to do the same.

"Is Harry coming?" I ask.

Her eyes dart away from mine. "No. We, uh, we're taking a break."

"Wait, what?" I'm not shocked, but I am a bit surprised she didn't tell me.

Her phone buzzes. "Taylor." Rae shows me her phone. "I'm gonna go meet her and your parents outside. Benny, go help Rhett hold down the fort."

"Why does she keep asking me to hold down a fort?" Benny asks, hooking her arm in his. "Are we at war? Am I a straight soldier? I'd probably blow a straight soldier."

"Oh, you and your ways."

Rae pulls him out, and I watch them walk to where Rhett is sitting. He's now fully having a panic attack, legs and arms spread as wide as possible, fighting off seat stealers.

"You're really dropping a Harry-size bombshell and leaving?" I shout.

"Not now, baby," she says. "This is your moment."

With that, she's gone.

Chloe and Sofía go over the notes for our short speech, which

I'm supposed to give to introduce the project, but I can't focus on any of that right now. There's way too much happening in my world for this. My parents are about to see my work. Rae broke up with Harry. Taylor's here. The mentorship is literally within reach.

Professor McPherson places a hand on my shoulder. "You nervous, Gray?"

I nod.

"Good." She smiles warmly. "You should be. Nerves are a sign of humility. If you weren't nervous in this industry, I'd say you weren't prepared for it."

I glance back out at the crowd and see Leila taking a seat somewhere in the middle. There's a bittersweet look on her face. More bitter, less sweet, all Leila.

"I feel you holding your breath," Professor McPherson says. "And that's okay for a time, but eventually, you'll have to get used to releasing your art to the world."

"I mean, I have experience with that after my virals. But it's weird because it's not really mine anymore."

"It'll always be yours," she says. "You made it. It's your heart. Sure, people will see themselves in it and call it theirs, and people will be challenged by it and reject it. Others will tell you it's been done before and derivative and—" She waves her hands in a dismissive manner. "But that's the whole idea behind it in the first place."

"I know all that. I do. It's just . . . you put so much of your heart into something, and then someone who doesn't understand just how important it is rips it to shreds," I say.

"Welcome to the biz, kid." She slaps my back, and the lights in the house go low. A spotlight appears on stage in front of the screen.

"You got all the heart you need. Never stop bleeding for your art, no matter what anyone else says. You're gonna do great."

She clears her throat, straightens out her retro sapphire-blue blazer with protruding shoulder pads, and walks out on the stage to a wave of applause. Once she steps up to the microphone, the noise from the audience dies down.

"This semester has been a highlight of my career, not just as a distinguished visiting professor for the animation program, but because"—she mumbles a number nobody can hear, and the crowd laughs—"years ago, I graduated from this program when it was in its infancy. We didn't even have a wing, let alone an entire beautiful building and an incredible roster of dedicated faculty. So to be asked back is an honor. Last night was our senior showcase, but tonight I get the privilege to preview our freshman talent."

As she talks, I spot Xavier. Then Rae with Mom, Taylor, and Dad. No sign of Dad's girlfriend, though, which is totally fine since I barely know her anyway, and I'm not upset about it.

"Every single one of these students was paired with two rising-star juniors. They worked their asses off for what you're about to see, and all I have to say is that Mickey Mouse better hold on to his ears because these kids are coming for his job. At the end of the show-case, there will be a mocktail hour during which you will have the opportunity to cast your vote for your favorite short of the evening, which will be announced at the end of our event, along with the winner of the mentorship. So please stick around and mingle and tell these incredible artists just how much you love their work!"

One by one, she briefly introduces my classmates. Chloe and Sofía are standing beside me now, and if they move, I'll probably keel over.

Every single one of these shorts is incredible. Mind-blowing. One is told from the point of view of an 8-bit video game character from the 1980s, and it's all traditionally hand-drawn but looks three-dimensional. Another looks like a damn Jackson Pollock painting, where paint splatters are personified, and, thematically, it's about not staying inside the lines and being different. But my favorite is done in the style of traditional comic book art. It's very Warholian, and it features a Wonder Woman–like character who saves the world from a sentient chicken nugget with a blond toupee who I think is supposed to represent a certain ex-president. It's hilarious, if a tad nonsensical.

More applause, louder than ever, and Professor McPherson calls my name, and it's all I hear until the *thud thud thud* of my heartbeat drowns everything else out.

Chloe and Sofía urge me to walk out first, but I want them with me, next to me. This may be my project, but it's ours, *theirs*, just as much.

I stand at the microphone, and everything I thought I'd say has been deleted from my memory banks.

Oh shit.

Everyone is staring. Waiting. Watching. Ready to tear me apart.

Sweat beads my brow and snakes down my back.

Sofía leans in. "Breathe. You got this."

"Find someone in the crowd and talk to them," Chloe whispers.

I scan the heads, looking for a pair of kind eyes. But all I see is standing room only along the back wall . . . and now I'm panicking because there are more people than I expected and—

My gaze lands on Jack.

He came.

He remembered.

After everything, he's here.

Leaning against the doorframe, arms folded, he looks all sorts of handsome and casually cool, backpack slung across his shoulder. He smiles that crinkly smile that he knows captures every bit of me, and suddenly I'm breathing a little easier.

"I'm not nervous at all. Can you tell?" I stammer, and Benny and Rae whoop and holler from the front row.

I hear Mom shout something that sounds like, "You're doing great, sweetie," and it makes me—and everyone else—laugh.

"Before you watch my short, 'The Prince Who Captured Lightning,' I want to thank my partners, Chloe and Sofía, who are two of the most brilliant artists and storytellers I've ever met, and without whom this never would have come together. They challenged me and understood my vision. This short is a love letter to everyone out there who dreamed about finding their prince or knight in shining armor and wanted to be part of something bigger than the background but never thought it was possible because they didn't see themselves in the fairy tales we grew up watching or reading because we were gay or queer or had a different body type." I look to Professor McPherson, and I realize just how hot the spotlight is, but I'm standing in it. "I'm a proud nonbinary animator, and I hope you enjoy my world."

I book it backstage and watch as my short starts playing. The prologue is set to grand orchestral music that Benny composed for me at the last minute in which Thunder and Lightning dance across the skies as lovers, there's the misdirect of the Witch being evil and the introduction of the Prince.

I keep my eyes trained on Jack, who watches, mouth agape as the story I'd told him about in bits and pieces plays out for him. At the very end, as the screen fades to black on the Prince and Knight together, "And they lived . . ." appears in white.

As the house lights come up and the applause rattles me, I feel a calm I haven't felt in a long, long time.

I exhale. It's over. I did it.

And I lived.

During the hour-long reception after the shorts, I try to search out Jack, curious to hear his thoughts. But he's nowhere in sight. My stomach cramps as I realize he probably left after seeing our fictionalized happy ending—yet another instance where I scared him off.

Not that I care.

Because I'm totally enlightened now.

Or something.

The one person I cannot avoid is Dad. I gave him a tepid hug, and Mom told me to "be nice." (I'm always nice.) Now we're all standing in a circle—me, Mom, Taylor, Dad, Rae, Benny, Rhett, Xavier, Chloe, and Sofía—and they're all talking about how impressed they are that my work looks so professional and blah, blah, blah.

Taylor yanks me to her level. "I had a looooooooong talk with Dad."

"About what?" I say, a little too loudly.

"You'll see." She offers a pity-me half smile, and my stomach does flips.

Right on cue, Dad breaks formation and asks me to step

outside. I follow behind him until we're safely out of earshot of any of the event's attendees.

"Krissy and I broke things off." He looks a bit older than he did a couple months ago. A touch grayer, a little more beat down, and a little fuller around the waist.

"Sorry to hear that," I lie. I barely knew her. Hardly said two words to her anyway, but he looks sad about it, and as angry as I am at him, I want to give him a hug.

I don't. But I want to. I think that's progress, right?

"Right after Turkey Day. The holidays are always rough," he says.

Then nothing.

But.

Awkward.

Silence.

Until: "I got your email."

My heart races. "What email?" I haven't sent him anything. *Unless* . . .

My fingers are numb as I paw at my phone in my pocket. I haven't given one ounce of thought to the email I drafted to my dad that night after my first session with Dr. Sweatervest, and I definitely didn't press send. But I pull up my Sent folder, and there it is. My fingers must've pressed the send button! This is why you don't type an actual email address into a pretend letter you never intend to deliver.

Oh crap.

"I, uh, didn't mean to—" My head is throbbing, and I want to grab the nearest tray of meat and cheese–filled puff pastries and shovel all of them into my gullet.

"It's okay, Chase," he says, not an ounce of malice or jest in his voice. He even uses my name, not Taters. "I'll admit I was angry when I opened it and read it, but your mother—and Taylor—helped me understand where you were coming from."

What? This is . . . new. All the harsh things I said to him, and he's not flying off the handle?

"I didn't realize what I was doing was harming you. I was trying to help you. I thought I was, anyway." He avoids making eye contact.

Time to stand my ground and not give him an inch. "You weren't."

"I won't call you that name anymore." He puts his hand on my shoulder and squeezes. "And I don't remember telling your mother that nobody would love you because of how you looked, but she reminded me of how I can get when I'm upset. I'm not sure how to apologize here because your letter was pretty chilling, kid." He tries to laugh, but it's wrapped in nerves and a bit of sorrow. "I'm sorry for all the horrible things I said. There's no other way to put it. And I promise to be better, if you'll let me."

It's all I ever wanted from him. To just be a real, sympathetic dad.

So I hug him. No other words needed.

When we pull apart, his eyes are a bit red.

As we walk back in, he says, "I was surprised to see Jack here. Taylor told me you two broke up. Wish he'd come over and say hi, but I get it." Dad pauses. "I liked him."

"It's nice he showed. I miss him." A few hours ago, if you would've told me I'd be this level of honest with Dad, I would've laughed until I choked.

He cocks his head and squints. "He didn't leave."

Dad points toward the stage, and there's Jack, fumbling with the microphone. The audio screeches, nails on a chalkboard.

He's dressed in a cheap prince costume, the material wrinkly and droopy and oddly rigid all at once. The metallic fabric catches the light in all the wrong ways. His empty backpack is open and crumpled on the floor by the stage.

"What the hell is he doing?" I gasp.

Benny looks to Rhett and smizes. They know something. "I wish I had popcorn for Jack the Snack's Big Moment."

Rae pulls out a snack bag of Smartfood from her purse. "I always come prepared."

Benny grabs her cheek and plants a wet smooch. "I love her so much!"

"I'm right here," she says. "But hush—Jack is about to make a fool of himself."

Screeching feedback commands everyone's attention. A quiet falls over mocktail hour.

Professor McPherson's face is panic-stricken, and she starts calling for security. Holy shit, I did *not* see this coming at all, but Jack looks anxious and out of place up there. Then I see Leila talking to Professor McPherson, and she seems to calm down. Leila turns to me and offers a small smile. A token.

"Sorry for the interruption, uh . . ." His voice is shaking as he clutches the microphone. "I have to do this before I lose the nerve. I'm not really the one for grand romantic gestures, but there's someone here who has quite profoundly become the center of my world." He sucks in a quick breath. "No, my universe. And I messed things up big-time. I don't know if he'll forgive me or if I even deserve forgiveness, but I have to try because, Chase Arthur, you are the best part of me. You've opened me up to worlds I've never seen before. You deserve everything, and, well, I'm kind of stepping on the poem I wrote for you, and security is giving me the eye, so I'll read this really quick."

Everyone turns to look at me. Mom is crying. So is Taylor. And Benny. The three of them are practically clinging to one another, looking at Jack like he's Henry Cavill holding a basket full of floofy kittens or something.

I look to Dad, who nods. "Hear him out. Can't hurt."

Rae grabs me and says, "Remember what love is supposed to feel like."

Jack clears his throat.

You remind me of
red cardinals and majesties unknown
faraway lands and magic spells,
words I've yet to learn
that haven't been invented
because with you
I'm an unwritten novel
reborn in your margins
under night skies,
and rainy-day puddles.
we exist
in the breath between
lightning and thunder
where the end is a beginning,

that starts with three simple words
a poem by your name that goes
I love you
I love you
I love you

The whole of Taughannock Gallery erupts in applause and whistles that follow me as I snake my way to the front of the stage where Jack stands. Then the cheers morph into a chant: "Kiss him, kiss him, kiss him!"

My heart is beating so fast, I might pass out.

He holds out a sweaty hand like a damn Prince Charming.

I take it, but it's clear he expects a kiss. Instead, I say, "Can we talk outside?"

28

Jack and I walk out, and I drop his hand.

I'm careful not to look at him because even though I want to kiss him, it's taken a lot for me to get to a point where I feel like I could live without him, and I don't want that progress to vanish. Not before I hear him out in more words than one of his poems.

His shoulders are slumped, almost as if he's struggling to keep his body upright.

"That was beautiful." My lips quiver. I didn't plan on getting emotional, but tears sting the corners of my eyes.

"I know it's not enough," he says.

"I just want to know why." I don't even know what I'm asking, specifically. I want to burrow deep into his mind and mine the recesses for answers to everything. I've already said what I needed to say at Aguyack Mountain. It's his turn now.

"It's complicated, but I'll try to untangle." He takes a deep breath. "I'm so torn up, Chase. I'm so deeply, ridiculously sorry for what Callum said about you and how I treated you. I'll regret that for the rest of my life." Jack's shaking—his voice, his hands, everything. Pain is etched on his face. "Our history is complicated. He's my best friend. He's been treated like a part of my family, and people think we're brothers. He has this hold on me, and I wasn't expecting to see him here. I thought maybe I could come to CIA, and my life here would be my life here, and my home life would be in the past, separated."

"I get that, but it doesn't work like that."

"I know." Jack motions for us to sit on a bench. "I remember being on the playground, and a couple of older kids were picking on me, and Cal just showed up like Captain America or something and told them to leave me alone. He was two years older than me but three years younger than my older brother, so he kind of just fit in between us in the family, like some long lost sibling. It didn't matter to Cal that I was young. We were inseparable. He took me under his wing. He helped me navigate high school and my first girlfriend and . . ."

Jack's voice trails off. I give him time to calibrate, not bothering to press further until he's ready. His eyes are big and open and ready to be honest in a way he hasn't been before.

"I didn't really realize that I was doodling our names together in the margins of my notebook or that the poems I was writing while I should've been paying attention in math class were about Cal. You know, overwrought stuff about how his eyes were bluer than the sky and that he was a blooming flower in a meadow of dead grass."

I roll my eyes. Do I really need to hear this? *Try to be supportive, Chase.*

Jack notices my discomfort, though, and looks away. "One day, I was sitting on the bleachers by the track field, writing, watching his football practice. I was a sophomore, and he was a senior. A legion of football players came up behind me and dumped an entire cooler of lime-green Gatorade on me. They grabbed my wet note-book and started tearing out soggy pages. One of the roided-out dudes read it out loud, 'JR hearts CT. Who's CT—Callum Tag-gart?! Oh shit!' And that's how the rumors started. I told them it meant Courtney Thomas because I had clearly thought about who CT could be if I had to in a pinch, which should've been a sign, you know? But I didn't want to confront my feelings.

"But that wasn't the first time. In middle school, I spent a lot of time at Cal's house. We were watching old sci-fi alien movies, the kind where cockroach-shaped creatures burst out of humans' stomachs, and we accidentally stumbled upon some unblocked porn channels. The girls looked so plastic, and the guy was more into himself than her. I spent most of the time staring at the wall behind the TV, tracing the streaks in the paint.

"But Cal had his hand down his pants, and I went to the bath-room to splash cool water on my burning face. Once Cal got off, we went outside and played a game called *Gladiator*, where we'd balance on this stone ledge on the side of his house and battle each other; the first one to push the other off won. He always won, but not that day.

"When Cal bowed to me, impressed, and stared at me with his big blue eyes, I don't know why, but I told him I loved him. He called me a fag and slammed me to the ground against the ledge. Searing pain shot through my shoulder, and burgundy blood oozed like a chemical spill on my chest. I passed out. Woke up in the hos-pital to my dad telling me that I had twenty stitches and asking me, 'What the hell happened?' He told me that crying and carrying on wouldn't fix anything, not for me, not ever. He told me to *never* cry.

"I couldn't tell him what happened because I was so

embarrassed. I thought Cal would never talk to me again and that it'd be all over school. I told him Cal and I were wrestling and got carried away, which I guess is what Cal said, too. But then Cal showed up at the hospital. In my room. And he told me he loved me like a brother, but if I ever came on to him again, he'd tell everyone and do worse than slam me into the pavement. He said I needed to 'get my head right,' and that I was confused and hated myself because of my 'unnatural urges.'"

That's insidious as hell. I break my embargo on touching him and take him in my arms, holding him tight. "I'm so sorry, Jack. Why did you stay friends with him?"

His mouth is pressed to my collarbone. "After that day in the hospital, everything was normal. Like it never happened. He never said another word. I started dating girls like Courtney Thomas. And Cal and I were closer than ever. He started working for my dad and basically lived with us at the farm and came to church with us, and Dad loved that because I was never big on going. But I started to like it because Cal was there, and I got to be near him. Sounds fucked up. The more he came with us, the more devout he became, and suddenly he'd be over for dinner and preaching the gospel. At some point, it just became too much for me because I was battling all this inner stuff." His voice gets quiet. "Being gay." He goes silent for a few moments. "I think that's why I didn't go to school in Vermont."

"You left to forget him?" I ask, but it's more like a statement.

"To get over him. To get away from him. I love him, but when I met you, I realized how toxic and wrong that love was. And then he showed up, and it was like that day all over again." Jack picks his head up and looks me dead in the eyes. "I hurt you because I was hurting. It felt like my whole life was collapsing around me because of the hold he had. I didn't realize that what we had, what we were building, was stronger than all that and could withstand it. And it took therapy and coming out to my parents and finally releasing Cal's hold over me that I saw that you saved me. You made me feel like I was enough."

It's funny how so many of us struggle with the same stuff: feeling like we're not enough. Not good enough to be loved. Not beautiful enough to be worthy. Not talented enough to be accomplished. Not significant enough to feel important or seen. Without the proper words to tell another that we love them, that we hate them, that we something-in-between them, that they hurt us when they think they love us. Hearing Jack say that what we have can withstand all that bad stuff makes me realize I've had it wrong all along.

Fairy tales are nice because they paint a rosy picture of love: Meet, sing a cute song, and bam! Marriage. But that's not love. That's fantasy. This? Facing the hard, gritty shit together, realizing you can survive the trials on your own, yet don't need to because someone is willing to hold your hand as you grow? That, I think, is real love.

And I love Jack.

"I didn't come out for you," he continues, his blue eyes piercing my damn soul. "I did it for me. I knew by then that there was probably zero chance you'd take me back, but I think that losing you made me realize everything I was willing to sacrifice for lying to myself. And to them."

"How'd they take it?"

He snort-laughs. "Funny story. I told them when Cal wasn't around—he'd left to pick up my brother—and it came out so fast that they didn't register what I said, and they were sort of stunned, I guess? And they asked me to repeat myself, and I just lost it on them. Started screaming that I was gay."

Jack laughs *hard* now. Meanwhile, I'm absolutely horrified.

"They still didn't say anything. Not a word. But the look on my father's face said it all. I freaked out and just grabbed my stuff, which I had packed already, just in case they threw me out. I grabbed my shit and booked it. Huffed it to the bus stop and just kept going until I ended up back here. The stupid thing is, my parents ended up being fine with it. I didn't hear from them until I got back from the ski mountain Friday night, and when I did, they were there waiting for me. Not Cal. Just my dad and mom." His eyes are watery. "Told me they loved me and that they wished I had stayed around. That they were shocked, but that I overreacted."

Jack reaches behind his head and scratches his neck. He looks like a cute farm boy I want to kiss.

A warmth stretches over me. "So they're cool?"

"My dad needs a bit more time to really get used to it, but for the most part, yeah. He even said, 'Any god that doesn't love my son is no god to me.'" Jack tears up, but he doesn't wipe them away. "I told them about Cal, and that's a bit of a thorny issue right now, but at least they know." He looks to the ground and licks his dry lips. "I also told them about you." I brush his tears away with my thumb.

"What'd you tell them?" I try to suppress a smile, but it peeks through anyway.

"That I met someone and fell so deep in love that I ruined it."

"A tale as old as time." I motion for him to come closer.

"I guess that makes me the Beast?"

He's being cute. Too cute. This is dangerous. "I'm sure as hell Beauty," I say.

He leans in. "That you are."

I raise my hand and put a finger to his lips. "Nuh-uh."

He winces. "Sorry. I read our"—he gestures between us— "energy wrong."

"No, you didn't. But before I officially take you back, I wanted to apologize to you."

His brows crinkle. "For what?"

"For not being more there for you."

"I didn't let you," he says.

"True." I let the silence linger between us.

"Is there more?"

I nod. "I want to be the best version of myself for you, and right now, I'm a work in progress. I feel like I'm in a growth spurt."

He grabs my hand. "Me too. Grow together?"

I squeeze his hand back. "Grow together."

This time, I lean into him, and our lips meet softly, tenderly, and it's every single firework display, every musical montage at the end of a Disney movie, every bolt of lightning across the night sky. It's not onstage in the middle of some grand romantic gesture, but it's perfect.

"I love you," he says.

Just then, Rae and Benny burst through the doors and, upon seeing us so close, apologize profusely and then bump into each other like windup toys scuttling across a wooden floor, unsure where to go.

"Sorry, I, uh—" Rae mutters.

"Ohmygod, cute! We should—" Benny stutters.

I want them to leave so I can have more time with Jack, but it's like they're actively trying to not leave. I mean, it's not that hard to turn around and beat it.

"What's up, y'all?" I ask.

"We, um," Rae hums. "Actually, you—"

Then I hear Professor McPherson over the speakers. It's muffled, but it's clear as the night sky: "The winner of the mentorship is Chase Arthur. Or, as I like to refer to him, Gray."

I blink. "Did she just say . . ."

"Anyone have eyes on Gray?" she shouts.

Benny is jumping up and down, hardly able to contain himself. "Yes, binch! That's why we're out here interrupting your moment! Your professor has been looking for you—I guess she couldn't wait to announce your name!"

I stare at Jack, eyes wide, and open my mouth, but no words come.

"You deserve this," Jack says.

"He's right," Rae adds as Benny purses his lips in a "don't test me" way.

I clear my throat. "If y'all would've let me talk, then you would've heard me say that damn right I deserve this."

I walk to the double doors and take a breath. Chloe and Sofía are onstage with Professor McPherson. Mom, Dad, and Taylor crane their necks to find me. Everyone is waiting on me. *For* me. To celebrate *me*.

It's okay to allow myself the space to enjoy every single delicious second of this.

29

✵ FIVE MONTHS LATER ✵

I used to daydream of princes and knights and faraway lands populated by dragons and brimming with magic. I grew up imagining I was a princess in a tower waiting to be rescued by a debonair man on a noble steed, and we'd have a lavish wedding. Over time, I realized that no man will ever be perfect, that love doesn't develop overnight, that it's something that has to be tended to daily, and that there are no princes or knights or happy endings. There is only here and now. I'm learning every single day how to love myself, the skin and body I'm in, and that it's okay to be a work in progress.

The balls of my feet gently push against the wooden front porch of Jack's parents' house in Vermont, and the porch swing rocks back and forth as the sun sets behind dense, towering pine trees and tall mountains. A symphony of crickets chirp around me, and the air somehow feels warmer and sweeter than it did a few hours ago. If there is such a thing as magic, this place comes pretty close.

Jack kicks open the screen door and backs out with arms full of snacks and two glasses of unsweetened iced tea. He sets everything down on the small table beside me and checks to make sure his parents or sister aren't around before leaning in for a kiss. Even though I've been here for two days, and they know we're together, I have to sleep in a guest room on the first floor of their house, and he's still a bit squeamish about PDA. I allow him that space because there are infinite other ways he shows me that he loves me—every square inch of me and my body and my mind. I don't need a public kiss or a hand to hold.

"It's about to rain," he says with such authority that I have to laugh.

"How the hell do you know that?"

"Listen," he says quietly, leaning sideways as if he's extending his ear. "The crickets are chirping faster than they were before."

I stare blankly, though admittedly, it's hard not to grab him and kiss him because of how damn cute he is when he gets all serious like this.

He rolls his eyes and flashes that crinkly smile. "When crickets chirp faster, it means the temperature is warmer." He points toward the sky, and I swore a second ago it was clear, if a bit hazy. "Look at the dark clouds rolling in. When it gets warm and humid like this so fast, a thunderstorm is about to roll in. Hopefully, it'll be gone by morning."

He sits back, and I put my feet up onto the seat and burrow into his side as he takes over rocking for us.

"Our moms and sisters are in the kitchen obsessively double- and triple-checking our flight itinerary for tomorrow."

We leave in the morning for Los Angeles, which Rae keeps telling me is a once-in-a-lifetime opportunity, but I know she'll miss not having me at home while she's still figuring out how she feels about Harry, all these months later. I know she misses him, and I can tell she loves him by the way she talks about him, like a long-lost Nicholas Sparks message in a bottle. But she has a lot of pride. Maybe time apart from each other will do her good.

My all-expenses-paid summer internship with Professor McPherson at her animation studio starts in two days, and Jack managed to get an internship at a small literary agency in Hollywood. He told his parents it was a coincidence that I was going to be in LA at the same time, but he could have easily found an internship on the East Coast, in Boston or New York. He chose me. And I'm pretty sure his parents, who are actually not the assholes I thought they were that day in the dining hall, saw right through Jack's hetero-charade. At the start of the spring semester, his father apologized for the comments he made when they came to visit CIA. I think being here and seeing their family dynamic has allowed me to understand all the god stuff more, especially because they told me their family now attends an LGBTQ-friendly church. Still, they're giving him money to sublet an apartment with me for two months. His dad even sat both of us down to give us a "this is a very adult decision" talk, but we assured him that it's only for the summer, and we're not living together at CIA for the fall semester. I could never leave Benny; I'm bonded to him for life.

This is a temporary adventure, a fantasy that Jack and I get to create for ourselves.

Jack's parents were nice enough to invite Mom and Taylor to stay for a few days, too, so that our families could get to know each other. Callum isn't around. He quit sometime in January, and Jack hasn't heard from him since. Though he doesn't talk about Cal at all, I get the sense that he misses his friend and that he hasn't quite processed his feelings, but I don't press him. When—and if—he's ready to talk about it, I'll be here.

Thunder rumbles in the distance.

"Told you."

"All right, no need to get cocky," I say.

His fingers find mine. "You wish."

"There'll be plenty of time for that."

He takes a deep breath. "You decide what you're working on with McPherson yet?"

"I think I wanna tell the Witch's story. Who doesn't love a misunderstood drag queen? But we'll see what she thinks."

"She's going to *love* it." He lets go of my hand and leans forward. A hush falls over the trees, and it feels like the forest around us is collectively holding its breath. He sucks air into his lungs and slowly breathes out. "Hear that?"

The sky is dark now, between the missing sun and the gathering clouds, and straight ahead, over the mountains, is a gauzy haze that looks like it's moving toward us. The sound is low at first, a pitter-patter that's barely noticeable, but in just a few short moments, it washes over the Reid property like a tidal wave.

We're protected by the porch, but the rain comes swift and hard.

Lightning bolts streak across the sky.

Thunder cracks immediately.

We're right under the storm.

Jack looks at me.

We *are* the storm.

Wordlessly, he holds me as we watch and listen to the titans dance around us.

When I would daydream of princes and knights and magic, I never imagined this. It may not be happily ever after, but what is? Regardless of what comes next for Jack and me, I know that I love him, and that's enough. But more than that, I love me. The whole of me, the nonbinary person with masculine energy, the person with a lifetime of work ahead to love his body, the person who uses art to show the world exactly who Chase Arthur is.

Which is kind of the whole point, right?

This *is* the adventure.

Once upon a time, Jack and I were two people who were sort of lost when we met, found ways to love ourselves, and then each other. And then *lived*.

we exist
in the breath between
lightning and thunder
where the end is a beginning
that starts with three simple words
a poem by your name that goes
I love you
I love you
I love you

A NOTE FROM THE AUTHOR

Chase Arthur is a character who has lived in my head since I was fifteen years old when I created him as an alter ego, a way to be unapologetically gay and fiercely artistic and comfortable in my overweight body. In reality, I was suffering from severe depression and battling body dysmorphic disorder (BDD). I have been struggling with weight issues my entire life, and, as a teen, I crash-dieted, sought out fad diets, binged, and studied the monstrous distortions I saw in the mirror and convinced myself I was too disgusting and unworthy to love or be loved. I would often not be able to recognize myself or see what others supposedly saw. I constantly analyzed every part of my body and gave in to the voices in my head that told me I would never be beautiful, that I would always be unworthy. I spent most days agonizing over my appearance and my body, covering my stomach and chest with oversize clothes and pillows and positioning my body in uncomfortable ways where I thought nobody would see the parts of myself I hated. I sought constant reassurance and resorted to extreme measures to "fix" my body due to shame and anxiety (which only fed into the suicidal ideations that came with concealing and suppressing my queerness) after being bullied for my weight.

As I got older, my body-image issues worsened, and the body dysmorphia became so extreme that I resorted to laxatives and more extreme crash diets that caused drastic and unhealthy weight fluctuations, including starving myself and compulsively over-exercising. While, for a spell, I appeared to be "skinnier," beneath the surface, my body was in pain. Concurrently, I fought against internal homophobia, gender identity struggles, and depression that came as a result of all the storms swirling inside my head. Eventually, my depression became so bad that the pendulum swung in the other direction, and instead of obsessing over losing weight, I gave in to my depression and binged, and my weight ballooned to the point of being clinically declared "morbidly obese"; my weight was threatening my health in innumerable ways that caused me to seek professional help. Through years of therapy and subsequent weight-loss surgery, I was able to curb and manage the unhealthy, life-threatening disorders that only exacerbated my depression. While I still suffer from BDD, and probably always will, I have learned to love myself *and* my perfectly imperfect body.

If you are battling body dysmorphic disorder or an eating disorder or just need positive, body-affirming reads (as I wish I had), check the following resources.

BOOKS:
- *Dumplin'* by Julie Murphy
- *Every Body Shines: Sixteen Stories About Living Fabulously Fat* edited by Cassandra Newbould

- *Faith: Taking Flight* by Julie Murphy
- *Fat Chance, Charlie Vega* by Crystal Maldonado
- *Hunger: A Memoir of (My) Body* by Roxane Gay
  (TW/CW: past sexual assault)
- *Wintergirls* by Laurie Halse Anderson
  (TW/CW: Features the grisly and deadly impacts of
  eating disorders. Please note that this is a tough read and
  does not feature body positivity)

RESOURCES:

- Psychology Today—
  Search for LGBTQ-friendly therapists around you
  who focus on cognitive behavioral therapy (CBT)
  https://www.psychologytoday.com/us/therapists
- Humantold Psychotherapy Services—
  if you live in the New York City area
  https://humantold.com
- Body Dysmorphic Disorder Foundation
  https://bddfoundation.org/support-groups/

Additionally, I've always had a complicated relationship with
gender. A lifetime of pain and the suppression of my own queerness
until I was twenty-three prevented me from fully mining my gender.
It took me until I wrote my debut novel, *Can't Take That Away*, to
pick apart and explore the layers of my own genderqueerness.
Carey Parker knew who they were. I am a proud gay, genderqueer
person, and now I know who I am. Chase Arthur, however, is still
figuring that out, and this story is yet another layer and exploration
of [my] gender. Chase is gay and nonbinary and uses he/him

pronouns. Because that's what he's comfortable with. He toys with the idea of they/them pronouns but hasn't landed on them as a permanent part of himself.

It was important for me to show a concurrent yet separate journey of someone figuring out who they are while also struggling with BDD. The answers aren't always clear or finite, and sometimes the lines blur—to be clear, gender dysphoria and body dysmorphia are *not* the same and aren't connected. At its heart, this sweet gay romance is a story of self-love, and Chase is still figuring out who he is by the end and will be for probably a long time. And that's okay. I promise it's okay to be in the process of figuring it out. I still am.

If you're struggling with your gender identity, here are some gender-affirming books and resources for you to consider.

BOOKS:
- *Can't Take That Away* by Steven Salvatore
- *Felix Ever After* by Kacen Callender
- *Between Perfect and Real* by Ray Stoeve
- *Symptoms of Being Human* by Jeff Garvin
- *I Wish You All The Best* by Mason Deaver
- *Out of the Blue* by Jason June

RESOURCES:
- CenterLink: The Community of LGBT Centers— Find your local LGBTQ center and attend one of the many incredible support groups or events they offer or volunteering.
  www.lgbtcenters.org/LGBTCenters

- The LOFT LGBTQ+ Community Center—
  (Westchester, New York)
  www.loftgaycenter.org
- The Trevor Project's TrevorLifeline (866-488-7386)
  https://www.thetrevorproject.org
- National Suicide Prevention Lifeline (800-273-8255)
  https://suicidepreventionlifeline.org/help-yourself/lgbtq/
- Crisis Text Line—Text HOME to 741741 from anywhere
  in the United States to text with a trained crisis counselor.
  https://www.crisistextline.org
- The LGBT National Youth Talkline (800-246-7743)
  https://www.glbthotline.org/youth-talkline.html
- Trans Lifeline (877-565-8860)
  https://www.translifeline.org

Remember: No matter what you're going through, you are not alone.

We are here, waiting for you.

Much love,
Steven

ACKNOWLEDGMENTS

I grew up daydreaming of fairy tales and magic and white knights on noble steeds. I immersed myself in the Technicolor worlds of animated Disney films and sang along to bold musical numbers as I danced around my living room in costume. In my head, I was a princess waiting for my prince, but I also held this deep fear that, because I was queer (though I didn't have the words to describe myself at a young age in the '90s), I would never get my happily ever after. Then, I met my husband, Steve, and he swept me off my feet. Steve, you've allowed me to live in a fairy tale of our own design since the day we met, and though there have been many twists and turns and chapters to our story, you've never failed to rescue me from burning towers and fire-breathing dragons and forces of evil that sometimes only exist in my own mind. You've encouraged and propped me up every step of the way. You have seen me through nearly every iteration of this book. You are my prince, my knight, my bolt of lightning, and I'll love you with all my heart until The End. I know love because you *are* love, and this book exists because you love me.

There are not enough words to say how much my rock star agent Jess Regel means to me. Jess, when you read the opening chapters of this book, you knew this was The (Next) One. You are a calm in my never-ending storm, and I'm so happy you're at the helm of my career (see what I did there? ☺). Your advocacy is unmatched, your advice is always the best remedy to my anxiety, and your belief in me as a writer lifts me up when I'm feeling unsure or like a fraud. Thank you a million bajillion times over. You are beyond. *Beyond* beyond!

This wouldn't be a true fairy tale without a fairy godmother/Jiminy Cricket–style mentor who so perfectly sees my potential, gives me the tools I need to execute my vision, and expertly steers me through all obstacles. Luckily for me, I had a team of mentors: Cindy Loh, your passion and love for *And They Lived . . .* made this the book I always knew it could be. Working with you was an absolute joy, and I'm grateful you gave Chase and Jack the opportunity to live. Claire Stetzer, you never missed a beat and were always right there to help guide me forward. Thank you for everything you did! It was a pleasure to get the chance to work with you. And, of course, the brilliant Allison Moore, whose unbridled enthusiasm for me and my books has kept me going. I'm so lucky to have you in my corner. Your vision for me as an author has been invaluable in helping me see my worth and value. Thank you!

For the entire team at Bloomsbury, who always goes above and beyond for me, you've brought this book to life, a book I've been writing since I was nineteen years old. This is a dream come true! Phoebe Dyer, Lex Higbee, Erica Barmash, Oona Patrick, Jeanette Levy, Donna Mark, and the brilliant copyeditors, Jon Reyes and Manu Velasco: Y'all are EVERYTHING! You make magic happen!

To Andi Porretta for a brilliant cover design! Seeing (a thicc) Chase and Jack on the cover embracing brings tears to my eyes. It's like being struck by lightning!

To EVERYONE who has ever read a draft of Chase's story (and there have been many!) over the past sixteen years: THANK YOU AND I AM SO, SO SORRY! I wrote the first draft of Chase's story in 2006, and it has seen seven completely new ground-up rewrites, countless revisions, and a rotating cast of characters. **Five Fun Facts:** (1) The only constant has been Chase, though his last name has changed more times than I can count; (2) In the first draft, Chase was straight and in love with Joey from *Can't Take That Away*; (3) Jack was introduced in the second ground-up revision when I was ready to write a gay character after I finally came out; (4) Leila's name used to be Vivianna; (5) Draft one's timeline spanned from middle school to college, drafts two to four took place in New York City, and drafts five to seven were a cross-country road trip.

Nicolas DiDomizio! You binch! This book is as much yours as it is mine, as I have bothered you with every single draft, revision, and edit since 2013—remember our first manuscript swap? It was the first time you met Chase! You've continued to believe in Chase's story as it evolved and completely shifted gears more times than I can count, even when I was certain Chase would never have his day in the sun. Your friendship, guidance, and critiques are EVERY-THING, and I cherish you more than you'll ever know. Thank you for being one of the greatest surprises and best friends I've ever known.

Jessica Verdi, I will NEVER stop thanking you for years of motivation and encouragement and time spent yanking me out the mud. Multiple times. You believed in Chase back in the *How I Set*

Myself on Fire days, gave me so much hope, and never allowed me to give up. Much love, friend.

Jason June! Our friendship has meant so much to me over the past year. You have been an incredible source of comfort and support, and a great sounding board for all my ideas and life woes! I don't know what I would have done during debut year without you! Thank you for being fiercely you. You inspire me beyond words.

For Becky Albertalli, the sweetest, most sincere and purely wonderful human who has ever walked this earth: Thank you for your friendship and support. You've given me so much love, and I'm constantly in awe of the good that you do. Thank you × 1,000,000!

To my family, who has believed in me every single step of the way and has cheered on me and my writing career, especially for Chase, I wouldn't be where I am without you. Mom, Giselle, Carole, Dad, Sandy, Missy, Uncle Bobby, Chris, Christopher, Adriana, Marissa and Brian (and Huddy Buddy and Harper), Nikki and Kevin, Mike and Patti, Queen Maria, Samantha, Elizabeth, Melissa, Carolyn and Joe, Jenna and Mama Becky, Jackie Boobie, my Ithaca girls (Sylvia, Fallon, the 15-05 girls—Caite, Katlyn, Brea, Vera— Amanda, and Laura Blondiepants, who cheered on Chase back in 2006–2007), and everyone else I can't possibly list but haven't forgotten, I love you all.

Cheers to incredible new friends who were such invaluable support systems during my debut year: Jacob Demlow (my PBF partner-in-crime; you're stuck with me, bestie), Charlie Murphy (I'll never forget what you did for me and Carey Parker), Michael Araújo (your willingness to fight on my behalf always cheers me up), my Bloomsbury siblings Alex Richards and Phil Stamper (both of whom made me feel welcomed and supported). Dahlia Adler and Julian Winters for being the most incredible souls and supporting this book, and Anthony Nerada and PJ Vernon for being fabulous friends and allowing me space to vent! I would have been completely lost without each of you.

A special shout-out to my former Ithaca College professor and friend Diane McPherson, who saved me in so many ways just by being visible.

And to the person I fell in love with once upon a very long time ago, who now exists only in my mind, who inspired Jack Reid: Wherever you are, whoever you are today, I wish you every happiness in the world. Thank you.